He sat at the other end of the couch, crossing one leg over his knee.

"So," he said. "What's a nice girl like you doing in a place like this?"

He was trying to relax her, make her smile. She could do neither. She forced her voice to stay steady. "You tell me. What *am* I doing in a place like this?"

Montana shrugged nonchalantly. "You're keeping out of trouble."

She met his gaze. "It's big trouble, isn't it? How big?"

His eyes didn't waver. "We don't know. Maybe not so bad. Let's hope so."

His calmness irritated her and so did his evasiveness. "Don't hold out on me," Laura said. "You've forced us to hide away like—like prey. I've got a right to know what we're hiding from."

His smile slipped away. "All right." His expression was impassive. "If word gets out that the kids saw what they did, it could be dangerous for them. These people don't care who they hurt. If you get in their way, they hurt you."

From the moment she'd seen him, she knew his face could be hard if he chose, his eyes cold. She just hadn't expected how hard, how cold. . . .

SEE HOW THEY RUN

SEE HOW THEY RUN

BETHANY CAMPBELL

BANTAM BOOKS
NEW YORK TORONTO LONDON SYDNEY AUCKLAND

SEE HOW THEY RUN

A Bantam Book / February 1996

ISBN 0-553-56972-4

Published simultaneously in the United States and Canada

Bantam Books are published by Bantam Books, a division of Bantam Doubleday
Dell Publishing Group, Inc. Its trademark, consisting of the words "Bantam
Books" and the portrayal of a rooster, is Registered in U.S. Patent and Trademark
Office and in other countries. Marca Registrada. Bantam Books, 1540 Broadway,
New York, New York 10036.

PRINTED IN THE UNITED STATES OF AMERICA

OPM   0 9 8 7 6 5 4 3 2 1

SEE HOW
THEY RUN

ONE

"YOU CAN SET YOUR WATCH BY HIM," ONE OF THE TEACHERS had said.

That's exactly what the twins did every weekday afternoon on the playground. The boys were eight and very handsome. They had dark hair and blue-gray eyes fringed with black lashes. They wore identical military watches, large and unbreakable.

Each day when the tall old gentleman appeared, rounding the corner, the boys' eyes glittered with interest. They would look first at their watches, then at each other. The watches should say 2:07, and if they did not, the twins adjusted them, because the old man *always* appeared at 2:07.

The old man carried himself with great dignity and walked with a silver-headed cane. His white hair was expertly barbered, his jaw always cleanly shaven. It was winter, so he wore an expensive overcoat of dark gray, a white muffler, a black fedora, and black leather gloves.

He came from the direction of the really expensive brownstones, and that's where Laura imagined he lived. She recognized his shoes as Guccis, six hundred dollars a pair. This meant that each shoe had cost exactly twice as much as her winter coat. She smiled wryly whenever she thought of that.

The boys counted the number of steps that took the elderly gentleman down the block past the school. On the average, it was 339. On the one-hundred-first step, he reached the edge of the schoolyard with its high wrought-iron fence.

The twins clung to the black bars of the fence like two solemn monkeys, staring at him and counting with all their concentration.

Every day the old gentleman gazed straight ahead, his face unreadable, as he passed them. Yet he always acknowledged the boys. He would raise his hand and tip his black hat, ever so slightly, as he reached the place they stood, grasping the fence.

"*Good* afternoon," the old gentleman would mutter, without making eye contact. "*Good* afternoon."

Perhaps, Laura thought with amusement, it was his habit to repeat himself, or perhaps he meant to give a separate and equal greeting to each twin.

The boys did not smile, and kept their faces as dignified as his. They hated wearing hats, so had none, but touched their fingertips to their foreheads in a return salute. "*Good* afternoon," they would chorus back, mimicking his tone. "*Good* afternoon."

Then, at approximately his one-hundred-twenty-fifth step, the old gentleman would turn his face slightly, his dark eyes meeting Laura's hazel ones. Although he was nearly seventy, he was still a handsome man, and he knew it, she could tell. He'd nod at her and touch the brim of his hat. She'd smile and nod back.

"He's got the hots for you," Herschel, one of the other teachers, had once said.

"Rich, old—and with the hots for me?" Laura had replied with a rueful smile. "I should be so lucky."

But the elderly gentleman's glance almost did seem to convey sexual interest, and she admired him for harboring youthful thoughts, even felt a certain affection for him, although they'd never spoken.

She was still young—twenty-eight—and knew she was fairly attractive, but New York was full of women who were younger and far more beautiful. She didn't care; she wasn't hunting for another husband. She'd had one, and he had been more than enough.

Her only vanity was her richly colored auburn hair, which was thick and waving; she wore it long. She used little makeup and let her freckles show. She always had freckles, even in winter.

This afternoon, the wind was cold and brisk, so she'd used her plaid muffler as a scarf, covering her ears and tying it under her chin. She stood a few yards from the twins, watching them, her hands deep in her pockets. Behind her came the shouts of other children playing.

The gray sky had started to spit needles of sleet. Laura would be grateful to see the old gentleman round the corner, for that meant recess was almost half over, and soon she would be back in the warmth of the classroom.

The twins, as usual, clutched the fence rails, ignoring the other children, watching for the man. Their winter jackets and gloves were alike in all but color. As usual, Trace wore blue and Rickie red. The boys were so identical that many people could tell them apart only by this color coding. They seemed even to breathe in unison, their breath rising in synchronized plumes toward the sky.

Their hands tightened on the fence when they saw the man coming. The air was so cold that his ears were red and his usually controlled face looked almost pained. His white muffler was wound around his neck, and his coat collar was turned up. He seemed to exhale smoke as he walked, as if he were an elderly and benign dragon.

Perhaps because of the cold, he walked a bit more swiftly than usual, and Trace frowned, trying to keep count of the man's steps. When the old man passed the boys, he lifted his hat, just barely.

"*Good* afternoon," he said, not looking at them, striding on. "*Good* afternoon."

They saluted stiffly, their eyes following him. "*Good* afternoon," they echoed. "*Good* afternoon."

He kept moving briskly. One of the other children, Janine, ran up to Laura, asking for help in retying her shoe. "Of course," Laura said, putting her hand on the girl's shoulder. But she waited, first, to exchange her usual silent greeting with the old gentleman.

His dark eyes met hers. He raised his gloved hand to his hat. He nodded.

Then a long staccato burst of noise split the winter air, and the side of the old gentleman's face exploded into blood. His remaining eye rolled upward, his shattered jaw fell, as if to cry out, but no sound emerged.

Blood blossomed on his chest like red carnations sprouting in full bloom, and blood spurted from his legs, which danced, sinking beneath him. He lurched like a broken puppet toward the street and fell in a ruined heap. His wounds steamed like little mouths exhaling into the cold.

The children screamed, the teachers on the playground screamed, pedestrians screamed, and one woman with a Lord & Taylor shopping bag sat on the sidewalk, screaming as blood poured down her face.

Laura moved on sheer instinct. She wrestled Janine to the ground before the old gentleman hit the sidewalk, and she held her there, her body thrown over the girl's. *Shooting,* Laura thought in horror, ducking her head, *somebody's shooting at us.*

A bullet ricocheted shrilly off the pavement of the playground, and one of the children—William, perhaps?— screamed even more loudly.

Her face hidden, she heard Herschel's agonized cry. "He's hit! He's hit!"

Then the shooting stopped and she heard the squeal of tires. Without the shots, the air seemed to ring with silence—except for the screams, of course, but they hardly registered on Laura's consciousness any longer.

"He's hit! He's hit!" Herschel's voice was broken. She looked over her shoulder, biting her lip. Herschel knelt above William, who flailed and writhed, holding his arm.

The other children were crying as teachers tried to drag them back inside the safety of the school.

Numbly Laura clutched the sobbing Janine closer to her chest. She forced herself to look at the old gentleman again. He lay motionless on the sidewalk in the welter of his blood.

His beautiful overcoat is ruined, she thought illogically. And just as illogically, a line from *Macbeth* ran through her head: *"Who'd have thought the old man to have so much blood in him?"*

So much blood.

Then, with a shock, she realized that Trace and Rickie still hung onto the fence as if hypnotized, staring at the corpse. They alone of all the children were not crying or shrieking.

They regarded the dead man, the dark pool of blood, the screaming wounded woman, with wooden faces. Their hands still gripped the fence bars, and a slow, thin stream of scarlet ran down Trace's cheek, dropping to stain the bright blue of his coat.

Oh, God, he's shot, Laura thought in panic. She rose and stumbled to the boys although Janine screamed out for her to stay.

Quickly she examined Trace's cheek. It bled profusely, but he didn't seem to notice. He acted irritated that she had pulled him away from the fence.

Janine got to her feet and lurched toward Laura, hysterical. She grasped her around the waist and wouldn't let go. "Shh, shh," Laura told the girl, her voice shaking. "We'll go inside. We'll be fine inside."

Rickie, too, was annoyed to be pulled away from the fence rails and clung to them more tightly. "Shots," he said. "Shots. The man got shooted on the hundred-and-twenty-ninth step."

"Yes, yes," she said impatiently, wrenching him from the fence. She was terrified that whoever had opened fire would return and shoot again.

She wrapped one arm around the bleeding Trace, the other around Rickie. Janine still hung onto her waist, wailing hysterically.

In the distance, sirens shrilled. "The police are coming," she told the children, struggling to herd them inside. "The police will be here, and we'll be safe."

"The car come by," Rickie said, frowning studiously. "The car shot. Hit the man."

Trace touched his own cheek, then regarded his bloodied glove impassively. He nodded. "The car shot. Hit the man."

A drive-by shooting. Here—in front of our own

school, in front of these poor children, Laura thought. *The world's gone crazy. The world's mad.*

Somehow, Laura maneuvered her little brood inside the school. Shelley Simmons, the speech therapist, had collapsed onto the hall floor and leaned against a wall, holding one of the younger children, his face hidden against her chest. Both wept uncontrollably.

"I've called nine-one-one," Mrs. Marcuse, the school's director, said, struggling to exert control. "The police will be here. An ambulance will be here." She held up her hands as if beseeching them for peace, but there was none.

Jilly, the oldest student, crouched in a corner, hugging herself, her expression full of terror. She covered her eyes with her hands, as if she could block out what she had witnessed.

Oh, my God, that they should see this—Laura thought, still in shock—*that children should see such a thing.*

Fanny Mayberry, the cook, appeared, staring at the chaos without comprehension. Herschel had William's thin body stretched on the floor, and was using his own jacket as a compress to stop the bleeding of the boy's arm.

"Fanny, take Janine," Laura said, trying to thrust the clinging girl to the other woman. "There's been a drive-by shooting. Trace is hurt, too."

"My Lord, my Lord," Fanny said, folding Janine in her arms. "What a world! You come to Fanny, honey, you be fine."

Laura knelt before Trace. She snatched off her muffler and dabbed it against his cheek. "Does it hurt?" she asked.

He ignored her question. He frowned at the door. "Car shot thirty times," he said, jutting his lower lip out petulantly. "Hit the man nineteen. The man didn't finish the walk. Got to finish the walk."

"He can't finish his walk. Trace, look at me. Tell me if you're hit any place else. Do you hurt anywhere else?"

Stolid, he didn't answer. He stared at the door instead, and Laura thought that maybe the wound in his cheek was only superficial. She kept her muffler pressed against it, willing her hand not to shake.

"I saw the license," Rickie said quietly. "It was MPZ one oh four eight one nine."

Trace nodded. "MPZ one oh four eight one nine. The man should finish the walk."

The hall was overwarm, almost stifling, but Laura suddenly went cold. Once more a peculiar silence enclosed her, blocking the riot of sound.

"What?" She clutched Trace's jacket by the lapel. "Say that to me again."

He frowned more irritably. "MPZ one oh four eight one nine. The man should finish the walk."

Her heart beat painfully hard as she turned to Rickie. "You saw the license number?"

"MPZ one oh four eight one nine," he said.

My God, she thought with a rush of adrenaline. *They both got the license number. Of course. Of course.*

The knowledge gave her a numbed comfort. The police would be pleased. They would find the monster who had gunned down the kindly, dignified, harmless old man, wounded the woman on the sidewalk, hurt William and Trace. They would catch the gunman, lock him away, make the world safe again.

But when the police came, they were not pleased.

"Now calm down, calm down," ordered the officer in charge. His name was Detective Valentine, and Valentine was an unlikely name for him. He was a tall, disheveled, heavy man who needed a shave and gave off an aura of sweat and cynicism. He had gathered them in the school cafeteria.

But few of the children calmed down, and Shelley Simmons still could not stop crying. When an officer tried to comfort her, she slapped at him and cried harder because he wore a gun. The medics should have given her a sedative, but in the confusion, nobody had thought of it.

The woman on the sidewalk had been critically wounded, and the bone in William's upper arm had been nicked. Both the woman and the child had been strapped onto gurneys and loaded into ambulances that sped screaming away. The school had been bedlam.

Trace's cheek had been cleaned and patched, and now Laura sat beside him, trying to keep him from scratching at his bandage. He muttered to himself, his dark brows drawn together. Rickie sat on Laura's other side, humming.

"Listen!" ordered Valentine, eyeing his weepy audience with disgust. "Did anybody see the whole thing? Just answer me that."

Nobody replied. Janine set up a fresh wail, and Herschel leaned his elbows on the table and put his face in his hands.

"I *said*," Valentine repeated, his lip curling, "did *anybody* see the whole thing?"

Laura waited, her heart hammering, to see if any of the other adults had witnessed the shooting, but nobody spoke.

"We did," she said so quietly nobody seemed to hear her. "We did," she said again. She had her arm around Trace, the better to restrain him from scratching at his cheek.

Trace didn't want to be touched and tried to squirm free. His brother stared impassively at the detective and kept humming.

Valentine had dark, bulging eyes that reminded Laura of a bulldog's. He trained them on her with no friendliness. "All three of you?"

"Yes." She nodded. "They got the license number. They saw the gunman clearly."

The room suddenly became quieter. Valentine stared at Trace and Rickie. They ignored him. Trace muttered. Rickie hummed.

"They seem calm enough," Valentine said, almost grudgingly. "Will they talk?"

"Yes. I—think so."

He nodded. He looked askance at Janine blubbering in Fanny's embrace, at Jilly huddled in the farthest corner, at Shelley Simmons still openly weeping.

"Where can we talk?" Valentine's voice wasn't kind.

"In my office. Down the hall," Laura said. "Room One-E."

"Room One-E," said Rickie.

"Room One-E," Trace repeated, trying to shake off Laura's hand.

One of the children, Fergus, began to make a strange, mournful yipping noise. "I want my room!" Fergus cried. "I want my bed! My room! My bed!" He yelped again, more stridently and unhappily than before.

Valentine sighed. "Let's go to One-E," he said. Weariness mingled with contempt in his voice. "Eagan, take over here. Oliphant, come with me."

He and Oliphant, a slim young black officer in uniform, accompanied Laura and the twins to her office. Trace muttered, frustrated that he couldn't scratch at his bandage. Rickie kept humming.

Laura's office was small but cheerfully decorated. Looking down from the walls were framed posters of Mr. Spock of *Star Trek,* Ariel the Little Mermaid, and Simba the Lion King. In the corner stood a small work table with a child's colorful, simple puzzle on it. Four shelves were crammed with books, both adults' and children's.

Tacked on one bulletin board were children's drawings and snapshots of the students and staff. On another bulletin board, student charts displayed gold stars. Some charts had many gold stars. Some had few.

Valentine lumbered to Laura's desk and, without asking, sat down heavily in her chair. She didn't like that. The uniformed officer, Oliphant, pushed aside a pile of her papers and sat on the corner of her desk. She didn't like that, either.

Both men stared at her. Valentine raised his hand and made a beckoning motion, as if coaxing her to respond quickly and without nonsense. "You?" He nodded at Laura. "Who are you? What's your job here?"

"I'm Laura Stoner. I'm a teacher."

"Age? Address?"

She told him she was twenty-eight and gave him her address, which was in a neighborhood far more modest than the school's. With an air of industry, Oliphant wrote the information on a notepad.

"How long you worked here?" Valentine asked. He picked up her appointment book and flipped through it idly. His presumption irritated her.

"We can do a puzzle," Trace said suddenly. He spoke so loudly that it startled Oliphant, who darted him a questioning look.

"We can do a puzzle," Rickie agreed. He had begun to fidget. She held both boys by the hand, and both were squirmy.

"Stand there," she told them firmly. "Be still. You can do a puzzle in ten minutes."

Both immediately looked at their watches. Rickie nodded, a bit sullenly. Trace continued to try to pick at his bandage.

"Don't touch your bandage, Trace," she said, just as firmly. "Look," she said to Valentine, "can you hurry? They're restless. And upset."

"Let 'em do the puzzle," Valentine said without smiling. "And you—you can sit." He nodded at the chair opposite the desk as if it were his office, and he was giving her permission to use her own furniture. He apparently found something of interest in her appointment book. He stared at the page, nodding idly.

Laura, shaken as she was, felt a stab of anger. She had intended to help the police, not be patronized by them. She held herself straighter.

"They'll do their puzzle when I tell them they can," she said evenly. "I don't want to sit—you're in my chair. I'll stand. And please put down my appointment book. You're not here to investigate *me*."

Valentine, unsmiling, only raised a brow. Oliphant slipped her a noncommittal glance. "He asked you how long you've worked here, Miss Stoner," Oliphant said in a velvety voice. "You didn't answer."

"Three years."

"Before that?" Valentine said. He glanced at a few more pages in the appointment book, then made a show of setting it back on her desk, but not in its original place.

"Before that I was getting my master's at Columbia," she said. "And before that I taught public school. And before that I was in college at Penn State. And before that high school in New Castle, Pennsylvania. And before *that*, junior high in New Castle. And before that grade school in New—"

"All right," Valentine said, cutting her off. "Now, I got to question you. One at a time. The kids first. I don't want any allegation they were coached. So leave and wait outside the door—"

"That isn't possible," Laura said. "They won't talk without me here."

Valentine stared morosely at the twins. He tented his fingers on the desktop. He attempted a fatherly smile, but it seemed merely sarcastic. "What are your names, boys?"

Neither looked at him, and neither answered.

Valentine leaned toward them, still trying to smile. "What are your names, boys?" he repeated.

Trace stared at the floor. Rickie squinted at the ceiling.

"They're upset, and they won't talk to strangers," Laura said. She was right, and she knew it. "Ask them whatever you have to. I won't coach them. And I haven't."

"This isn't regular procedure—Miss Stoner."

"This isn't a regular day for us—Detective Valentine."

He sat back in her chair. He still wore his hat, brim pulled down, and his overcoat, unbuttoned. He took off the hat and set it on her stack of papers. His hair was thinning and slicked tight to his scalp. It gleamed, as if oiled or dirty. "What are their names?" he asked tonelessly.

"Tell the man your name, Trace."

Trace glanced at his watch, stared at the floor, and said, "My name is Trace Francis Fletcher. I'm eight years old. I go to Stephenson School. I live there." He gave his address and telephone number.

"*Very* good, Trace," Laura said, smiling. "Now you, Rickie."

Rickie continued to study the ceiling with narrowed eyes. "My name is Richard Mark Fletcher. Call me Rickie. I'm eight years old. I go to Stephenson School. I live there."

He gave his address and telephone number in the same singsong voice that Trace had used.

Oliphant stole another glimpse at the boys. His expression had grown guarded, measuring.

Valentine, who clearly didn't understand children, gave them another small, false smile. He put his elbows on the table and folded his hands together. "Now, boys, suppose you tell me what you saw this afternoon on the play-ground. Can you tell me what you saw? If you do a good job, I'll have Officer Oliphant here buy you some ice cream."

"Ice cream?" Trace said, his voice shrill. "Ice cream!"

"No, Trace," Laura said calmly, "you can't have ice cream. You can have juice. Tell what you saw. Tell what happened to the man with the cane."

Trace frowned harder. Laura repeated her instructions. Trace took a deep breath. He cast an unfriendly glance at Oliphant but still did not look at Valentine. "The man turned the corner. The man took one hundred and twenty-nine steps. The man fell down."

Valentine pursed his lips and stared at Trace with dis-satisfaction. "What is this—a hundred twenty-nine steps?"

"They're interested in numbers," Laura said and pressed on, choosing her words carefully. "Trace, tell what you heard when the man fell."

"Shots," Trace answered without hesitation. "Thirty shots."

"Tell what the shots did," Laura said.

"Now, wait," Valentine said, irritably, "you're prompting him—"

"Nineteen shots hit the man."

Oliphant looked up again. "That's flukey, man. He got hit about twenty times, all right. How he know that?"

"Trace," Laura said quietly. "Tell me where the shots came from."

"The car," he answered. "The car was big. The car was blue. The car said 'Cadillac.' The car said 'de Ville.' "

"Now—wait a minute," Valentine interrupted. "What'd he say? We got all kinds of conflicting witnesses on that car. Is he *sure*? Is he one of those kids that knows cars—?"

Oliphant's face had gone taut. "Jesus," he said under his breath.

"Trace," Laura said. "You said you saw a license num-ber. Tell me the number."

"Now, wait a minute—a license number?" Valentine asked, skepticism in his bulldog eyes. "He's just a kid—"

Trace cocked his head as if Valentine's voice annoyed him. "The number was MPZ one oh four eight one nine."

Rickie nodded absently. "The number was MPZ one oh four eight one nine."

Oliphant scribbled furiously. "Jesus Christ," he said. "Sweet Jesus."

Valentine merely stared at Trace, his brow furrowed, his mouth set cynically.

"Thank you, Trace," Laura said. "That was very good." She turned to Rickie. "Rickie. What happened today to the man with the cane?"

Rickie stopped staring at the ceiling and began to stroke his own cheek, one finger at a time, never using his thumb. He answered her questions as Trace had, almost verbatim.

"Tell me the license number," she said at last.

"MPZ one oh four eight one nine," said Rickie.

"MPZ one oh four eight one nine," Trace echoed.

"Go radio headquarters," Valentine ordered Oliphant. "Tell them to put an APB on the number."

Oliphant got up swiftly from the desk and gave the twins a wary look. "Like, that's *spooky,* man."

"Like, that's *spooky,* man," Rickie repeated as Oliphant left the room. His childish voice mimicked the officer's inflection.

"Like, that's *spooky,* man," Trace said.

"What is this?" Valentine demanded. "This is weird. I never saw nothing like this. Can I believe these kids?"

"Can I believe these kids?" asked Trace.

"Absolutely," Laura said with confidence.

"Absolutely," repeated Rickie in the same tone.

"Why are they saying everything we say?" Valentine asked, his nostrils flaring.

"Why are they saying everything we say?" Trace said.

"Why are they saying everything we say?" Rickie said.

"Why are they saying everything we say?" Trace said again.

"Don't echo, Trace," Laura said, shaking her head. "Don't echo, Rickie."

"We can do a puzzle," Trace said, looking at his

watch. Rickie, too, looked at his watch. He pressed his lips together and nodded.

"Yes," she agreed. "You can do a puzzle. Sit at the table."

They marched to the table, pulled out the two chairs, and sat. Rickie pushed the child's puzzle away.

Laura went to a shelf and took down a jigsaw puzzle. "It's a new one," she told them, taking the cellophane from the box. "It doesn't make a picture."

They waited stolidly. She was proud of finding the puzzle. It was labeled "Highly Difficult" and contained a thousand pieces. On both sides, it was black.

Carefully she poured the pieces of the puzzle to the middle of the table. The boys began to spread them out, sorting. Rickie immediately found four pieces that fit and locked them together.

Laura moved to her desk and set down the puzzle box so that Valentine could see it.

Trace, who was obviously more tired than Rickie, began to mutter loudly. "Blue rhubarb," he said emphatically. "Blue rhubarb, blue rhubarb."

"Cows can fly," Rickie said, apropos of nothing. "In outer space. Cows fly in outer space."

Valentine looked up from the puzzle box and at the twins. He regarded them with something bordering on horror.

"Why do they talk like that?" he demanded. "What's this 'blue rhubarb'? What's he mean, 'Cows fly'? What's with the repeating?"

Laura pressed her lips together and searched for words.

"Blue rhubarb, blue rhubarb, blue rhubarb," chanted Trace.

"Cows can fly," Rickie said, sounding bored. "MPZ one oh four eight one nine. MPZ one oh four eight one nine."

Valentine swore, his expression more horrified than before. It was as if he was staring at two serpents, not two little boys.

He swung his head so that he faced Laura. "These kids

aren't right in the head, are they?" he challenged, contempt in his voice.

"These children are special," she said. "And I have to get them their juice. I promised them."

She went to the small refrigerator on the counter and took out two containers of apple juice. She opened the snap tops and carried the juice to the table.

Mechanically Rickie muttered, "Thank you."

"Thank you," Trace said, quickly fitting the puzzle pieces together. "Blue rhubarb, blue rhubarb, blue rhubarb."

Valentine stared at them again as if repelled. "These kids are retards—*retards*."

Laura turned to face him, putting her hand on her hip. She knew his contempt could not hurt the boys. It would not even register on them. "The correct word is autistic, Mr. Valentine. But I'd prefer you use the word 'special,' as the staff does."

He swore and turned his gaze back to her, his eyes glittering angrily. "That's what the 'special' in this school means? It's a school for morons and nut bars?"

Laura gave him a withering look. "This school serves children with special needs. What kind of school did you *think* it was?"

"I don't know," Valentine almost snarled. "Some of 'em was crippled or something. I thought it was a cripple school. Only these two look so normal, I didn't know—how'm I supposed to know—?"

Laura crossed her arms and looked away angrily. She didn't tell him they didn't use the word "crippled," either. Some of the children had cerebral palsy in addition to mental retardation. And Fergus, who had been brain-injured in a car accident, was in a wheelchair.

"For a minute," Valentine said angrily, "I thought I got dream witnesses here. Kids who know cars. Very observant kids. With good memories. I thought maybe this is a school for the special smart. Now you tell me they're loons."

Laura swung back to face him. "Don't call them names," she ordered. "They *do* know cars. They *are* observant. They *do* have good memories."

"Yeah?" Valentine challenged, his mouth twisting. "How do I know they aren't just repeating what they're told? They're like two parrots, goddamnit."

"No," she argued. "They're children with a condition. Sometimes they repeat what they hear. It's called echolalia."

"Yeah?" Valentine said again. "So how do I know it ain't you they're echoing, or whatever the hell you said? I mean, who's gonna believe a kid who says 'blue rhubarb' all the time, or that cows fly? Christ, lady, you realize you just had me send in a report based on the testimony of two—two retards?"

Laura clenched her fists atop the desk and leaned toward Valentine. "I said, don't use language like that. What they said is right. I'd swear to it. They're never wrong about numbers. They may be handicapped in some ways, but they're gifted in others. In observation. In—in dexterity. In spacial perceptions. But especially in numbers. About numbers they're never wrong—never."

"Oh, shit," Valentine said bitterly. "Why'd I get outta bed this morning?"

"Believe me," she said earnestly. "It's true. They're never wrong about numbers."

Valentine looked away from her. He put one hand to his temple. "Shit," he said again. "Shit and blue rhubarb."

"I can't tell you how many steps that man took," Laura pleaded. "But they can. It's what they *do*. I didn't notice the sort of car. I didn't count the shots. I didn't see a license number. But they could, and they did."

Valentine swore again. "What's this supposed to be? They're like that guy in that movie? That Tom Cruise thing? These kids are like that—that *Rainman* guy?"

"Yes," Laura said, eagerly springing on his words, even if they weren't quite accurate. "Like *Rainman*. Exactly. Some people call them 'idiot savants,' wise idiots. They're below average in some skills, but in others they have a sort of genius—"

"Wise, schmize, a idiot's a idiot," Valentine said blackly. "Besides, a movie's a—a work of *fiction*. That rainman guy wasn't *real*."

"He was based on real people, people like these boys,"

Laura argued. "Look at that puzzle. Could you do it? I couldn't."

He glanced with distaste at the twins bent over the puzzle. They were working swiftly, and had assembled almost a fifth of it already.

"I wouldn't *want* to," he muttered. "I got enough puzzles in my life."

"That's not the issue," Laura said. "Could you do it? That fast?"

He shrugged. He swore again. He still had his overcoat on, and sweat was starting to bead his face.

"When was your birthday?" Laura asked.

He scowled. "What? Now we're gonna play astrology?"

"I'll show you what they can do. When's your birthday?"

"April twenty-seventh, 1941," he muttered. "Curse the day."

Laura rose upright again and turned to the work table. "Rickie—tell me what day of the week was April twenty-seventh, 1941."

Rickie did not look up from the puzzle. "Sunday," he said without hesitation.

She turned back to Valentine. "Well?" she said.

He looked both displeased and startled. "He got lucky."

"Try him on anything," she challenged.

"My sister got married in 1963," he said, narrowing his eyes. "September seventh."

"Rickie," she said, "what day of the week was September seventh, 1963?"

"Saturday," Rickie replied without looking up.

She picked up her appointment book. She looked back to the first part of the year. She pointed to an entry in January. It said, "Rickie excused. Dentist—filling. 1:30."

"Rickie," she said carefully, "the dentist gave you a filling. Tell me the time and place."

Rickie took a drink of juice and wiped his mouth. He picked up a puzzle piece. "January eighth. Friday—one-thirty. The office has an aquarium. Thirteen fish. Six striped ones. Four black ones. Three gold ones."

She flipped through the book. She saw the entry reminding her of Herschel's birthday party in July. She pointed it out to Valentine. "Rickie, when was Herschel's birthday party?"

Rickie yawned. "July fourteenth. Wednesday—three-thirty."

She reached to her desk, picked up her calculator. "Rickie, tell me the number of candles on Herschel's cake."

"Twenty-nine."

Laura held the calculator so that Valentine could see it. She punched in the numbers. "Rickie, what's twenty-nine times twenty-nine?"

As soon as she said it, she hit the *equals* button.

"Eight hundred forty-one," Rickie said, almost as quickly as the number came up in the calculator's window.

"What's eight hundred forty-one times eight hundred forty-one?" she asked, punching in the numbers.

The number 707,281 displayed almost simultaneously as Rickie said it.

She kept throwing challenges out to Rickie. He met them effortlessly, until Valentine seemed impressed in spite of himself.

She started to push in another set of numbers, but Valentine gestured for her to stop. "No more," he said, shaking his head. He gave Rickie another cold look. "He's a goddamn freak."

Laura was infuriated. But Oliphant opened the door and reentered. Because now she and Valentine had an audience, she tried to temper her reply, but she still spoke with passion.

"He's not a freak," she said. "*They're* not freaks. They're human beings, just like you and me."

"Human beings," Valentine muttered, as if he held the entire species in contempt.

Laura clenched her fist. "Listen," she said from between her teeth. "They can help you find out who killed that lovely old man. He was always such a gentleman. He never really talked to us, but he was always so nice—"

Oliphant cleared his throat. He walked to the desk. He

gave Laura an ironic sideways glance, but he spoke to Valentine. "They got a make on the victim."

"Yeah?" Valentine said. "Well?"

"Well, hang on to your ass. It's 'Saint Frankie' Zordani."

The name meant nothing to Laura, and she was surprised by Valentine's strong reaction. "The hell you say," he said, as if in a mixture of shock and awe. It was the first time she had seen the man show an emotion other than suspicion or disapproval.

Valentine turned his attention back to Laura with a smile that was close to a sneer. "Well, well," he said with false pleasantness. "This wasn't your average 'Let's drive by and kill somebody' shooting. This wasn't random. This has got *interesting*."

"Interesting?" Laura said, doubt in her voice. What she had seen was terrible, shocking; how could he find it interesting?

Valentine's superior smirk stayed in place. He nodded. "Your 'lovely old man'? 'Such a gentleman'? Who was 'so nice'?"

"Yes?" she asked with a frisson of foreboding.

"A drug lord," Valentine said with satisfaction. "This wasn't any random violence you witnessed. This was planned. It was a hit. A major drug war hit."

Her scalp prickled, and a cold lump formed in her throat. She couldn't speak. *Planned? A hit?* she thought sickly. *A drug lord and a drug war?*

"The D.A.'s office wants a statement. Then they want those kids in protective custody. Maybe the woman, too," Oliphant said. "Immediately."

Valentine nodded. He rose and picked up his hat from the desk. He looked Laura up and down.

"Get your coat," he ordered. "And the kids'. They're material witnesses in this—if what they say can hold up in court. Let's go."

"Protective custody?" Laura said, stunned. "Material witnesses? Court? You mean these children might be in danger?"

"Worry about number one, lady," Valentine said. "You might be in trouble yourself. You got yourself in the middle of something big. Oh, you've done it up right, no mistake."

A tide of horror swept her. It had never occurred to her that she had to do anything more than have the boys tell the police about the license number. Now Valentine was talking about courts and witnesses and drug wars and protection—it was incomprehensible. "But—" she protested. "But—"

Valentine gave a snort of cynical laughter. "The D.A. ain't gonna believe *this*. We got witnesses—but they're eight-year-old idiots."

Don't use that language, Laura wanted to say, but the words stuck in her throat. She could only stare at Valentine's unsympathetic face.

"Blue rhubarb, blue rhubarb, blue rhubarb," said Trace.

"Cows fly in outer space," said Rickie.

TWO

HIS NAME WAS MONTANA, BUT HE WAS FROM NEW YORK.
He'd been born on a Friday the thirteenth when it was
raining. His mother, who was superstitious, had cried, believing he would die young.

But Montana had been one of those people convinced
he was immortal, so he became a cop. They say a cop is
washed up the day he learns he *isn't* immortal.

Montana had realized he was merely human one night
in a dark alley behind a crack house when he was twenty-
seven. It hadn't washed him up; rather it had baptised him
in lightning and fire. He had nearly died. But he had risen,
born again, more scrappy than before.

His injury would keep him off the street, where he had
been crazy about the adrenaline rush of pitting himself
against the Bad Guys.

Well, as his Uncle Eddie always said, there was more
than one way to skin a cat. Montana hung out now with
the Federal Attorney's office, an assistant. He was still after
Bad Guys. He still had a slightly fanatical gleam in his eye.

Of late he needed fanaticism to fuel him. He'd been
assigned to help make a case against an annoying young
marijuana czar, Dennis Deeds. Building a case against
Deeds was like building a wall out of clouds. The guy had

come out of nowhere and kept dodging back into it. He was as elusive and insubstantial as a ghost.

Montana missed the thrill of a big-time hunt. He wanted a case that was large, sweet, and juicy. The Deeds investigation was small, dry, and plodding. But this afternoon, something had come down in the attorney's office, something big.

Montana's superior had temporarily taken him off Deeds's ephemeral trail and sent him over to West Fifty-seventh, to the Organized Crime Task Force offices.

Frankie Zordani had been clipped. The task force wanted to talk to Montana, and he had no damned idea why.

Now Montana sat cooling his heels in the waiting room of Isaac Conlee, no less, who was the highest-ranking FBI man with the task force. *Frankie Zordani* had been clipped—Montana couldn't get over that.

As Mafiosi went, Zordani was a nice old gentleman. He hardly ever killed anyone unless it was absolutely necessary. The task force had been trying to nail him for years but couldn't touch him.

Now he'd been nailed to the sidewalk in his own blood. God, not the task force, would have to sort out his sins. Montana idly wondered if God viewed income tax evasion as seriously as the IRS did.

Conlee's secretary, a pale, prissy-looking blonde with a long nose, listened to a low voice on her intercom, then looked at Montana, as if sizing him up. "You may go in now," she said.

I *may* go in, Montana thought. *My, my.* He rose and crossed the office. The door to Conlee's office was metal and needed a new coat of paint. He opened it.

Conlee, behind his desk, rose to greet him, shook hands, and pretended not to notice that Montana shook left-handed.

"Michael Montana?" Conlee said. "I'm Conlee, FBI liaison."

"I go by Mick," said Montana. Conlee was about forty, short for an FBI man, only five foot seven or so. But he was powerfully built, and he had that FBI *look*—the conservative haircut, the clear, cold eyes, the three-piece suit, the air that said he voted Republican and would do so unto death.

Montana was taller, six feet even, and deceptively lean. He looked one-hundred-percent Italian, which he was, and nobody would ever guess he had spent his youth serving as an altar boy, which he had.

"Have a seat," said Conlee, and gestured at the institutional-looking chair before the desk.

Montana sat and remembered not to slump or cross one leg over his knee. He had spent seven years on the vice squad, a division not noted for its etiquette. He still had trouble tolerating wearing a suit every working day.

Conlee sat again at his desk. His office conveyed the usual FBI spartanness. On the wall behind him, a framed photograph showed the President looking noble and presidential.

"I'll get directly to the point," Conlee said, his cold eyes taking Montana's measure.

"Good," said Montana, measuring Conlee in return.

Conlee stared at a report on his desk. "This afternoon, at approximately fourteen-oh-eight, Francis Zordani was shot to death in front of the Stephenson Special School. The weapon was an Uzi. The car was a Cadillac de Ville. Two witnesses got the license number. We haven't found the car yet."

Montana's adrenaline gave a small rush. An Uzi? That probably meant something ominous.

Conlee nodded, as if he could read Montana's suspicions. "Colombians, we think," he said. "We traced the license. The car was stolen, probably two days ago, but not reported."

"You're sure it's Colombians?" Montana asked. When it came to bloodshed, he'd rather deal with the Mafia any day. The Mafia had standards, at least. They were incredibly low, but they were standards. The Colombians were wild men, crazy as coots. They'd kill you if they didn't like the way you tied your shoes.

"Yeah," Conlee said with weary disgust. "We found the guy the car belonged to. Their idea of a joke, we suppose, to use his car. He was another Mafioso, Markie

Scarlotti. Waterfront enterprises. His body was found this morning. They gave him a necktie."

Montana sat up straighter. A necktie was a form of cut throat, a signature of the Colombians. The murderer slashed the victim's neck so widely he could shove the tongue down through the wound.

Conlee said, "A neighbor walking a dog saw three Hispanic-looking guys—young, well-dressed—going into Scarlotti's place two nights ago, late. He said they were speaking a foreign language. It sounded like Spanish to him. He didn't know what they were saying."

Montana narrowed his eyes.

"Right," Conlee said, "it could be a drug war. We don't know if this is a Cartel or just a couple of crazy cowboys. We hope it's just a few loose cannons."

"Both Scarlotti and Zordani hit? Do you have any idea why?"

"No. None." He paused and gave Montana another of his chilly stares. "But this is probably gonna get ugly before it's over."

"I'd agree," Montana said.

"The reason I called you in is that I've got witnesses to protect."

Montana was surprised but tried not to show it. If the witnesses were important, the Colombians would try to kill them. It was as certain as the law of gravity. But why drag in an attorney?

"Why me?" he asked. "You've got your own men."

Conlee frowned. "The task force wants to make this an interdepartmental effort. More flexibility. Less predictability."

More red tape, less control. He doesn't like it, Montana thought, but said nothing.

"Officially, it's still on NYPD turf," Conlee said. "But it looks like it'll be our case. We're stepping in now because this could involve both the Mafia and the Cartels. So we want to be like God. To move in mysterious ways. We don't want anything we do to be anticipated."

Again Montana said nothing, waited for Conlee to go on.

"We also," Conlee said, "want the Colombians to

know if they move against us, they aren't fucking around with one of us. They're by God fucking around with *all* of us. Maybe even they'll think twice."

"I see," said Montana.

The Colombian drug kingpins had so much money they thought they were omnipotent. They didn't like people who got in their way, and if they couldn't buy somebody off, they killed him. It was a simple system and highly effective.

But the central task force wasn't merely people. It was a monolith composed of other monoliths, the FBI, the IRS, the NYPD, the Federal Attorney's office. It could tap into the DEA, as well—the whole big alphabet soup bowl of law enforcement.

The central task force had been formed when South American cocaine began pouring into the States. The coke problem had been too big, the players too many and too rough for any one agency to handle.

Ah, thought Montana nostalgically, for the good old days when heroin alone was the menace. How simple the heroin trade of yore seemed in comparison, how almost innocent.

"We've got a safe house," Conlee said. "We've got three witnesses, two kids and a woman. We want to put them there—at least temporarily. We need men with them."

Montana nodded but thought, *Are you going to say you want me? This is odd. This is very odd.*

Conlee picked up a file. "This is on you," he said. "There's one on every federal attorney. Yours is—unusual."

Montana said nothing. Again he waited.

Conlee opened the file. "This right? You were with the NYPD vice squad seven years?"

Montana nodded.

Conlee studied the pages, nodding. "A good record. Some impressive commendations. You helped uncover the Sicilian connection?"

Montana nodded. He had, and it had nearly gotten him killed. He'd been playing a bad cop, a bought cop, trying to line up some crack houses for a bust.

Accidentally he'd stumbled onto information of a turf war within the Mafia, Sicilians rolling into New York territory. NYPD loved that news. So did the District Attorney. Even the FBI was interested.

Go deeper, he was told. Get more.

He went deeper, got more; it was working like a charm. Then one night he'd been coming out the back door of the crack house after midnight. And damned if somebody didn't shoot him.

His first reaction had been amazement, not pain. His second was a surge of anger so primitive it was like a panther screaming inside him.

He'd been *set up*. The Mafia didn't run the crack house, but they owned and protected it, and somehow they'd found out about Montana. He knew it, even as his midsection was ripped by bullets.

Somebody had blown his cover. Somebody had betrayed him. He'd felt a wave of hatred both hot and cold. And then he'd felt nothing.

He'd awakened in a hospital bed, missing part of his lung, part of his spleen, and most of the feeling in his right hand. Part of his little finger was missing, and so many small bones had been shattered and nerves blown apart that the surgeons told him they almost hadn't saved the hand.

He was lucky to be alive, they said. By all rights he should have been dead, and whoever popped a cap on him should have put a bullet through his brain to make sure. But they hadn't—why? Too dumb, too green, too scared?

Now his hand was a disfigured claw. His ring finger and what was left of his little finger were permanently curled together, like a pretzel made of scar tissue. His middle and index fingers were unbendable, so stiff that they seemed welded together in a permanent accusing point. His thumb alone moved.

His days on the streets were ended, and he hadn't wanted to be shuffled into some division office to drive a desk until retirement.

Instead, he quit, took his disability allowance, and went to law school. Now the U.S. Attorney's office had him doing legwork, because it was what he knew best.

But someday Montana would be in the courtroom, prosecuting the Bad Guys. And he would stab those permanently pointing fingers into their faces as if God's own relentless hand was damning them.

"You had a reputation for being tough," Conlee said. "That right?"

It was right. Montana merely shrugged.

"And for being incorruptible—you gotta lot of priests and nuns in your family—that why?"

That was why. But Montana only shrugged again. His uncles Ernest and Bill were priests. He had four cousins who were priests and one a Dominican brother. He had two aunts who were teaching nuns, and a cousin who was a missionary nursing nun. His brother John had just been ordained a Jesuit.

"You a religious man, Montana?" Conlee asked.

"So-so," he said. He didn't much believe in God or the afterlife. He no longer attended church. But he hadn't shaken off all of his upbringing, and he didn't want to.

There was good, there was evil. There were Bad Guys, there were Good Guys. His aunts and uncles and cousins and brothers waged a holy war in their peaceful way. He waged a secular one and played as rough and dirty as he had to.

"I see you still shoot," Conlee said, turning a page in the file.

Montana kept his bad hand curled in his lap. "I can shoot left-handed. I go to the range three times a week."

"Why?" Conlee raised his eyes from the file.

Montana met them. "I was a good shot. I didn't want to lose it."

"You miss the force?"

"Sometimes. I like where I am." It was the truth, although most police officers hated prosecutors. The prosecutor's office fucked them up. Montana had signed on to fuck it back, make it serve police work, not thwart it. This did not make him popular in his office. He didn't care.

"I want somebody with the U.S. Attorney to help guard these witnesses," Conlee said. "You got the background I'm looking for. Are you up to it?"

Oh, Oh, Oh, that old adrenaline rock and roll, sang Montana's blood. But logic had priority over rock and roll.

"The attorney's office isn't law enforcement," he said. "We're not enforcement. We're lawyers and clerks."

Conlee pushed back slightly from his desk, adjusted his navy blue tie. "We may have a few legal knots to untie about these witnesses," he said with something like reluctance. "This is an unusual situation."

"Unusual how?"

Conlee explained about the twins, and when Montana heard the word "autistic," it was as if somebody poured ice water into his brain stem.

He knew what autism was. His sister Cindy's second son was ten years old, autistic, and in the children's unit at Bellevue. He couldn't dress himself or speak a coherent sentence, but he could name every kind of dinosaur that ever walked the earth. It was like his mind was a haunted movie house where *Jurassic Park* and nothing else played forever.

"Jesus," Montana said, showing emotion for the first time, "you can't put kids like that on the stand. Normal kids are dicey enough, unreliable. They'll be ruled incompetent—"

Conlee interrupted him, shaking his head. "Not necessarily. In matters of memory, especially numbers, these kids might be ruled plenty competent. Besides, they saw the face of the gunman. A dark man, they said. With three moles on his face. Like this."

Conlee held three fingers to his cheek, indicating the pattern of a triangle. "Besides," he said, "it doesn't matter if they get to court or not. If the Colombians know there are potentially dangerous witnesses, they'll come for them. To make an example of them. So the next time there are witnesses, they'll come down with a case of very bad memory."

Montana resisted the desire to swear again. "You can't let word leak that there are witnesses."

"We'll do everything possible to insure against leaks," Conlee said. "But I can't guarantee anything. There are cops on the take out there. You know it. I know it."

Montana tried not to glance at his ruined hand. Oh,

yeah, there were people who'd sell you out. There always were, always would be.

"Look," Conlee said, the line of his mouth going bitter, "*every* agency's got leaks. Between the money and the intimidation, the dealers get to people. The cocaine money —it's endless."

Montana shook his head impatiently. He knew all this. "You're still not saying why you need somebody from the attorney's office."

"All right," Conlee said. "Look—we can't find these kids' father. The mother's dead and the father's in Bora Bora or some damn place. When we do find him, God knows how fast we can get him back."

"*What?*" Montana said. "You can't find any *parents?*"

Conlee made a gesture of disgust and frustration. "He's some big-shot jeweler or jewelry designer. He's island hopping, something to do with pearls. We haven't been able to catch up with him. The best we can do is this: We got a judge to declare these kids temporary wards of the state—for their own protection."

"Great," Montana said sarcastically.

"Yeah?" Conlee said, raising an eyebrow. "Well, it gets greater. I said we're holding a woman, too. Now she didn't really see anything. She's a teacher at the school, but she was out on the playground when it happened. The thing is, Montana, we got no parents for these twins. We got no guardians. And they are *not* normal kids."

"I'm aware of that." Montana thought of his nephew, the dinosaur boy. He was a strange, good-looking kid who treasured his privacy and routine. When either was threatened, he could scream like a banshee.

Conlee set his jaw. "We got nobody trained to handle individuals like these. The woman, she's trained. They know her. They're comfortable with her. She can communicate with them. We can't. We got her in protective custody not because she saw anything, but because we *need* her, the kids need her."

"Jesus, Conlee," Montana said with distaste, "you can't do that."

"It's been done. She's agreed to help. She's soft where these kids are concerned. She feels responsible for them."

Montana gave a disgusted sigh. "Did anybody tell her how much trouble she could get into?"

"No," Conlee said, "not in so many words. She'll figure it out, fast enough. In the meantime, I want you there to talk her down, keep her calm, keep everything on the legal up-and-up."

Montana muttered several curse words in Italian.

"Hey," Conlee said from between his teeth, "it's her own fault. She's the one who told NYPD the kids knew the license number, counted the shots. *She* got them into this."

"She's a civilian," Montana countered. "She's a schoolteacher, for Chrissake. She probably thought she was doing her civic duty. How could she know what she was getting into?"

"*That* is not our problem. Protecting her and the kids is," Conlee said flatly. "Now, let me brief you about this safe house. It's not ours, it's not NYPD, it's DEA. Like I say, we're going to move in mysterious ways."

"So what happens," Montana persisted, "when the Colombians find out about these twins and the schoolteacher? If they're called as witnesses, you can't keep it secret."

"We can try. For the grand jury, we'll go for a deposition on videotape. See if the judge will allow the kids on videotape; don't show their faces, just silhouettes. Then they're home safe, they're home free," Conlee said. "Let's hope that's the way it happens."

We better do more than hope, Montana thought cynically. I better call up all my churchly relatives to pray.

Montana went home, packed a suit carrier and a duffel bag, and strapped on his holster. He called his sister Isabel and said he was on special assignment; he'd be incommunicado for a while.

She sounded aggrieved. "Oh, no, Mick. I thought those days were gone for ever."

He only smiled at her tone and said, "Not quite."

Dark had fallen by the time he reached the precinct house. He identified himself and said he'd been assigned by the task force. An unshaven detective, ill-tempered and

See How They Run / 31

with the unlikely name of Valentine, came for him and told him it was about time.

Montana, said Valentine, was the last of the four guards to show up. The FBI, Valentine said pointedly, had been *prompt*. So had NYPD. The lawmen waited upstairs. So did the woman and kids.

Montana had been told with whom he'd be working. An NYPD homicide investigator, M. J. Stallings, belonged to the special District Attorney's squad. This was no mean distinction. Stallings had come up through the Seventy-third Precinct, the city's toughest and most volatile.

The two FBI men were Becker and Jefferson. Conlee had said they were used to this sort of duty and had pulled it before.

Montana met the three of them in a room that seemed too small to contain them. They were all big men. Montana, at six feet, was the shortest. He'd always been lean. Next to their muscle and bulk, he felt gaunt.

Stallings was almost six foot four, with broad shoulders, a bland face, and big hands. He had clear blue eyes and the sort of healthy pink cheeks seldom seen in New York. Although he looked like an overgrown farm boy, his accent was pure Brooklyn.

Becker was about six foot two and built like a packing crate. He had the inevitable FBI suit, haircut, contained expression, and icy eyes. Jefferson was his black clone. The two could have hired out as oversized salt-and-pepper shakers.

Montana introduced himself; they introduced themselves. It was formal, it was professional, but Montana knew they were sizing each other up like soldiers about to enter battle together, not wanting any illusions.

The others had met the woman and the twins. Montana alone had not. Valentine, plodding like a man who is much put upon, led Montana down the hall to another small room.

"These kids," he said scornfully, "are *sensitive*. We're introducing you one at a time. Make your entrance. Meet 'em. Then you're taking off. We got cars for you."

He swung open the door and let Montana enter first.

Montana kept his scarred hand in his overcoat pocket. He didn't want to put off the kids.

He saw the woman sitting on a metal chair. The twins were huddled in similar chairs, one on either side. They leaned against her and she had an arm around each.

Her face was pale, her eyes wide and wary, and she pulled the twins to her more tightly. The boys' faces were clouded with confusion. They stared up at him as if they were at his mercy. One had a white Band-Aid across his cheek.

Christ, Montana thought with an unexpected surge of emotion. He thought of his nephew, Joey, in Bellevue. These kids were just like him—there was something not quite human in their eyes, yet they were good-looking. His sister Cindy had said that autistic children were often unusually attractive. She was right.

The twin with the bandage looked more tired, frightened, and sullen than the other. Otherwise the kids were phenomenally alike.

They had thick dark hair, nicely trimmed, that fell over their foreheads. They had straight dark eyebrows and thick black eyelashes. Their eyes were an almost unearthly blue-gray. Beautiful kids, who looked whole and normal.

"This is Rickie, this is Trace," Valentine said, pointing first at the uninjured twin, then at the one with the Band-Aid. He sounded bored, as if all of this was dull and stale news to him.

"This is Laura Stoner," Valentine said and nodded at the woman. "This is Michael Montana. Mr. Montana'll help take care of you."

Laura Stoner stared at Montana, and he stared back. She wore little makeup and had freckles. Her eyes were troubled, as if she was just starting to realize the enormity of what she'd gotten into.

She had an angular but elegantly boned face, and could have been a looker if she'd tried. Her eyes were deep-set and a clear hazel. Her white blouse had blood on it, but she didn't seem to realize it.

She had long hair that was dark red; he guessed the color was called auburn. It made her face look even paler.

"Hello, Laura," Montana said softly. He knew from

his cop days that when people were dazed or frightened, you got friendly fast. He nodded at her encouragingly. "Just call me Montana. I'm with the U.S. Attorney's office. I'm here to help watch out for you and the boys. We'll take good care of you."

Her eyes held his for a moment. He had the eerie sensation that she could see inside him. It was an illusion, he knew, because nobody saw inside him. He didn't allow it.

Then she nodded, as if she accepted him. Odd, he thought, because although she might be scared, she was going to take care of those kids, damned *good* care. He sensed a certain quiet ferocity in her.

He smiled at her, although he knew he wasn't gifted at smiling. She managed a half-smile back. *Good girl,* he thought.

He moved toward them slowly, then dropped on one knee before her and the twins so he could look into the boys' faces. He didn't try to touch them. He knew his nephew didn't like being touched. He was surprised they tolerated the woman holding them as she did. Maybe it was because she was the only familiar being in a strange new world.

"Hello, Rickie," he said quietly. "Hello, Trace."

They said nothing. They stared past him as if he were an apparition that might be either good or evil, one that it was safest to ignore.

What's going on in there, boys? he thought. *How do I reach you? Can I reach you?*

On impulse he said, "Tyrannosaurus rex. Brontosaurus. Stegosaurus."

He thought he saw a light of interest flicker in the eyes of Rickie, the unwounded twin. The other said nothing. Looking tired, the boy tried to twist away from Laura Stoner's grasp. She held him tight.

Montana concentrated on Rickie. "Triceratops," he said, "Pteradactyl. Velociraptor." *Come on, kid,* he thought. *I'm running out of dinosaurs. All kids love dinosaurs. Even you in there, I bet.*

"Horned toad," Laura Stoner said in a soft voice. "Iguana. Monitor lizard. That's the sort of thing they like."

He looked up at her. She nodded. She was letting him know that the kids liked their reptiles alive and well, not extinct.

He nodded back. He looked into Rickie's blue eyes again. "Yeah," he said. "Monitor lizard. Lizards? Tell me about lizards."

Rickie cocked his head, looking at the ceiling, not at Montana. "Chuckwalla," he said in a clear, strong voice. "Gila monster. Spiny-tailed iguana."

He turned abruptly to stare at his brother. "Spiny-tailed *iguana*," he said, as if Trace had missed his cue. *"Spiny-tailed iguana."*

Trace shifted uncomfortably. He hung his head and muttered, "Flat-tailed horned lizard. Regal horned lizard. Round-tailed horned lizard."

Ricky took up the list in a more singsong voice, then Trace took his turn again. Lizards, lizards, they reeled them off mechanically, by the dozen.

We have achieved lift-off, Montana thought. He looked up again at Laura Stoner. He had the weird sensation that the four of them were united by a strange language that the twins knew best, the woman knew fairly well, and he was just learning.

His eyes met hers again. *Nobody's going to hurt these children. I won't let them,* her gaze said.

I'll die before I let anybody hurt you or them, he tried to tell her with his own. He meant it. It was his job to mean it. But he wondered how long she'd feel protective, once she realized how serious the situation was.

"Enough with the lizards," Valentine said cynically. "We got to get you vehicles."

"I'll see you, boys," Montana told the twins. They took no note of him; they were still taking turns listing night lizards.

He rose. "I'll be back, Laura," he said. She gave him the nervous twitch of a smile, but did not speak.

"Everything's going to be fine," he told her. Then he turned and went with Valentine.

In the hall, Montana said, "This has to stay quiet. If word gets out, these kids are targets. The situation's serious. Extremely."

Valentine swore. "I know that," he said. "I gave the school a cover story for 'em and orders not to talk."

"If word gets out," Montana said in his toughest voice, "and we find the leak came from here, your collective ass is grass. I hope you know that."

Valentine said as far as he was concerned, if they found any leaks in his precinct, the D.A. could plug them with hot lead, freshly fired.

Ten minutes later, Montana, along with Becker, Jefferson, and Stallings, ushered the woman and the boys out of the station house and into its garage. The department had given them two inconspicuous cars, a green-gray Chevy Lumina and a tan Ford Aerostar.

Becker, the white FBI man, was senior officer. He decreed two men would go with the woman and children, two men would follow. Nobody else had been able to get the twins to talk, so Montana was assigned to travel with them. Becker and Jefferson were used to each other, so the pink-cheeked homicide man, Stallings, volunteered to go with Montana.

Becker and Jefferson were to take the Chevy. As the group moved through the passage that led to the parking garage, Montana looked again at Laura Stoner.

She held each twin by the hand, and she walked with her back straight, her chin up. Her dark red hair swung as she walked, as if it had a life of its own, like a dark flame. She looked shaken, but determined.

Come on, God, Montana thought. *She shouldn't be in this at all. And they're just kids. No leaks, okay? If you're up there, cooperate this time—no leaks.*

They stepped into the coldness of the garage.

If God heard Montana's plea, He gave no answer, made no sign.

THREE

THE SAFE HOUSE WAS NOT A HOUSE, LAURA WAS TOLD, AND it did not sound particularly safe.

It was an apartment over a luncheonette near the garment district, the man named Montana said. He drove and did most of the talking. He spoke in the easy, trust-me tone that reminded Laura of a policeman talking a would-be jumper off a ledge.

The comparison made her uneasy. She did indeed feel like someone trapped on a high ledge, like a sleepwalker suddenly wakening, not knowing how she got there, not knowing how to get off. And, somehow, she had two children with her.

The boys, she kept thinking. *I have to take care of the boys.* That thought alone helped her keep her composure. She couldn't tell if Montana's too calm voice made things better or worse.

But at least he talked. The other agent, Stallings, barely spoke. He was intimidatingly large, with close-cropped blond hair and pink cheeks. If his eyes hadn't been so cold, he would have looked like a strapping, wholesome Scandinavian farm boy.

Montana, by contrast, seemed completely of the city. His lean darkness and New York accent made her think of city neighborhoods as Italian as Rome, and he moved with the edgy grace of a man who knows the streets.

"They tell me this place isn't much," Montana said, catching her eye in the rearview mirror. "But it's only temporary. If we need to detain you longer, we'll move someplace more comfortable, more out of the way."

If we need to detain you. Laura swallowed.

The boys sat on either side of her, slumped in their seats. They usually loved riding in a car, but both were tired and disoriented. Trace fluttered his fingers aimlessly against the collar of his blue jacket. His head hung down, and his eyes kept closing sleepily.

Rickie, more alert, stared without emotion at the passing streets. He hummed tunelessly to himself. Somewhere he had found a white paper napkin and was shredding it into tiny pieces without looking at it. Normally, she would have stopped him. For the time being, she let him do whatever gave him peace.

"How long—" she hesitated. "How long do you think you might keep us?"

Montana's gaze met hers in the mirror again. His eyes were unreadable, despite the friendliness in his voice. "I couldn't say. Don't worry. We'll keep you safe. That's what counts."

She leaned forward, pulling her coat more tightly around her. She put her hand on the edge of the driver's seat. Somewhere along the way, she had lost her gloves. So had Rickie, so had Trace.

Three little kittens who've lost their mittens, she thought irrationally. *But I won't begin to cry. I can't begin to cry.*

"Listen," she said to Montana. "How much danger are we in? You can tell me. The boys won't understand. But I need to know."

She thought she saw Stallings' big shoulders flinch slightly at her question. Rickie hummed more loudly and tore the napkin into tinier pieces.

Montana gave a casual shrug. "Rest easy. We don't know that you're in any danger. We're just taking every precaution, that's all."

Her fingers pressed more deeply into the seat's upholstery. "Please. Don't be evasive. I asked you a frank question. I want a frank answer."

He shook his head as nonchalantly as if they were discussing the weather. "The truth is that at this point there *isn't* any answer. The important thing is that word of this doesn't get out. If it doesn't get out, we've got no problem."

Laura persisted. "And if it does, just what kind of problem do we have?"

"Nothing we can't deal with," Montana said.

She leaned back against her seat grimly, letting her hands fall into her lap. Montana wouldn't give her a straight answer. Probably nobody would.

But she was still thinking clearly enough to know that being swept off into hiding by four men of the law was no cause for optimism. The boys were in big trouble, and so, somehow, was she.

All she could do was pray that what Montana said was true. She was out of practice at praying, but she tried anyway. She closed her eyes. She heard Rickie's tuneless humming. She felt Trace's body fall softly against hers, felt the evenness of his breathing. He was asleep.

Please, God, she thought. *Don't let anybody know about them—please. Keep them safe. Haven't You dealt them a hard enough hand?*

Her mother had told her once that hypocrites prayed only when they wanted something. She supposed that made her a hypocrite, but she didn't care.

When she opened her eyes, she saw that Montana had been watching her again in the rearview mirror.

"We're going to take care of you," he said. "You'll be fine. All of you."

But she didn't believe him.

The *World Weekly Record* was a tabloid newspaper, the sort sold at supermarket checkout stands. The paper had a hot line, and each week it paid five hundred dollars to the reader who phoned in the best tip.

A middle-aged reporter named Tim Finnegan was manning the hot line that evening. He chain-smoked as he punched up a story about a famous blond rock star who was afraid she had AIDS. She did not have AIDS as far as Finnegan knew, but every year the *Record* ran a variation on the story, and it always sold papers. The jealous public, apparently, *wanted* her to have the disease.

The hot line phone rang, and Finnegan sighed cynically. Half the time the information was neither new nor important, and the other half, the callers were clearly hoaxing.

But there were people out there who had access to dirt, sometimes surprisingly interesting dirt, and they desperately wanted that five hundred dollars.

Finnegan answered the phone in his most bored voice. *"World Weekly Record,"* he said. "News Hot Line. Tim Finnegan. You got something I should know?"

There was a moment of silence, then a young man spoke. He sounded excited and nervous, as if he had some telephonic form of stage fright.

"This is big," the caller said shakily. "You know that killing in front of Stephenson Special School today? Well, the police have three secret *star witnesses*. People that saw it. From the playground."

Finnegan grew suddenly less bored. He'd heard about the shooting. A Mafia drug lord whacked. Big stuff. It had happened shortly after two, less than six hours ago. "Star witnesses?" he asked. "Three of 'em?"

"Yes," the caller said in his excited, unsteady voice. "One's a teacher. Laura Stoner. I think it's Laura Ann Stoner. The other two are students, twins, boys."

"So how do you know this?" Finnegan narrowed his eyes against the cigarette smoke.

"Because I'm—I'm a staff member there," the caller said. "I heard her talkin' about it—"

"What kind of 'staff member'?" Finnegan prodded. "How do I know you're on the up-and-up?"

The caller paused. "I'm the—assistant maintenance engineer, like," he said at last. "I saw almost the whole thing. Through the window. I heard shots. I saw the blood and everything."

The janitor, thought Finnegan with dark amusement. *I should have known. All the better janitors read our paper.*

"You got a name, maintenance engineer?" he asked.

"Yeah," said the caller, sounding more nervous. "But I don't wanna say. I could get in trouble."

"I don't know who you are, buddy," Finnegan said. "But what you say sounds interesting. So if this is the Tip of the Week, how do I get the money to you?"

"Look," the young voice said, sounding reluctant. "I already told you too much. If I win, I'll come round myself, pick up the money in cash."

This amused Finnegan, but only slightly. "How'll I know it's you?"

The caller hesitated. "I'll give you a code word—'Atlantis.' I'll say, 'Stephenson School story,' then 'Atlantis.' You'll know."

Atlantis, thought Finnegan. *Shit, it's one of our readers all right.*

"Go on," he said.

"I saw 'em on the playground. It was like a movie or something—all this shootin'. Afterwards, I heard her talk about it, and she said the twins saw everything, a guy's face and everything. I saw the police take her away. Her and the kids. The head of the school called a meetin' later. She said they wasn't comin' back. Cops came and took the kids' stuff. The woman's, too. From her office."

Finnegan knew about the shooting. The story was already on the Associated Press wire service, and out of idle curiosity he'd checked out the school.

He said, "The students you got there—at Stephenson. These kids don't play with a full deck. You telling me you got witnesses not playing with a full deck?"

"Well, yeah," his caller said, sounding defensive. "But it's not like they're total morons, see? It's like that movie *Rainman.* These kids are geniuses with numbers and things. They got the license number and everything—a whole bunch of stuff. They got photogenic memories."

"Photographic memories?" Finnegan asked from between his teeth. He was interested in spite of himself.

"Yeah. That's what I said. The guy that did the shooting. They saw his face. And they never forget *anything,* man."

Finnegan stayed on the offensive, grilling him.

"Twins? They got the license number? They saw a face? That's what you're saying?"

"Yeah," the caller said, sounding happier. He probably already felt the five hundred dollars in his hand. "That's right. This teacher, Laura Stoner—and these *Rainman* twins—they saw it all. The cops took 'em away and then come back for their things. They got 'em in protective custody, I bet. Like on TV shows. That's what they call it. Protective custody."

Finnegan let a beat of silence pass, weighing, calculating. "What's the woman look like?" he asked. "Would you say she's pretty?"

The voice sounded almost resentful. "Yeah. You could say that. I wouldn't kick her out of bed for eatin' crackers."

Finnegan let the silence stretch as far as suspense allowed. Then he asked, "Could you get pictures?"

The caller sounded more confident. "Sure," he said. "She's got a bulletin board. All kinds of pictures. I could get you pictures. Easy."

"Okay," Finnegan said. "Okay. Now you and I, we'll need to talk again. Is there a phone number I can get you at?"

The caller went momentarily silent again. "I'll call you, instead," he said.

"Okay," Finnegan said, all business. "But talk to me, nobody else. I'll give you my hours. I'll give you my home phone. Got a pencil? Take it down."

The caller agreed, sounding conspiratorial and eager. Finnegan could hear the happy greed trembling in his voice.

When Finnegan hung up, he lit another cigarette and frowned. He studied the spiral notebook on which he'd scribbled his notes. The caller had sounded like a flake to him, a smug, stupid, hyper flake.

But something about his story rang true, and it jibed with the trickle of information coming over the wires.

The kicker, for Finnegan, was that the twins were "idiot savants." He dealt in the bizarre for a living, and he understood the twins' affliction. Retarded as hell, they could crunch numbers like computers, and their memories were infallible.

And the woman, the caller had said, was pretty, maybe even very pretty. Pretty women were always good copy, and Finnegan knew it. His reporter's instincts were starting to clamor, *Go for it.*

Shit, Finnegan thought, dragging on his cigarette. The cops or even the feds could come down hard on the paper for printing this—if it were true.

But that's what the first amendment was for. And the paper retained a flock of overpaid attorneys to block any legal backlash over a story. The lawyers, shysters to a man, were good, very good. They kept penalties light.

Finnegan cocked his head meditatively. At the worst, he'd alert the world that there were some witnesses hiding away out there. So? It wasn't his job to protect them. That was the law's. Finnegan's job was to get the news out. News, the more grotesque the better, sold papers.

The longer he weighed it, the more he knew this was a story the paper couldn't afford to resist. He wanted to see a picture of the woman, especially if she *was* pretty. The kids, too.

He could already see the headline: AMAZING *RAINMAN* TWINS SEE MOB DEATH! The subhead could be "Twins and Beautiful Young Teacher Fear for Lives!"

It'd sell a lot of papers. The devil take the consequences. The devil usually did, but Finnegan had trained himself not to care.

In the meantime, he supposed he'd fork over the five hundred bucks to the shaky-voiced kid who wanted to call himself "Atlantis."

Happy blood money, kid, thought Finnegan. And he marveled for the thousandth time at how cheaply human beings sold out their fellows.

The air of the safe house smelled stale and oily, redolent of years of cooking grease from the luncheonette downstairs.

The Ghost of French Fries Past, Laura thought, wrinkling her nose. She held each twin by the hand, and she could feel the tension rising in them as they faced yet another unfamiliar territory.

The apartment's living room was dark and joyless, its furniture worn, its overhead light fixture dimmed with grime. Montana seemed to have taken charge of her and the twins. She decided she didn't like this; she was a woman who preferred being in charge of herself.

"It's not much," Montana said, nodding in the direction of the hall. "But it's got three bedrooms. You and the boys take the biggest."

"No," she said firmly. "It'd be too different for them. I want their room the way it is at school, as much as possible. I'll sleep on the couch."

"There's no need for that," Montana told her. "We'll arrange something—"

Laura cut him off. "I'll sleep on the couch," she said with finality. She felt as if these men had seized control of her life. She could not resist trying to wrest it back, bit by bit, in any small ways she could.

She studied the gloomy living room and wished her heart didn't hammer so madly.

Rickie tried to free his hand from hers. "Don't like it here," he muttered pettishly. "Stinky. Stinks."

Trace scowled and scratched his Band-Aid. "Stinky. Stinks," he repeated. "Laura—*home*. Go school, go *home*."

She tried to make her voice sound sure and cheerful. "Don't pick the Band-Aid, Trace. We'll stay here a while. We'll all have fun together, Rickie and Trace and Laura."

"Want home," Rickie insisted, trying harder to twist away from her. She knew both boys were tired, confused, and ready to burst into tears.

"Look," she said brightly. "A television and a VCR! You can watch cartoons. For two whole hours."

"Two hours," Rickie murmured, seeming to weigh this. "Two hours."

But Trace glowered at the television's dark, dusty screen. His lower lip jutted out. "No," he said. "No, no, no. Watch television at *home*."

"For a while, this is home," she said in the same falsely

hearty tone. "You'll see. And everything's fine. Laura's here."

Trace took a deep, shaky breath, and she knew that he was on the edge of tears. If he cried, Rickie would, too.

"We'll have a party tonight," she promised, trying to ease their dismay. "A popcorn party. All big boys like popcorn parties. Cartoons and cocoa and popcorn. And bedtime books."

Slowly Trace let out his breath. His chin quivered, but he didn't cry. Not for now, anyway. "All big boys," he said dubiously.

"Yes," she answered, squeezing his hand. "All big boys like popcorn parties. Trace and Rickie are big boys."

"Big boys," Trace echoed wanly.

"Yes," she said. "Laura's big boys."

Her nerves prickled as she realized that Montana was watching her, almost as if he was measuring her ability to handle the situation. She felt another twinge of resentment toward him and his vague, easy answers. She cast him an accusing sidelong look.

What are you doing to these children? Do you know what you're putting them through? she wanted to demand. *What's to become of them? Of me?*

If he read her thoughts, he ignored them, and his face told her nothing.

The boys' possessions, packed in boxes, stood stacked against the bedroom's bleak wall. Laura had been adamant with Valentine, saying the boys needed everything: sheets, bedspreads, books, toys, even the decorations off the walls. He'd gone off to get them himself, along with Oliphant, and had grumbled about it.

She set about unpacking the boxes and trying to re-create their room at school. Montana, who seemed intent on winning her trust, helped her.

The boys loved Looney Tunes cartoons. Even as she worked, they sat in the living room, watching their treasured videocassettes. Laura could hear Daffy Duck singing an opera aria, lisping wildly.

Silently she and Montana made the beds, hung the

curtains. The boys' curtains and sheets and pillow slips were bright with pictures of cartoon characters. Rickie's bedspread was red, and Trace's was blue.

The rug that went between the beds depicted Wile E. Coyote chasing the ever-elusive Road Runner. Montana hammered nails into the walls so she could hang the plastic plaques of Daffy Duck, Bugs Bunny, the Tasmanian Devil, and Sylvester the Cat.

The twins had a Marvin the Martian clock they insisted sit in the exact center of the dresser top, and a Bugs Bunny lamp that had to be on a table between the beds. For reasons that Laura couldn't fathom, Bugs had to face the wall.

Any illusion she'd had of Montana as a comforting, homey sort vanished when he stripped off his suit jacket and hung it over the desk chair. He wore a shoulder holster, and the gun in it was large, heavy, and lethal-looking.

Laura couldn't help staring, slightly horrified. He'd knelt to unpack a box of books. When he glanced up and saw where her gaze rested, he studied her face a moment.

"Yeah," he said quietly. "It's okay. I'm trained to use it."

"I thought you were a lawyer," she said.

"I used to be with the police force."

She looked into his eyes, and uneasiness rippled up her spine. She had a sudden intuition that beneath his seeming compassion, he was the hardest and most dangerous of the four men.

Quickly looking away from him, she concentrated on hanging the twins' clothes in the closet. *Routine, routine,* she thought. *I've got to make all this seem ordinary, safe, secure.*

She'd gotten the boys to settle down in front of the television set, clutching their favorite toys, little plastic lizards in bright primary colors. The boys never actually played with the lizards, but they liked to carry them, finger them, stuff them into their pockets, keep them near.

The boys and their cartoons and their lizards, she mused; that should seem normal enough. But not when three men as large as football players sat in the kitchen in their shirtsleeves, their holsters in plain sight.

She'd heard snatches of the men's conversation. It was shop talk, and the wares of their shop were drugs, death, crime, and punishment.

"Where does this go?" Montana asked. He held a photograph in a gold frame.

"Oh." She moved to his side and took it from him, staring down at it.

The photo showed a handsome, sandy-haired man, a pretty blue-eyed woman, and the twins as toddlers. The couple sat posed stiffly, each holding a child. The man's cheerful expression seemed forced, the woman's smile tense.

The boys were only three in this picture, but already their faces hinted at their emotional distance. Neither looked at the camera or at their parents. Both had their eyes focused on some otherwordly point that only they could see.

She put the photograph on the dresser beside the Marvin the Martian lamp. "Their father and mother?" he asked, nodding at it.

"Yes," Laura said. "She died. Two years ago. It hurt her to put them in the school. But she knew it had to be done."

"And him?" Montana asked, tapping the man's picture. "What about him?"

"Him?" she said, her jaw tightening. "Ever since she died, he's been hiding in a bottle. He doesn't come see the twins any more. He travels a lot. He sends postcards. That's it. He pays the bills, and he sends postcards."

"Too bad," Montana said.

"When are you going to find him?" she asked. "It's wrong, all this happening, and him not knowing."

"We're working on it," he said.

"He should be here, not me," she said. Then she sighed philosophically. "Maybe some good will come out of this. Maybe this will make him stop running from things and face them instead."

"Maybe it will," said Montana.

He opened another carton and started unpacking books. He asked no more questions about the Fletchers, for which Laura was grateful.

The silence seemed to weigh on the room. At last Montana said, "We brought a computer. It can pull up mug shots of everybody we have on record who's connected to the Colombians. We want the boys to look. When can we start?"

"Not before tomorrow," she said. "They're tired. They've been through too much for one day."

"Whatever you say." Once again he gazed at the picture of Burton Fletcher and his late wife.

She swallowed. "You said Colombians. How can you be sure?"

He shrugged casually. "We can't. It's a hunch. If it fails, we try other mug shots."

"What if they identify someone?"

"We've got a video camera," he said. "We'll make a tape of the ID for the record. If the court accepts a tape as a deposition, we'll make another video, have their faces and voices electronically masked. The public never has to know who they are."

"And how long do we have to stay here?" she persisted. "In this—place? It's like being held prisoner. How long do I have to stay? Until Burton Fletcher gets here, I suppose. I mean, I didn't really see anything."

"Later we'll sit down and talk about it," he said, and opened another carton. "After the kids are asleep."

We'll talk. After the kids are asleep. How innocent, how normal, how wholesome it sounded. But the words seemed an ominous parody of real family life.

Montana turned to her, and gave her the companionable smile that she was learning to mistrust.

His arm was full of children's books, but his holstered gun gleamed in the soft light that fell from the Bugs Bunny lamp. The gun seemed to dominate the room, making everything else insubstantial, meaningless.

In New York, the winter night was black and cold, and the sleet had turned to stinging snow.

But on the island of Bora Bora in French Polynesia, it was early afternoon. Clear blue waves sparkled and danced, mirroring the flawless sky.

Burton Fletcher sat at an outdoor table of the Bora Bora Yacht Club staring blindly at the turquoise water. He had not touched his food, only his wine, and the bottle was three-quarters empty.

Many people called Bora Bora the most beautiful island in the world. Thick vegetation covered its jagged volcanic peaks, robing them in a deep, glowing green as rich as velvet.

The lagoon that surrounded the island was as blue and crystalline as the mountains were green. But Burton could see none of this. He wanted to care for beauty but could not; it no longer registered on him.

He refilled his glass and signaled for another bottle of wine. For a moment he let his gaze rest on the small, shallow pool that had been created beside the deck. In the pool's confines a trapped shark swam back and forth, back and forth, for the amusement of the customers.

Burton, in his growing drunkenness, identified with this shark. He felt as if his life consisted of some cramped, fetid space from which there was no escape.

He kept pointlessly moving even though moving took him nowhere, and he remained caught in the same murky, empty circle.

He was cold-blooded like the shark; he felt hungers and animal drives, but he no longer felt emotions. The shark needed water to exist; Burton needed alcohol. They both could sustain themselves only in their liquid element, although why they should bother to sustain themselves, neither knew.

Burton raised the last of his Beaujolais to the shark and said, "Here's to cold fish." The shark swam back and forth. Burton drank.

An hour and a half ago, in the open-air lounge of the Hotel Bora Bora, Burton had been approached by a heavy-set young Polynesian in a tan police uniform. The man's wide bronzed face had looked grim when he'd said, "Mr. Fletcher?"

Oh, damn, Burton had thought irritably. *The police? What now?* He wondered if he'd had a fender-bender last night with his rented car in the parking lot. He couldn't remember getting back home after drinking at Bloody Mary's.

"What's wrong?" he'd asked.

The policeman's face had gone even more stolid. "We had a fax from Papeete, Mr. Fletcher. It's about your sons. There was a drive-by shooting in front of their school. Your sons are fine, but they saw a man killed."

In accented English he droned out the story, ending with the news that police had the boys and their teacher in protective custody.

Burton had stared at the policeman uncomprehendingly. "Protective custody? Then they're all right. So why—"

The man had shaken his head. "The man killed was in the Mafia, Mr. Fletcher. New York police think he was killed by hit men. That maybe there's some kind of drug war. You need to go back. They'll put you into protective custody with your boys. There's a plane leaving for Tahiti in six hours. We can get you on it to catch the night flight to the States."

Burton could feel nothing, nothing at all. He simply stared.

"I'm sorry, but it's true," said the policeman. "You're requested to go back to the States."

Burton took a long pull from his morning drink, then looked the officer in the eye. "Why should I go back? What good would it do?"

The man seemed taken aback by the question. "Why? To be with your children. *Vos enfants. Tes enfants.*"

Burton said nothing because there was nothing to be said. How could he tell this man that he did not want to see his children? How could he say that he had stopped loving them, had stopped loving anything? That he wished, ardently, his children had never been born? He would gladly sacrifice them if it would bring his wife back, but nothing could. She was gone forever.

So he drained his drink, stood, and clapped the young policeman on the shoulder. He said he would be on that afternoon plane to Papeete and from Papeete he'd depart for the States.

Then he'd come here, to the pretentiously named

Yacht Club, to be alone and embalm himself in liquor before he had to go back. The waitress brought him another bottle of wine, but gave him a disapproving look.

Burton didn't give a goddamn. He was past caring, and he was long past tears. That was the odd thing. When he'd learned that his boys would never be normal, he hadn't cried, his eyes hadn't even moistened. He didn't cry when he sent them off to live at Stephenson, although his wife had. He couldn't even cry when his wife died, although he'd wanted to.

No, he could not cry. He was no longer capable.

He poured a fresh glass and raised it to the captive shark swimming through water fouled by its own wastes. *To those who have no tears*, he thought, and drank as deeply as he could.

FOUR

THE BOYS FELL INTO UNEASY SLEEP AT LAST. THE BUGS
Bunny lamp would stay on all night; that's what they were
used to. Beyond its soft glow, the corners were full of
shadows.

Laura rose from her chair, shut the book, and laid it
aside. She walked down the dim hall and into the living
room where the lights blazed.

The FBI men Becker and Jefferson sat hunched over
the coffee table, playing cards. Both had the sleeves of their
white shirts rolled up and ties loosened. Both wore guns.

"Gin." Jefferson yawned.

"Lucky bastard," Becker muttered and tossed down
his cards. "I'm too tired to think straight. I'm going to
bed."

When Becker saw Laura, he stiffened. "Excuse the language, ma'am. We didn't know you were there."

She tried to smile, almost succeeded. "It's all right."

She glanced about the room. Montana lay stretched on
the green couch, his head on a dingy sofa pillow. An open
book was propped on his chest.

Stallings, the apple-cheeked, cold-eyed man from the
NYPD, was nowhere in sight. Becker and Jefferson sat
eyeing Laura warily, as if she might be about to make
trouble.

But Montana's voice was easy when he spoke. "The boys asleep?"

"Yes," she said.

He closed his book, swung his feet to the floor. "Both of them?"

"Yes," she repeated. Her heartbeat speeded, and her throat tightened. *This is really happening,* she told herself. *I'm in this seamy room with three strange men with guns. This is not a nightmare. This is real.*

"Good," Montana said with a small nod. "You want a sandwich or something?"

The thought of food made her queasy. "No. Thanks."

"I'm hitting the sack," Becker said and got up.

Jefferson rose, too. "Likewise."

He moved toward the door, but paused when he reached Laura. Becker also stopped. She felt dwarfed by the two big men, overwhelmed.

Jefferson, the black agent, gave her a kindly smile. He said, "Good night. And don't worry. We'll take good care of you and those boys."

"Thank you," she said, and wished her voice didn't sound so stiff and unnatural.

Becker said only, "Good night," then moved on. He was a serious-faced man, with permanent worry lines etched across his brow.

Jefferson patted her shoulder, winked at her, then followed Becker.

She stared after the two men, then turned to Montana, who stood by the television. He was putting a Bugs Bunny videocassette back into its box. Like the other two men, he'd rolled up the sleeves of his shirt, unbuttoned his collar.

He was so lean that his face was gaunt. It reminded her of the paintings of El Greco, the portraits of dark, ascetic-looking men who seemed beyond the temptations of the flesh.

"You said we'd talk," she said.

He smiled. It was a small, disarming smile, but she didn't allow herself to be disarmed.

"Sure," he said, and gestured toward the couch. "Join

me? Can I get you something? There's half a pot of coffee left."

She shook her head. Caffeine was the last thing she needed. She crossed the room and sat down at the end of the green couch. It was hard and lumpy, and the fabric looked grimy from years of neglect.

He sat at the other end, crossing one leg over his knee. His hair looked jet black in the bright light, and so did his eyes.

"So," he said. "What's a nice girl like you doing in a place like this?"

He was trying to relax her, make her smile. She could do neither. She forced her voice to stay steady. "You tell me. What *am* I doing in a place like this?"

He shrugged nonchalantly. "You're keeping out of trouble."

She met his gaze. "It's big trouble, isn't it? How big?"

His eyes didn't waver an iota. "We don't know. Maybe not so bad. Let's hope so."

"That detective, that Valentine man. He said what we saw was a drug killing. Was it?"

"It's a major possibility. Look, you're sure you don't want something to drink?"

His calmness irritated her and so did his evasiveness. "Don't hold out on me," she said. "You've blown our lives apart. You've forced us to hide away like—like prey. I've got a right to know what we're hiding from."

His smile slipped away, his face went somber. "All right. How much did Valentine tell you?"

"He said the old man was a drug lord. That the killing was planned, that it was a—a hit. He said something about a drug war. Is that true?"

His expression was impassive. "Maybe so. Yeah."

"And the twins are in danger because they got the license number, saw the gunman?"

"Yes," he said. "And you saw it, too."

She shook her head, confused. "No. I saw him die. That was all. It was terrible. That's all I remember."

"But you saw it," he said. "And if word gets out that the kids saw what they did, it could be dangerous for them."

"Somebody would really harm children?"

"These people don't care who they hurt. You get in their way, they hurt you."

She drew in a long, shaky breath. She could think of nothing to say.

He said, "These same people, this same organization, drove a van into a mall in Florida. Yeah, you heard right. Drove it right *inside* the mall. Opened fire."

She stared at him as if he were making up a horror story, an unbelievable one.

"They were mad at the guy who ran the liquor store. Shot the store to pieces. Killed four people. Kept firing all the way out. They gunned down a sixteen-year-old kid in the parking lot, killed him. A bag boy, carrying groceries out of the supermarket. It was lucky they didn't kill more."

She kept staring at him. "And these people are Colombians?" she asked. "Like—like the bad guys on *Miami Vice*?"

"We think so. What this is about, we don't know. Are they moving in on Mafia turf? What's coming down? We don't know."

"And if they find out about the boys?"

"The Colombians don't like witnesses. So we want to keep this thing under wraps. They move against the boys, they move against *us*. All of us."

"All of you," she said, not comprehending.

"All of us. Jefferson, Becker, Stallings, me—we're from different parts of the Organized Crime Task Force. And the force wants you safe. All of you."

May the Force be with you, she thought. "Why me? I'm not really a witness."

He looked her up and down as if measuring her. "You saw enough. And we need you. The kids need you."

Slowly the realization dawned on her. "You're not going to keep me because of *them,* are you? You don't intend to keep holding me after their father gets here?"

From the moment she'd seen him, she knew his face could be hard if he chose, his eyes cold. She just hadn't expected how hard, how cold.

"You got them mixed up in this," he said. "You're the one who got them into it."

She looked away, her heart thudding. Why had she been in such haste to be Ms. Good Citizen? What had she done to herself—and to the boys?

If she'd stayed quiet, they'd be at Stephenson now, safe in their own beds, locked into their usual ordered existence. The events of their day would run in as smooth and inevitable sequence as the numbers they loved: breakfast, play, roll call, salute the flag, lessons—one, two, three, four, five.

And she would be home in her spartan apartment, living a life as sequestered and narrow as theirs. Her apartment was clean and well lighted, and she kept it as bare as possible. She liked it that way. After work, she returned to it and lived in it as snugly as a hermit crab in its shell.

If only she'd kept quiet, tomorrow she would arise and go about her pleasantly predictable tasks. She would take her morning coffee break with Herschel and Shelley Simmons.

Herschel would be cheerful and full of good-natured teasing. He always had what he called "the joke of the day," and it was always bad. Shelley, who was to be married next month, would be fretting about wedding arrangements.

Most important, she would work with her special group of students—not only the twins, but Fergus, Janine, and Brian—children to whom she was fiercely devoted. She did not love them; that would be unprofessional, but she put their welfare above all else.

The children would need her tomorrow because today had been so violent and upsetting. They wouldn't understand why she was gone.

If Laura wasn't there, how would Janine learn to tie her shoes? How would Fergus master writing his name? How would Brian finally learn to talk?

Other people's children, her ex-husband had once said to her in frustration. *Your whole life is other people's children.*

She locked gazes with Montana. "I was stupid to tell the police," she said bitterly. "I shouldn't have said anything. I wish I could turn back time."

"It doesn't turn back," said Montana.
Down the hall, Rickie cried out in his sleep.

Rickie lay on the unfamiliar, lumpy mattress, dreaming. Even in dreams, his world had no order; it was like a wild and boundless sea on which he sailed in a tiny boat.

He had no map for this sea. He did not know in what direction he sailed or toward what shore. Laura might say, *go this way, go that way.* Laura was his only compass.

Laura talked with her voice and her face, but Rickie did not know the language of faces. *Like this,* Laura would say, showing him a picture of a smile face. *This is happy.*

In Rickie's world, clocks ran smoothly, but time itself was broken. Clocks talked in numbers: twelve hours, sixty minutes, sixty seconds.

But time gibbered nonsense and ran wild. Time had eaten up Mama and wouldn't give her back.

Mama said that death is like a door in the clouds. Mama is in the clouds now, but where is she when the clouds are gone? Mama is behind the sky. She went through a door in the clouds. What took her?

A bird, huge and vicious, with a sharp beak and wide beating wings. Rickie had seen a picture in a storybook of such a bird carrying a child up into the clouds.

In his dream, Mama was at first with Rickie and Trace, and Laura was, too. The four of them stood on the playground, and far away on the edge of the sky Rickie saw a dot, a moving dot. It flapped nearer, taking on a terrifying shape.

Rickie couldn't move; he could only stand and watch the bird grow bigger, bigger, until he saw in detail all its ferocious features: the knifelike beak, the yellow eyes, the terrible claws. . . .

The bird swooped, but it didn't take Rickie. Instead, it took Mama. It flew up, up, with her, and the sky turned sunset red, and a door opened in the fiery clouds . . .

Rickie screamed, screamed long and hard.

But then he was awake, and Laura was there. She held him so tightly that she was more real than the bird, but still he could not stop crying, although he could not say why.

• • •

Laura sat on Rickie's bed, hugging him.

Montana had followed and stood in the doorway watching. He made her self-conscious, and she was sure his presence only upset Rickie more. Over her shoulder she said, "This would be easier if you'd go away, Montana."

He nodded silently and left. It took her perhaps fifteen minutes to get Rickie back to sleep. She heard the phone ring and the low mumble of Montana's voice, but couldn't understand what he said.

What are these children doing here, going through this? she thought resentfully, rocking the boy. *What am I doing here? It's mad.* But at last Rickie's eyes were shut, his face peaceful, his breathing even.

Wearily she rose and returned to the living room. Montana, looking restless, stood by the sofa, his dark eyes trained on her face. "You were holding him," he said. "I thought they didn't like that kind of thing."

She sat on the arm of the sofa and shook her head. "Mostly they don't. But sometimes being held tight calms them."

"How do you know when to do it or not?"

A good question, Laura thought, rubbing her forehead tiredly. "Instinct," she said. "That's all."

"Fletcher's been located," he said. "We've sent word to him. We're waiting for a reply."

Laura's fatigue melted and a sudden alertness seized her. The phone call—she'd forgotten about the phone ringing.

She said, "Once he's here, I'll go—right? You can't really keep me."

"We'll take it as it comes," he said vaguely. "Tell me about him, about Fletcher. What's the story?"

She resented the change of subject, the continuing evasiveness. "You're the ones with the files on everybody. Don't you already know everything?"

"Not everything. What happened to their mother?"

"I told you—she died."

"How?" he asked.

"Can I go home when he gets here?"

"That's not my decision. I'll do everything I can for you. How'd she die?"

Laura put her fingertips to her temple. Her head ached. "She was walking. Near Times Square. The light was against her, but she stepped into traffic. In front of a taxi. It couldn't stop in time."

"An accident?"

"Nobody knows. It was six months to the day that they'd put the twins in school. She was devoted to them, completely. She always seemed like the strong one in the family. You know, the one who held things together."

"Maybe she was tired of being strong."

Laura had often asked herself if this was so, but the answer was beyond her. "Nobody knows. Sending them off to live at school hurt her. A lot, you could tell. Maybe it hurt her more than she could stand."

"And their father?"

"Their father—I don't know. I think he blames them. Or he can't understand why this happened to them. Maybe he's just given up. It's hard to say."

"That's why he drinks?"

She looked away and shrugged. "I don't know. Like I said, she was the strong one. And then—she was gone."

"I see," said Montana. He seemed to be watching her closely, and it made her nervous.

"Listen, Montana," she said impatiently. "How long do you intend to keep the boys, anyway? Do you know how hard this is on them?"

"Death's harder," he said.

His words shocked her, and perhaps he had meant them to.

He said, "If we're dealing with Colombians, we don't want them even to know these kids exist."

She swallowed. "Do you really have control over the news getting out?"

"Some," he said. "We have some control."

"That means you don't know how much. Doesn't it?"

"We'll see."

Her head throbbed more wickedly. "So many people already know," she said. "Everybody at school. The police. This—this task force, the four of you. Your families know where you are, surely? What you're doing?"

He shook his head. "No."

She couldn't believe him. "Your own families don't know?"

"Becker never tells his wife everything. It's how he plays the game. Jefferson's divorced. Stallings isn't married. He's got a fiancée, but he doesn't tell her. That's the way it's got to be."

"How can you live like that?"

"It's how we live. That's all."

"What about you?" she asked, studying his face. He looked calm and concerned, but he had an actor's face, she thought; it could show emotions that never touched his heart.

"I'm single," he said. "When I was a cop, having a family didn't seem right. I was undercover. A wife and kids? That'd be giving hostages to fortune."

"And now?"

"I still don't give hostages to fortune."

She looked away from him. Montana could be kind when he chose; he could be perceptive. But there was, at his center, something implacable. Of the other men, only the pink-cheeked Stallings seemed to share this hardness.

"Where's Stallings?" she asked, glancing toward the hall. "I didn't see him."

A half-smile touched the corner of Montana's mouth.

"Stallings lifts weights for half an hour, has a glass of something made out of seaweed, then goes to bed. He doesn't drink, smoke, or touch fat, sugar, or caffeine. I hope he also doesn't snore. I have to bunk with him."

"Are you staying up much longer?" she asked. "I want to sleep. I'm taking the sofa. I found extra blankets in the closet."

She touched the grimy sofa with distaste. She imagined a long, restless night ahead of her, and she didn't even know if she had a nightgown or pajamas.

Someone at the precinct house had sent a policewoman to Laura's apartment to get her things. Laura hadn't even yet had time to open the suitcases. She had no idea what possessions or clothing she had with her.

"Go ahead, stretch out," Montana said. "I stay up until three-thirty."

"Why?" she asked, nonplussed.

"We drew lots. It's my turn to take watch."

"Oh," she murmured. She could think of nothing else to say. Of course, there would be a watch. These men were, after all, guards.

"Go to sleep," he urged. "You're tired. I see it in your face. Things will seem better in the morning. You'll get used to this."

"No," she said. "I won't. I don't see how anybody could."

"You get used to it," he said, nodding. "Trust me."

I don't want to trust you, she thought bleakly. *I don't want to trust anybody except myself.*

A man may be so intent on other matters that he may sow the seed of a great folly and not notice.

Don Mesius Estrada had sown such a seed, ironically, when he was striving to spurt his far less metaphorical seed into a most delicious blonde of eighteen.

"My cousin wants to be in the Cartel," she'd said, as he undid her lace bra. "He's an assassin. He's only eighteen, but he's killed."

"I have all the assassins I need," Estrada had mumbled against her white, round breasts.

"He could start out free-lance," she'd whispered. "If someone needed something done, you could recommend him. He could work his way up."

"Would it make you happy?" Estrada had asked, pulling down her lacy panties.

"Oh, yes, yes," she'd said with a breathy sigh.

"Then it is done," Estrada had said, and marveled that she was truly blond all over.

A week later, a customer of the Cartel's, a good customer, told Estrada he wanted two men "taught a lesson." That was precisely the phrase the customer used: "I want these guys taught a lesson."

And Estrada, still bewitched by blondness, had given

him the name of his mistress's cousin, a boy he'd never met.

Now Estrada, who had until now built his empire unerringly, was threatened by the foolishness of a silly boy from Bogotá, who, along with his friends, had thought it would be fun to kill. Estrada was enraged.

He had had phone calls from half a dozen different informants today. Each call sickened him more. This bully-boy had only needed to threaten. Instead he had killed.

Not only that, he had taken friends with him. He had even let a friend use the gun. Reynaldo Comce had shot down Francis Zordani like a dog in the street—Reynaldo Comce!

Estrada had become almost ill when he heard this. Then he was told that the police had witnesses, and that Colombians were suspected. *Madre de Dios,* his life passed before his eyes.

These spoiled schoolboys had created this mess, this abomination. He swore to God they would clean it up. Coolly, all graciousness, he'd summoned them, and they had come to him, as nervous and eager as suitors.

He greeted them silkily and with elegance. When they entered, his stomach knotted and he felt poisoned, but he looked at his guests and smiled sublimely.

You will undo the evil you have done, he thought, gazing on their foolish young faces. *Then you will die—and not easily.*

"Gentlemen," he said. "Welcome to my home."

They smiled back uneasily. Well might they be nervous, he thought. And let them smile while they had heads to smile with.

But none of his rancor showed, not a jot. He was as charming as if he loved them deeply. He was a man of station, and he acted it.

Mesius Estrada's address was exclusive; a famous rock star had once lived in this building, and his widow still did. It was an enclave of the wealthy and powerful.

Estrada's living room was lavish. A chandelier dripped crystal, and the reflection from its hundred lights glimmered from the silver candelabra and golden bric-a-brac. The drapes were of satin so deeply crimson the shadowed folds seemed black, and the furniture was upholstered in velvet.

His guests, the three young men he had summoned, looked callow and unsophisticated. Reynaldo Comce was not with them, of course. They thought Reynaldo Comce was their little secret.

Their leader was the blonde's cousin, a slender baby-faced boy known as Paco. He had frightened eyes, this Paco. Did he guess his pretty neck was in the noose?

I have wines older than you, thought Estrada, smiling down at Paco. *And worth far more.*

Estrada was well-built and of medium height. He was fair-skinned and dark-haired, and his piercing hazel eyes were fringed with lashes as long as a film idol's. He wore jeans and a simple blue sweater, but gold glistened at his throat and from his fingers.

Mesius Estrada was young for so important a position, only thirty-two. Unlike these bumbling provincials he had been bred for power. He had felt the weight of its responsibility from childhood.

These three privileged brats were only—what was the pungent Yankee phrase?—they were mere *wannabees.* Like children, they had played at being outlaws. Now he would work the little bastards like puppets to make them undo the damage they had done.

Estrada walked to the ormolu liquor cabinet, took out a bottle of Tia Maria, and poured four glasses. "Come," he invited. "We'll drink to you. I've heard you had a successful day—is that right?"

"Yes, Don Mesius," said Paco. "We hope it was." He took his glass in a hand that was not wholly steady.

The other two youths followed suit. Their names were Puentes and Diaz, and they had all come from Bogotá together, ostensibly to attend college.

All three had flunked out, although they had not told this fact to their families. They aspired to greater things than college. They aspired to the Cartel.

An unprepossessing lot they were. Paco was narrow-shouldered, and his face was childish, round and smooth with no trace of a beard. Puentes had a thick, dull, oxlike look to him. Diaz was mean-eyed and cocky and already bore himself like an up-and-coming young assassin.

Puentes and Diaz aped Paco, smiling when he smiled, drinking when he drank. They came from families far less well-to-do than Paco's. Puentes's father managed a coffee factory, and Diaz was little better than a servant, come to New York to keep Paco company and see to his needs.

Estrada gave Paco a conspiratorial look. "So. You're the ones who did the job for the *norteamericano,* eh? The one who went to Florida. He's hiding now. Everyone is looking for him, no?"

"I—I don't know," Paco said. "We weren't given details. We were told to go after two men, and we went."

"I see," Estrada replied. "Alas, a job's not always as simple as it seems. There's always the unexpected, isn't there?"

Paco blinked hard in apparent surprise. A wary expression shone in his eyes. "What?"

Estrada put his hands in the back pockets of his jeans and paced to the center of the room, his pose thoughtful. "There seems to be a problem," he said.

Paco swallowed. "A problem, Don Mesius?"

A problem. Estrada could see the word sent terror skittering along Paco's nerve endings. *Yes, something is wrong, little man. Very wrong.*

Estrada gave Paco a mild look from under his long lashes. "Yes. There were witnesses. Something has to be done about them."

Paco's face was a study in confusion. Clearly, the news stunned and frightened him. He stared at Estrada, his face pale. "Witnesses? Who?"

Estrada strolled to the window, lifted the drape, and stared at the jewellike lights of the city. "Three witnesses," he said. "A teacher, a young woman. And two children. They saw everything, noticed everything."

"Children?" Paco said stupidly. He kept repeating everything Estrada said, as if he had no words of his own.

Estrada let the drape fall back into place. He turned to face the three young men. "They saw the gunman's face. They can identify him."

All three looked as if they had taken mortal blows.

Paco smiled sickly, as if he prayed to God Estrada was joking. "But Don Estrada, everything happened so fast. No one could identify—"

"These aren't ordinary children," Estrada said in his silky way. "They remember everything they see. The make of the car. The license plate. And the face they saw."

Paco shook his head as if dazed. "But—but . . ."

Estrada reached into the right front pocket of his jeans and drew out a piece of paper. He unfolded it. "The car you used. A Cadillac de Ville? License number MPZ one oh four eight one nine? They remembered this, you see. As well as a man's face. I'm told if they see him again, they'll know him. Without error, they'll know him."

Paco looked thunderstruck. Yes, Estrada thought bitterly. *I know what you're thinking. What curse of Satan is this? What sort of children are these, the devil's own?*

"Yes," Estrada said, shaking his head. "They saw everything. The police have them in custody, hidden away. Along with the woman."

Paco looked sick with fear and dismay. "I'm sorry, Don Mesius. What do you want us to do?"

The other two young men held themselves so tensely that Estrada thought their spines must hurt.

"I want there to be no witnesses," said Mesius Estrada with a smile. "And you must want the same thing. It's you they can identify—no?"

"Yes," Paco blurted. "Yes, of course."

No, you little liar, Estrada thought. *It's Reynaldo Comce they can identify, and if that happens we are all dead men. You have fucked us, Paco. You have totally fucked us.*

"Now," said Estrada with a careless gesture, "this isn't really my problem. It's yours. And the *norteamericano*'s. He started this business. You'll have to finish it for him. Dispose of the witnesses."

Paco seemed physically shrunken, as if his body had aged decades in the last minutes. "But if they're hidden, how do we find them? How can we get to them?"

Estrada regarded him solemnly for a moment. Then he held up the piece of paper with the Cadillac's make and license number. "I can find out any number of things.

When I tell you where and when, I want you to kill them. Them and anyone who tries to stop you. Understand?"

"Yes, Don Mesius," Paco mumbled, looking sick with repentance. "I understand."

"And this isn't Cartel business. You're finishing it up for the *norteamericano*, not us. That's clear?"

"It's clear, it's clear," Paco nearly babbled.

He thinks I don't know about Reynaldo, Estrada thought, marveling at Paco's naivete. *Oh, Paco, Paco, you and your friends should have stayed with your school-books and left killing to men who understand it.*

"As a favor to the Yankee," said Estrada, "I'll help your search. And as a favor to you. But I repeat, this was never a Cartel matter."

"No," Paco said. "Never."

Estrada walked to Paco and put his hands on his shoulders. He looked into Paco's eyes. "If you're success-ful, you'll have indeed proved yourselves. Then it will be time for you not to work for the *norteamericano* any longer. Instead you'll join us."

The pulse in Paco's throat leaped visibly. Estrada looked at that jumping vein and thought with satisfaction of slicing it open.

"We'll make a place for you." Estrada smiled. "Just kill the witnesses."

FIVE

AT BREAKFAST, LAURA STRUGGLED TO PRETEND THINGS were normal. She cajoled the twins to eat their cornflakes, not play with them, to drink their orange juice, not gargle it or blow bubbles in it.

She herded them into the bathroom to brush their teeth and left them there. Grateful for a respite, she hurried back to the kitchen to finish her coffee.

Montana was there, leaning against the kitchen counter as if waiting for her. The other men were gathered in the living room, setting up a computer.

The computer's for the mug shots, she thought with a sinking sensation. How would she ever make Rickie and Trace sit through dozens of mug shots?

She squared her shoulders. "The boys need to go outside, have some exercise. Or they'll be wild. It has to be done."

Montana's dark gaze rested on her face. "Later. You and I have other things to talk about."

"Other things?" she asked, suddenly apprehensive. "What?"

"I've got good news, bad news."

"What's the good news?"

"We've heard about Fletcher."

She sighed in relief. "That *is* good news. When will he be here?"

"That's the bad news. He wrapped his car around a coconut tree yesterday afternoon. They had to fly him to a hospital in Tahiti."

She could only stare at him, wordless with shock.

He took her coffee cup from the table, refilled it, and handed it to her. She took it from him numbly, but only held it, did not drink.

"He's got a head injury," Montana said. "He's not going anywhere for a while."

"A head injury? How bad?" Laura said in disbelief. "He can't come back? For how long?"

"Laura," he said, "I'm sorry. He's seriously hurt. There's nothing we can do about it."

She ran her hand through her hair in frustration. Burton Fletcher in the hospital? Who else did the twins have? One set of grandparents in Florida, with the grandfather dying of cancer. A sickly grandmother in Pennsylvania. An aunt and uncle working for an American oil company in Belgium.

"Drink your coffee," he said in a voice that was gruff, yet kind.

But she couldn't drink. She set the cup aside.

Montana shrugged, almost casually. "We can have you appointed as their temporary guardian," he said. "We've got a judge working on the order."

"Me?" she asked, astonished. *"Me?"*

"I'm sorry." He shrugged again, just as nonchalantly. "The kids need somebody. You're all they've got. Let's face it."

She sat down at the table in stunned silence, her coffee untouched before her. Montana's face was grim. She expected he might at least try to look sympathetic, but he didn't.

"I don't know why you're so stony-faced," she said. "I'm the one caught in the middle."

"We're all caught in the middle," he said. "Fletcher's in bad shape. That's all there is to it."

"How'd it happen?" Laura asked with a toss of her head. "He was drunk, wasn't he?"

"Yeah," Montana said. "He was."

Laura crossed her arms and gave him a disgusted look. "He was probably feeling sorry for himself. As usual."

"Maybe he was," Montana said without emotion.

"I was hoodwinked into this whole mess, wasn't I?" she said. "The only thing you need me for is to take care of the twins. You didn't have Fletcher, so you drafted me."

"We'd need you even if he was here," he said. "Could he handle the boys? No. Only you can."

She was too dismayed to speak. Her thoughts whirled crazily. Montana stood watching her expression the way a scientist might watch a lab experiment.

Then shrieks and splashes sounded from the bathroom. The boys were playing in the water, a bad habit she'd worked hard to break.

Without a word, she left Montana and ran to the bathroom and turned off the rushing water. She snatched a towel and began to dry the boys' dripping hands and faces.

Now I'm supposed to be their guardian. Bleakly she dried Rickie's ears as he grimaced and wriggled to get free.

How ironic it was, she thought, making him hold still. Her marriage had broken up because she couldn't have a child. Now, suddenly, she had two—they just didn't happen to be hers.

But they're not really my responsibility. I haven't signed anything. Not yet. And I won't.

She toweled them both dry, thinking furiously the whole time. Yesterday, she had been caught in emotional tides that made her feel enormously protective of the boys. In the cold light of a new day, she had to think about herself.

She led the boys to their room, made them strip off their wet flannel shirts, and put fresh sweatshirts on them. Trace's was blue with a picture of Bugs Bunny on it, Rickie's identical except that it was red.

Of course, Montana was right, she thought—that was the damnable part. What good could Burton Fletcher do if he were back?

Burton couldn't control the boys; he could barely communicate with them. He was helpless in their presence.

Well, that problem was Montana's and the law's, not hers. She saw her situation with a fresh, cold clarity.

She was ready to charge back to the kitchen and tell Montana she'd seen through his double-talk, his pretense of concern, his mind games. Did he think he could play her emotions any way he wished? Did he think she was that simple? Oh, she would tell him, all right.

But Trace's shoe had come undone, so first she had to sit him on the bed and crouch before him. She tied the lace in a bow and double-knotted it, but her mind wasn't on shoes or laces.

She would march out the apartment's front door and away from this mess; the task force had no legal right to stop her. After all, she had a job to keep, her rent to pay, a life of her own to live. . . .

Trace reached out and took a thick strand of her hair in his hand. He didn't pull or twist, just held it, rubbing it gently between his fingers.

"Laura," he said, his voice plaintive, "take Trace home. Home *now*, Laura."

Her fingers froze over the knotted lace, and she looked into his eyes. Tears welled in them. He kept fingering her hair, a quick, nervous motion.

She knew she should move his hand away and tell him firmly that he must not do that. But she didn't. She felt almost humbled by his touch. Stroking hair was one of the few ways he showed affection.

She'd thought she'd broken his habit of stroking hair; she'd had to. It wasn't appropriate behavior; it wasn't normal; it wasn't acceptable. But for a moment she let him, because it gave him comfort.

Rickie came to her side. "Ossbim, Laura," he said. "Ossbim. Ossbim." It was a nonsense word he used that meant he was unhappy and wanted to leave. He had dozens of such words; who else would understand them except her?

"*Ossbim,*" Rickie said with emphasis.

"Laura," Trace implored, rubbing her hair more desperately. "Take Trace home."

"This is home for now," she told Trace, taking his chin

and making him look her in the face. "Don't cry. Laura's here, and for now this is home."

She knew they couldn't understand the concept of *for now;* time and language about time mystified them. She searched for words to explain, but could find none.

Trace repeated her words mechanically. "Don't cry. Laura's here. This is home."

Rickie nodded and stared at the ceiling. "Laura's here. This is home. Ossbim. Wavy gravy."

She swallowed hard. *Oh, hell,* she thought.

She wasn't going to leave them, couldn't leave them. What would they do without her? They needed her. Perhaps they were the only people in the world who actually needed her.

In a brisk, no-nonsense tone she said, "Laura has to talk to Mr. Montana. In fifteen minutes, Laura and Rickie and Trace take a walk."

Rickie stopped staring at the ceiling and squinted at his watch. "Walk," he muttered softly. "Walk, walk, walk."

Trace, too, turned his gaze to his watch. "Walk, walk, walk," he echoed.

Gently she made him let go of her hair. He rubbed the unshed tears from his eyes and stared at the sweeping second hand, counting.

She stood and gazed down at them a moment. Then she turned and went back to the kitchen. Montana looked her up and down.

"Well?" he said.

"I have to take them for a walk. In fifteen minutes. How many of you have to come along? Will we look like a parade?"

The two of them stared at each other for a charged moment.

He said, "I don't think that's a good idea, them being seen together. It'd be better if they weren't seen at all. Better take them one at a time or not at all."

Laura's chin jerked up in rebellion. "They'll explode. They're not used to being apart that way. They're already facing enough change."

"And I said—"

"I don't care what you said," she answered. "You want me to stay, but you can't make me. That's true, isn't it?"

He gave her a smile that seemed sympathetic, but she saw the coldness flicker to life in his eyes. "It's not true, Laura. We can detain you. Absolutely."

"No," she said. "I'm not a witness. I haven't signed anything that makes me a guardian. You have no right to hold me."

He shook his head. "You're the only one who can communicate with them, so *ipso facto* you're a material witness. A material witness can be held against his—or her—will. It's in the law books."

"I'd like to call an attorney and find out."

"Save your money," he said. "An attorney'd tell you the same thing."

"I doubt it. I only have to stay with these children if I want to. And I refuse to stay unless my word on their welfare is final, do you understand?"

She glared at Montana, who seemed unphased. He gave her a mild little smile, as if she were some harmless featherhead he was forced to patronize.

She wasn't deterred. She glanced at her watch, then looked him in the eye again. "If you want me to be their guardian, I have to be in charge of them. And I say they go for a walk—in nine minutes. What's your answer? Yes? Or no?"

Montana gave a lazy shrug and smiled more patronizingly. "I'll have to talk to Becker," he said.

He strolled off to the living room, leaving her alone.

Her heartbeat had speeded from this confrontation; the pulses in her temples drummed. She had won, she sensed it, and it gave her a giddy rush of triumph.

The price of triumph, of course, was that she would sign the guardianship papers. She would stay with the twins. She had become a voluntary prisoner.

It's all right, she told herself. After all, nobody in the outside world would need her or miss her. Since her divorce she'd made herself into an emotional hermit. She'd cut herself off from life as much as Burton Fletcher had.

Perhaps, in her way, more.

. . .

Montana had tried to jive her, and he'd failed.

She was smart, and once her shock had worn off, she'd caught on to the truth all too fast.

She wasn't about to forgive him, either. She avoided him as much as was possible in a five-room apartment, and she struck up a friendship with Jefferson, the black FBI man, instead of him.

Montana didn't care. She'd signed the guardianship papers, and that was what counted. She was staying on.

Her work was cut out for her, because the kids were edgy, badly out of sorts. They needed structure in their lives and lots of it. Laura Stoner knew what sort, and she created it for them.

She alone could truly talk with them. Sometimes the twins said strange, incomprehensible things. She was the only one who understood and could answer.

Only Laura could coax them into looking at mug shots on the computer screen. She had to work hard at it because the kids disliked the task; it bored and irritated them.

After two days, the kids had seen over eight hundred mug shots. They'd said the same thing about every one: "No."

"Look for the man who shot the gun," Laura would say patiently. "Say when you see the man."

A new photo would fill the screen, a new face with a new name and number beneath it.

"No," Rickie would say vaguely. The faces did not interest him. Instead he wanted to play complicated games with the criminals' numbers.

Trace, solemn and sometimes surly, would say the same thing: "No." Like Rickie, he found the numbers more interesting than the faces.

They always wanted to change the pictures faster, yet they seemed to be going through them at such a dizzying pace the men couldn't believe they were really looking. "They can go faster still," Laura argued. "Their perception doesn't work like ours."

But Becker's order was no, the pictures couldn't be speeded up any more. Once Trace's frustration burst out. "The man got three moles," he said impatiently. He pressed three fingertips against his cheek for emphasis. "Moleman," he'd said. "Moleman, Moleman, *Moleman.*"

Jefferson had laughed. "So that's who we're looking for—Moleman. Wasn't he the bad guy in a Flash Gordon movie?"

So the killer was dubbed Moleman, but mug shot followed mug shot with never a glimpse of him.

Becker and Stallings grew pessimistic and lost faith the boys would ID anybody. Their hope eroded almost completely after they learned the twins didn't understand age. When asked how old they thought Moleman was, Rickie said, "Eight," and Trace said, "Three."

"We're getting nowhere fast," Stallings grumbled at one point.

"If there's a picture of him, they'll know him when they see him," Laura insisted.

"We don't even know if they were right about the car or license," Stallings said, looking sour-tempered.

"They were right," Laura told him. "You can bank on it."

"Optimism," Jefferson nodded. "We need optimism here. Gotta accentuate the positive."

Montana said nothing, but he'd seen his nephew's phenomenal memory at work. He believed Laura was right. When the twins saw the killer, they would know him.

Subtly, sides were taken within the confined apartment, allegiances formed. Both Stallings and Becker kept clear of the twins as much as possible. Becker acted almost hurt by the kids' aloofness, and Montana sometimes caught Stallings regarding the twins as if they gave him the creeps.

Jefferson was another story. Once things settled into routine, Jefferson had dropped his guarded expression, lost his distant attitude. He joked with Laura and was patient and friendly with the twins.

Jefferson, divorced, had two sons of his own, and he instinctively knew how to win the kids' interest. He could recite endless sports statistics, which fascinated the twins even though they didn't understand sports.

Jefferson was an inveterate reader of newspapers, and he didn't mind reading the boys the columns of basketball statistics in the *Times*. They memorized rebounds, assists, and free throws without knowing what they were.

Copying from the kids' books, Jefferson could draw lizards, either realistic or comic ones. The twins preferred realism.

Jefferson could make a coin seem to walk across the back of his dark knuckles, a feat both boys struggled to imitate. Montana could get them to recite long lists of reptiles for him, but that was all. His own early success with the boys was eclipsed by Jefferson. And of course Laura ate it all up.

Montana was amazed to feel the faint stirrings of something resembling jealousy. He ignored it.

What he couldn't ignore was his growing doubt about the safety of the safe house. At last he felt compelled to speak to Conlee about it on the phone.

"Conlee, I don't like this place. The kids have to spend time outside, and they're too conspicuous. They act up, people look at them."

Conlee sounded bored and unconcerned. "Relax, Montana. This is New York. Nobody'll notice."

"People notice. Trust me. I don't like it."

"It's the best I can do. The task force hasn't got funds for things like this. The state's got no funds. Beggers can't be choosers."

"Any word on the car?"

"None."

"Any hard information of any kind?"

"Some. We keep getting street talk that the Colombians didn't do the hit. That it wasn't Mafia infighting, either. But that's only rumor."

Montana shook his head. "It seems damn stupid for the Colombians to have done it. But it's got all the earmarks."

"Sit tight. We'll get to the bottom of it. In the meantime, stop sweating the location. You're safe."

Montana didn't contradict him. But he didn't believe him, either. Working the streets had made him cynical.

"How's the teacher?" Conlee asked. "She doing her job?"

"Yeah," Montana said without emotion. "She's doing her job."

Laura slept again on the couch, an uneasy sleep because a light stayed on and there was always a man in the room. Early in the dark hours of morning, someone kept coughing. The phone rang. A door opened, a door closed.

The phone rang again; again a door opened, a door closed. Men talked in hushed voices. She tried to ignore the sounds, to escape into a dreamless void.

She was awakened by a hand shaking her shoulder. "Wake up," Montana said. "Pack. We've got to get out of here."

She raised herself on one elbow and blinked at him sleepily. "What?" she said. "No. It's night."

He shook her harder. "Get up and pack. We have to leave—fast."

Groggy, she glanced at her watch. It was not yet six in the morning. Only one light was on, and by its muted glow, she saw that Montana needed a shave. Stubble shadowed his sharp jaw. This fact, however, was not interesting enough to keep her awake. She tried to sink back to the sofa.

"Come on," he said impatiently. This time he shook her so hard it jarred away all muzziness. Her eyes flew open in surprised anger.

She tried to wrest away from him. "Stop."

"This is crazy," Jefferson said, appearing behind Montana. "Who took the news? You?"

"Stallings," Montana said from between his teeth. He brought his face close to Laura's. "Listen. You've made the headlines. The *World Weekly Record* went to press last night. They're doing a story on you and the kids. Pictures, everything. We've got to get out of here, because we've been seen walking these streets, and people will remember."

"My God," Laura said, stunned. "You mean—you mean—?"

His good hand still gripped her shoulder. "We tried to keep you secret. It didn't work. We need to get you out of here."

For a moment she was too dazed to think clearly. "Where—where are we going?" she asked, her heart beating hard.

"Valley Hope," he said, and he must have seen the reluctance in her eyes because he said, "It's a private hospital on Long Island."

"Valley Hope?" she said in dismay. She knew the name. The place was a scandal, on the verge of having its license revoked.

"You can't take them there," she said. "It's a snake pit. No."

"Don't fight us, Laura. It's the only place Conlee could set up at this short notice."

"No—" she tried to argue, but he cut her off.

He fixed his gaze on hers. "We've got no choice."

The way he looked, the way he spoke, the way he held her, she knew he meant it.

They had no choice.

Hurry, hurry, hurry, said everything in the apartment's atmosphere. Even the beat of Laura's heart seemed to repeat the command: Faster, faster, faster. From the corners, the very shadows seemed to whisper it.

She struggled to seem calm. She knew the twins sensed the uneasiness in the air, and it set them on edge.

Montana had said, "Give them breakfast. Then we're outta here."

Down the hall, she heard the men ripping apart the cheerful room she had so carefully reconstructed for the boys. Drawers slammed, curtain rods clattered, and packed boxes thudded as they were stacked.

Montana came into the kitchen. "Are you going to be all right?" he asked.

"It's not me I worry about," she said. She turned to

Trace. "Don't play with the toast. Eat the cornflakes. When the cornflakes are gone, we'll go for a ride."

Trace squinted at her, his sleepy face dubious. "Go for a ride," he echoed tonelessly.

"Yes," she promised. "But eat the cornflakes."

"I'm sorry to do this to you," Montana said. "I'm sorry for them, too. It's twice as hard on them."

No, she thought. *Not twice as hard on them—three, four, ten times harder. Maybe a hundred times.*

"Who'd do such a thing?" she demanded, watching Trace. "Exploit them, put their pictures in the paper? What kind of people would do such a thing?"

"People who sell papers," he said.

"How did the paper even get the story?" she asked. "And pictures? They really have our pictures? How?"

"The *World Weekly Record* gives five hundred bucks for the best news tip of the week. You were it."

He went to the kitchen's small window. He parted the slats of the venetian blind with his scarred hand and looked out. The sky was still dark.

"Five hundred dollars?" she asked in disbelief. "Somebody would sell out two children for five hundred dollars?"

He let the blind's slats fall back together. "No," he said, turning to her. "They sold out two children and a woman. You know anybody from the school who needs money that bad? Or wants it that much?"

"No," she said, horrified by the thought. "Why should it be somebody from school? What about the police?"

"It's a possibility."

He said it as calmly as if he was discussing the weather.

"Will it snow again?"

"It's a possibility."

"Will it be a lethal snow? Will it kill us?"

"It's a possibility."

She looked at the boys and pressed her lips together in a tense line. Rickie was uneasy, and Trace looked angry.

Both still dawdled over their cereal, and Trace talked to himself. "Blue rhubarb," he whispered as he watched the light glint on his milky spoon. "Blue rhubarb, blue rhubarb."

If only I hadn't said anything, she thought, angry at herself, angry at the unfairness of it all. *Nobody would know. But, no. God, God, why didn't I keep quiet?*

Montana must have sensed her growing despair. He moved beside her, put his good hand on her shoulder. "Look—" he said, "At least the *Record*'s a weekly. It's distributed nationwide. It won't hit the stands for a couple of days. And if it's any help, you've been doing great, more than great, you've—"

He didn't finish the sentence. Stallings came into the kitchen, dressed in a suit and tie. His usually pink cheeks were pale, his eyes watery.

"We're set," he said to Laura. "Everything's packed. So when you're ready, we can—"

He was cut off by howls of pure anguish, each more shrilly piercing than the last.

Stallings stopped, openmouthed. The shrieks ascended in a piercing spiral, more frenzied, more pained.

Rickie screamed uncontrollably. He dropped his spoon, knocked over his cereal, and fell to the floor with a crash.

He scuttled backward into a corner and crouched there like a small, trapped animal, tears streaming down his face. He howled and swatted out wildly at the air.

"It's the swan," Laura cried to the bewildered Stallings. "He's terrified of swans."

Stallings wore a beige tie with a black swan printed on it. She practically snatched it off him. He gaped at her as if she were a madwoman and Rickie were her demon spawn.

But she finally convinced Stallings it was the tie. Rickie was terrified of large birds, even pictures of them, and nobody knew why.

Reluctantly Stallings pocketed the offending tie and went down the hall to hide it in his suitcase. He grumbled that it had been a present from his fiancée, that it was a really nice tie.

Laura took Rickie into her arms and held him tightly. "The swan's gone far away," she consoled him. "The swan went to Japan, and Godzilla ate it. It'll never come back."

By the time Rickie quieted, Trace was upset, his eyes flashing dangerously. Just when she thought she had them both calmed and took them into the bathroom so they could brush their teeth, they *both* threw tantrums. Becker had unwittingly packed their Bugs Bunny toothbrushes away before they could use them.

Laura's patience was stretched to its limit by the time they got into the van. Both boys were irritable and exhausted.

Rickie looked frightened of Stallings, as if any minute Stallings might pull the evil swan tie from his pocket. Stallings was moody because in spite of all his seaweed and vitamins, he was coming down with a cold, a bad one.

Jefferson volunteered to switch places with Stallings and go with the twins, Laura, and Montana. Laura was grateful. Jefferson was far more genial.

It was snowing hard, and traffic crawled. Laura couldn't wait to get out of Manhattan, through the tunnel, and onto Long Island.

Jefferson had left a few books unpacked for the boys, but they were more interested in a road map they found under the backseat. Laura was content to let them study it and play an incomprehensible game with highway numbers.

"So is he over his scare about the swan?" Jefferson asked. The windshield wipers shuffled back and forth, clearing snow from the glass.

"Pretty much," Laura said, although she could tell both boys were bewildered by another sudden change.

"Is he afraid of anything else?" Jefferson asked. "I mean, don't be scared to say. Forewarned is forearmed."

She took a deep breath, and pushed her hair back from her face. "Yes," she said. "Swans. Penguins. Owls. All big birds. And they're both afraid of Santa Claus."

"Santa Claus? I never heard of a kid afraid of Santa Claus. Why?"

"We don't know," she told him. "And they can't tell us. Maybe someday, but not yet."

Jefferson shook his head. "That beats all. What else?"

"Bathing suits. Trace is frightened of people in bathing suits."

"Well, at least we don't have to worry about *that* this time of year."

She leaned back against the seat, closed her eyes. How paradoxical, she thought. Rickie hadn't screamed or cried at the gunfire or the blood when Zordani was shot. Yet even the picture of a large bird could send him into paroxysms of terror.

She wished she could experience, for just a little while, what it was like to understand the most complex problems in math, but not comprehend the simplest of wordless human signals, a smile, a wink, a hug, a kiss.

Montana's voice interrupted her futile wondering. "We'll get you out of Valley Hope as soon as we can."

"It can't be soon enough," she replied as evenly as she could. "I'm sorry, but that's how it is."

She hated the thought of the boys at Valley Hope. She'd seen it once, on a tour of residences for the mentally handicapped.

The hospital was ancient, three stories high, its liver-colored brick dingy with age. A high, thick wall of the same brick surrounded it, and the windows were barred with rods of rusty iron. The inside was cheerless, dirty, and evil-smelling.

Montana said, "I don't know where they'll send you after there. You may be put in the charge of federal marshals by then."

Her eyes flew open, and a strange hollowness took possession of her. "You'll leave us?" she said.

Without realizing it, she'd become used to these four men. "You've been good to the boys," she managed to say.

"Thanks," Jefferson said. "It's been a pleasure."

"The marshals will treat you right," was all Montana said.

A disturbing thought crossed her mind. "They're not going to relocate us, are they? You won't send us off and change our names and everything—will you?"

"I don't think it'll come to that," Jefferson said cheerfully. "Don't worry about it."

She couldn't help it; she had to worry. As soon as the twins' names and pictures were published, the whole country would know about them. Any hope that their testimony would be anonymous was forever gone.

Contracts, she thought. Wasn't that what drug dealers did to someone they wanted eliminated? They put a contract on him, a price on his head.

A price on their heads, she thought, her stomach queasy. She gazed at the twins, bent over their road map. Their straight, glossy hair fell over their foreheads, and their dark lashes were so long they cast shadows on their cheeks. *They're so helpless,* she thought. *So completely helpless.*

Once past Queens, the two-car caravan made a brief stop on Long Island. Stallings signaled that he wanted to halt, and both cars pulled into the parking lot of a strip mall.

Stallings came to their car and said he wanted to get aspirin and cough drops; he felt lousy. Laura thought he was starting to look seriously ill.

Although the twins grew restless as soon as the car stopped, Montana warned her to keep them inside. He didn't want anyone to catch sight of them.

Rickie and Trace, bored, began to squabble, and she put all her energy into making peace. She separated them, making one sit on either side of her, and she commandeered the map, which they had torn.

The van was crowded, the rear stacked with the video equipment, the television, and the boys' belongings. Looming up over the rear of the backseat were the wall plaques of a grinning Daffy Duck and a snarling Tasmanian Devil. *We're trapped in the world of Looney Tunes,* Laura thought darkly, and she wished sanity would return to life.

At last Stallings, wiping his nose, came out of the drugstore, a bag clutched to his chest. Once again, they got under way. Stallings and Becker's car was as crowded as the van, for it carried the adults' baggage and the computer.

The snow fell more heavily. The radio repeatedly issued travelers' warnings. Highways were treacherous, and side roads were drifting shut.

Each slow, snowy mile took them closer to the mis-named Valley Hope. She let the twins, reconciled, sit to-gether again. Once more they studied the map and giggled about highway numbers.

"Love is strange," Rickie kept singing over and over. It was a phrase they'd picked up from an oldies station on the radio. The one line was all they ever sang.

"Love is strange," Trace would echo. "Love is stra-a-ange."

"How much farther?" Laura asked, staring at the thick veils of snow. It was as if the car were completely curtained by swirling whiteness, and the world were a wasteland of cold.

"Six miles," Montana said. She could see the tension in him. More than once the van had skidded.

"Six miles," Trace echoed without emotion.

"Six miles," Rickie said and laughed.

A sudden gust of wind shuddered the van and made the falling snow churn like flakes in a shaken snow globe. Laura's heart jumped, Jefferson swore under his breath, but Montana said nothing. The twins didn't notice. "Love is stra-a-ange," Rickie chanted, then bent lower over the map.

Montana drove the last six miles at a cautious crawl. The snow kept falling, and the wind whipped harder. The van rocked with each fresh gale.

Even Valley Hope will look good, she thought as an-other gust shivered the van. *It's come to that. It's that bad.*

But then, at last, the van came to a halt. She could see the blurry shape of the Chevrolet stopped in front of them, its red taillights glowing.

"What now?" she asked.

"We're there, but the gate's shut," Montana said. "Becker's opening it."

Through the driving snow Laura could see the iron bars and crossbars of the gate. It had a medieval stoutness and would have made a fine entrance for a prison, which was, of course, exactly what Valley Hope was.

Becker, hunched against the cold, came and rapped at the window on the driver side. Montana rolled the van's window partly down and narrowed his eyes against the swirling snow.

The cold had made Becker's face apple red. "Gate was shut but not locked," he said, his breath pluming up. "Wind keeps blowing it shut. I'll hold it open."

Montana nodded, but Laura sensed tension in him.

"I hope they got coffee in this dive," Jefferson muttered.

"Yeah," Montana said absently as he rolled up the window.

Becker jogged to the gate and held it open. If hell had a gate, Laura thought, it would look like the one to Valley Hope.

Ahead of them, Stallings put the Chevrolet in gear and inched through the gate. His wheels hit an icy spot, spinning uselessly, and he gunned the motor, trying to gain momentum.

The car lurched forward, and Becker waved for Montana to follow.

Just as Becker's hand reached the top of its arc, there was a strange, distant popping sound, and Becker's fingers turned into bloody stumps, spewing scarlet.

Becker's forehead erupted in vivid red; his reddened cheeks disappeared beneath the rain of his own blood, and from his chest and belly gushed fountains of red.

The Chevrolet, with Stallings at the wheel, shivered and was suddenly pocked with holes. Its rear windows cracked into complex webs.

Laura was too horrified to scream, even when she saw the shattered rear window of the Chevrolet spatter with crimson. Stallings had to be mortally wounded for so much blood to spray the glass.

"Shit!" Montana swore. He threw the van into reverse so fast that she felt it twist her spine.

Instinctively she flung herself over the twins, who cried out in surprised anger. Jefferson grunted with pain.

"Hell, man, I'm *hit*," Jefferson said. She was vaguely aware that the car was colder. Looking up fearfully, she saw that Jefferson's side of the windshield was shot through.

Montana shifted, spun into a sliding turn, and took off at an insane speed.

Behind them, Laura heard the roar of another vehicle, a truck perhaps, and a fresh assault of gunfire. The back window cracked, and she pushed the twins farther down against the seat. Rickie wailed; Trace struck at her hand.

"Man, I'm hit." Jefferson's voice was choked.

"Get down," Montana said, "or you'll be fucking dead."

Another volley of shots smashed through the rear window. The twins wailed in protest. Laura dragged them down to the floor, pressing them hard against it despite their screams.

Something struck her back, but bounced away harmlessly. Her eyes had been squeezed shut, but she looked up, dazed. She'd been hit by the plastic plaque of Daffy Duck. It had been knocked onto the seat.

Half of Daffy's carefree face was ripped away by gunfire. He grinned a broken, insane grin.

SIX

THE VAN SKIDDED DOWN THE STREET, VEERING CRAZILY.

In the rearview mirror, Montana saw a white panel truck in pursuit, and he hoped to hell he wasn't going to take a fatal slide that would leave them a sitting target.

Jefferson, curled in a fetal position half on the floor and half on the seat, was bleeding badly. The shoulder of his tweed overcoat was sodden with crimson.

The kids' screams ripped the air. Montana could not see them in the mirror, or Laura, either. Had they been hit?

"Laura?" he yelled. "Are you all right? The kids?"

"I think so." He barely heard her above the din.

The white truck was gaining on them, although it, too, lurched and slid in the snow.

The window on its passenger side was rolled down, and a man in a black watch cap leaned out. He aimed an assault rifle at the Ford.

"Stay down!" Montana yelled. He veered to the left so hard that he went over the curb and onto the sidewalk, then slid back into the street, spinning like a top.

A volley of shots burst out. The windshield on Jefferson's side turned into a web of fractures. A hole exploded through the upholstery, just above Jefferson's head.

Swerving, the van swung out and jumped another curb. Montana, desperate, let it slide, then floored it again, wrenching the wheel into the spin. The van pivoted 360 degrees, then plunged onward, weaving first left, then right, running a stop sign.

A snowplow came trundling down the street toward them, and Montana struggled not to smash into it. He maneuvered around the plow, barely missing it.

Once he hit the plowed street, he accelerated as hard as he could and headed for the first cleared side street.

In his mirror, he saw the truck, still following. The truck swung out to give the snowplow a wide berth, hit an icy patch instead, and careered straight into the plow's scraper blade. It ricocheted off the blade with a metallic, ripping sound.

Then, with an almost dreamlike slowness, the truck skidded on two wheels until it crashed sideways into the thick metal post of a street lamp. It shuddered to a stop, falling back heavily on all four wheels.

The snowplow driver stopped his machine and leaped to the street. A wiry, older man, he ran gingerly toward the van, apparently to check the passengers.

He got as far as the curb before a blast from the gun hit his chest and blew clear through his back. He pitched forward, collapsing facedown into the snow.

Montana didn't wait to see more. He was doing sixty in a twenty-mile zone, the kids were still screaming, and Jefferson was bleeding like a stuck pig. He swung around the next corner, the axles shuddering in protest.

Montana didn't think the truck was in any shape to come after them; he hoped it wasn't. But he wanted another car—as fast as possible. Nine blocks from the wreck, he saw a four-wheel-drive vehicle, a blue Bronco, coming down a side street, and he brought the van to a screaming halt crossways in its path.

"Give me your badge," he ordered Jefferson. Jefferson looked weak and befuddled, but he nodded. He pulled the badge's leather holder from his inside pocket and handed it to Montana. The case was slippery with blood.

Montana sprang from the van, flashing the badge with his right hand and holding his gun in the left, pointing upward. The Bronco ground to a halt. Its driver was a dark, bearded young man in a plaid jacket. He stared at Montana with utter incomprehension.

"Open the door," Montana commanded. When the driver didn't respond, Montana leveled the gun at him and motioned for him to get out. White-faced, the driver opened the door and stepped out, raising his hands.

"FBI," Montana said. "I need this car. Government business."

"Hey," the man said in protest, but he looked more frightened than resentful.

"There's been shooting, there may be more. Get inside someplace. Don't be seen near this car." He nodded at the Ford van.

"Hey," the driver said again. "You can't just—"

"Help me move my partner. He's hurt. We'll have to lift him."

The man frowned, gave Montana an impotent glower.

"Help me," Montana said, gesturing with the gun. "That's an order."

Reluctantly the driver obeyed and went with Montana to the passenger side of the Ford. Montana opened the door, and when the man saw Jefferson, crouched and bleeding, he said, "What the hell—?"

"Help me," Montana repeated, hoisting Jefferson from the car. He tried to ignore the screaming of the twins.

"Jesus, he's bleeding all over. Don't put him in my car—"

"Shut up," Montana said. "Take him under his good arm."

The driver shook his head, supported Jefferson's right side, and together they maneuvered him into the passenger seat of the Bronco.

"God, he's bleeding all over my sheepskin seat covers. Who's gonna pay for this? Somebody's gonna pay for this."

"Laura," Montana barked. "Come on. Do you need help?"

She'd already opened the door. She held Rickie, struggling, in her arms. "Get Trace," she said. "And the boxes."

He sprinted to the Ford, snatched up Trace, and carried him, kicking and hitting, to the backseat of the Bronco.

"Get the boxes!" she cried. "We've got to have them."

"We haven't got time," he snapped. "Get in and shut the door." He didn't think he'd see that white truck swinging around the corner, but he didn't want to take the chance.

"We *need* them." She had a wild, stubborn light in her eyes. "I'll load them myself, dammit." She was already halfway out of the Bronco.

Montana shoved Trace into the backseat, none too gently, and the boy screamed in frightened outrage. Montana could have gladly flung Laura in beside him.

But she was already in the van, kneeling on the seat, yanking boxes from out of the back and piling them beside her. She did it so frantically that boxes fell, tumbling into the street. One came open and spilled the children's videos onto the packed snow.

"Get in the damn car," Montana snarled at her. "Or I'll throw you in."

She shot him a rebellious glance and went on grabbing boxes from the back. The broken plaque of Daffy Duck clattered to the street beside the videotapes.

"They need their things," she insisted. "I want *all* their things."

She was crazed, a woman possessed, but Montana knew she meant it; she wasn't going to go without the twins' possessions. In the meantime Jefferson was probably bleeding to death, and God only knew where the white truck was.

"Goddamnit, help him. Try to stop the bleeding," he ordered.

Laura seized an armload of boxes, staggered back to the Bronco, and threw them inside. She started for the van again.

Montana blocked her way. "Help Jefferson."

She tried to push past him. "We need their things!" she insisted. "They have to have their things."

"Help Jefferson," he said. "I'll get their damn things."

She looked at him with disbelief but backed toward the Bronco.

"Help him!" Montana said, furious.

She whirled and ran to the Bronco, climbing in beside Jefferson.

"You," Montana said, turning to the driver. "Help me."

"What is this?" the driver demanded. "Kids? What—?"

"Load the Bronco," Montana said with such ferocity that the driver blanched and hurried to the van.

Together they loaded the back of the Bronco, swiftly and haphazardly.

The driver had two clean white shirts in a clear plastic laundry bag hanging in the back. Montana saw Laura seize one and wad it into a makeshift compress. When she peeled back Jefferson's bloody coat and saw the wound gaping in his shoulder, she looked faint.

But she hung onto herself. She pressed the cloth against the wound and held it fast.

Montana shoved a last armload of boxes into the back of the Bronco and slammed the door shut. There was no more room, even though boxes were still piled in the back of the van, and the videos and the broken Daffy still lay in the snow.

"There's more," Laura protested.

"That's enough." His jaw clenched, he headed for the driver's seat. "We're getting the hell out of here."

"What about my car?" the driver demanded. "How do I get my car back?"

"You'll get it. But don't call the police. Just get out of here. Before you get hurt. I repeat: Don't call the police."

Montana got in and slammed the door. He thrust the key in the ignition, put the car in gear, and hit the accelerator. The tires shrieked against the packed snow, and the Bronco shot down the street breaking the speed limit.

"I'm all right," he heard Jefferson say to Laura. "Climb in back with the kids."

"No. Hold still," Laura said. "Don't move."

Rickie and Trace were wailing, and Trace kicked hard at the back of the driver's seat.

"Help the kids," Jefferson said.

"Shh," said Laura. "Shhhh."

Montana made up the route as he went along, and he tried to make their flight as tricky as a fox's. His heart beat like a jackhammer in his chest.

"Where are we going?" Laura asked over the twins' crying. Their sobs were lower now, as if they were finally exhausting themselves.

"Get Jefferson to a doctor," Montana said, not taking his eyes from the road.

"Where's the nearest emergency ward?"

"No," Montana said. "I don't want any admission records. We were set up. We've got to run."

"But Jefferson," she protested. "Can he hang on?"

Jefferson, sitting between them, sagged forward, then fell back heavily against the seat. He flinched with pain. "I can hang on," he said. "He's right. We were set up."

Montana gave Laura a sidelong glance. Her face was white, but her eyes were as alert as a wary animal's.

"What do you mean, set up?" she asked.

"I mean set up," Montana said with bitterness. "Somebody leaked word we'd be at Valley Hope. That's the only way this could happen. Jesus."

"We walked right into it," Jefferson said, grimacing. "Laura, you got any more shirts back there? I think I bled through this one."

"Oh, God, yes, yes," she said. Montana stole another glimpse at her. She looked as if she was going to cry, but she didn't. She pulled the shirt off the hanger, folded it into a tight square, and pressed it against Jefferson's shoulder. The white material reddened immediately.

Montana's mind raced, considering options.

"I know a doctor, a retired doctor in Queens," he told Jefferson. "I'll take you there."

Jefferson nodded and closed his eyes.

"How do you know the doctor's home?" Laura asked.

"He's always home," Montana snapped. "He's too old to go out."

"There's a car phone back here," she said. "We could call."

Montana almost bowed his head to give thanks. For a moment he was in love with her, her and the divine gift of the telephone.

He glanced at the mirror. Rickie was slumped, curled into one corner and whimpering, rubbing his eyes. He seemed spent and was perhaps crying himself to sleep.

Trace sat in the opposite corner, his knees up, his face hidden, his fingers fluttering in a frantic dance over his cheeks and lips. He banged his head against the backseat, and between sobs he muttered something unintelligible.

Montana took a deep breath. "Okay," he said, turning his gaze back to the snowy highway that led back to Queens. "Can you reach the phone?"

"Yes," Laura said. Keeping the compress against Jefferson's shoulder, she leaned over the backseat.

"I'll give you the number," Montana said. "Dial it. When he answers, tell him Mick Montana needs him. Then hand me the phone."

He told her the number, which he still knew by heart.

Laura pushed the buttons, then waited. "He doesn't answer," she said. "It's rung nine rings."

"It takes him time to get to the phone," Montana said.

"*Ten* rings," said Laura, looking worried.

"Great," Jefferson said from between his teeth. "For a doctor, I get a two-thousand-year-old man. He'll give me a transfusion of dinosaur blood."

At that moment, Laura said, "Doctor? Mick Montana wants to talk to you."

She handed the phone to Montana, then put both hands on Jefferson's compress. "Stay still," she said. "Easy."

Jefferson closed his eyes more tightly, then relaxed. He had sunken into unconsciousness.

Dr. Marco DeMario was a widower, eighty-two years old. He lived in a tall, narrow house in a neighborhood that had been elegant forty years ago, but no longer was.

The house's peeling white facade looked dirty against the pristine brightness of the snow. The evergreen hedge that enclosed the small yard had run wild, untrimmed for years.

Montana pulled the Bronco into the drive and into

DeMario's open garage. He'd told DeMario that they'd bring Jefferson in through the back door.

The boys were both asleep in their separate corners of the backseat. Montana was strong, but Jefferson was a huge man, and Laura had to help half carry, half drag him up the back stairs of the old house.

At every step Laura flinched, fearing they were hurting him more. She'd wrapped the cleaner's bag over his shoulder to try to keep from leaving a trail of blood.

Montana rang the bell, supporting Jefferson against his shoulder like a man holding up a drunk.

Laura was surprised at how quickly the back door swung open. DeMario must have been watching for them.

"Get him up on the counter, close to the sink," DeMario said in his creaking voice. "It's going to be messy."

"There's a lot of blood," Montana said.

An understatement, Laura thought, dazed. When Trace's cheek had been grazed, her coat lapel had been spattered with blood. Now the shoulder and front of her coat were smeared and glistening with it. Montana's topcoat was almost as bad.

DeMario bent over Jefferson and expertly stripped away the coat and shirt from the wound. He used what might have been a scalpel, or for all Laura knew, an old-fashioned straight-edged razor.

DeMario was like his house, tall, lean, and unkempt. A shock of thin white hair hung over his brow, and his face was a collection of wrinkles. But behind his trifocal glasses, his eyes were black and bright.

Delicately he peeled the last of the shirt away from the wound, and Laura had to look away. She hated herself for feeling queasy, but she did.

"It's veinous blood," she heard DeMario say. "No arteries hit."

"Good," said Montana.

"I got a bottle of ether on that counter," DeMario said. "Old as hell, but it'll do. Saturate that rag with it. Don't put it over his face until I tell you."

"Ether?" Laura said, raising her eyes. "Isn't that awfully—primitive?"

"Hell," DeMario said, "I've worked under worse conditions. I followed General George S. Patton across half of Africa and a damn lot of Europe. Operated eighteen hours a day sometimes. The wounded were stacked up like cordwood. Hmmph. World War Two—we *won* that son of a bitch."

Laura could think of no answer. She stared numbly at DeMario's ancient instruments, ranged on an old kitchen cart. They twinkled in the light spilling from the dusty light fixture overhead.

"You can help him?" Montana asked.

"Hell, yes," DeMario said. "I mean, it isn't gonna be pretty. Just get the lead out and sew up the holes. I could do it in my sleep. In my day, we didn't worry about the *cosmetic* aspects."

He gave Laura a sharp look. "You wouldn't happen to be a nurse?"

"No," she managed to say. "A teacher."

"Well, if this is going to make you faint or some damn thing, you should leave. Mick, you stay. I need help here."

He picked up something that looked like a torture instrument and began to probe the torn flesh.

"Laura," Montana said with surprising gentleness, "why don't you wait in the van. Let the kids sleep. I'll help you bring them in when it's over."

Gratefully she turned away and left through the back door. She saw that the plastic bag hadn't done its job. Drops of Jefferson's blood spotted the unpainted boards of the glassed-in back porch.

But the snow still fell thickly, and the trail of blood across the yard was already disappearing under a mantle of white.

Montana had left the garage door open, the Bronco's heater was on, and the inside of the car was warm. She got into the backseat again, careful not to wake the boys.

She was exhausted but didn't know if she'd ever sleep again. When she closed her eyes, nightmare images danced in her mind: *blood, blood, and more blood—was there no end to it?*

At last Montana appeared and opened the door. Cold flooded into the car.

She blinked at him. The sky was a dark cloudy gray behind him. "Is it over?" she asked, trying to read his face. She kept her voice low so as not to wake the boys.

He nodded. "It's over. Let's bring the kids inside."

"Is he all right? Jefferson?"

"He'll be fine. We stay here tonight."

"Here?" she asked, startled. "Is it safe?"

"It has to be. Jefferson needs to rest. I don't want to leave him. When we move on, we're going to need him."

"When we move on?" she asked. "To where?"

For a moment his eyes held hers. "I don't know, but it had better be good. Let's get the kids inside. I've got to dump this car. It's hot."

"But the driver," she said. "You told him not to call the police."

"That won't stop him. I've got to get rid of it."

"But—" she said.

"Trust me," he said.

"But how—?"

"When I get back, we'll talk. I promise. Now let's get the kids inside. Will you be all right alone with them for a while? Marco's got to go on an errand for us."

He gathered Trace into his arms, lifted him. She nodded. She slipped her arms around Rickie. Following Montana, she carried the boy in the back way.

"I don't know what sort of mood they're going to be in when they wake up," she said to Montana. Rickie stirred in her arms and rubbed his cheek.

"Does DeMario—" she groped for words"—does he know about the twins? Will he understand?"

"He knows," Montana said. "He'll understand. He's seen it all."

"I thought I'd seen it all," said Marco DeMario, crossing his thin arms. "But I've never seen this. I've read about it. Heard about it. Never seen it."

He nodded at the twins. They sat quietly on the worn living room rug.

It was as if Valley Hope was only a fading dream to them. They played with total absorption, lost in a game of their own devising. DeMario had given them each an old quart jar, filled to the brim with pennies. He'd returned from the mysterious short trip he'd taken for Montana. He offered no explanation of where he'd been or what he'd done, and Laura didn't ask him.

The twins looked at the coins one by one, saying the dates and adding them up as they went.

"1962," said Trace.

"Three million and eight," Rickie answered without hesitation. He selected a penny. "1991," he said.

"Three million, one thousand, nine hundred and ninety-nine," Trace answered. "1936."

Rickie immediately answered, "Forty-four," which both of them found inexplicably funny.

"They just lost me," DeMario said, peering at them as if they were as exotic as unicorns. "Did they just suddenly switch to a square root? I believe they did."

Laura shrugged, not knowing. She wasn't thinking about numbers. She was worried about Montana, who'd been gone for hours.

"By criminy, I think they did," DeMario said, almost cackling. "Pulled a square root out of thin air—just like that. Real idiot savants. Wise fools."

Laura gave him a feeble smile. People didn't call them "idiot savants" or "wise fools" these days. But she didn't want to correct DeMario. He had been too kind.

"Mick's nephew," DeMario said with a sage shake of his head. "Joey, in Bellevue. He's worse off than these boys. A lot worse off. These kids are much luckier."

At the moment she considered the boys' luck to be in very short supply, indeed. "They can read and write," she said. "But they're not always cooperative. They can dress themselves. They've come a long way."

"Amazing," DeMario said, tenting his thin fingers.

His hands, she noticed, had a marked tremor; they quivered constantly and sometimes twitched. It seemed impossible that such trembling hands could have operated on Jefferson only a few hours ago.

But although his hands quavered, his mind was steady and sharp. He saw the direction of her gaze. He held out his right hand. It fluttered delicately, like a moth trying to hold a stationary position in the air.

"You're wondering how a shaky man can do surgery. It's simple. I had a shot of hooch before you showed up. I learned that following Patton. Not a good trick. But sometimes a necessary one."

"I—thought maybe it had just been a long day for you," she said. "We've put you through a lot."

"At my age, I'm glad to be put through anything besides the home for old poots."

"You took us in," she said. "People are after us. Aren't you scared?"

"Of what? Dying before my time?"

She gazed somberly at the twins, intent on their game of pennies and numbers. Then she turned to face DeMario. "I don't want for us to put you at risk."

His face showed no emotion. Behind his trifocals, his eyes were black as Montana's.

"Mick'll cover his tracks," he said. "He's a smart one." He tapped his temple with one finger. "His mind is never *la dolce far niente*. You know what that means?"

"No," she said, "I don't know Italian."

He tapped his temple again. "His brain is never in a state of happy idleness. That's his curse. That's his gift. He's always thinking."

She studied the old man and thought he must have been handsome once, tall, lean, with such snapping black eyes, such an intelligent face. Age had not made him ugly, but it had sapped him, made him look frail in spite of his spirit.

"Mick," she said hesitantly. The name felt strange on her lips. "You've known him a long time?"

DeMario nodded. "Since he was a bare-ass baby. Excuse my French."

Laura almost smiled. It was impossible to think of Montana as an infant.

DeMario nodded. "He was a serious kid. But funny. I know that sounds like a contradiction in terms. But he was. Serious. And funny. Marched to a different drummer."

She wondered how DeMario knew him so well. "Are you related?"

"Naw," said DeMario. "He used to hang around with my grandson. We were pretty much raising him. His mother was divorced. It wasn't her fault. She ended up living with us. She and Mike. Mike was the grandson. Mike and Mick. Mick and Mike. The M and M's we used to call them."

He smiled faintly. "What'd they play? Cops. They always played cops. Day in, day out. Like they were joined at the hip. Like they were twins."

He stared at the twins playing on the hearth rug, and his smile faded.

"Where's Mike?" she asked. "Did he grow up to be a policeman? Or a doctor like you?"

Suddenly DeMario looked older, frailer than before. "Mike didn't grow up," he said. "He died. Seventeen years old. A diving accident. Two and a half weeks in a coma. He never woke up."

"I'm sorry," she said, wishing she hadn't asked. DeMario obviously still grieved for the lost boy.

"I cried," he said. "Everybody cried. Except Mick. Mick was one of the pallbearers. He was the strong one."

"I'm sorry," she said again.

He put his hand to his trifocals, shook his head. "It's a terrible thing to be a doctor and stand there, helpless, when someone you love is dying. I did it two more times. When my daughter died. Mike's mother. She couldn't stand up to it, Mike's dying. She took to drink, and it killed her. I couldn't stop that, either. She was the only one that could. But she didn't. Or she didn't want to."

"I'm sorry," Laura said, feeling like a broken record. Impulsively she reached out and took his hand. His flesh felt as dry as parchment, his bones as fragile as bird bones.

He didn't look at her. He stared at the twins piling pennies in a system only they understood. "You would think," he said, "a man who's seen as much dying as I have—the war—would get used to it. But, you see, those boys, those soldiers, were strangers. Still, I never got used to that, either. I thought if I got used to it, the doctor in me would die. I had to care. It's important."

She nodded and squeezed his hand more tightly. She understood why Montana had turned to this man.

DeMario stared at their joined hands. "I cried when my wife died. I went away so nobody saw. But both times, for my daughter, my wife, Mick was there again. He was a pallbearer again. I thought, 'He must get tired of carrying my dead.' "

"I don't think he'd look at it that way," she said. She thought, *I have no right to say that. I don't know him that well.* But still, she thought it was a true thing to say.

"No," DeMario said, gazing at the twins again. "He wouldn't. You're in good hands. Which is a funny thing to say, with his hand cripped up so bad. It doesn't matter. You're still in good hands."

"I know," she said, her throat tight. Montana was a mystery to her, a paradox, and she knew he didn't always tell her the truth. Yet she had literally trusted her life to him, and the twins' as well. An instinct deeper and more primal than any reason told her that DeMario was right.

DeMario kept staring at the twins, not looking at her. "I like seeing you with these boys. Yes. You're good with them. They're in good hands with you, too."

His words embarrassed her, and she changed the subject to what concerned her most. "I'm worried about Montana," she said. "He should be back by now. Shouldn't he?"

"What should be done, he'll do," DeMario said. He drew his hand from hers. He stood and took a moment as if gathering strength and insuring his balance.

"I'm going to check on your friend," he said, nodding toward the bedroom where Jefferson rested. "Then I'm going to have another shot of hooch and go to bed. I'll sleep in the same room with him. My wife, at the end, she wasn't comfortable sleeping in the same bed. We got twin beds. It was easier on her. I'll keep an eye on him."

"Thank you," she said. He had already showed her the room that would house the boys. Once again she'd put the familiar sheets on the bed, hung the Looney Tunes curtains on the window. She'd put up their plaques and bulletin board and even hung some of their clothes in the closet, although she knew she'd soon have to repack everything.

"I'll leave the Chianti bottle on the counter," DeMario said. "Help yourself if you want. Make Mick have a drink. He'll need it. Even if he won't admit it."

"I will," she promised. She stood and took his hand again. "Thank you, Dr. DeMario. I don't know what we would have done without you."

Once again he drew his hand away. He gave her a rueful smile. "Don't go sentimental on me. I can spill my guts all I want. I've got an excuse. I'm senile."

She put her hand on her hip and regarded him. "You're not a bit senile."

"Put it in writing, will you?" he muttered. "So somebody can read it to me when I can't remember who I am or where I'm going or why."

"You're too hard on yourself," she said, smiling.

"I'm a cynic," he said. "I have been since World War Two. But I'll tell you one thing. We won that son of a bitch."

He waved a vague good night and went to check on Jefferson, then hobbled into the kitchen for his drink. He did not acknowledge her again.

The boys went to bed with remarkably little fuss, although they insisted on keeping their jars of pennies.

She read to them from their lizard book. Although they knew it by heart, they always liked to hear it. They hardly seemed to remember what had happened that afternoon. For this, Laura was grateful.

It struck her that although DeMario's house was old and ill-kept, the place had an air of hominess. She felt at home herself, for reasons she could not explain, and she was sad that they must move on.

Rickie had fallen asleep first, then Trace, still clutching his jar of pennies. Gently she took it from him and set it next to the Bugs Bunny lamp so he could see it as soon as he woke up.

DeMario had given her the room next to the twins'. Everything was dusty, and the ruffled green spread on the double bed had faded to the color of bread mold. Yet, paradoxically, again she felt at home in the room. It was as if she were visiting the house of a favorite grandparent.

She paused by Trace's bed. Gently, so gently he would not feel it, she stroked his hair. Then she turned and lightly kissed Rickie on the forehead. He turned and frowned in his sleep, then went still again, as if sinking more deeply into his dreams.

She left their Bugs Bunny lamp on, then went downstairs to wait for Montana.

He didn't return until after eleven o'clock.

He knocked at the kitchen door and said, "Laura? It's me. I should've given you a password. What can I say? Your eyes are hazel, the twins' are blue. The Bugs Bunny lamp always has to face the wall; we don't know why. Okay?"

She unlocked the door and swung it open. His too-lean face seemed almost handsome to her.

He wore an old leather jacket of Marco's because his own coat, like hers, was stained with blood. Snowflakes glittered in his dark hair. He carried two brown paper bags of groceries.

"How's Jefferson?" he said.

"Marco says good. He can be moved tomorrow if he feels like it."

"Good. And the twins?"

She sighed with relief. "Better than I could have hoped. They act like it was a bad dream. They don't realize what happened. I got their room set up. They're asleep."

"That's good," he said, setting the bags on the counter. "How about you?"

She said, "I was worried about you. You were gone a long time."

"I had to lay a false trail. I drove back to Long Island. I used the car phone, called a bunch of numbers. Like motels, hotels, doctors. And car rental agencies. To confuse anybody looking for us."

She still felt half giddy over the miracle of his return. "You got another car?"

"Yeah," he said, putting a carton of milk and a carton of orange juice in the refrigerator. "I borrowed it from my uncle. He doesn't know it yet. I left a note."

"You borrowed it without him knowing?" she said, appalled. "You mean you stole it?"

Montana didn't answer directly. He said, "Every year he takes his wife and flies to Florida for six weeks. He won't be using it."

"But how? Did you have the keys?"

"He keeps a spare set in a magnetized case under the front bumper. I picked the lock to his garage. There was the van, there were the keys. He won't be home for a month. Nobody knows the van's missing. It's clean, nobody'll notice it."

"Your uncle—won't he get angry?"

"That's then. This is now."

"What about the other car, the Bronco?" she asked, worried about all this larceny.

"I changed the plates and dumped it. The airport parking lot. I hope it takes a while for anybody to notice it's abandoned."

"How did you get from the airport?"

"Took a cab to a hotel. From the hotel I took a different cab to a bar in my uncle's neighborhood. From the bar, I walked to his house and picked the garage door."

"What if you'd set off an alarm?"

"I keep telling my uncle to install a guard system. Maybe now he'll listen."

His audacity frightened her, and she hoped her fear didn't show on her face.

"The van's in Marco's garage, out of sight," he said. "We should leave early, so nobody sees. Can you do it? Get the kids ready early? I got groceries for their breakfast and stuff." He nodded toward the two sacks on the counter.

"I'll do my best." She pushed her fingers through her hair, a nervous gesture. "But how can you think of all this —even groceries?"

"It's my job. Like it's yours to teach the kids. They're really okay? Calmed down again?"

"Really. The worst thing, they think, is I pushed them down and scattered their lizards. And it's like Marco gives off an aura. Somehow, he made them feel safe."

"Yeah," Montana said, as if he took it for granted.

"Montana," she said, her brow furrowing, "are we putting him in danger? It scares me."

"I've done my best not to. It scares me, too," he said. "But I don't gamble wild, I gamble careful. He knows that. He trusts me. And besides, he's not afraid."

She swallowed, looked away. "I know he's not. Why?"

"Because he's old," Montana said. "Older than he ever wanted to be. But he's brave. He was born brave. He'll die brave. What happens in between is the same to him."

She stared down at the worn linoleum. Jefferson's blood still spotted it, a red-brown trail from back door to kitchen to hall to bathroom.

"I'm not brave," she said, "I'm frightened. I saw Becker get shot. He has to be dead. What about Stallings?"

"Stallings is probably dead, too," he said without emotion.

She put her hand to her eyes, trying to shut out reality for any length of time, even a second. "We were lucky, weren't we? That's the only reason we're alive. Sheer, dumb luck."

"Maybe," he said.

She let her hand fall away, and she looked into his eyes. "I'm terrified for the boys. You said we were set up. That's how we got ambushed. Who did it? Who can we trust?"

"I don't know who did it. I don't know who to trust. Somebody, somewhere sold us out. We're on our own."

"The newspaper," she said. "Breaking the story on us. Is that how they found us?"

"Hell, maybe the newspaper was set up, too. I don't know. All I know is for now we're on the run. I'm sorry, but that's how it is."

She looked away from him. "Oh, damn," she said. "I don't want that. Not with the boys. They're not meant to run."

"I know," he said. "But that's how it is."

She walked to the counter, put her hand on the Chianti bottle. "Marco left out the wine," she said. "He said to make you take a drink. That you'd need it."

Montana came to her side. "Marco's had his nip, I know," he said. "He didn't overdo it, did he?"

"No," she said, regarding the bottle. "He didn't. But he's right. You probably need it."

"That's not what I need," he said.

And she knew what was going to happen. She'd known from the moment he came in the door.

He put his arms around her. He kissed her. The touch of his mouth made her dizzy with a hunger for life. She kissed him back, almost ravenously.

"Montana," she said against his lips, "don't worry. I won't fall in love with you or anything stupid like that."

"This isn't about love," he said. Then he kissed her again, harder and more desperately than before.

SEVEN

Hᴇʀ ʟɪᴘs ᴘᴀʀᴛᴇᴅ sᴏ ᴛʜᴀᴛ ʜᴇ ᴄᴏᴜʟᴅ ᴛᴀsᴛᴇ ʜᴇʀ ᴍᴏʀᴇ
completely. She tasted him back.

Stop, he told himself. *Or in another sixty seconds you
won't be able to stop.*

For a crazy moment he didn't care.

But she was the one who drew back. He forced himself
to try to breathe evenly and not to pull her into his arms
again. He looked into her hazel eyes and at her mouth. His
groin tightened another notch.

"You're right," he said, but he still held her by the
upper arms. "We don't need more complications."

Her expression was wary. "No. We don't."

"Maybe I just wanted to prove we're both still here."

She looked away. She seemed embarrassed, yet she
didn't move away from him.

He dragged his gaze from her and found himself staring at the Chianti bottle on the counter. "Let's sit, have a
glass of wine. We need to talk."

"Yes," she said. "We should talk."

He released her with reluctance. She stepped back, almost as if she felt the same hesitation.

He went to a cupboard, and took two of the old jelly
jars that served Marco as drinking glasses. He half filled
each.

"This isn't fancy," he said, trying to sound casual, unconcerned. "I think when Marco's wife died, he gave all the china and stuff to his niece. Have a seat."

He pulled out a kitchen chair for her. She sat down rather stiffly and took one of the glasses. He seated himself across from her.

An uncomfortable silence fell between them. He sipped his wine, wishing it would calm his rambunctious blood. He'd kissed her. He'd liked it. For a wild moment, she'd seemed to like it, too.

Hell, he told himself, it was sex, that was all, and he couldn't afford to think with his dick; he'd been assigned to protect her, not get into her pants. Yet he knew more than hormones had pulled them together for that instant.

Today they'd seen Becker and Stallings killed and Jefferson torn apart. They all could have died, and they both knew it. Last week she'd seen Zordani blown away, just as nastily.

Violence, he thought, all the damn violence and pain and death. When you see enough of it, when you're threatened long enough by it, something snaps. You've got to have the opposite. Pleasure. Affection. Life. Sex.

That's what he'd felt. It was what she'd felt, too, even if she didn't understand. And part of Montana's mind kept whispering, *What's so wrong with wanting it? What if we don't make it out of this? Would it matter so much if we fucked? What the hell?*

He searched for something neutral to say. "Did Marco feed you okay? You and the kids?"

She nodded, still seeming shy with him. "All he had were SpaghettiOs and cheese and crackers. But the twins were happy. Still, you'd think a doctor would eat better."

Montana shrugged, took another sip of wine. "He says nothing tastes the way it used to."

"What about you?" she asked. "Did you eat?"

"A couple candy bars," he said.

They fell silent again. She looked at him, worry in her eyes. "Montana? What are we going to do?"

He tried to sound nonchalant. "We've got some problems. What we do is go to earth. We hide. Like a fox does."

"How long?" she said, looking more worried than before.

"I don't know. As long as it takes."

She picked up her glass and took a drink of wine. "I watched the late news. The story about the shooting was on. They haven't caught the gunmen. But they didn't mention us. Not a word."

He nodded. "They didn't mention us on radio news either. They're keeping it quiet."

"Who are 'they'?"

"Authorities. Somebody high up."

"Why—to protect us?"

He felt a muscle twitch in his cheek. "Maybe. Or to protect themselves. They screwed up."

"Have you called anybody?" she asked. "Do they know we're safe?"

"I called Conlee from the car phone. They can't trace a cellular phone. I told him we're alive, that the kids aren't hurt. That's all. I don't want them to know more."

A futile bitterness filled him. Conlee had said there was no clue to the identity of the killers. They'd escaped.

But how did somebody crash into a goddamn snowplow, kill its driver, and still escape? What did they do—walk away down the street? Hail a cab? Charter a plane?

She set down her glass and pushed it away. "The task force is made up of different agencies. Does that mean anybody, in any part of the system, could have betrayed us?"

"It's possible."

"Then who can we go to for help?" she asked. "Who's *not* involved?"

That was the question that haunted him. He rose and refilled his glass.

"Who's not involved? Everybody's involved. The police. The district attorney. The federal attorney's office. And the attorney's office can tap or be tapped by all the federal agencies. FBI. DEA. More. There are moles all over the place. Moles and snitches and sellouts."

She looked up at him. "My God," she said. "Can't we turn to anybody?"

"I don't know," he said. "And I don't know why what the kids saw is so important. Was it the car? The license? Or the gunman? Maybe all three. Whatever it is, somebody doesn't want them talking."

She looked bewildered. "Then all we can do is run?"

In spite of himself, he took her hand in his good one, held it tightly. "Yes. We run."

"For how long?"

"I don't know."

"But they'll all be looking for us. The law. And the Colombians, too."

"Yes. They will."

"So what do we do?"

"We throw them off the trail. I've already started."

"You mean by switching cars, calling doctors?"

"That and more," he said. "I used Jefferson's Visa card. I called American Airlines, made one-way reservations on a night flight to Philly. Two adults, two children. You went to school in Philly, right?"

"Yes," she said, looking bewildered. "But you don't mean . . ."

"No," he said. "My sister Cindy's picking up the tickets, checking in. She won't use them, but there'll be a record we checked in. It'll take them time to find out nobody went."

She nodded. She raised no objections about Jefferson's credit card. That was good. She was learning fast to be hardheaded.

He said, "I mailed Jefferson's credit card and two of mine to Cindy. She'll drop one of mine in the bus station in Manhattan. She mails one to my sister Susie in L.A. Susie does the same thing. Pretty soon they got crazy credit patterns on two coasts. They won't know what to trust."

She swallowed and nodded again. "Aren't you afraid to involve your family?"

"Yes. But I never did when I was undercover, and they won't expect me to now. We do nothing that they'd expect."

"They won't expect you to come here, to Marco?"

"They shouldn't. I know half a dozen doctors on the

wrong side of the law. I called one. I mailed him another one of Jefferson's credit cards. Told him to take a nice vacation. Immediately."

"So what do we do—really?"

"They'll expect us to panic, to bolt. And to leave Jefferson behind. We do none of those things."

"We take Jefferson because we can't leave him with Marco?"

He paused, then nodded. "That, and we may need him. Now this is what I think we should do. Find a place to lie low a few days, get our act straight. Then we go someplace, keep a low profile, and establish new identities. We don't hurry it. We do it right. It takes time, and they don't expect us to take time."

Her face was strained. "It'll be hard on the boys. Really hard."

He gripped her hand more tightly. "I know. Just keep on doing what you've done. Can you?"

She didn't answer yes or no, but she raised her chin to a determined angle. He liked the way she looked when she did that.

"So," she said, "where are we going to hide?"

"We'll find somewhere," he said. "We just need an out-of-the-way place to light for a few days. We'll find one."

She took a deep breath. "I thought about it. While you were gone. We can't go to a hotel or motel. They'd want a driver's license, the van's plate number. We'd leave a trail."

"That's right. There may be an all-points bulletin out on us. We don't know."

She stared at their locked hands. "Like I said, I thought about it—hard. I might know a place. It's primitive, but it might be safe."

He was dubious, yet he knew she was smart. "Okay," he said. "Tell me about it."

As if by mutual consent, they kept their hands joined, resting on the tabletop.

And she told him of the place she knew.

.　　.　　.

Don Mesius Estrada sat in his library at his desk, and in his palm he held a cross of gold and emeralds with a golden chain. He played grimly with this chain, studying it with distaste.

A dark, cadaverously lean young man with a scabrous face sat in the leather chair on the opposite side of the desk. His name was Santander, and he was Mesius Estrada's sometime bodyguard and his most feared henchman.

When Santander had first heard the word "henchman," he hadn't liked it; it had a cheap, insulting sound. But he had looked it up in Estrada's big English dictionary, and it had said "a loyal and trusted follower."

The word had once meant the "page of a prince." It pleased Santander to view himself this way, as the messenger of the prince. The message that he frequently delivered was a final one. He had done so today, three times over.

But tonight his prince, Estrada, looked half ill with rage. He threw the chain and cross across his desktop in disgust.

"*Santo Domingo,* how could they do such a thing? Tell me again."

Santander started to rub his jaw, then stopped himself. His dermatologist told him he mustn't scratch his face. "Suarez and I took them to the park on Long Island. The truck was there, keys under the seat. Like you said."

Estrada nodded coldly. Santander knew Estrada had executed his side of the bargain as scrupulously as possible, in fact, flawlessly.

Santander's mouth crooked contemptuously. "They were at Valley Hope at the right time. They were in the right place. They must have opened fire too soon, before the van was inside the gate."

"*Los imbéciles,*" Estrada said. "Why'd I think the little shits could right their own wrong?"

Santander wondered this himself. By trying to contain the damage the three fools had done, Estrada had only compounded it. Perhaps now the prince had learned his lesson.

"They came back to us crying like kittens," Santander said. "You gave them no time to plan, they said. Personally, I think they were hung over. The big one, Carlito—he had breath like a fart."

Estrada rose and paced to the shelves that held his philosophy books. "Go on."

"They whined about the snow," Santander said. "They couldn't see good, they couldn't drive quick, the snow made them skid. If it weren't for the snow, they would have come back heroes."

Santander gave a disdainful little laugh. "So it was your fault. It was the weather's fault. It was God's fault. It was anyone's fault but their own, the pricks."

Estrada looked as if he tasted gall. "The Yankees have a proverb: Don't send a boy to do a man's job. I should have killed them right off and sent you and Suarez."

Santander ducked his head slightly, as if bowing in acknowledgement. Once again he resisted the desire to pick his face.

He said, "The one who shot the snowplow driver was Carlito. The big one, the stupid one. He panicked and fired."

Estrada nodded, his expression more sour than before.

"They crashed the truck, but not bad," said Santander. "It still ran. But they panicked. They came back to the park to drop the truck and escape. With us. They came like dogs with their tails between their legs."

Estrada picked up a volume of Miguel de Unamuno. "They came back," he said, shaking his head. "They actually expected sympathy."

"They bitched like women," Santander said. "They thought they'd get another chance."

Estrada opened the book. His eyes fell on words that obviously displeased him. " 'Being right is a small thing,' " he quoted in contempt. "Unamuno was a fool. Being right is the only thing."

He slammed the book shut, shoved it back on the shelf. He turned to Santander, his face grim. "They didn't even know who they'd killed and who they hadn't."

Santander shrugged. It was true. They hadn't.

"I have it on the best authority that the twins escaped," Estrada said bitterly.

He looked at Santander and seemed to choose his

words carefully. "The Cartel's position is delicate. We mustn't be blamed for spilling the blood of these witnesses. But we must be sure they die."

"Yes," Santander said. He asked no questions. He had his opinions, but he knew his place.

"You will be my *capitán* in this," Estrada said. "I'll get you killers who can do the job. But this has to be done with discretion."

"I understand," said Santander.

"I've found these twins once. I'll find them again."

Santander believed this. Finding them might take longer this time, but Estrada could do it. He was a powerful prince, and Santander would have served no other sort.

Estrada leaned back against his bookshelves, his gaze as cold and flat as a cobra's. "When I locate them, kill them. We'll put the blame on the *norteamericano*. And then he'll have to be killed."

Santander nodded.

"The three young buffoons," Estrada said. "They were surprised?"

Santander smiled crookedly. "The baby-faced one, he cried. He didn't want to, but he did. The big one pissed his pants. The other one swore and called us Judases."

Under other circumstances, Estrada might have smiled. "And you did what I said?"

Santander nodded. "We cut off their heads. We have them on ice. In a Styrofoam cooler."

"Good," said Estrada. He would send the severed heads to the Mafia, a gift of good faith. We, your friends in the Cartel, have tracked and killed those who preyed on your organization.

He picked up the golden chain and cross again. The emerald at the cross's center glittered. That morning, the cross had adorned the neck of Paco Paredes.

Estrada regarded it with contempt. Paco had no more need of necklaces. Nor did his friends.

"And their bodies?" he asked.

"To Zarate's Funeral Parlor. They'll be burned—how do you say?"

"Cremated," Estrada said, regarding the cross. "It's good to be rid of them. I should have done it sooner."

Santander was wise enough to say nothing.

Estrada shook his head, musing. "Did they say *why* they took Reynaldo Comce with them? My God, the stupidity."

"They said he wanted to come. They said, 'How do you say no to somebody like Reynaldo?' "

Estrada studied the cross, then threw it back to his desktop. "Madness," he said with scorn. He raised his eyes and met Santander's. "The woman and twins die. And the men with them. The man. There are two, but one's wounded. They'll leave him behind."

"Of course." Santander was careful to keep his expression neutral. Killing a man was standard procedure, nothing special. As for the twins, they sounded like the spawn of a *diablero* to him, a wicked witch. He could kill them as easily as he would crush a pair of insects.

But he was seldom asked to kill women, and the idea of killing women secretly excited him. He liked to read books and magazines about it, true stories of serial murderers and sex killers and men who cut apart women's bodies. He liked to look at the pictures.

He had dreams, and often the dreams left him with sticky wet spots on the bed clothing. He thought of the schoolteacher and raised his hand to his face. He allowed himself to scratch his cheek deeply, just once, for the pure, forbidden pleasure of it.

Morning was gray outside the bedroom window.

"I can't take this," Laura told Marco DeMario. "It's a real fur coat."

"What's the matter?" Marco demanded. "You're one of those women who won't wear fur?"

He held out a jacket to her with his slightly shaky hands. The fur was silvery white. It was still beautiful, even though it had the air of being old.

Laura shook her head in consternation. She *didn't* approve of fur coats, or at least she supposed she didn't. She'd never had the money to buy one if she'd wanted.

"Genuine silver fox," Marco said. "It was my wife's.

A Christmas present. Years ago. You disapprove? You think these pelts belonged to personal friends of Bambi?"

"Well, there's that," Laura said, "but even more—"

"Pretend these foxes died of old age," Marco told her. "If left to natural causes, they would have by now."

"It's more than that," Laura objected. "That must have been very expensive."

"It turned out to be a very expensive meal for moths. Take it. I offered it to my niece, but she's so short, she was like a fur ball. She looked like something the cat coughed up."

"I wouldn't feel right—"

He made a sound of impatience. "You can't take your own coat. It's bloody. It's like wearing a sign saying, 'I've been shot at recently.' You go without a coat, you'll catch pneumonia, then where will those boys be? Take it."

With a sigh she relented. Time had dimmed the luster of the jacket's satin lining, made it musty, riddled it with tiny moth holes. But the fur itself was still thick and silky.

"Thank you, Marco," she said. "But no more now— please. You've given me enough."

But he did give her more. While she'd coaxed the boys through their breakfasts, Marco had rifled through his dead wife's closet. From its long-undisturbed depths, he'd pulled over a dozen items that were still wearable, blouses, slacks, and sweaters. There was even a pair of furry mukluk boots, a bit ratty, but warm.

The clothes were fifteen years out of fashion, but well made and wearable. Marco had even gone through his wife's bureau and found a few changes of underwear, yellowing with age, but still perfumed with the fading scent of sachet.

Lastly, he talked her into taking the jacket. All her clothes, as well as Jefferson's and Montana's, had been in the car with Stallings and Becker.

"You're built like my wife," he said gruffly. "All long legs and no real meat to you. But on her it looked all right. You, too. Does me good to see you in it."

She wasn't so sure it did him good, because she thought she saw unshed tears in his eyes when he stood there looking her up and down. She wore a pair of his wife's dark plaid slacks, her navy sweater, the mukluks, and now the silver-white fur.

But his expression was not one of pathos. His head was high, his nostrils pinched, the set of his mouth critical. He looked almost ferocious, like a very old hawk who still had fight in him.

"Laura!" It was Montana's voice, and it startled her. "Laura, are you ready? The kids are antsy."

"Go," Marco said. "You've got to go now."

"Thank you for everything," she said. She leaned and kissed his cheek. It felt soft, cool, and fragile beneath her lips.

"Enough of that," he said, waving her away. "I'll carry your suitcase downstairs."

"No, I can manage," she protested. But he insisted. To argue with him, she felt, would insult his masculinity.

He huffed, he gasped, he swayed and frightened her on the steep staircase, but he made it to the landing. Then Montana saw them, came up the stairs, and took the heavy suitcase.

Marco followed them downstairs to the back door. The boys, in fresh jeans and their jackets, waited at the door, looking sulky with sleepiness and confusion. But they held road maps—Marco had found one for each—and they still clutched their quart jars of pennies. Marco refused to take them back.

Jefferson had already been helped into the car. Marco told the boys good-bye. After Laura's persistant coaching, they said good-bye and thanked him. Both the good-byes and the thanks sounded mechanical and perfunctory, and neither boy looked Marco in the face at all.

But the old man didn't seem to mind. He smiled at them, even if they wouldn't smile back. He understood. Laura felt choked. How could she bid him good-bye, perhaps forever, after all he had done? How could she thank him?

But he didn't seem to want her to try. Perhaps he didn't want her to see any more of his emotion. Impatiently he gestured for her to be on her way. He allowed her to give him one more peck of a kiss.

Then she was herding the twins down the back porch

stairs and into the van's long middle seat. The new vehicle, which was red, seemed to intrigue them. They peered at it, eyes narrowed. She glanced back and saw Marco and Montana in the doorway. They were silhouetted against the kitchen light.

They embraced each other, an embrace that struck her as heartfelt and very Italian. Then Montana released the older man, clapped him on the shoulder, and loped down the stairs and across the snowy yard. He got into the driver's seat, and began backing out of the drive.

She saw the silhouette of Marco's body against the rectangle of light in the doorway. He watched after them until they were at the end of the drive and turned on the street. She waved, but if he saw her, he gave no indication.

Then he closed the door. She stared at his house until she could see it no more. A sick feeling of homelessness filled her when it was out of sight.

The twins, full from breakfast and drowsy from being awakened too early, clutched their penny jars and road maps and seemed ready to fall asleep again. Ricky hummed for a while, then his humming faded into silence.

Jefferson, full of pain pills, was asleep in the front seat, snoring gently. Coatless, he had a quilt wrapped around his big shoulders. His own coat was ruined by blood, and Marco had nothing but an old zippered sweatshirt large enough to fit him.

Marco had enough pain pills to keep Jefferson comfortable until the afternoon. He'd written a prescription for more, as well as one for tranquilizers for the twins if they were needed. Laura strongly resisted the idea of drugging the boys, but she'd accepted the prescription, just in case.

Snow had begun to fall again. She supposed, in a way, that was good. It would slow them down. But it would slow down any pursuers as well.

For a quarter of an hour they rode without speaking, listening to the drone of the car's motor, the rhythm of the windshield wipers, and Jefferson's drugged snore.

At last Montana broke the silence. His voice was low,

but it startled her. "You're awfully quiet back there," he said. "What are you thinking about?"

She crossed her arms and pulled the jacket more closely about her.

"I was thinking," she said, "that this is one hard way for a woman to get a fur coat."

EIGHT

THEY CROSSED THE TOLL BRIDGE THAT SEPARATED QUEENS from the Bronx, and cut a northward path through Connecticut.

The twins, awake again, played complicated number games with their maps and pennies.

"Let me get this straight, man," Jefferson said in a pained voice. "We're going to *Bible* camp?"

"It's her idea," Montana said, nodding in Laura's direction.

Laura put her hand on the top of the front seat and leaned close to Jefferson. "My grandparents lived close to this little town in Vermont, East Jamaica. I used to visit them in the summers."

"And they sent you to Bible camp? Oof. Ouch."

"Don't try to turn around," she said, putting her hand on his good shoulder. "The camp was outside of town. My grandfather hauled wood there once a week. I'd ride with him. Sometimes we'd get invited to lunch. Sometimes he let me stay and play. I got to know it pretty well."

"Wood? Why was he hauling wood in the summer?" Jefferson asked.

"For cookstoves," Laura said. "It was all very back-to-nature. I mean, the camp was in the woods; still, they didn't want to cut down their own trees. But they had to have a constant supply of wood."

"Oof," said Jefferson.

"You should take another pain pill," said Montana.

Rickie told Trace some impossibly high number, and they both began to laugh giddily. Trace shrieked.

"Shhh," Laura said firmly. "Not so loud. It's all right to laugh, but not so *loud*."

"Jeez," said Jefferson. "They're giving me a headache."

"They're just being kids," said Montana. "Take a pill."

"I want to hear about this camp first," Jefferson said, then grimaced with pain.

The twins subsided into giggles. "That's better," Laura said. "That's good." She turned to Jefferson again.

"I stopped going to my grandparents' after my grandpa died, years ago. Then my grandma got Alzheimer's disease. She didn't know us anymore. She had to be put in a home."

Rickie pointed to something on the map, and he and Trace began to giggle harder.

"My grandmother died last summer," Laura said. "I was in charge of the funeral. I stayed afterward to put her affairs in order. But I'd take these sentimental journeys, you know? Like to the farm where they'd lived. And one day I went to the Bible camp."

"I hope it got turned into a Holiday Inn," said Jefferson.

"Would you take a pill?" Montana asked, irritation in his voice. "Or am I going to have to shove it down you?"

"I'll tell you what to shove and where," Jefferson groaned. "Let me hear about this camp, okay, dammit?"

"Don't swear in front of the kids," Montana said. "Laura, tell him fast, okay?"

"The camp's still there. But it's out of business and for sale. I met a real estate agent. He said he didn't think it'd ever sell. For one thing, it's a white elephant. For another, there's a dispute about a property line. A dispute that's going to be messy to solve."

"So maybe some idiot who likes messy white elephants bought it," Jefferson said from between his teeth.

"No," Laura said. "I got a Christmas card from this same person. Less than a month ago. He wrote, 'I've still got your camp for you, bargain price.'"

"What's he sending you Christmas cards for?" Jefferson asked. "He got the hots for you, or what?"

"Yes," Laura said matter-of-factly. "But he's married. So I don't have the hots for him. Anyway, this camp is isolated, and it's empty. We can go there until we figure out someplace better."

"Quebec sounds good to me," Montana said. "Does anybody speak French?"

"A little," Laura said, certain that her little was far from enough.

"French?" demanded Jefferson. "I'm shot full of holes, you're taking me to *camp,* and now you want I should speak French? Ouch!"

Jefferson nearly doubled up, and he ground his teeth.

Laura winced at his suffering, but the twins, still playing map games, laughed together.

"Take your goddam pill," Montana said.

"Take your goddam pill," Trace echoed. "Take your goddam pill."

He and Rickie laughed hysterically.

Jefferson groaned.

Laura held her breath when they crossed the border into New Hampshire. Montana took the straightest path to the nearest city of any size, Nashua.

She tried to keep the twins amused when he stopped at one of Nashua's outlet malls. He had to buy clothing that would fit Jefferson. He also had to provision them with camping supplies. The deserted Bible camp had neither electricity nor gas.

He must have spent a small fortune, Laura thought when he returned. He and she had to repack the van, and the boys were as curious as monkeys.

Montana had anticipated the boys would be restless and had brought them a Chinese checkerboard with its set of colored marbles. Laura could have kissed him. The boys didn't care about the game, but they loved the marbles and arranging them in patterns on the board.

She and Montana worked out a circuitous route of back roads to reach the camp, and they set out again. The board and marbles kept the twins absorbed, for which she offered up a prayer of thanks. Jefferson slept, snoring lightly.

They reached the camp in late afternoon, and the sky was already growing dark. They had passed through the village of East Jamaica and were in the foothills of the Green Mountains.

The camp was located far off a back road that saw little traffic. The lane to the camp was almost four miles long, full of twists and turns and precipitously steep in places.

Snow had not fallen as deeply here as in New York. The day must have been sunny, for the road was nearly bare, though badly rutted from neglect.

Their progress was slow and jolting, and it woke Jefferson, who grimaced when he looked out the window. "I never saw so many *trees*," he said, not sounding happy.

But the trees were good, thought Laura. The looming pines, the bare maples, and the silvery birches formed a fortresslike wall between the camp and the outer world.

Never before had she seen the Vermont woods in winter. The ground was bare except for dead vines and the remains of old snow, and the needles of the tall pines were so dark that the trees looked black against the graying sky. The place felt so empty that it almost felt safe.

"A guy could die of loneliness out here," Jefferson said.

"There are worse ways to die," said Montana.

The camp, or what remained of it, was more rundown than Laura remembered. It was, in fact, in ruins. She thought it was no wonder no one had bought it. No one ever would.

Ramshackle, its roof sagging, the main lodge still stood. So did the old barn made of logs, although its roof had caved in. A totem pole, its paint weathered, stood at a drunken angle.

They all got out of the car. Jefferson looked about in obvious dismay. "Lordy," he said softly to himself, shaking his head.

The twins, full of restless energy from the long day, stood a moment, then exploded into action. Rickie ran in large circles around the tilting totem pole. Trace stuck his arms straight out and whirled like a dervish. "Blue rhubarb!" he yelled.

"Cows fly!" Rickie shouted back. He kept running, Trace kept twirling, and both of them cried out phrases that had meaning only to them.

Laura didn't try to stop them. Like Jefferson, she could only stand and stare in dismay. She remembered when the camp was smart and trim and had been full of children's laughter. Now only the boys' wild cries echoed through the darkening air.

Permanent tents had once stood, a dozen of them, ranged with military precision between the lodge and the stable. Now the canvases were gone, and only a few wooden platforms still stood, in various states of disrepair.

"I didn't remember it being this bad," Laura said, putting her hand on Jefferson's arm. "I guess it looks different in summer. . . ."

Jefferson only nodded. She thought, *That's it. When I saw it last, it was summer and the sun was shining. The trees were in leaf, and there were wildflowers in bloom; it didn't seem so desolate.*

"It'll do," Montana said shortly. "Let's unpack."

Snow had began to float down in thick white flakes.

Laura took a box of boys' clothing from the van, but she couldn't restrain a sigh. Everywhere they went, evil weather seemed to follow, like a cold, malicious ghost.

The inside of the main lodge was in better shape than Montana expected. Teenagers had partied there, leaving behind beer cans, wine bottles, and graffiti.

The windows had been boarded against further vandalism, the doors bolted, but he'd had little trouble getting in.

The interior was dark, dusty, and cloaked with cobwebs. The litter flowed from room to room like a dirty, silent river. But the building was dry and tight. No wind blew through any crack, no snow fell through the roof.

Best, there was a main fireplace with dry wood stacked beside it, three rooms with battered bunk beds, and a kitchen with an old-fashioned cookstove, a pump, and an antique wooden icebox. There were even a few battered cooking and eating utensils left.

In Nashua, Montana had bought battery-operated lanterns, a small chemical toilet, a propane stove and heaters, and sleeping bags. He'd also bought a couple of gray sweatsuits for Jefferson, a winter jacket, and a pair of size fourteen basketball shoes.

He put the chemical toilet in an old pantry, and in doing so, scared out a mouse. "I feel like I'm back in the projects," Jefferson said without enthusiasm.

Laura played outside with the twins as long as possible. Then she made them soup and sandwiches and cocoa. While they ate with Jefferson, she and Montana worked once more to recreate the bedroom the boys had at school.

She swept with a cast-off broom, and he moved the old beds to the right positions. He found a crate to serve as a night table, and put the Bugs Bunny lamp on it, facing the wall. There was no electricity to plug it in, and Bugs was starting to look the worse for wear. Montana hoped that it was the thought that counted.

Together they made up the beds with the Looney Tunes sheets, putting the zipped-open sleeping bags on for extra cover. They hung the Looney Tunes curtains.

Montana found a kitchen drawer that held a cache of rusty nails. Using the tire iron from the van, he hammered them into the walls so they could hang the cartoon animal plaques and bulletin board in place.

There was no dresser, so they piled the boxes of the boys' clothes where the dresser should have been. There were no desks, but Montana found two more crates, and Laura used them as a substitute for desks, and set out the boys' books.

"Home sweet home," she said, looking at the make-shift room by lantern light.

"We're getting good at this," said Montana, adjusting the plaque of the Tasmanian Devil.

Laura shook her head. "It doesn't look so good to me. Where will we do it next? A cave?"

"That's what we figure out."

She looked up at him. Her face seemed younger and more vulnerable by lantern light. "Did you mean what you said about Quebec? Canada?"

"Yeah. But when we make a move, it's got to be right."

Her expression grew rueful. "I'm sorry about this place. I really didn't remember it being this run-down."

"Hey. You don't take care of places this far north, they go to hell fast. Excuse me. I shouldn't swear. It's a bad habit."

"Just so it's not in front of the boys," she said. "I don't mind. Don't apologize."

He put his bad hand in the pocket of the jeans he'd gotten from Marco. They were tight and faded, but they'd do.

The lodge was still chilly, and he'd kept on the old leather jacket. His sweater, an old blue one of Marco's, was too small, but it was warm.

He said, "I'm surprised. About the kids, I mean. This much change. I thought they'd be more upset. You're really good with them."

She shook her head. "No. They've been to camp before. A special camp in New Jersey. They liked it. They caught lizards and turtles. I had to explain that the lizards and turtles are asleep now."

"Like I said," he said, "you're good with them."

"Thanks." It was a simple compliment and an honest one, but she seemed embarrassed.

Maybe she was looking at him differently since last night. He realized he was doing the same thing to her; he couldn't stop thinking of sex. It might not be the wisest way to act, or maybe it was. *Whatever gets you through the night,* he thought fatalistically.

"I should get them in bed, give poor Jefferson a break," she said, turning to go.

"Wait," he said. She stopped in the doorway, but kept her back to him, and didn't turn to look back at him.

"You haven't eaten. You and I, we could eat together."

"Sure," she said.

"And then," he said, "maybe we could sit by the fireplace, have a glass of wine. I bought a bottle of wine in Nashua. What do you think?"

She stared out into the main room where flames crackled in the ancient fireplace. "I think I'd like that."

"Good," he said. "Fine."

Jefferson was more than ready for Laura to rescue him from the twins. He took another pain pill and unrolled his sleeping bag on a sagging bunk in the front bedroom. The walls were covered with graffiti, and he grumbled that he didn't even want to think of the things that had happened on that mattress. He was asleep before the twins had on their pajamas.

The twins were put off and irritated by their bedroom. They were angry that the Bugs Bunny lamp didn't light, but Laura put a lantern on the crate in front of it, and that mollified them somewhat.

She read to them from the lizard book. Rickie, worn out, was asleep after five pages. He had his jar of pennies and his map on the crate between the bunks.

Trace, drumming his fingers lightly against his face, lasted for eleven pages. Then his fingers went still, his breathing grew regular, and his closed eyelids fluttered as he sank into sleep. He cradled his jar of pennies in the crook of one arm.

Laura closed the book, and put it in its place among the others. She took the penny jar from Trace and placed it beside the other one, so he could see it when he woke.

Montana was waiting for her in the kitchen. He'd made cheese sandwiches and instant coffee, and heated a can of minestrone soup.

The electric lantern gave the kitchen a warm glow, even though it left the corners in shadows. She sat on a rickety bench across from Montana. In Nashua he'd bought plastic dishes and cups, plastic knives and forks and spoons. He seemed to have anticipated every need, which impressed her.

The table was old and trestle-style. Its top was scarred with carvings: initials, declarations of love, silly phrases, obscenities.

Montana looked at her over his sandwich. "So tell me. What's 'blue rhubarb' mean? And why do they say that cows fly in outer space?"

She cocked her head slightly, bemused. "I don't know what 'blue rhubarb' means. He just seems to like the sound. Rickie does that a lot, too. It's like they make up their own poetry."

Montana shrugged. "I've heard worse. I've got an aunt that writes poetry. Worse. Much worse."

She smiled, even though smiling made her feel shy and self-conscious. "Sometimes he says it when he's upset. It's like a magic word to shut out what bothers him. Sometimes he uses it to tease. Once he followed a little girl around for two days, saying, 'Sneak snake puddle, sneak snake puddle.' She punched him so hard he got a nose-bleed."

Montana shook his head. "Sounds like love."

"I think it was. Only her parents moved and took her to San Francisco. He missed her. He got up every morning looking for her."

"I thought these kids didn't form attachments. That's what people say."

"But they do," she said with feeling. "In their way. But they don't know how to express it. Trace went through a phase of touching people's hair if he liked them. It was hard to teach him not to."

"So why's Rickie talk about the cow?"

"These kids are very literal," said Laura. "If you say, 'It's raining cats and dogs,' they think puppies and kittens really fall from the sky. If you say somebody has money to burn, they think that person really sets fire to money."

"And the cow?" asked Montana.

" 'Hey-diddle-diddle, the cat and the fiddle, the cow jumped over the moon.' One of their books shows a picture of the cow jumping over the moon. It's real to them. They don't seem to understand imagination. That's fairly typical."

Montana nodded and crossed his arms on the scarred

tabletop. "So in their world, cows fly. And the dish really runs away with the spoon."

"Exactly," she said. "If they see a cartoon of a dancing frog in a high hat, they'll say frogs dance and wear hats."

She paused for a moment. "There are other things, too. They have trouble with pronouns, especially 'you' and 'me' and 'I.' That's why I use names instead."

"How do you understand all this?" Montana asked. "How do you know what goes on in their heads?"

"I read everything I can. I watch. And listen. It's like being a detective. That's what you did before, right? You were a detective."

He frowned, shook his head. "That was different."

"Why?" she asked.

"I never helped anybody. I just busted people. Punks and pushers and hookers and junkies."

He sounded cynical, and she didn't understand. "Well, that helped, didn't it? It stopped *some* crime."

"It didn't make a dent," he said. "It didn't change a thing. It didn't matter at all."

He meant it. His years as a vice cop hadn't mattered in the big scheme of things. The people he'd busted got right back on the streets, plying the same crimes. If they didn't, somebody else took their place. Nothing had got any better. It only got worse.

She, in contrast, actually did *good*. This intrigued him. It also bothered him, because he had helped drag her into danger, and it was wrong she'd been pulled into this morass. But she didn't bitch and moan, she didn't complain. She was a good soldier, better than many men might have been.

He'd propped an old mattress against the wall so they could lean against it, watching the fire. He realized this was not merely a romantic move, but a corny one. He'd done it anyway.

They went to it and sat before the fire, a bit stiffly. He uncorked the wine awkwardly. A man needed two good hands to uncork wine properly. But he got it done, and he filled a plastic glass for each of them.

"Even drinking glasses," she said, taking hers. "You thought of everything."

"I tried," he said wryly. Toilet paper had been a minor victory of planning, he thought. It would have been a hell of a thing to have forgotten toilet paper.

I'm a great Don Juan, he thought. *Here I sit in the firelight with a pretty woman, drinking wine and thinking about toilet paper.*

"You even remembered toilet paper," she said. "I'm glad you didn't get colored. The twins don't like it colored. I forgot to tell you that."

He laughed. She looked at him, puzzlement on her face. "What's so funny?"

"Nothing," he said. He liked the way the firelight played on her even features, sparkled in her hair.

"To getting out of this mess," she said, lifting her glass in a toast.

"I'll drink to that," he said and clicked his glass against hers. They each took a sip. Then a silence fell upon them. The only sound was the wind moaning at the boarded windows and the crackle of the fire.

"The smoke," she said, at last. "What if somebody sees smoke coming out of the chimney?"

"Nobody will while it's snowing," he said.

She settled back against the propped-up mattress, but she looked tense. "And when it stops snowing?"

"I bought three propane heaters. If that's not enough, I drive back to Nashua, get another."

"Where's the money coming from? You can't be using checks or credit cards. Somebody could trace us."

"Marco had a bunch of CD's in his safety deposit box. He cashed them in, gave me the money. He gave me his bank card, too. I'll use it if we have to, but only in an emergency. It's too easy to trace."

"God love him," she said, shaking her head in wonder. "What would we do without him?"

"God love him indeed," said Montana. "Yeah. I think, deep down, he thinks this is fun. Not for us, I mean. But it gets his juices going."

She took another sip of wine as she gazed at the flames. He watched the firelight play on her profile. She had a nice profile, a straight nose, not too long, not too short, a well-set mouth, a firm little chin.

Once again he listened to the groan of the wind, the snapping of the fire. "So," he said, at last. He gave a casual shrug. "What's your story? Got a boyfriend back there, worrying where you are, how you are?"

She kept gazing at the flames. "No. Nobody."

He digested this information, nodding to himself. "So," he said again. "Wasn't there ever anybody? Boyfriend? Husband?"

She was silent a moment. Then she said, "Husband. There was a husband."

He gave another nod. "Okay. What happened?"

She said nothing.

"I'm sorry," he said. "You don't have to answer."

"He left me for another woman," she said, her face impassive.

Shit, thought Montana, and he gave himself a grade of F in conversational skills.

"I'm sorry," he repeated, but an apology seemed worthless. He'd hurt her by bringing up the subject; he could tell by her voice.

She held her glass up, regarding the glint of the red wine in the firelight. "It happened after I lost a baby," she said, her voice under perfect control. "It would have been our first. It happened in the fifth month. The doctors said I couldn't have any more. And I won't. They removed that part of me."

She kept staring at the wine. "He wanted children. He really did. He was an instructor at NYU. He fell in love with a graduate student. He got her pregnant. He divorced me, married her. They had a little girl. A beautiful little girl, I hear. That's all. That's my story."

Montana cleared his throat. He refilled his wineglass. He gazed at the fire a long time.

"You loved him?" he asked. He was unused to asking such questions, and he felt he was bad at it.

"Yes." She gave a bitter little laugh. "And I was so *happy* to be pregnant."

He stared into the flames for another moment. He had one more question. He made himself ask it. "You still in love with him?"

"Yes," she said. "I am. Don't ask me why."

"What about the rest of your family?" he said. "I know your grandparents lived around here. What about your parents? Brothers? Sisters?"

She shook her head. "My parents got divorced when I was five. After that, my father and his side of the family never had much to do with us. He went back to Texas. We don't communicate. My mother died my senior year in college. She was an only child. So was I. I'm the end of that particular line. It's like nature is a lifeguard, and he blew his whistle and said, 'Hey, you—out of the gene pool. You're out of the swim.' Well, that's the way it is."

She turned to him. "So what about you? You didn't get through life without falling in love once or twice, did you?"

"I fell in love a couple of times," he said with a shrug. "Then I fell out."

"That simple?" she asked. "That clean?"

"No. Usually she'd fall out first. My job. What I did. Dirty work. Rotten hours."

"You said 'usually.' You mean once it didn't happen that way?"

Damn, he thought. She was too sharp. He said, "Once I made the classic vice-cop mistake. Absolutely classic. She was a hooker. I thought I'd make an honest woman of her. I thought wrong."

"What happened?"

"She couldn't kick her habit. She'd say she would. She wouldn't. Finally I said, 'Choose. Me or the shit.' She chose the shit."

"What happened to her? Or do I ask too many questions?"

He took a long pull of wine. "She's dead. An overdose. It was inevitable."

"I'm sorry."

"Don't be sorry for me," he said. "Be sorry for her."

Laura gave him a questioning look, and he knew what she wondered. *What was she like, this girl?* A good question. He was still trying to figure out the answer.

He said, "She was the prettiest little thing I ever saw. Puerto Rican. She wanted to be a model. She should have been. But it was more than that. It sounds stupid, but she had a kind of innocence. Yeah. That's stupid. But it's true."

Laura put her hand on his arm, so lightly that her touch was ghostlike.

He gazed at his scarred hand, which was gilded by the firelight. "Know how she got the money for an OD? By selling me out. I should have known. I knew it was a dirty world. I got down in it, as dirty as anybody."

For a dozen heartbeats, Laura left her hand on his arm. Then she took it away. When she did, he realized he'd been holding his breath. He let it out slowly.

"Your husband," he said, looking her in the face, her lovely face, "was a real fool."

She gave him a tight smile. "Thank you."

"You're welcome," he said. Then he leaned to her and kissed her. He put his left hand to her face.

She kissed him back. She took his right hand, the stiff, deformed one, and drew it up so that it, too, touched her face. That surprised and touched him.

He kissed her more hungrily. She put her arms around his neck. She parted her lips, and her tongue, her mouth, tasted like red wine.

She drew back, momentarily. She touched his face, and looked up into his eyes. "I meant it, Montana," she said. "I don't expect you to fall in love with me or anything."

"We've been there, done that, haven't we?" he said.

She nodded.

He lowered his face to hers, and covered her mouth with his own. He nudged the mattress to the floor and, taking her in his arms, lowered her to it.

She wound her arms around his neck, tracing her tongue silkily over the inner curve of his upper lip. Her touch made him crazy, and he reached under her sweater to feel the warm swell of her breast.

She sighed shakily against his mouth, and he kissed her more hungrily. They made every move as silent as possible, so that no one would awake.

The wind mumbled at the windows. The fire crackled.

NINE

LAURA WANTED TO RESIST, YET COULDN'T. SHE HAD A WILD hunger to touch and be touched. Reason pulled her one way, but desire, a hundred times stronger, pulled her another.

Her misgivings only made her blood beat more wildly. Montana didn't love her, and she didn't understand what she felt for him; she knew only that she wanted to feel alive in every part of her body.

Shy and reckless at once, she desired his naked body against hers, yet, her fingers shaking, she stopped him when he had half unbuttoned her blouse. The fire cast too much light on them; they were too visible.

"The boys," she whispered against his mouth. "Or Jefferson. What if they wake up? What if they see us? We can't."

"We'll go to your bedroom."

He rose and drew her to her feet. Haltingly, almost desperately, they kissed and fondled their way into the furthest bedroom. He closed the door behind them, and drew off his sweater.

There in the darkness, he finished unbuttoning her blouse, pushed it from her shoulders, and let it fall to the floor. He kissed her bare shoulder, his hands cupping her breasts. She shivered.

"Take off your bra," he murmured, his lips moving to her throat.

She did. He kissed and touched her until she was half faint.

"Unbutton my shirt," he whispered. She did.

Her fingers trembled, but he was patient. When the buttons were undone, he shrugged out of the shirt and gathered her close, so that her breasts were pressed against the naked hardness of his chest.

The chilly air made his body seem all the warmer. They kissed and caressed each other in urgent silence. The imposed secrecy of their acts made their need keener.

Her shyness dissolved, leaving only yearning. She trembled from the outer cold and inner heat.

"Lie down with me," he whispered.

"Yes." The word came out in a ragged breath.

They lay on the narrow bunk. Awkwardly, they struggled out of their remaining clothing until they were naked and could join each other completely. He kissed her almost fiercely. She kissed him back with something akin to despair.

Each thrust of their bodies was like an affirmation that said, *We're alive, we're alive, we're alive.*

Afterwards, he held her tightly, and neither of them spoke. She should have felt ashamed, but didn't. He stroked her hair. She lay with her cheek against his bare chest. They slept in each other's arms.

Montana was up before anybody else in the lodge the next morning. He phoned Conlee. Conlee got straight to the point.

"I've been told to order you to turn yourselves in," he said.

"The hell you say," Montana retorted.

He glanced around the lodge's dilapidated main room. He'd refused to tell Conlee where they were or to admit Jefferson was hurt. But Conlee knew about Jefferson. The owner of the blue Bronco had talked, just as Montana knew he would. He'd told the police about the big black man who'd bled profusely.

Montana lied glibly, saying they'd left Jefferson behind, but he wasn't saying where. "Hey, he's got a lot of friends," was all Montana would say about it.

The Bronco hadn't yet been found. Conlee persisted in asking if Montana still had it, but Montana wouldn't comment.

Conlee's voice grew almost pleading. "Listen, Montana—you're positive the teacher and kids are all right?"

"They're fine."

"Tell me where you are. Federal marshals will bring you in. The bureau and the task force are pledged to guarantee your safety."

"You can't guarantee our safety," Montana countered. "Somebody inside the organization doesn't care if these kids die. I care."

"Are you still inside your region's jurisdiction?" Conlee asked.

"Neither affirmative nor negative," said Montana.

"Montana, you're to turn yourself and your party over to the marshals. That's an order."

"The last time I followed orders, two of our men died. The kids could have got it. The woman, too."

"Montana, I'm conveying an *order*."

"It's an order I can't follow in good conscience," Montana said.

"Fuck your conscience," Conlee said. "It's not your choice to make."

Montana ignored him. "The next time I call you, I want a list of everybody who knew we were going to Valley Hope. Understand? Everybody. Somebody on it's rotten."

"We're checking. You think we're not checking?"

"I want a list."

"Fine, fine."

"And I want to know why the Colombians mixed it up with the Mafia. Why'd Zordani get shot? Is anybody talking?"

"The hit may have been hired," Conlee said. He sounded uneasy. "By an independent. Not the Cartel."

"Which one? What independent?"

"Your independent," Conlee said.

"Mine?" Montana said dubiously. "Dennis Deeds? He deals marijuana, for Chrissake. He's still back in the hippie days, selling love and happiness. He never killed anybody in his life. He's never had anybody killed."

"Yeah? There's a first time for everything. Nobody's found him yet. He's hiding, like you. Only now he has to hide from the Mafia, too. If you run into him out there, give him my regards."

Montana frowned. What Conlee said made no sense. Deeds was a major grass dealer, but a quiet and elusive one. His main business was not hard drugs but recreational ones; he ran his organization like a conservative corporation, and he never played rough.

"Where'd you get your information?" he asked Conlee.

"Florida. We got a couple people in Fort Lauderdale we're leaning on."

"Lean harder," said Montana.

"We're doing all we can, believe me."

"How's Fletcher?"

"Semicomatose. When he talks, nothing comes out that makes sense. He thinks his kids are babies again or something. Nobody understands him."

Jesus, Montana thought. Just what the kids needed. A vegetable for a father.

"Montana, if you don't come in, they'll put a federal warrant out on you. You've already impersonated an FBI officer. You illegally seized a citizen's vehicle. Now you're defying a direct order. If you don't come in, do you know how many charges they can slap on you? Obstruction of justice—"

Montana hung up. He walked to the front door, opened it, and looked out. The snow had stopped, but fog had closed in, obscuring the world even more.

Something in Conlee's tone hadn't rung true. There was too much bluster in it, too much grandstanding. Conlee couldn't personally guarantee their safety, and he and Montana both knew it.

His gut instinct was that Conlee didn't want him to come in. Conlee, as well as anybody, knew there was a leak somewhere, and nobody was safe until it was plugged.

But Conlee's tip about Dennis Deeds hiring Colombian free-lancers, that was interesting—if it was true. Now Deeds had the Mafia after him? That was more trouble than a prep school pipsqueak like Deeds was prepared to handle.

In the meantime, Montana was dead set against handing Laura and the kids back to the government. He wouldn't do it until he could be certain they'd be safe.

And he knew, full well, that day might never come.

When Laura arose, Montana was already up, and Jefferson had just awakened and limped into the kitchen. Montana gave no sign that anything had happened between himself and her. Neither did she.

Montana gave them the news. Conlee had ordered them to come back under task force protection. Laura blinked hard and tried not to flinch.

Jefferson shook his head. "Man, we can't go back. No way, and Conlee knows it."

"Right," Montana said. "But he can't say that. That call was monitored. He'll say what he's got to."

"They can't guarantee our safety," Jefferson said. "We were supposed to be safe before. We were sitting ducks."

"Laura?" Montana said.

She stared down unseeing at her coffee cup. She kept thinking of all the people who had been surrounded by security but still had been shot—even presidents.

"We can't go back," she said. "There's no use even discussing it—is there?"

"No," said Montana, meeting her eyes. "There isn't."

Jefferson, in spite of his night's sleep, looked weary, and dried blood spotted his sweatshirt. He must have bled during the night.

"We gotta find someplace to go," Jefferson said, shifting uncomfortably in his chair. "But I'm damned if I know where. Oof."

Laura tried not to wince at his pain.

"I'm thinking of a place," Montana said. "I've got to check things first."

Laura wanted to ask *What place? What things?* but

Montana looked as if he intended to keep his own counsel for now. And then, suddenly, the twins were up, confused, disoriented, and making a dozen demands on her.

She hustled to get them calmed down and to feed them breakfast. Montana told her only that he needed to drive back to New Hampshire. There were details to tend to, he said, options to check.

She nodded, acting as emotionless as he did, wondering if last night had been only a dream. Her body, still tingling, told her it had not.

But nothing's real anymore, she thought rebelliously. *None of this is real, so what we did doesn't matter.*

After Montana had gone and the boys finished breakfast, Jefferson kept her company at the scarred kitchen table, nursing his second cup of coffee.

By the fireplace, the boys played with pennies and marbles and the Chinese checkerboard. They'd heaped their plastic lizards between them in a bright pile. Laura had told them they could play half an hour before lessons began.

Jefferson finished his coffee and stared morosely at the empty cup. "I hate camp," he said with comic gloom. "Call my mama. I want to go home."

She smiled. "How do you feel? Any better?"

"Not bad," he said. "I heal fast. That old sawbones got the job done. The stitches itch. That's all."

She searched his face, knowing he was in more pain than he admitted.

"Heck of a fog outside," he said.

"Yes," she said. The fog, thick and cottony, shrouded the outside world. But the fog was good luck; as long as it lasted, they could keep the fires in the hearth and the cookstove going.

Even with the two fires and the propane heaters, the big room was chilly. She knew they could not stay here long. It was not a healthy place for the twins or for Jefferson, who was still weak, no matter what he said.

Once the weather cleared, their situation would be even more hazardous. Anyone might stumble on them, snowmobilers, teenagers looking for a spot to party, a deputy making a routine check.

"Did you reach your wife?" she asked Jefferson. She corrected herself. "Your ex-wife, I mean."

Earlier, while the twins were eating, Jefferson had taken the cellular phone into the bedroom, closing the door behind him. He'd wanted to phone Chicago.

He didn't look happy. "I reached her."

"Did she know about what happened at Valley Hope?"

His eyebrow lifted cynically. "She heard. The bureau told her. Said if I called, she should try to find out where I am. I told her you people left me in New Jersey. She pitches into me, gives me holy hell, tells me she doesn't want to hear, not to drag her and the kids into it."

His tone was derisive, but she could see the brooding hurt in his eyes.

"At least your children know you're all right," she offered. "You have two, right? Boys?"

"Right. Nine and seven. Only they got a step-daddy now. One with a safe job with regular hours. He's an *accountant.*"

He studied the boys as they played by the fire. "She goes, 'What you doing, getting shot up guarding somebody else's kids? Don't you care about your own? You don't care about anything but your stupid job.'"

Jefferson's expression grew bitter. Laura didn't know if he was angry with his ex-wife or with himself.

"I'm sorry," she said.

"I can't blame her. She was always scared of this. She said, 'It was bound to happen.' She said, 'What'd you expect?' She said, 'I told you so.'"

He shook his head sardonically. "So I say, 'Fine. It happened. You happy now?' You know what? She starts *crying.* She is the most contrary woman I know. She goes, 'Are you in such trouble you can't get out? Have you finally gone and done it?'"

Laura bit the inside of her lip. She wanted to ask the same thing: *Will we get out of this? Will we survive?*

Instead she said, "Do you think Montana's right? That we should go to Quebec? Is that still what he's thinking of?"

He lifted his eyebrow higher, his gaze still on the boys.

"Canada? Maybe. Or we could go to Portland, take a plane to the Caribbean. St. Thomas, St. John, some American possession where we don't need passports."

"What's the advantage of that?" she asked.

He turned to her, gave her his lopsided smile. "For one thing, I wouldn't stand out like a sore thumb. Not many black dudes this far north. I am *unique* here. Besides, it's warmer down there."

She stared down at the tabletop and idly traced out the carved words "God is Love."

"I don't know how the twins would act on a plane," she said. "They're on edge. Trace is close to throwing a tantrum, I can tell."

"It's chancy. We're recognizable," Jefferson said. "The Colombians are looking for us. Our own people, too. And that damn paper's coming out. But Canada? It could buy us some time, maybe. I don't know."

"How would we get over the border?" she asked. "We'd have to show papers. We don't have any."

"Montana knows how to get them," Jefferson said.

"And once we're there?"

"At least we're not here."

She rubbed her temples with her fingertips. Her head was starting to ache.

"Montana's smart," Jefferson said. Her gaze met his, and suddenly she realized he knew what had happened last night between her and Montana.

"He's good," Jefferson said. "It'll be okay."

"I hope so." She turned away and stared at the flames dancing in the fireplace. She could feel Jefferson studying her. "I wish he was back," she said.

"He'll be back," Jefferson said. "And we'll take care of those boys. I promise you that."

The day was too cold to let the twins stay outside for long, but Laura was desperate to keep their energy level down. She took them out after their afternoon reading lesson.

The fog had thinned slightly. The three of them played fox and geese in the pristine snow, running and chasing.

She taught them to fall over backwards in the snow and make the print of a snow angel, and they made dozens. The drifts beside the lodge were marked with the shapes of angel after angel, each the size of a child.

When the boys grew bored with angels, she began a snowman. The three of them were putting on the finishing touches, pine cone eyes, when she heard the sound of a motor approaching.

She was terrified that it might not be Montana. But where could she and the boys hide? Nowhere, really. When she saw the red van coming through the white mist, her heart started beating again.

The twins showed no interest. They were rearranging the snowman's face. They put his nose on his forehead and his eyes on his chin.

Montana parked and got out of the van. He came to where she stood shivering as she watched the boys. She expected him to say something neutral and businesslike.

Instead he bent and kissed her mouth. His lips felt warm as sunshine to her.

"You're freezing," he said. "You should take this show back inside."

"I'm trying to wear them out. It's working the other way around. You were gone a long time. I was worried."

"I've been checking out things, laying false trails," he said. "We'll talk about it later."

He took hold of the lapels of her jacket, drew her close, and kissed her again. She knew she would be in his arms again tonight.

"We shouldn't do this in front of the kids," she breathed.

"They don't notice," he said.

"They notice more than you think."

He turned to the boys, who now had the snowman's face resembling something from a cubist painting.

"Yo, Rickie, Trace," he said. "Hi. How are you?"

Neither answered. They were busy making the snowman's mouth go sideways.

"Rickie—Trace," Laura said with all the authority she could muster, "Mr. Montana said 'Hello' and 'How are you?' Answer him."

Rickie squinted harder at the snowman. "Hello. I'm fine. How are you?"

"Fine, thanks," Montana answered with a nod. "And you, Trace. Hello. How are you?"

"Hello," Trace answered absently. "I'm fine. How are you?"

"I'm good," Montana said. "Do you care if I kiss your teacher?"

"Montana," Laura whispered in rebuke.

Rickie looked in Montana's direction with a vague frown. "Mamas and daddies kiss," he said. "Mamas kiss. And Laura kisses. Laura's not a mama."

He spoke with innocence, but his words stung. She started to draw back from Montana. "We should go inside."

But he didn't release her. "Men and women who like each other kiss," he said. "It doesn't have to have anything to do with mamas and dads. It doesn't take skill to have a kid, just luck. What's hard is caring for them."

Rickie looked up at the treetops. "Kissing's yucky," he said flatly. "Hasten, Jason, bring the basin. Urp, slop, get the mop."

"Urp, slop, get the mop," Trace repeated. It was a rhyme they'd learned in the schoolyard.

Montana gave her a one-sided smile. "The best thing about me," he said, "is my unfailing talent for finding a romantic atmosphere."

"Hasten, Jason, bring the basin," Rickie chanted. "Urp, slop, get the mop."

"So I see," Laura said, her gaze holding his. The outside world, the cold, the snowman, the teasing boys seemed to fade to unreality.

Why is this happening? she asked herself. *Is it because we're both afraid we're not going to get out of this? Are we starting to hold on to each other because there's nothing left to hold on to?*

He took her hand in his good one. "Come on," he said softly. "You're like an icicle. Let's get the stuff out of the van and go in."

She nodded mutely.

All afternoon and evening, the snow fell steadily. It

covered the fox and goose tracks, obscured the snowman's bizarre face, and buried the small, childish angels in the snow.

After supper, Montana watched Laura, who sat before the fireplace with the twins. They were having an impromptu lesson about recognizing emotions. She'd made a pack of flash cards that showed by turn a smiling face, a scowling one, a frightened one, dozens of different expressions.

Her clothes were old ones from the closet of Marco's long-dead wife. Her gray sweater had a hole in the elbow; her purple bell-bottom slacks looked like they were left over from the days of *Sgt. Pepper's Lonely Hearts Club Band*. Her auburn hair hung loose and glinted in the glow from the fire.

Two or three times Montana had seen Trace reach out and tentatively stroke her hair. He remembered she'd said that was how he sometimes showed affection.

Did they love her? He supposed they did, in their way. They trusted her, which was just as important. He had to trust her himself, and she him.

He wasn't used to trusting; he hadn't been for a long time. As for loving her, he didn't intend to. An affair was different. They were in this trap together. They would take what human comforts they could find.

She held Rickie's face so that he had to look at her. "Show 'happy,'" she told him. "Show Laura a big smile."

Rickie grimaced, a caricature of a smile, but a smile nonetheless. "Good!" she said.

"Now, Trace?" She touched the other boy's face, turned it to hers. "Trace, show Laura 'happy.' Show a big smile—there!"

Both boys now gave her a distorted version of a smile, but hers was real. "Rickie and Trace smile and make Laura happy, too. See?"

Rickie's forced grin faded. He tapped at his cheeks and looked at his watch. "Half hour, Laura," he said, almost sternly. *"Over."*

"Half hour," she said, giving his chin the gentlest of caresses. "Rickie's right. Play for half an hour now."

She gave Trace, too, a light, affectionate touch, then rose from the floor. "Play for half an hour," she repeated to them.

She came to the kitchen area, made herself a cup of instant coffee, then joined Montana who sat at the old trestle table. Jefferson sat across from him, scowling at one of the newspapers Montana had brought from Manchester.

"Well?" she said, "What do we do next?"

She said it with remarkable calm, Montana thought.

Jefferson shook his head at the *Boston Globe*. "Man, we don't exist," he said. "Not in the New York papers, not Boston, not New Hampshire."

"Any more on Valley Hope?" Montana asked. So far the only coverage had been limited to one short Associated Press release. It consisted of a terse paragraph that ended, "Authorities refused to speculate or comment."

"Not a word," Jefferson said, laying the paper aside with the others stacked on the table. "Somebody—Conlee —whoever—is sitting tight on this story. That's good."

"It is good, isn't it?" Laura asked. "Maybe nobody's after us yet." A look of hope crossed her face.

Montana was pessimistic. "It's a matter of time. Whoever was after us is already looking. I'd put money on it. And the feds are looking, too. And what the feds know, the Colombians know."

He watched her expression of hope die. She made no answer.

Jefferson said, "There could be more than one leak involved. Probably is. Could be human, could be electronic. Bugs, surveillance, who knows?"

"Yeah," Montana said. "Sure."

Laura was disbelieving. "Surveillance? You mean the task force itself could be bugged?"

"Task force, FBI, DEA, name it," Montana said.

"But how?" she asked. "You're the people who *do* the bugging. How can you be bugged yourselves?"

Montana felt an unpleasant surge of cynicism. "Anything we do unto others, they do unto us. There are bugs almost impossible to detect."

She still looked dubious, but Jefferson backed him up.

"They got a microcircuit a thousandth of an inch thick," he said. "Gets its power from radio waves in the air. You can have a transmitter so small, you can slit the edge of a playing card and slip it inside."

"Bugs like that cost megabucks," Montana said. "But the Cartel's got megabucks."

"There are these passive electronic devices that work in the microwave spectrum," Jefferson said. "Harder to find than a square egg."

"And the Colombians have more money than a lot of governments."

"We're not talking thousands of dollars here," Jefferson told her. "We're not talking millions. We're talking billions. The Cartel's got billions of dollars."

Laura looked slightly sick. "Do you bug them back? I mean to that extent?"

"Not us," Montana said. "The CIA gets the sophisticated stuff. We play with the Tinkertoys like pen registers and wiretaps."

"But," Laura protested, "your offices have to be the most secure in the country. How can anybody *put* a bug there?"

"You have enough money, you can buy almost anything," said Montana. "Or anybody."

"Exactly," Jefferson said.

Laura looked from man to man in dismay. "You mean they really could know an agency's every move? Even before it's made? That's how they might have known about Valley Hope?"

"Right," Montana said.

Montana saw Laura's gaze go again to the twins as they played by the fire. She said, "Then how long will we have to keep this up? Running away? Hiding? Will things ever be normal again?"

Montana said, "I don't know."

She swallowed, hard. "I mean, theoretically, it might be forever. Right?"

"Theoretically," he said. "And theoretically, it might be safe to go back tomorrow."

Jefferson said, "Let's not worry about forevers. Let's worry about this week."

Montana nodded. "We can't stay here. We've got to move on." He looked at Jefferson. "You feel up to traveling again? Tomorrow or maybe the next day?"

"No problem," Jefferson said, but Montana could see he was still in pain. That was unfortunate, but Montana couldn't afford pity.

"When the weather breaks, we go," Montana said. "As long as the snow or fog stays, we're safer here than on the road."

Jefferson nodded.

Laura's voice sounded tight, anxious. "Where do we go?"

"We've got options," Montana said. "I say we take the riskiest. It's the one they won't expect."

"What's the riskiest?" Laura asked.

"Canada," Montana said. "It takes a lot of trouble. We've got to establish new ID's, get paper. So we'll find a place to sit tight. That's Phase One. Getting to Canada is Phase Two. I know a guy there. He'll help. His name's Florent Porrier."

Laura's face grew more troubled. "What's Phase Three?"

He didn't intend to tell her Phase Three yet, because she wasn't going to like it. "We'll worry about that when we get to Canada," he said.

He gave Jefferson a quick, conspiratorial look that said, *Back me up. She doesn't need to know any more.*

The big man came through for him. Laura's hand rested on the table, and Jefferson covered it with his own. "In the meantime," Jefferson said, "we do the three musketeers thing. One for all. And all for one."

Montana put his good hand on Jefferson's. "Good enough," he said.

Laura swallowed again and gazed, first at Jefferson's face, then Montana's.

The twins had stolen up to the table. Rickie started to

riffle through the papers, looking for sports scores. He must have heard the last part of their conversation.

"Good enough," he said in a singsong voice. The words seemed to fascinate him, for he repeated them.

"Good enough, good enough, good enough," he chanted, and Trace joined him.

"Good enough, good enough," they sang.

But Laura didn't look as if such vows were good enough at all. She looked uneasy.

I'm hiding the truth from you, Montana thought. *It's what I've got to do.*

TEN

AT BEDTIME, THE LODGE WAS COLD, AND THE TWINS CLAM-
ored that they wanted to go home. They cried, and Trace
kicked over the box on which the Bugs Bunny lamp sat.

"Want the room at school," he said between sobs.
"Want bed at school! Room at school! Room! Bed!"

Trace set off Rickie, who cried harder still and started
sobbing, "Mama! Get Mama, Mama, Mama, Mama,
Mama . . ."

His words tore at Laura's heart, because he only called
for his mother when he was baffled and frustrated to the
point of terror.

Montana appeared in the bedroom doorway. "Can I
help?"

"You can try," she said, above the boy's screams.

She held Trace tightly and talked to him, trying to calm
him. At first he fought her, but at last, exhausted, he submitted to her embrace.

Still crying, he lay his face against her shoulder. His
arms went around her neck in an awkward embrace, and
his warm fingers fluttered against her skin, stroking her
hair.

"Trace is on vacation now," she told him. "Soon we'll
go in the van again. Trace will like that. Trace can see new
places on the map, and highways, big ones and little ones.

And we'll get more pennies—and maybe nickels and quarters, too."

On the other bunk, Rickie had let Montana put his arm around him, and Montana spoke to him earnestly. "We'll get in the van. We'll go someplace with a shower and a television. We'll—we'll sing. Do you know 'A Hundred Bottles of Beer on the Wall'? Rickie?"

Laura kissed Trace's cheek, right beneath the red streak that marked where the bullet had creased him. When he flinched only slightly, she kissed him again. His sobbing lessened. "Laura's here," she said. "And Laura will take care of Trace. Trace knows that."

Montana sang:
"A hundred bottles of beer on the wall,
"A hundred bottles of beer—
"If one of those bottles should happen to fall,
"Ninety-nine bottles of beer on the wall."

She was surprised that he had such a good voice, a strong, melodious baritone.

". . . If one of those bottles should happen to fall,
"Ninety-eight bottles of beer on the wall.
"Ninety-eight bottles of beer—

"Come on," Montana urged. "You sing, too." He squeezed Rickie's shoulders and nodded encouragingly.

Laura saw Rickie wince at the hug, but he tolerated it. His face stained with tears, he wiped his nose with the back of his hand. Then, in a quavering voice, he began to sing along with Montana.

"Ninety-seven bottles of beer on the wall.
"If one of those bottles should happen to fall—
"Ninety-six bottles of beer on the wall . . ."

"Good," Montana said. "That's it." The two of them kept singing, and Montana took out a handkerchief and wiped the boy's nose properly.

Trace went even more quiet in Laura's arms. He was listening, she could tell. When Montana and Rickie reached ninety-three bottles of beer on the wall, Trace pushed away from her and began to tap his fingers against his cheek.

His voice, wobbly and stuffy from tears, joined theirs. "Ninety-two bottles of beer on the wall.

"Ninety-two bottles of beer—

"If one of those bottles should happen to fall . . ."

Laura threw a grateful look at Montana, dug in the pocket of her slacks for a tissue, and cleaned Trace's runny nose. He shook his head, fighting off her attentions. He was becoming caught up in the song.

Montana flashed her a conspiratorial smile. She smiled back and began to sing in her off-key alto.

"Ninety-one bottles of beer on the wall . . ."

Rickie was nodding drowsily at seventy-nine bottles of beer on the wall; he was fast asleep by seventy. Trace lasted through the sixties, then sighed, lay down, and closed his eyes at fifty-eight.

"Thank God," Montana said. Laura pulled the covers up to Trace's chin, while Montana set the crate upright again and placed the Bugs Bunny lamp back on it.

"Bugs is starting to show signs of wear," said Montana.

"So are the boys." She stood, and he did, too.

She gazed up at him. "Thank you. You were a genius."

He smiled. "You won't think so when they've sung it for the thousandth time."

"I'll be like Scarlett O'Hara. I won't think about it now. I'll think about it tomorrow. Tomorrow I'll be able to stand it."

He touched her affectionately on the jaw. "Come on, Scarlett. We've got to plan a way out of Atlanta before the Yankees get us."

The three of them sat at the scarred table by lantern light.

"What's the weather like?" Montana asked Jefferson. "Have you looked?"

"The snow's stopped. I went to the van, listened to the radio. It's supposed to be clear tomorrow. Clear and sunny."

Montana studied Jefferson. "We should leave. You up to it?"

"Man," Jefferson said, "I'd be up to it if they'd shot my arm *off*. You know what the most beautiful words in the world are? 'Central heating.'"

The corner of Montana's mouth turned up slightly.

"I mean it," Jefferson said with feeling. "Happiness is a real toilet. Made out of real porcelain. I'm tired of whizzing in that overpriced bucket."

"We're upgrading accomodations," Montana said. "We'll establish ID's, get ready to leave the country."

Laura's emotions warred. All of this seemed so uncertain, so dangerous; what if they were caught?

In contrast to her, Jefferson seemed calm, almost stolid. "All right. Go on."

Montana nodded. "We keep the kids out of sight. The *World Weekly Record* hits the stands in two days. Once it does, the whole country knows what they look like." He looked at Laura. "And you. They'll know your face, too."

Laura winced. Whenever she thought of the paper, she was angry, sick, and frightened.

"I drove to Manchester this morning," Montana said. "It's the biggest city in New Hampshire. There's a village north, more of a suburb. Hooksett. That's where we're going."

"But where will we live? And how?" Laura asked.

Montana said, "I saw a realtor. We're renting a place in the country. North of Hooksett. We'll be off to ourselves."

Laura was appalled by his audacity. "*Renting?* Talk about dangerous. Talk about conspicuous—"

"We need a place, we need an address. What are we supposed to do? Check into a motel? We can't do that. You said so yourself. It leaves a paper trail."

"He's right," Jefferson said without emotion.

Montana gave her a challenging look. "Stay with friends? We haven't got any here. And if we did, would you move in on friends if you knew the Colombians were after you? What do you say? 'Oh—don't be surprised if some guys with Uzis come in shooting.'"

"We can't break into an empty house," Jefferson said. "A neighbor might notice. A cop. Or just somebody passing by."

"So we rent," Montana said. "It's chancy, but it's all we can do."

She tried to fight the anxiety that threatened to choke her. "What do we tell people?"

"As little as possible," Montana said. "I told the realtor we're a couple with one kid. We're back from three years in Berlin. I'm a computer programmer. I'm starting my own business."

"But what about Jefferson?" she protested, looking at the big man. "And there are two children, not one—"

"They don't know that," Montana said. "We keep to ourselves. Don't worry about cover stories. I'll come up with them. I'm used to lying. I can do it. You'll have to trust me."

"But who *are* we?" she asked. "I'm not a good liar. I don't know if I can—"

"You're Anne Orsi, and I'm Mike Kominski," Montana said. "We're married. If anybody there asks, we say we have just the one kid. We cross the border at night, with the kids asleep. We won't say they're twins, just flash their documents and split."

Laura put her hand to her forehead in frustration. "Wait. Slow down. If we're married, why is my name different from yours? What documents?"

He took her hand in his. "We say you kept your name when we got married. Lots of women do. I've sent for a birth certificate for Anne Orsi."

"A birth certificate?" she said.

Montana nodded. "Once you have the birth certificate, you can get a driver's license. And in this country, once you've got a driver's license you can get anything."

"That's right," Jefferson said.

Laura found it hard to think, hard to get her breath. "Who's Anne Orsi?" she managed to say. "Why that name?"

Montana held her hand more tightly. "My Uncle Dom's daughter. She died of a heart defect when she was a baby. I already wrote to the county records office for the certificate. It'll arrive in a couple of days. At the house in Hooksett."

"I'm a dead person?" she asked. It seemed ominous.

"It's the safest way," he said.

She licked her lips, which were dry. "And you're Mike—Kom—Kom—Kom—"

"Kominski," he said. "Marco's grandson. My friend

Mike. Marco gave me his birth certificate and his social security card. I applied for a New Hampshire driver's license today. You get yours as soon as you get the birth certificate."

All this duplicity, all these identities had her confused. "And the boys?" she asked, shaking her head helplessly. "Will they have dead people's names, too?"

"No," Montana said. "In Manchester I stopped at a religious supply store. I said I was a parish priest from upstate. I bought a box of baptismal certificates. We can name them anything we have to."

Jefferson said, "You four go over the border together. I'll rent a car and follow, meet you in Quebec. My name'll be Warriner. Sidney Warriner."

Laura eyed him warily. "And Sidney Warriner is . . . ?"

"A guy I went to college with," Jefferson said. "He died of leukemia."

She turned to Montana. "You've sent for that birth certificate, too?"

"Yes," he said. He nodded at Jefferson. "We talked about it yesterday."

"I—I feel like this is a séance," she said. "We're all turning into ghosts."

"It's how it's got to be done," Montana said.

Jefferson nodded.

"Aren't you worried about using Mike Kominski's name?" she asked. "Afraid of implicating Marco?"

"There's not a lot of choice at this point," Montana said. "I'll change it again after we get to Canada."

"More changes in Canada?" she asked in dismay.

"Yeah," he said. "A few."

"This friend of yours? In Quebec? Who is he? How do you know him?"

"Florent Porrier," Montana said. "He's Indian. I met him when he came to New York to claim his sister's body. She was a kid, she got in with the wrong people. Colombian coke dealers killed her. I helped take them down. Florent said, 'You ever need help, you come to me.' I'm doing it."

"But who is he?" she asked. "And how can he help us?"

Montana held her gaze. "He's a priest. He can get us papers. He can make connections for us that need to be made."

She pushed fingers through her hair in exasperation. "A priest? You're dragging a priest into this? How do you know he'll agree?"

"He's a very militant priest," Montana said. "He's got no love for the Colombians. And he doesn't like the government because of what it's done to his people. He's not afraid to break laws when laws need breaking."

"It seems like too big a risk," she said.

Jefferson shrugged philosophically. "Everything we do's a risk."

"We do what we have to," said Montana.

Mesius Estrada knew as much about the twins' whereabouts as the authorities did, which is to say that he knew precisely nothing.

Until now, Estrada had been able to buy or extort almost any information he wanted. But, when it came to the twins, he'd lost his best and most reliable source in the gunfire at Valley Hope.

He had no knowledge of the twins simply because none existed. It was as if the children had dematerialized.

Estrada, not a man to dawdle, had phoned Don Diego Carmago, the head of the Cartel in Bogotá. Don Diego had sent the Cartel's best man to New York from his base in Atlanta, Georgia: Jorge Hepfinger.

Jorge Hepfinger was plump and jolly-looking, with a round face, thick glasses, and thinning fair hair. His disarming appearance gave no clue of his profession. He was a hunter of human beings; he hunted them down for torture and killing, and he excelled at his work.

Now Hepfinger sat in Estrada's living room, his legs crossed, a mug of beer in one soft hand. In Atlanta he ran an "electronic information service" whose sole customer was the Cartel.

"What's this about, Don Mesius?" Hepfinger asked, smiling. He spoke perfect English.

"Don Diego didn't tell you?" Estrada asked, not believing him.

"I was told to get the story directly from you."

He wants to hear it from me, thought Estrada, his nerves prickling in suspicion. *Does he suspect I'm responsible? Does the Cartel?*

Hepfinger only smiled more amiably. Estrada smiled back but was not fooled by the plump man's resemblance to a clean-shaven Santa Claus.

Hepfinger was half German and half Venezuelan, and from boyhood he had been educated at the best schools in the United States. He was formidably intelligent and absolutely relentless. In Spanish his nickname was *el Podenco de Infierno,* the Hound of Hell. The superstitious said his sinister powers came from witchcraft.

Estrada chose his words carefully. He had painstakingly constructed a lie to hide his own guilt, and he must tell this lie just so.

He said, "We have a warehouse man named Nunez. A man came to him on behalf of one of our customers, Dennis Deeds. Deeds runs a large operation in marijuana and is expanding into cocaine. He wanted a favor."

Hepfinger picked at a stray thread in his sweater, which was well-worn, unfashionable, and slightly dirty. "Umm," he said mildly, a signal for Estrada to go on.

"It's a complex story," Estrada said with distaste. "Deeds came out of nowhere, a nobody. But he has boats—yachts, fishing boats, even freighters. He tried to buy a pier in New York."

"Enterprising," Hepfinger said and picked harder at the pesky thread.

Estrada plunged on. "One of Deeds's men, a certain Elton Milton, arranged to buy this pier. Deeds had a freighter on its way with fifty thousand pounds of marijuana. He had a fleet of eighteen-wheelers ready to roll up to the pier and be loaded."

"Marijuana," chuckled Hepfinger, as if the thought amused him.

Estrada smiled as if he, too, were amused, although he

was not. "At the last minute the owner of the pier changed his mind. Instead of selling to Milton, he leased to a man named Scarlotti, the owner of a fishing company."

"So Deeds didn't get his pier," Hepfinger mused. "This Milton must have been in a sweat."

"He was," Estrada said. "The freighter was due with no place to dock. So, acting like a legitimate businessman, Milton approached Scarlotti. Milton claimed he had a ship in need of repair and asked to rent the pier."

Hepfinger pulled the wrong thread in his sweater, accidentally unraveled it, and sighed. He hardly seemed to be listening to Estrada.

Estrada's heart quickened with anxiety. The tale of Deeds and the pier was a comedy of errors, and he imagined Hepfinger was full of carefully disguised scorn.

"Scarlotti agreed to let Milton use the pier—on the condition Milton's business was legal. Scarlotti was emphatic about this. The business *must* be legal."

Hepfinger was still engrossed with the threads of his sweater, but he nodded. "Um-hmm?"

Estrada sighed. "The freighter came in at three in the morning. It was unloaded, went its way. The trucks went theirs. Milton went back to his apartment. But Scarlotti's men came for him."

Hepfinger looked up at Estrada with a conspiratorial smile. It was as if Estrada was telling him a joke, but Hepfinger had already guessed the punchline.

"Scarlotti is—?"

"Mafia," Estrada said. "He'd leased the pier for Mafia, and he didn't want it dirtied up. Milton and Deeds had done just that, right under his nose. The Mafia was angry —and curious. Who was Deeds? Rich enough to buy a pier, to have his own freighter, to bring it so arrogantly to a borrowed pier."

"Oh, yes, arrogance," Hepfinger observed mildly. "It brings people down. It does."

Estrada toyed with the gold chain at his throat. He paced the room, then glanced back at Hepfinger, concentrating once again on his loose threads.

"So," Estrada said, "to teach Deeds a lesson, the Mafia kidnapped Milton. They phoned Deeds and said they wanted five million dollars ransom. *And Deeds paid.* That's the amazing part. He *paid.* The Mafia set Milton free. But they'd just begun."

Hepfinger looked up and smiled his cherubic smile again.

Estrada shook his head. The Cartel would never have paid such a ransom. They would have let the man die to punish him for being stupid enough to get caught.

"Now the Mafia was really wondering about Deeds. How could he hand over five million, just like that? Why did he have no fight in him? They began to stalk Deeds and try to steal his business, bit by bit."

"As well they should," Hepfinger said primly.

Estrada gave a sigh of weary sophistication. "They kept pushing Deeds. Finally, he felt he had to push back. Scarlotti's superior was Francis Zordani. Deeds was hiding in Florida by then. He told his New York people to hire him someone to teach Scarlotti and Zordani a lesson. That's why Deeds's man came to Nunez, asking for help."

Hepfinger plucked at his thread, his mouth pursing. "The Cartel has no business in such quarrels."

Estrada's stomach tightened queasily. "My thinking exactly. Nunez asked me to help Deeds. I told him it wasn't our place."

This was a lie, and Estrada was terrified Hepfinger would divine it. Carelessly, mechanically, Estrada had told Nunez to hire Paco Paredes and his friends. No one could confirm this but Nunez, and Estrada had made sure Nunez would never tell.

Nunez's friends and family believed he was on a business trip to purchase a fishing boat. In truth, Santander had driven him to the New Jersey pine barrens, shot him, and dismembered his body.

"But the story's not over, is it?" Hepfinger said with a twinkle in his eye. He waved his forefinger teasingly at Estrada. "This Nunez at the warehouse, he went against your wishes?"

Estrada's stomach knotted, but he kept his demeanor cool. "Yes. Nunez told Deeds's man the names of some amateurs, men who would work for hire. Colombians, unfortunately."

Hepfinger shook his head in disapproval.

Estrada made an impatient gesture. "Three fuck-up university students playing tough. Wanting to be *coqueros*. So Deeds had them hired. But—" Estrada paused, hating what he had to utter next.

"But what?" Hepfinger prompted.

"They were idiots," Estrada said bitterly. "Deeds wanted Scarlotti and Zordani to back off, that was all. Instead, the fools killed them."

As briefly and clinically as possible, Estrada recounted the murders and how the twins had witnessed the Zordani killing. And he told Hepfinger the damning truth about whom the twins had seen—Reynaldo Comce.

"I knew about Reynaldo from the start," Estrada said in disgust. "None of the three fired the gun. Reynaldo wanted to go with them, and they let him shoot. He bragged of it to a servant that same afternoon. The servant, a good man, phoned me."

"Reynaldo Comce," Hepfinger said, looking more regretful than surprised. "That's why he was sent home?"

"Yes. I told only Don Diego the truth. He ordered Reynaldo back. The cover story is that he was sent home because of the girl, the actress. That she was being used to get to him. As few people as possible should know the truth."

Hepfinger gave a nod of friendly concern. "Absolutely. And as for the witnesses, the Cartel can offer expertise and means. But the blame should be put squarely on this Deeds."

"Of course. He's the ass who started it."

"Exactly," said Hepfinger. "I'll do all I can. It's only a question of finding this Montana person, the twins, and the woman? The black man isn't with them?"

"Yes," Estrada said.

"You have records on them, files and such?"

"I have sources in the task force. We know everything they know."

"I'll need all that information, of course. All of it."

"It's at your disposal," said Estrada.

Suddenly Hepfinger's stomach growled, and he laughed with chagrin, his eyes crinkling at the edges. He placed his hand affectionately on the mound of his belly. "Would you happen to have some cheese? Some crackers or water biscuits? A nice Brie would hit the spot."

"Of course." Estrada pushed the button that summoned the maid.

Hepfinger regarded his beer mug, then took a drink that left a slight mustache of foam on his upper lip. He licked it off with relish.

"As for the twins and the woman?" he asked. "Consider them yours."

Laura watched, wary, as Montana used the cellular phone to call the realtor in Hooksett. He confirmed that he'd pick up the keys to the country house tomorrow.

Everything Montana told the man was untrue yet sounded plausible. He lied with such ease that Laura was taken aback.

When he hung up the phone, he gave Laura and Jefferson a tight smile. "We've got porcelain, Jefferson. Electricity, too."

"It's furnished?" Jefferson asked. "Real beds? Real chairs?"

"It's furnished. It belonged to a doctor in Boston. His family used it summers. He died last fall. It's got twenty acres and a pond. He fished a lot."

"Fishing," Jefferson said dubiously. "I never understood fishing. You want to eat a fish, buy one. Well, I'm not gonna think about that. I'm going to bed."

Jefferson took another pain pill. He stood at the counter, washing the pill down with a drink of luke-warm cola and grimacing at the taste. Then he turned, rubbing his shoulder, and lumbered toward his room.

A suspicion had begun to gnaw at Laura. She waited until Jefferson was out of sight to speak.

"Montana, you said Phase One is Hooksett. Phase Two is getting to Canada and this Florent Porrier. But you've never said what Phase Three is. Or exactly what Porrier's doing for us. There's something you're not telling me. I think Jefferson knows it, but I don't. What is it? Don't lie to me. Please."

Montana paused for a long moment, as if deciding how much to reveal. His face became unreadable. At last he said, "Florent can get new papers for me and one of the boys. Then we'll separate."

Laura's head jerked back as if she'd been struck. "Separate? What do you mean?"

Montana's gaze met hers. "I mean separate. You and Jefferson take one twin. I take the other."

She stared at him, stunned. "Separate them?"

"We split up. Don't travel together. Don't live together."

"But—for how long?"

"As long as we have to."

Laura felt as if the ground had been cut away from beneath her feet. "You can't do that. What about their feelings? They've never been apart for any length of time. You're not equipped to handle a child like that. There are lessons, there are—"

"We've got tranquilizers," Montana said. "I'll keep him drugged."

"That's inhuman," she protested. "I won't have it—"

Montana cut her off. "Together, they stand out too much. The most conspicuous thing about them is there are two of them."

"No," she said with passion. "I'm their guardian. I won't allow—"

Again he cut her off. "You saw what happened at Valley Hope. Do you want it to happen again? Do you want them alive—or dead?"

She looked at him in panic. His expression showed no emotion; it was perfectly controlled.

"But—" Laura said, then stopped, groping for words. Objections swarmed through her mind, too many to choose from, but Montana held the trump card, and she knew it.

"It's the safest thing," he said. "We do what we have to."

Her heart thudded faster. "Jefferson and I—and a white child?"

Montana said, "Say he's your second husband. Toronto's an international city, sophisticated. Nobody's going to look twice at a mixed marriage."

"But you?" she protested. "Alone with a child? A child with special needs?"

"I'll say my wife died, I'll say she left me. What's it matter? The world's full of single fathers."

"But you don't know enough."

"Maybe I won't need to," he said. "Maybe the task force'll have rooted out whoever informed and we can go back. We take this one day at a time."

Laura wasn't mollified. Montana suddenly seemed monstrously duplicitous to her. Was this the same man who had just helped her comfort crying children? Who had held her in his arms only this afternoon, as if he'd always stand by her?

She darted a resentful glance at him, then looked away, sick with a sense of betrayal.

"Want to sit in the other room? Talk it over?" He spoke as if nothing of import had happened.

"Montana, I can't accept this," she said. "Separating the boys, going different ways—I can't allow it."

"This place is damned cold tonight," he said. "It'll be good to get to a real house."

Anger flared within her. Wasn't he even going to answer her? She stared bleakly at the fireplace, which was empty except for a gray heap of dusty ash.

Montana had let the fire die because the snow had stopped and the sky had cleared. They couldn't take the chance of smoke being seen.

They'd put one propane heater in the boys' room. Jefferson had taken the second into the bedroom with him. One remained in the lodge's main section, throwing off only the faintest hint of warmth in the big room.

She shivered, not knowing if it was from the outer chill or some deeper inner coldness. "You never said we'd have to separate," she said, not looking at him. "Have you planned this all along?"

She meant *Did you have this in mind when you made love to me last night?*

Again he was silent a moment, and when he spoke, his voice was neither hard nor gentle. "I've thought it from the start," he said. "Before we got to Marco's, even. I had to. I wasn't going to tell you until the time came. But I thought I should. Maybe I was wrong."

"Oh," she said bitterly. "Just like that— 'By the way, we're splitting now. And, oh, I'm taking a kid.' How am I supposed to react?"

"Do you think it makes me happy?" he countered. "But it's not a matter of feeling. We've got to think. The law and the Colombians are both looking for twins. Twins, a woman, a white man. You tell me. Which is safer—to stay together—or split?"

Tears welled in her eyes, burning. She couldn't answer because she knew he was right. He was right, and she hated it.

Her chest tightened as if in a vise, and her thoughts spun. If they separated, it *was* more logical for Montana to take one of the boys. How could Jefferson do it? How could he explain himself, a lone black man in a foreign country with a white child, obviously not his?

"Who—who would you take?" she managed to say. "Which one? Trace? Or Rickie?"

He paused again before he answered. "Rickie's got an easier nature. He let me hold him tonight. Rickie, yes."

She couldn't help it, the angry tears spilled and crept down her cheeks. "I don't think I can stand it," she said. "Letting him go. Not knowing—"

She stood and was going to stalk away from him, but he, too, was on his feet. He caught her, held her so she wouldn't leave. "Laura, Laura," he said softly, "don't cry. I'll take care of him. I swear it."

"Leave me alone." She struggled feebly to break free from him.

He pulled her close. "Leave you alone?" he said in her ear. "It's the last thing I want. Not now, not in Canada. We'll get back together. I promise you that, too."

Paradoxically, for as much as he'd hurt and startled her, she wanted him more than ever. Perhaps it was because she needed another human being, any human being. Perhaps it was simply lust, because lust could temporarily cancel hurt and fear. Or perhaps she needed to be near him because she might lose him so soon.

"Laura," he said again, holding her tighter. "I'm sorry. I shouldn't have said anything. But I thought the longer I waited, the worse it'd be."

She clung to him, not knowing what else to do. She buried her face against his shoulder.

"Jefferson already knew," she said miserably. "Didn't he? I was the only one who didn't guess."

"We talked yesterday. When you were out with the kids."

"If you take Rickie, I'll worry about him all the time," she said, her voice tight. "And they'll miss each other."

"It can't be helped," he said.

"You can't drug him," she insisted. "I won't let him go if you drug him."

"It has to be done."

"No. I mean it. I won't let him go."

He drew back, took her face between his hands, and stared down at her. "There's no choice, Laura. It's better he's drugged than dead."

She blinked hard, refusing to let more tears fall. "Don't talk like that."

He shook his head, a troubled expression on his face. "It won't hurt him, not in the long run. Laura, you're so protective of them. Too protective. It's the reason you're here. You shouldn't be. You should have walked away when you had the chance."

"It's a little late for that," she said bitterly. "Somebody had to be here for them."

"Yeah," he said. "Somebody did. But it didn't have to be you. I conned you."

She didn't answer him. If she were honest enough, she would say, *I conned myself. I was as self-isolated as the children. I stayed with them because I was like them, caught inside myself. I didn't want to feel this much for them. But I do feel, and I feel alive again, and I want to stay alive.*

Montana gazed down at her, his face gilded by lantern light. She thought real regret was etched into his expression, that his dark eyes held something almost akin to sorrow.

But she couldn't know. How could she ever know what a man like him truly thought, truly felt?

"It's true," he said. "You didn't have to be here."

"What's done is done," she whispered.

"I watched your face when I was on the phone," he said. "You didn't like what you heard, did you?"

"You lie too well," she said. "It scares me."

Her ex-husband, too, had been an accomplished liar, and she knew how dangerous such men were.

"I worked undercover for four years," he said. "Do you know what that means?"

"No. What does it?"

"It means I can be a lying, scheming two-faced son of a bitch. It means I can convince somebody he's my best friend, then turn around and sell him down the river."

"That's a terrible way to live," she said.

"Maybe. I didn't think about it. I just did it."

"Because it had to be done?"

"Yeah," he said. "That's what I told myself. And still do."

His face was so near she could sense the warmth of his mouth hovering so close to hers. *I still want him,* she thought, bewildered. *And he wants me. Why? Why do I feel this way?*

She took a deep breath. "Montana," she said carefully, "if I'm what needs to be done, it's all right. It's nice to be wanted by somebody besides students. I don't care if you're pretending. It helps. It's fine."

He raised his bad hand to her forehead, stroked back her bangs with his knuckles. "That's not what I meant."

"Yes, it is," she said. She raised her chin, gave him an uncompromising look. "I suppose I'm using you, too."

He looked into her eyes. "This isn't about using."

She held his gaze. "Then maybe it's about needing. I'm scared, Montana. When I close my eyes, it's trite, but I imagine an hourglass with the sand running out. Maybe we need to make the most of time."

He gave her a strange one-sided smile that had no happiness in it. "You're unusual, you know that?"

"No," she said. "I just have the feeling there's no time to be coy. I'm not naive."

"No," he said. "You're not."

She set her jaw. "So maybe you're screwing me for my morale. Or maybe because you feel time is running out, too, and we better take what we can while we can. It's all right. Maybe you think you're a lying son of a bitch. Maybe you are. But you aren't when you're with the kids. You can't fake that. But I'll still fight you over Rickie. I will. All the way."

He frowned. "Laura . . ."

"We don't have to talk if you don't want to," she said and put her hand to his face. "We'll just play this out as it happens."

"We'll do what we have to do," he said, his voice even, controlled. Then he looked at her mouth, took a deep breath, and pulled her into his arms again, hard. He kissed her, almost roughly.

She didn't mind. She liked it. From here on out, everything *should* be intense, every breath of air, every bite of food, every second of vision. And every touch—like this.

She wound her arms around his neck and clung to him, kissing him back, as aggressively as he kissed her.

He pulled her against him so tightly that she could scarcely breathe. She didn't mind that, either, and wished he could do it harder still. He did. She gasped in a combination of pain and pleasure.

"I am not," he said against her lips, "doing this for your goddamn morale."

"Are you doing it for yours?"

"I'm doing it because I want you," he said. "You. I want you."

She didn't believe him. It didn't matter. Against everything that was sane, she still desired him. She knew she was alive because of him, and that his touch made her feel more alive, made her on fire for life itself with every atom of her being.

ELEVEN

THEY AWOKE IN EACH OTHER'S ARMS IN THE BLACK, NOISE-less hour before dawn. They said nothing, only drew closer, naked body to naked body.

Montana didn't know if he kissed her first, or if she was the one to brush her lips against his. He did not know who made the initial seductive caress; did he touch her, did she touch him? Or by some unspoken consent had they acted at the same moment?

It did not matter. In the cold, the silence, the dark, they made love again. There was desperation, a fierce need in their hunger for each other. But as their bodies locked together, straining, there was also an unexpected poignancy, a haunting sweetness that made Montana keep her tightly in his embrace afterward.

She lay with her cheek against his chest. All she said was, "I mean it, Montana. I'll fight you over Rickie." Her breath was soft and warm against his naked skin.

"I know," he said, his arms locking around her more possessively. "I understand."

He held her, his face buried in her hair and thought, *There's not enough time. There's not enough time.*

At last he left her for a cold, uncomfortable bed across from Jefferson's and a sleep full of evil dreams. When he woke, the twins were waking, too, resentful and cantankerous. He was plunged into the clamor of another unsettled morning, and of making ready for another confusing change for the boys.

From time to time, his eye caught Laura's, but her gaze told him nothing. He kept his own expression as inscrutable as he could.

She muttered that she was worried about Trace, that he seemed listless. Montana looked at the kid and thought he did seem sickly. So, for that matter, did Jefferson.

Jefferson kept coughing, which tore at his wound and made him wince. The big man didn't complain, but seemed weaker than he had been.

Shit, thought Montana, *what next*? He loaded all their possessions into the van and wondered if the police and the feds were yet looking for them.

But their trek toward Hooksett was more mundane than dramatic. They'd hardly been on the road half an hour when Rickie's voice came plaintively from the backseat of the van. "Rickie's got to pee-pee!"

"Montana . . ." Laura said apologetically.

"There's a town ahead," Montana said. "I'll stop as soon as I can."

"Pee-pee, pee-pee, pee-pee!" Rickie chanted with monotonous regularity. "Pee-pee, pee-pee, pee-pee!"

Jefferson covered his eyes with his hand and sank more deeply into his seat. "Why can't he take a whiz in the snow like other kids?"

"Because he's not used to it," Montana answered grimly. "He'd explode first."

"My head's what's gonna explode," Jefferson said and sank lower in his seat. "Lone Ranger never had to stop for a kid to go pee. Superman never had to. Rambo neither." He sneezed, dug in his pocket for a handkerchief, and blew his nose.

"Pee-pee!" Rickie yowled.

"Hush," Laura told him. "It's not polite to be so loud."

Montana pulled up the van to a stop in the parking lot of a convenience store east of Keene, New Hampshire. The day was bright and clear, but bitterly cold. Laura and Rickie got out and went into the store.

Montana narrowed his eyes against the glare of sunlight on the snowdrifts. He decided that while Laura took Rickie to the rest room, he would try to put a call through to Conlee.

He dialed the number and waited. Conlee didn't immediately answer. Montana cast a worried glance at the rearview mirror.

Trace looked more sluggish than before. He'd started coughing, and he showed no interest in his jar of pennies, the plastic lizards, or the marbles.

At breakfast, the kid had hardly eaten, and he'd spent the last fifteen minutes in the van dozing uneasily, sometimes mumbling in his sleep. What was wrong with him?

Hellfire, Montana thought, his teeth clenched. Stallings had been sick right before he'd been shot at Valley Hope. Had his goddamn germs lived on?

A distant receiver lifted, and a man's voice said, "Yes? Isaac Conlee here."

"Conlee, this is Montana. The boys are safe."

"Montana, where are you? What in hell are you doing?"

"I called to say the kids are fine," Montana answered. "I'll keep you informed, that's all I can do."

"Montana, what you're doing is illegal. Burton Fletcher could press kidnapping charges against you. That's a federal offense, a life sentence."

"I won't bring them in until it's safe," Montana said flatly.

"And what if you decide it never is? Are you going to stay on the run for the rest of your life?"

"If I have to," Montana said. "Tell me how Fletcher is. Make it quick."

"In a semicoma still," Conlee said. "When he talks, he makes no sense. But he seems to think his wife's still alive."

Montana had no time to waste on sympathy "What's the word on the Zordani case?"

"Listen carefully, Montana. There's important news on Zordani. The rumor's true. Dennis Deeds hired the hit. We've got a snitch. The Cartel is clean. One of Deeds's flunkies hired some loose-cannon Colombians, told them who to hit. Zordani'd been after Deeds, and Scarlotti started the bad blood between them."

Montana listened, his face stony, as Conlee told him the story of Deeds, Scarlotti, the pier, the kidnapping, and the ransom.

"So you're *not* up against the whole Cartel," Conlee finished. "It's just three, maybe four guys. Come in."

"No," Montana said contemptuously. "How did three or four guys without connections find out we were going to Valley Hope? The Cartel's got to be mixed up in this."

"I'm telling you this is contained. They had an extremely well-placed leak, that's all. We'll find it. We'll find them. We'll lock them up. It'll be over."

"It's a long way from over," Montana challenged. "Whatever leak they've got, it's a killer. Have you swept the task force for bugs?"

Conlee gave a sigh of angry resignation. "We've swept this whole building four times. No bugs."

Montana didn't buy it. "A good bug isn't found easy."

"We've got CIA technicians coming in for a fifth sweep. If they don't find it, it isn't here."

"What about that list?" Montana pressed. "I asked you for a list. Of everybody who knew we were going to Valley Hope. Do you have it?"

"I've got it," Conlee said. "And it's short. Who knew where you were going? *And* when? Only seven of our people. You, Jefferson, Stallings, and Becker. Me. Bitcon and Forstetter."

"Who are Bitcon and Forstetter?"

"Bitcon is full-time task force. He set up the deal with Valley Hope. Forstetter is NYPD. A task force investigator on the Zordani case. He was told because he was going to replace Stallings. Stallings was coming down with something."

"Somebody's dirty," Montana said. "Somebody talked."

"Nobody we can find, Montana. The bureau's run checks on everybody on the list, including me. They've run checks on the checks, and then checked those. Nobody's got a bank account in the Bahamas or a Rolls-Royce parked in his garage."

"Look," Montana said, his patience worn thin, "if it isn't one of them, it's somebody else. Somebody *knew*. The Colombians didn't just have a mystical vision of where we'd be—"

"The leak could have come from Valley Hope," Conlee countered. "We're checking. We're getting to the bottom of this."

"Yeah, sure," Montana said.

"Montana, where's Jefferson? Have you got him with you or not?"

"Not," Montana lied. "Why would I drag him along? I haven't got enough problems?"

"Then where the hell is he?"

"I left him in good hands."

"Why haven't we heard from him? Why's he not coming in?"

"Ask him, not me," said Montana.

"The FBI wants a federal warrant on you. I can't stall them forever."

"If they put a warrant on us while you've got the leak, you're playing right into the hands of the Colombians."

Conlee was silent a moment. "All right, Montana. You've been warned. If you're smart, you'll come in now."

Montana made no reply.

"Now," Conlee repeated, and he hung up.

Montana hung up and turned to Jefferson, but he was asleep again, his lungs rasping with each breath.

Outside Laura was ushering Rickie toward the van. Her vivid auburn hair fluttered in the breeze, and cold had brightened her cheeks.

She looked up at him and made a gesture that asked, *Can I keep him outside a while? Let him play?*

He nodded. The parking lot was deserted except for them. Few cars traveled the highway.

Laura raced him back and forth across the parking lot until she was out of breath. Then she stood with her hands in the pockets of the white fur jacket, watching Rickie. The kid began to spin himself around at the edge of the parking lot, his lips moving a mile a minute. Montana rolled down the window an inch to hear him.

"A hundred bottles of beer on the wall," Rickie sang loudly, twirling in unsteady circles.

"A hundred bottles of beer,

"If one of those bottles should happen to fall—"

Beside Montana, Jefferson coughed in his sleep. Montana reached over and touched Jefferson's forehead. It was burning hot. From the backseat, Trace, too, coughed. Stallings was dead, but his virus went marching on.

A dismal feeling swept through Montana. He drew his hand back and stared out the window again at Laura standing so straight in the cold, her long hair rippling.

"Ninety-five bottles of beer on the wall," Rickie sang. He looked up at the sky with a rapt, absent smile.

"If one of those bottles should happen to fall—"

Happen to fall, Montana thought darkly. He watched the little boy, and the line echoed in his mind. *Happen to fall. Happen to fall.*

Whenever Jorge Hepfinger came to New York, he stayed at the Plaza in a suite that overlooked Central Park.

Estrada sat on an ivory-colored velvet love seat, watching Hepfinger with ill-disguised impatience.

Hepfinger was hunched over a white-and-gilt desk, writing with painstaking precision in a leather-bound notebook. He was almost psychotically meticulous.

A sleek portable computer rested on the desk, plugged into the data port. Beside it a portable fax machine hummed, ready for action, its green light shining.

Hepfinger had asked Estrada to drop by because, he said, he wanted to show him some intriguing data.

But since Estrada's arrival, Hepfinger had told him nothing. He seemed rudely absorbed only in penning his notes. He reminded Estrada of a roly-poly maggot, greedily burrowing into his mound of dead facts, lost to all else.

"What have you learned?" Estrada asked at last. "Do you have something to show me? Or not?"

Hepfinger, startled from his reverie, straightened and turned to Estrada with a benign smile. "It's like a chess game. One gets wrapped up in the strategy."

"This isn't a chess game. It's a hunt," Estrada said

with an edge in his voice. "Speed is imperative. It's best if the law never finds those children."

Hepfinger folded his hands over his stomach. "As the Americans would say," he observed cheerfully, "the law is doing a piss-poor job."

"You can do better?"

He had given Hepfinger all the information that had come into his hands. Estrada had two excellent informants within the task force. They were quiet, unremarkable-seeming people who handled remarkable information, and they smuggled it out with boldness and ingenuity. But what good had it done?

"If only you hadn't lost your primary source," Hepfinger said sympathetically. "Valley Hope was unfortunate. Your baby gunmen hit all the wrong targets."

Estrada didn't need to be reminded. "We used them because we wanted to keep the crime tied to Dennis Deeds. It was a strategic decision."

Hepfinger shook his head as if to say, *It was a poor decision, a disastrous decision*. But his utterance was placating and mild. "We won't cry over spilt milk."

"The law thinks they've gone to Philadelphia," Estrada said.

"Correction." Hepfinger held up four pudgy, well-manicured fingers. "The law thinks four went to Philadelphia. Montana, Laura Stoner, the twins. And that the black man's been left behind."

Estrada narrowed his eyes. "You disagree?"

Hepfinger chuckled.

On Monday afternoon, someone using Jefferson's credit card had bought four one-way tickets on a red-eye flight to Philadelphia.

The tickets *had* been picked up and boarding passes issued; the airline computers confirmed this, but not if anyone had actually used the seats. Flight attendants were being tracked down, but so far, their memories were hazy. The flight hadn't been crowded. Neither empty seats nor full ones had been conspicuous.

Hepfinger rose and paced to the room's mahogany minibar. He opened it and took out a bar of Cadbury's chocolate with almonds. "A snack?" he asked Estrada hospitably.

Estrada shook his head, his mood dark. "I have men poised and waiting in Philadelphia. A word from me and they move. But are you saying they're not in Philadelphia?"

Hepfinger began neatly peeling the gold foil from his bar. "The trail's too clear. Therefore, it's false."

Estrada challenged him. "You can't know that."

"One never leaves a trail," Hepfinger said, his mouth full, "unless it's the wrong one."

"They were desperate," Estrada said. "They had no choice."

Hepfinger shrugged good-naturedly. "They had dozens of choices. Why, for instance, leave New York?"

"The black man," Estrada said. "Is he in New Jersey? He told his ex-wife he was in New Jersey."

"Perhaps. But if I were going to hide a black man, what better place than Harlem?"

"You think he's in Harlem?"

"Possibly."

"Possibly he's anywhere," Estrada said. "Possibly he's dead. This is all speculation, nothing more. I need facts."

Hepfinger walked to the desk and tapped a stack of folders. "It's one thing to procure information. It's another to evaluate it. One has to ask the right questions."

Estrada knew Hepfinger's reputation well, but he was finding the man insufferable. Irritation sharpened his voice. "What are the right questions?"

Hepfinger sucked an almond clean of chocolate, withdrew it from his mouth, and set it carefully in a crystal ashtray.

He said, "The obvious questions are, 'Where is Montana? Where does he have the woman, the twins?' Trails go a certain way, but they lead to nothing."

"Yes?" prompted Estrada.

"Attention should be paid to the key question. Where is the black man?"

Estrada frowned. Jefferson hardly mattered. Jefferson was beside the point.

Hepfinger smiled his bland, maddening smile. "Jefferson was wounded—badly. It's certain he needed medical attention. The Bronco's owner said he was bleeding 'like a stuck pig'—a colorful phrase, if vulgar. But I digress.''

You certainly the fuck do, thought Estrada.

Hepfinger took another large bite of his candy bar. "They had to get help for Jefferson. But from whom?"

"The law's asked that question," Estrada said. "The law's done background checks. I've given you the information. It's all there.'' He pointed to the folders.

Hepfinger waggled his hand, a gesture that said *Maybe yes, maybe no.*

The FBI was interviewing friends, relatives, neighbors, and fellow workers of Montana, Jefferson, and Laura Stoner. The bureau was running checks and double checks on any medical personnel the three had in their pasts. The job was time-consuming, tedious, and far from complete.

"Ahh," sighed Hepfinger, "who treated the black man? It's like searching for the proverbial needle in the haystack."

"Why's it matter? It's Montana, Stoner, and the twins I need."

"Bear with me," Hepfinger said, cocking his head almost coquettishly. "First, this person who treated the black man has shown loyalty. He—or she—has reported nothing. Second, for all we know, Montana, the woman, and your twins may still be with him. Third, if they've moved on, they'd need money, transportation, a safe destination. Their host may have provided any or all of these."

Estrada nodded, somewhat mollified.

"And if they've moved on," Hepfinger continued, "this is the crucial question: Was Jefferson left behind? Or is he still with them?"

Estrada said, "Why would Montana take him? A wounded man would only slow him down. And one so conspicuous? A giant—and black into the bargain?"

"Because he may have plans for him," Hepfinger said.

"Plans? What kind?"

"That," Hepfinger said with obvious satisfaction, "is my point. He would need him for only one reason."

"And that is what?" Estrada asked in exasperation.

Hepfinger sucked another almond clean and set it

aside. "He intends to split up the twins. The black man will go with the woman and one boy, to protect them. Montana will take the other."

"That's ridiculous," Estrada protested. "The black's still wounded. He's good for nothing."

"Wounds heal," said Hepfinger.

"They take time to heal."

"Time," Hepfinger said, his blue eyes twinkling. "Suppose this Montana is doing just that, taking his time? That means he's doing things carefully. He's been underground before. He's not an amateur."

"The five of them together? It's insane," scoffed Estrada. "Impossible."

Hepfinger ate the last of his candy bar, then licked its crumbs clean from his fingertips. "Then where *is* the black man? Whoever he's with may be able to tell us something crucial about Montana's *modus operandi*."

Estrada shook his head unhappily. Sifting through the list of medical connections was proving a daunting job even for the FBI.

The problem wasn't a lack of leads, but too many of them. Laura Stoner had lived in New York for four years and her work had brought her into contact with doctors, nurses, therapists. Jefferson's ex-wife and ex-girlfriend were both RN's. Montana, through family and friends, could be linked to a dozen nurses and doctors.

In addition, vice work had taught Montana in nasty detail about the medical world's slimy underbelly. There was, for instance, an MD named Falk who'd lost his license, but practiced without it. Montana knew of him, of two more just like him, and of a score of men and women who were far worse.

Hepfinger opened the folder that held the lists of medical people being questioned.

He said, "The pattern of the FBI's investigation concentrates on Montana's underworld contacts. And one of them, Falk, used Jefferson's credit card to go to the Bahamas. The FBI's looking for him. But I think they're wrong. I don't think Montana went to a criminal."

"Why would he drag innocent people into the situation?" Estrada objected. "It doesn't fit him. The police say as much. It's not his style."

"Who would you trust if you were in mortal danger?" Hepfinger asked smugly. "A criminal? Or a friend? And if you were in danger, would you do the expected? Or the unexpected?"

He picked up a sheaf of papers from the folder and handed it to Estrada. "These are the medical contacts the three had in a sixty-mile radius of Valley Hope. They couldn't have traveled much farther with a man that badly wounded. Even if the FBI has questioned these people, question them again. The answer may lie here."

Estrada scanned the list, which was penned in Hepfinger's flawless handwriting. Fifty-three names were divided into three columns, according to whom they were linked.

Laura Stoner	*Thomas J. Jefferson*	*Michael M. Montana*
Ira Klein, M.D.	Danella Miller, R.N.	Lynda Trentino, R.N.
Sally Butz, R.N.	Shelanna Cowpry, R.N.	Ed Rosen, Paramedic
Marcus Whitt, D.D.S.	Quentin DePew, M.D.	Cosette Kent, L.P.N.
J.L. Brainard, M.D.	Lola Hoch, R.N.	LeRee Smiley, R.N.
G. Lazenbee, L.P.N.	Lana Hoch, R.N.	S.K. Munk, Paramedic
DeLana Brown, R.N.	Casswell Depp, M.D.	Marcia Galli, L.P.N.
Treena Valdez, D.O.	Lea Mayberry, R.N.	Ferris Wong, M.D.
Copley, D.O.	U.S. McCall, D.D.S.	Wm. F. Ponti, M.D.
Alice Zamchow, R.N.	Fiona Lords, R.N.	Nan Rogers, L.P.N.
Jon Redmond, L.P.N.	I.I. Washington, M.D.	R.J. Epp, Paramedic
R.M. Fleet, D.M.D.	Candy Zangwell, R.N.	Forrest Serb, D.V.M.
Kara Gold, M.D.		

Tisha White, L.P.N.	Caitlin Moss, R.N.
Bessy Janeway, R.N.	Mary Ferarri, L.P.N.
K.O. Jefferson, D.V.M.	Marco DeMario, M.D.
W.B. Linway, D.C.	Lucian Martino, D.D.S.
Juan L. Perez, M.D.	

Estrada turned the page and began scanning data on the names. His expression was bleak. "My God," he said, "some of these people are fucking *veterinarians*."

"Veterinarians set bones," Hepfinger said. "They cut flesh, sew it up. And one is Jefferson's cousin."

"Dentists?" Estrada said with ill-disguised contempt.

"Dentists operate. They prescribe drugs."

Estrada read on and shook his head in disdain.

Hepfinger sighed. "Unfortunately, the list isn't alphabetized. Unfortunately, I haven't had time to arrange the names by some system of priority. Some, to be sure, are less likely than others."

"Look at this," Estrada said in disgust. "This woman, this nurse. Your note says she's seventy-nine. That she's crippled by arthritis."

"A crippled nurse is better than none."

Estrada flicked a finger contemptuously at Marco DeMario's name. "This one's even older. The bureau's already questioned him. It says he's palsied and—possibly—drunken. It says he had wine on his breath."

"A man can put wine on his breath with a single swallow," Hepfinger said. "A tremor can come and go. It can be faked, exaggerated."

"Very well," Estrada said in resignation. Hepfinger's love of detail would drive him mad. "What do you want?"

"A team of men. Smooth enough to impersonate officers and not call attention to themselves. More than one team would be better. There are many names."

"Too many." Estrada cast another disdainful look at the list. "And you want to double-check even those the bureau's dismissed? Veterinarians? Dentists? A crippled old woman? A shaking old man?"

Hepfinger gave a good-natured shrug and smiled, showing dimples in both his round cheeks. "You never know. Sometimes the heart of a mystery is plucked from the least likely place. An animal doctor. A dentist. A crippled old woman. Or a trembling old man."

"We'll see, won't we?" Estrada asked sourly.

"Yes," Hepfinger said. "We will."

TWELVE

THEY REACHED HOOKSETT AND DROVE TO THE OFFICE OF
the realtor, whose name was Freneau. Laura stayed in the
van, but watched Montana through the tinted glass. She
held Trace in her arms. He was burning with fever, so sick
that he submitted to her embrace without protest.

Montana stood on the doorstep of the office building,
laughing and joking with Freneau, who leaned in the doorway.

She cradled Trace more protectively and thought,
*Hurry, Montana. How can you act so casual? How can
you act as if everything's normal, nothing's wrong?*

Jefferson, who'd been dozing in the front seat, awoke
and straightened. Immediately, he slumped again, putting
his hand over his face. He shivered violently as if wracked
by cold, even though the van was warm.

She leaned forward and clasped his good shoulder.
"Montana's getting the key. We're almost there. Then
we'll get you to a real bed."

"Damn Stallings," Jefferson muttered. "First he ups
and dies, and now he's tryin' to take me with him."

Stallings, Laura thought with a pang. He'd been dead
only a few days, and his family and fiancée must still be in
shock. But to her, it seemed as if Stallings and Becker had
died eons ago, in a different century, a different world.

Beside her, Rickie fidgeted and tugged at her sleeve. He'd been staring at the map, frowning and mumbling to himself.

Now he said, "Laura, make Trace play. Make Trace play pennies. Laura, tell Trace about—"

"Shh," she said as patiently as she could. "Trace is sleeping." She was relieved when Montana opened the door and got back into the van. He tossed a set of keys into the air and caught them with a flourish. "Let's go home, troops," he said, putting the keys in the pocket of his leather jacket.

Rickie quieted as soon as the motor started. She felt both gratitude and a pang of affection. She always counted on him to be the more cooperative and even-tempered of the boys.

She swallowed, her throat tight. Rickie was the one Montana wanted to take from her. What would her world become without Rickie? And without Montana?

Trace stirred restlessly in her arms. His eyes were closed, but his lids fluttered. "Mama?" he said sleepily. "Mama?"

Laura's heart beat faster as she touched his hot forehead. "Montana," she whispered, "I'm scared."

The house was two miles out of town, off a dirt road and down a long, twisting lane. On either side of the snowy lane, pines rose like dark walls. The house, a small barn, and a corral stood in a clearing surrounded by pine woods.

The house itself was a bungalow, white with red shutters, a carport, and a big front porch. When Montana opened the door and switched on the lights, the interior seemed cheerily bright, even welcoming. The furniture didn't match, the appliances were old, out-of-date newspapers and tabloids were stacked by the fireplace, but everything looked solid and comfortable.

There was a kitchen with a real refrigerator and stove, and a bathroom with real fixtures. There was a large bedroom with a double bed, a smaller one with twin beds, and in the living room, an old green sofa that made into a bed.

Montana watched as Laura lowered Trace to the sofa and covered him with the afghan that had draped its back.

When Rickie saw the television in the living room, he cawed with raucous laughter. Laura switched on the set, and he immediately plunked down on the braided rug with his treasures: his penny jar, his marbles, and his plastic lizards. He stared at the screen in enchantment, even though only a commercial was on.

Jefferson took two more aspirins, then collapsed into the double bed, not bothering to undress.

"Let me check your shoulder," Montana said. "You're bleeding again."

"Later. Leave me alone, okay?"

"Let me see," Montana ordered. He unzipped the sweatshirt; blood was soaking through the dressing Marco had applied.

"I'm gonna have to change this," Montana told him.

"Man, I'm an albatross," Jefferson said in disgust, "I'm no good for nothing. You should have dumped me."

"Shut up and heal," said Montana. "We've boarded a train we can't get off."

Montana helped Laura haul the twins' things inside, then helped her arrange the room so it would seem familiar to the boys. They each knew their part of the task; it had become ritual to them.

She seemed distracted as she unpacked the Looney Tunes sheets, pillowcases, and curtains yet again. Her face was pale, which made her freckles stand out. And she was quiet, as if she was thinking hard about something.

At last she spoke, saying exactly what he'd hoped she wouldn't.

"Jefferson needs a doctor. He's wounded—now this. It's some kind of flu, a bad one. He could get pneumonia. He could die."

Montana stopped unpacking the dog-eared books. He straightened and looked at her, wanting her to meet his eyes.

She kept on hanging curtains, her back to him. He could see the tension in her body.

"We can't take him to a doctor," Montana said. "Conlee can't hold off the bureau forever. The law's going to be looking for Jefferson, for all of us."

Carefully she smoothed the pleats in the curtains. Then she repeated the motion, as if unaware she'd already done it once.

"Last year," she said, "a little girl at school got flu and it turned into pneumonia. She had to be hospitalized."

She turned to face him. "What if that happens? What if Jefferson gets so sick, he needs a hospital?"

"He'll have to do without," he said. "We can't take the chance."

From the next room, he heard the pained, ragged sound of Jefferson's cough. She heard it, too, and winced. Her eyes were sad and stormy, both accusing and pleading.

Montana shook his head. There were few blacks in New Hampshire. Drag a black man with no identification and a poorly-patched gunshot wound to the hospital? They might as well advertise their location.

"What if he dies?" she challenged. "What happens to your plans then? And what about Trace? What if he keeps getting worse? Will you let him suffer, too?"

He studied her face, and he thought, *I'll sacrifice whoever I have to.* But he couldn't tell her that. She was just learning to understand these things, and she hated them, couldn't accept them.

What, he wondered, if she were the one in Jefferson's place? Would he be as cold, as ruthless? Would he sacrifice her welfare for the others if he had to? The thought made him edgy, slightly sick.

"Montana?" she said, raising her chin.

"Yes?" He was careful to keep emotion out of his voice.

"There's *nothing* we can do? Jefferson's trying to play it down, but he's really hurting. The way he was bleeding again—it scared me. I'm scared for Trace, too."

Montana looked about the little room. The Bugs Bunny lamp, its shade dented and smudged, sat on the night stand, casting its golden light. The rug with the cheerful picture of the Road Runner lay between the beds.

Tweety Birds and Sylvesters stared at him, smiling, from the curtains.

Innocence, he thought bleakly. *It'd be easier without all the damned innocence.*

In the neighboring room, Jefferson hacked, an exhausted, tearing sound. As if in answer, from the living room Trace coughed. Mixed with those sounds was the manic theme music from the Bugs Bunny cartoon Rickie was watching.

Montana's innards knotted, and he had a surreal image that inside him there was an old, cold snake, tired of winter and hunger and darkness.

He said, "I'll call Marco."

She looked reluctant and hopeful at the same time. "You could," she said. "But you don't really want to, do you? You don't want to involve him again."

Montana shook his head. "I'll be careful."

He left her and went to the small dining area where the cellular phone rested on the corner of the table. He picked it up and dialed.

At the room's far end Rickie sat on the braided rug, hypnotized by the television and fingering his lizards. He bobbled his head back and forth, humming to himself.

On the couch, Trace lay curled in a fetal position, his eyes screwed shut and his forehead shiny with sweat. *Hell,* Montana thought in frustration, *the kid's sick as a dog.*

He dialed Marco's number. The phone rang thirteen times before the old man answered.

"Marco, it's Mick. One of the kids is sick. So's Jefferson. We think it's flu. What do I do now?"

"Just keep 'em in bed," Marco said. "Aspirin helps. And fluids, lots of 'em. But mostly just rest. Is the other kid okay?"

"Fine so far."

"I'll phone in a prescription for amantadine. Start getting it down him as soon as possible, and he should stay fine. What about you and Laura? Have you had flu shots?"

"Yeah, yeah," Montana said. The thought of Marco phoning in a prescription made him profoundly uneasy.

"Listen," Montana said. "This hit Jefferson hard. He's been bleeding again. Laura's scared he'll get pneumonia."

"Pneumonia's a distinct possibility," Marco said in his quavery voice. "What about the wound itself? Any pus? Excessive swelling? Inflammation?"

"No. But I think the coughing made him tear something loose."

"Okay. I'll give you prescriptions for amantadine and an antibiotic for the wound and an antitussive for his coughing. It's a narcotic; don't give it to the kid."

"Okay," said Montana. "I understand."

"Keep his wound clean," Marco said. "Fluids'll help keep the coughing down. The other important thing is to let him rest. The kid, too. Are you settled in someplace? Are you in the city? What name are you using? What's the closest pharmacy?"

Montana hesitated. He'd dreaded these questions. He didn't want to say, and it was best Marco didn't know.

"What are you trying to do?" Marco asked sardonically. "Be noble? Protect me? From what? Nobody saw you come here, nobody saw you go. I'm safe."

"And nobody turned up to question you?" Montana asked.

Marco hesitated a moment. "Oh, hell," he finally muttered. "Two clowns from the FBI showed up. Day before yesterday. I gargled some wine, blew fumes at 'em, and jittered like an aspen. They couldn't get away fast enough. Now where the hell are you?"

Shit. The FBI, Montana thought, gritting his teeth. Marco was naive about such things. The authorities could be watching the old man, could even have his phone tapped. The thought wrenched Montana's stomach with a primitive, evil-feeling twist.

"Jefferson's weak, and he'll get weaker," Marco scolded. "You got one sick kid, and if you don't do what I say, you'll have two. This flu going round's a bad strain, a strong bugger. Now—where are you? And what name're you using? The one I think?"

Montana set his teeth. He knew it wasn't likely Marco's phone would be tapped; it took major red tape to get a wiretap. "Yeah," he said, "the name you're thinking. Which drugstore? Let me look one up."

A telephone book lay on the dining room table. Montana opened it to the yellow pages. He picked a pharmacy in the village of Goffstown on the other side of the river, a good long drive away.

He gritted his teeth harder and gave Marco the number. "Don't call from your own phone," he said. "Just in case they ever start investigating phone records. Use a pay phone, okay?"

"You've got it," Marco said.

"Clark's Family Drugstore," Montana said, dragging the words out of himself. "Goffstown, New Hampshire. Six-oh-three, five-five-five, six-one-two-one."

"Wait—let me write it down. Goffstown, New Hampshire? Where in hell is Goffstown, New Hampshire? What are you doing, heading for Canada? Don't try it. It's too crazy."

"Don't worry. The FBI should think we're in Philly."

"The FBI asked about Philly," Marco said. "They were very interested in you and Philly."

Good, Montana thought. *Let them stay interested.*

Marco said, "They're also very interested in Jefferson. They act like they think you're not together. Why?"

"I don't want them to think we're together," Montana said. "It doesn't matter why."

"Do you need money?" Marco asked, sounding concerned. "Use the damn card. Use it all you want."

"I will, Marco," Montana lied. "Now I'm getting off the phone. It makes me edgy. Just phone in the prescriptions. Like I said. Don't try anything cute."

"God be with you, boy," Marco said roughly.

"You, too," Montana said. He hung up.

He stood for a moment, staring at Rickie who sat swaying and humming before the television screen. The kid gaped happily at Bugs Bunny cavorting through the woods.

Montana wondered if he'd be arrested by state police as soon as he walked in the door of Clark's Family Drugstore in Goffstown. He wondered if even now authorities were starting to mobilize, readying to close in on them.

Small towns were the worst places in the world to hide, he knew. He would have given his good hand to have everybody's papers, to be over the border and safely split up in Canada.

He put on the old leather jacket and went to tell Laura he was driving to Goffstown.

"Let me go instead," she said. "I need to get used to being out on my own. I have to do it."

He shook his head. "No. It's night, it's a strange town, it's icy, and you've got no ID, nothing. You'll get your chance soon enough. I promise."

She looked up at him, concern on her face. She laid her hand on his jacket arm, as if she didn't want him to leave.

"Don't worry," he said gruffly. He brushed his lips against hers, a kiss meant to reassure. But when he drew back and gazed down at her again, he could still see the anxiety in her eyes.

"Don't worry," he repeated. He buttoned up the jacket, went outside, got into the van, and headed toward Goffstown.

He was careful, his every move sure. When he reached the drugstore, he was studiously casual. He called no attention to himself.

He acted as efficiently and nervelessly as when he'd worked undercover vice. But he felt haunted and powerless, as if what little control he had over the situation was slipping away.

Laura was almost sick with relief when she heard the van pull up in the carport. There were footsteps on the porch, then Montana's voice.

"Laura? It's me. Bugs Bunny faces the wall, okay?"

She unlocked and unbolted the door, swung it open, and flew into his arms as soon as he was over the threshold. "It seemed like you were gone forever," she said against his shoulder.

He gave her a swift but intense kiss. His mouth was cold and stung her lips, but the sensation seemed delicious.

"You're okay?" he asked, pulling her closer. "Nothing happened?"

She shook her head. "Nothing. Is that the medicine?"

"Yes. How's Trace?"

"The same." She undid the buttons of his leather jacket, and he slipped out of it, hanging it on the back of a chair. Laura took the medicine vial from the bag and read the dosage.

She filled a glass with water. Montana followed her into the boys' bedroom. She had everything in its right place. In the light from the Bugs Bunny lamp, he saw that Rickie slept peacefully on his side, his penny jar on the night table next to the lamp.

But Trace, sweat shining on his forehead and upper lip, had kicked away his covers. His hair was damp, and he frowned in his sleep.

Gently Laura woke Rickie and made him sit. He was so sleepy that he barely fought against taking the pills. He swallowed them on the second try, then tried to wriggle out of her embrace. She took her arm away, and he sank back to the pillow, his eyes already closed in sleep.

She rose and gave Montana a weak smile. "That's that," she said and held up the medicine. "This doesn't help people already sick?"

"Marco said no—just rest and fluids. Let me get this other stuff down Jefferson so he won't cough."

She nodded. Together they left the children's room.

Montana went to Jefferson, and she headed for the kitchen. She rinsed Rickie's glass, dried it, and put it away. Then she leaned against the counter, waiting for Montana, her heart beating unaccountably hard.

He appeared and looked her up and down. "You want a drink?" he asked. "It's been a long day."

She nodded. "Too long."

Opening a cupboard, she took out two glasses. "We have wineglasses, everything, here," she said. "Even a washer and dryer. This place feels like a palace after the lodge."

She busied herself opening and pouring the wine. He stood so near to her that she was overly conscious of him.

"Laura?" he said in a strange tone.

"Yes?" she asked, pouring the wine.

"What's Jefferson's gun doing on the coffee table?"

Slowly she raised her gaze to his. "I took it. In case—in case something happened."

His eyes searched hers, and she knew what he was looking for. He said, "Could you use it if you had to?"

She swallowed. "I don't know."

He shook his head as if dubious that she could. "Have you ever shot a gun?"

"Yes," she said. "I had a boyfriend in college. He said everybody should know how. He used to take me out to practice. We'd shoot at cans, bottles, things like that."

"But could you use it on a person?"

Confusion rose within her. "No," she said, looking away. "Probably not. But I thought if I had it . . . Oh, I don't know what I thought."

For a moment Montana said nothing. "Whatever happened to him? The guy who taught you how to shoot?"

"I threw him over for a pacifist with really great blue eyes," she said.

Then he tipped her face up to his, and smiled, and so did she, although a bit sadly.

She turned back to the table, picked up her wineglass.

"Here's hoping nobody has to fire at anybody," he said, and clinked his glass against hers.

"I'll drink to that," she said, her heart still beating hard. She took a sip. It was a red wine, strong and rich, and she savored its taste and the afterglow that followed it.

Everything tasted different when you were in danger, she thought. Tasted, sounded, felt different. The sky had been blue this afternoon. She thought she'd never noticed how blue it could be. She'd kept staring through the car window, wondering how many more blue-skied days she might live to see.

She hadn't really been hungry tonight, but she'd found herself almost spellbound by the taste and texture of canned peaches. It seemed miraculous how smoothly her spoon sliced through the golden flesh, amazing how sweet the fruit tasted.

I'd like to eat strawberry shortcake with fresh spring strawberries and real whipped cream, she had thought. *I wonder if I ever will again?*

And when Montana held her or kissed her, his touch affected her so strongly it shook her through. It was the danger, the constant danger, that intensified every sensation. She wondered if this intensity was only an illusion. Or had nothing in her life been real until now?

She looked at the play of light in the depths of her wine. "Did you ever?" she asked, her voice choked. "Kill somebody, I mean?"

She raised her gaze to his again.

"Yes," he said.

"Was it hard?" she asked, then tried to swallow the knot in her throat.

"Let's not talk about dying," he said, taking her face in his hands. "Let's talk about living. Talk to me. Tell me about the twins."

She put her hand over his scarred one, pressing it more tightly against her cheek. "Because you'll be taking Rickie?"

"I've got to learn," he said. "I need you to teach me."

She closed her eyes, took a deep breath, and willed herself not to tremble or cry or weaken in any way.

He said, "You understand them. You make them understand you. My nephew, nobody could ever do that for him. What goes on in there, inside their heads? Explain it to me."

She opened her eyes and met his steadily. "I can't see into their minds. But I know—sort of—how their thought processes work. There are different levels of autism. It doesn't sound as if your nephew is as lucky as they are."

She paused, musing over the absurdity of calling the twins *lucky*.

His hands moved to her waist. He lifted her and set her on the countertop next to her wineglass. He insinuated his body so close that he stood with his body between her jeaned knees. He handed her the wineglass.

"Go on," he urged.

She took a drink of wine and relished its taste, the warmth it stirred in her.

"Autism's mysterious," she said softly. "The most obvious problem is communication. They don't *understand* communication. So I have to teach them as well as I can."

"How? How do you teach that?"

She twirled the stem of the wineglass between her fingers, thought of how she could explain such a complex thing.

"All right," she said. "The first thing is to try not to confuse them. Their logical and perceptive processes are very different from ours. They understand things like 'who' and 'what' and 'where.' They could tell you that I'm Laura and you're Montana."

She paused. "I showed Rickie on the map when we crossed the state border. He could tell you we're in New Hampshire, not Vermont, or that this is a house, not the school."

She took a meditative sip of wine. She said, "What they can't tell you is *why* or—in a way—*when*. They have trouble understanding cause and effect. Ordinary children would know that we're on the run for a reason. They don't."

He said, "Then maybe, for once, this thing's a blessing for them."

"Maybe," she said, but the thought gave her no comfort. "They don't really understand that they've seen people killed. If we went back to school tomorrow, they'd expect to see Mr. Zordani again, the same as always."

"What about their mother?" he asked. "She's dead. Do they understand that?"

She shook her head. "We told them she'd gone to heaven. But how much they understand, I don't know."

He drew her closer, and ran his hands from her waist, down her thighs and back again. "You said they don't understand the concept of *when*. What'd you mean? They sure understand those watches."

She searched for the right answer, wishing his touch wasn't so distracting, yet glad it was. She set aside her wine and rested her hand on his shoulder, felt the reassuring hardness of his body.

She said, "They know numbers. But the flow of time's a mystery to them. They have trouble with ideas like 'before' and 'after.' Words like 'someday' and 'then' and 'later' bewilder them."

"So that's why you always say 'At eight o'clock' or something specific. Not like 'in a little while,' or 'when I have time.'"

"You have to be precise," she said. "And careful. Once Rickie asked one of the aides when he could have more juice. She said, 'In two shakes of a lamb's tail.'"

She paused, remembering. "They actually believed there was a lamb at school. They asked about it for days." She gave a small laugh of rueful affection.

"It's nice to hear you laugh," he said.

"You have to be able to laugh," she said. "Or it'd break your heart. And funny things do happen— Once Trace was nagging a teacher. She said she wasn't going to change her mind, not if he argued until the cows came home. He was so excited. He thought cows would come to the school."

He said, "We put things in crazy ways. In a jiffy. A snail's pace. Time flies."

He looked her down, then up again. "Once in a blue moon," he said. "That's a good one. Once in a blue moon."

She smiled. "Yes. Any phrase like that— Paddle your own canoe. Hitch your wagon to a star. You can bet your boots. The cat's got your tongue."

They were silent a moment. His hands moved to her arms, caressing them.

"Laura," he said, "what happens to them? My nephew's going to spend the rest of his life in places like Bellevue, unless a miracle happens. What about them?"

She gripped his shoulders more tightly. "If we can teach them enough, they'll be able to live in some sort of halfway house, have simple jobs, have some independence."

She hesitated a moment. "When they're older, they'll have to be separated, of course. That's why I don't want it to happen now, not yet. They get so little time together. It seems wrong to make it less."

She felt his muscles tense beneath her hand. "What do you mean?"

"The doctors say it's best. If they can always turn to each other, it could slow their social skills. That's probably right."

"Probably right?" He sounded dubious. "Do you believe that?"

"I don't know. It sounds right. But that wasn't supposed to happen until they're grown. Until then, they were supposed to have each other."

He moved closer to her, brought her face closer to his. His breath on her lips made her flesh tingle. "I don't want them to be apart," he said. "I don't want us to be apart."

"I know," she said, fighting the catch in her voice. "I don't want you to leave us. Or to take him."

"But they're not apart yet." He nuzzled her cheek. "They're not alone yet. Neither are we."

He kissed her just beneath the ear. Then he put his hands on her waist again and drew her down from the counter to stand next to him.

He slipped his good hand to the back of her neck, sliding it beneath her hair. He started to lower his mouth to hers.

"Montana—" she said shakily "—Mick? We're just doing this because it's the path of least resistance, aren't we? And because it feels good? And because, what if there really isn't a tomorrow?"

His hand caressed her nape. "There'll be a tomorrow. You have to believe that."

She kept her hands tense and still on his shoulders. Part of her wanted to keep him at a distance, yet a far deeper part of herself wanted him nearer, as near as possible.

She wanted to explain her paradoxical feelings, but knew she couldn't. "If we're lucky," she said, "there'll be a future. But not for this. Not for you and me. This is just for —comfort, right?"

He ran the knuckles of his scarred hand over her hair, stroking it. He kept doing it. The feeling was nice, almost hypnotic. "More than comfort," he said. "I like you. Do you want me to say I love you? I love you."

Her mind whirled drunkenly, even though she'd had but little wine. She suspected he would say whatever he had to say to make things work, to keep them bonded, working together, not giving up. They didn't love each other; they simply needed each other on the most primitive level, that of survival.

She didn't care. He was smart; he knew the words they had to say to each other, what they had to pretend.

"I love you," he repeated, bending once again to kiss her.

"I love you, too," she whispered. *For here, for now,* she started to say.

But his mouth was upon hers, silencing mere words, and his arms were around her, embracing her so tightly that her breasts were crushed against his chest.

They kissed hungrily. The cabin seemed to melt away; all of snowy New Hampshire dissolved; the solid, threatening world faded to nothingness, and the only real things were herself and him and desire.

"Please," she managed to say, "the lights. We should get under the covers or something. The children . . ."

He stared into her eyes, his gaze dark and hungry. He seemed reluctant to let go of her. He led her to the sofa. With an almost uncanny efficiency, he pushed the coffee table out of the way, swept the crumpled afghan to the floor.

He pulled the cushions from the sofa and leaned them against the wall. He pulled the sofa bed open, so that it unfolded into a mattress, complete with sheets and blankets.

He took off his sweater, tossed it so that it rested on the cushions. He turned to her, his eyes burning into hers.

That look made her want him so much she was stunned. She supposed, vaguely, that tomorrow she would be ashamed for feeling such naked need. She didn't care. But for a moment, she pretended to.

"There are pillows and extra blankets in the hall closet," she said, almost primly. "I'll get—"

He unbuttoned the first two buttons of his shirt. "Later," he said. He reached over to the end table and switched off the lamp.

They were plunged into sudden, velvety darkness. She felt his hand close, gently but possessively, around her upper arm. She let him draw her closer, until the warmth of his nearness prickled through her. His arms enfolded her again.

"Once we're apart," she whispered desperately, "we may never see each other again—"

"I won't let that happen," he said, unfastening the top buttons of her blouse.

"But—" she gasped.

"I won't let it happen. Tell me that you love me again. Say it."

He kissed her between the breasts, then on the mouth. His breath was fragrant with wine. "Say it again. Like you believe it."

"I love you," she said in a shaky whisper.

"Good," he said. "Good."

His lips took hers and shook her to her heart. She kissed him back, no longer knowing truth from lies, no longer caring.

THIRTEEN

MONTANA WAS A LIGHT SLEEPER. WHEN THE NIGHT WIND shifted, when the cold made the cottage creak, he instantly awoke.

He lay in the darkness, holding Laura, listening until he was sure the sounds were natural, not made by intruders. Only then would he relax, draw her nearer, and fall back into a sleep too light for dreams.

As dawn began to lighten the east, he gently released her and left the sofa bed. He wore his jeans and a T-shirt, because he knew it wasn't wise to sleep naked; the night might hold surprises. He took up his holster, but didn't strap it on.

He prowled to the closed hall door. The sleeping bags were stacked against the wall beside it, and he picked up his. He carried it to the side of the room farthest from Laura, unrolled it, and climbed in.

He could smell her scent on his body. He fell asleep with it haunting him and his good hand resting on his gun.

When the sun had risen and the sky turned gray, he was the first in the house to wake. He rose as silently as possible. He made himself a cup of microwave coffee and a bowl of cereal, then sat at the kitchen table.

He sipped his coffee and stared into the living room where Laura lay, a curved shape beneath the blankets.

His stomach tightened. There was nothing noble about his relationship with Laura. The closer they were, the longer she'd hang on, the harder she'd fight. And so would he.

Laura stirred on the sofa bed. She stretched and turned over. After a moment, she raised herself on her elbow and smiled across the room at him.

"Good morning," she said, running her fingers through her tumbled hair.

"Good morning," he said. "Want a cup of coffee, piece of toast or something?"

She sat up, yawned, then stretched. "Are you buying?"

God, he thought, she looked nice even with no makeup and her hair all rumpled. "I'm buying."

She got out of bed. After they'd made love last night, she, too, had risen and slipped back into her clothes, an old pair of gray bell-bottoms and a blue sweatshirt. She even had on her socks, which strangely touched him: *Laura, ready to be on the run at a moment's notice.*

Maybe he stared with an interest too proprietory, because she lowered her gaze and fumbled in her suitcase until she'd gathered an armful of fresh clothing.

"I'll change," she said. "And take a shower. I hope it's not too early."

"Go ahead," he said. "It's almost eight."

Keeping her head ducked down, she hurried into the hall. He looked after her, musing. In bed, she was warm, ardent, giving—even adventurous. Out of bed, she was modest to the point of shyness. He liked the combination.

But almost as soon as the sound of the shower came from the bathroom, Jefferson was up, moaning, groaning, and standing at the kitchen sink, washing down aspirins with orange juice. He looked like hell warmed over.

"Feel better?" Montana asked.

"Very funny," said Jefferson. "Who's in the bathroom? My bladder feels like its got Lake Superior in it."

"Laura. Give her a minute."

Jefferson didn't answer. He lumbered to the bathroom door and knocked on it hard. "You gonna be in there long?" he demanded, then coughed.

Laura came out in less than two minutes, her face

flushed, her hair damp. She was buttoning up one of Marco's wife's out-of-style blouses and wore a different pair of slacks. She hadn't taken time to put on lipstick, yet once again Montana was conscious of how desirable she seemed.

There was no time to reflect on this. Suddenly Rickie was up, banging on the bathroom door impatiently, demanding Jefferson get out so he could get in. "Rickie's got to *pee*!" he said with passion. "Pee-pee, pee-pee, pee-*pee*!"

Jefferson opened the door and scowled at the boy. "Well, you ain't the only one," he said. He put his hand to his forehead and shambled into the living room. He picked up the papers Montana had bought yesterday in Manchester, then half sat, half fell into the easy chair.

Laura, barefoot, sat on the edge of the sofa bed, putting on her socks and boots. She gave Montana an amused, diffident look.

"Come eat," he said gruffly, "I'll put your bread in the toaster. The coffee's made."

She rose and made her way to the kitchen area, stopping beside Jefferson. "Are you hungry?"

Jefferson shook his head and kept staring into his newspaper. "I'm not feeding this virus *nothing*. I'll starve the booger into submission."

He waved her away.

She came to the little kitchen table and sat down across from Montana, who was nursing his second cup of coffee. The toast popped up, and they each took a piece.

"Sleep all right?" Montana asked gently.

She had no chance to answer. From the bedroom came Trace's voice, wailing her name.

She jumped up and ran to him. Soon she was at the bathroom door, leading Trace by the hand. She knocked, telling Rickie in no uncertain terms to get out. Trace stood, his shoulders slumped, rubbing his eyes.

Rickie strolled to the breakfast table and squinted accusingly at Montana. "Get some juice," he demanded. "Get some cornflakes. Get some bananas. Get some toast. Get some jelly."

For a sinking moment Montana didn't feel like a fugitive or an attorney or an ex-cop. He felt like a father trapped in a too-small house with too many people for a day that was going to be too long.

But he rose and poured Rickie's cornflakes.

For the moment, this was family, and it was all that they had.

Marco DeMario awoke feeling as weak and wasted as an old insect facing winter. Sleep had not refreshed him; dreams of deaths and loss had assailed him all night long.

Last night he had executed everything that Montana had asked—and more. Doing so had filled him with headiness and a sense of purpose; he'd felt a rejuvenating rush.

But the rush had eddied and died, leaving him spent. He'd hardly been able to make his way home and to bed. Now, when he arose, he felt as fragile as if all his bones were made of blown glass.

Bleary and exhausted, he dressed himself in wrinkled trousers and a shirt in need of laundering. He did not bother to shave. He did not bother with shoes or socks; he wore scuffed leather slippers on his blue-veined feet.

He shuffled into the kitchen and made himself a cup of instant coffee and a piece of toast, which he buttered then promptly forgot. He sat down stiffly at the table and sipped his coffee. It was tepid, but he was too tired to rise and heat it.

Last night Marco had gotten in his old car and driven through the snowy streets to the nearest service station. He drove as seldom as possible, and never on snow or at night if he could help it, but Mick had told him to use the pay phone.

Marco hated pay phones because they were newfangled and confusing. They had buttons instead of dials, and half the time when you wanted to talk to an operator, you got an incomprehensible recording. He refused to use a phone credit card, which he considered a sort of numerical witchcraft, instead of good, solid, clinking coins.

So he'd dug into another of his jars of change, filled his pockets, and phoned in the prescriptions. By the time he'd finished the call, his heart was thumping so hard it quaked his ribcage. His blood hummed, and his mind seemed lit by a preternatural alertness.

He folded the paper with the Goffstown number and shoved it into his coat pocket. Mick didn't want him to get more deeply involved; Mick probably thought he was a coot, a codger, a weak old man who would wear out.

But Marco's mind, lively and in fighting trim, spun with activity. *He was part of a war again. It was like being young again.* Fearfulness edged his excitement, but only edged it; excitement was stronger.

Mick was struggling to lay false trails, was he? Marco could help. He looked up a number in the phone book that was chained to the telephone platform. He picked up the receiver again. The night was freezing, the phone out in the open, but Marco did not feel the cold.

He fumbled in his pocket for more change. With hands that had, oddly, stopped shaking, he arranged the coins on the metal shelf beneath the phone.

He dialed the local police, and when a woman answered, Marco lowered his voice to a hissing whisper. He sometimes watched mystery movies on the Late Show. He knew calls from pay phones could not be traced, and a whispering voice was hardest to identify.

"I saw something you should know. On the day of the killings at Valley Hope. I saw about those killings on TV."

He sensed a sudden tense interest on the other end of the line. "Who's calling?" the woman asked. She had a deep, calm voice, full of authority. "Your name, please?"

"I don't want to say," Marco whispered. "I'm afraid. But the day of the shootings, I saw a car—a blue Bronco—drive up to the back of this nursing home. A white man helped a black man get out. The black one was bleeding."

"A Bronco, you say?" the woman asked in her deliberate way. "Did you happen to get a license number on that?"

"No, no," Marco whispered. "The white man came out and got back in the Bronco. He was dark. Like Spanish or Italian. He drove off."

"Sir, where is this nursing home?"

God, Marco thought, his nerves suddenly going skittish on him, *how can she sound so businesslike, so laconic?*

"New York. I don't want to say any more."

"New York State or New York City?"

He hesitated a moment, then said, "New York State. I don't want to talk any more. I don't want to get involved."

He hung up and found he was panting for breath. His knees threatened to buckle beneath him, and for the first time he was conscious of the cold.

But triumph surged through him, making him giddy and frightening him with his own boldness. There, he thought—let them report that. Let them investigate every nursing home in the entire goddamn state of New York. That ought to keep them busy.

Marco's hands had started to shake, but he was determined to buy Mick more time still. He would call the FBI itself.

He would again disguise his voice. This time he would say he had talked on the phone to a cousin in Philadelphia. This cousin, he would say, claimed he knew about the shooting at Valley Hope.

Marco would say the cousin also claimed that there were two adult fugitives from the shootings, a man and a woman, and they had some children with them, and that this cousin had helped them get away to the Virgin Islands.

Years ago Marco'd had an old army buddy in Pennsylvania, a back surgeon with a light plane. He'd often sent Marco postcards from the Virgin Islands, his favorite destination. Marco thought the story would have the ring of truth and would send the FBI on a pretty good goose-chase.

He looked for the phone number of the FBI in the book and was confused when he found not one, but several—they seemed to have offices all over the damned state. Albany, Manhattan, all the boroughs. . . .

Marco felt the cold more deeply now and began to tremble with it. He chose the Manhattan number, but then realized he'd read the phone book wrongly, and had dialed the number of a different branch. *Let it be, it'll do,* he thought.

An operator's voice came on the line, demanding more money. Shakily he inserted the coins into the slots, cursing his own frailty.

His call was answered on the second ring, and he tried to muffle his voice.

"What?" said the man on the line. "I can't hear you, sir. You'll have to speak more clearly."

Marco swore silently and took his hand away from his mouth. He whispered again. "This is about the shooting at Valley Hope. The newspaper said if anyone had information to call—"

"I can't hear you, sir. Are you speaking into the receiver?" The man had the same maddening sort of voice as the woman had, unhurried, unemotional, almost uninterested.

Marco rebuked himself again. "This is about the shooting at Valley Hope. The newscaster said if anyone had information—"

"You're calling about the shooting at Valley Hope in Long Island. I see. Go on."

Marco hesitated. Suddenly this call didn't seem like a clever piece of strategy at all. It seemed a damned fool thing to do, and he was the damned fool doing it. He held the receiver, pondering if he should say more or simply hang up.

"Sir, are you still there? You have information about the Valley Hope case? I'm listening."

Sir, Marco thought with a pang of fear. His whispering hadn't fooled his listener. He stood, his mind racing. "Philadelphia," he mumbled. "The people you want are in Philadelphia. A man, a woman . . ."

"Let me confirm this. You say that the people we want are in Philadelphia. What people do you mean, sir? The perpetrators?"

"The innocent ones," Marco said with a desperate hiss. "Philadelphia. They're in Philadelphia. A man, a woman, two children."

"Which people, sir? Can you speak up?"

An operator's voice interrupted them. "Please deposit another dollar, twenty-five cents."

Marco automatically reached toward his stacked coins, but his hand quivered and twitched, knocking them to the ground. Some rolled away, some sank into a pockmarked patch of snow, and some splashed into the trampled slush.

"Please deposit another dollar, twenty-five cents," the operator droned.

But Marco's trembling hands had betrayed him, and his mind seemed to fly apart in confusion. He forgot what he'd meant to say to the FBI, he was afraid he couldn't retrieve enough coins to feed the phone, and the phone itself suddenly felt as dangerous in his hand as a cobra.

He hung it up, and breathing hard, his heart and his pulses rocking his body, he hobbled back to his car.

"Hey, Dr. DeMario," called the station attendant. "Ya dropped some money there—"

Marco ignored him and almost stumbled getting back inside his car. He drove home feeling disoriented and frightened. Mick had said something he should remember. But what? What? He was so shaken that twice he almost drove off the road.

Once home, he was so unsteady, he could barely get his key in the door to unlock it, and it took him two tall glasses of wine, drunk quickly, to calm him.

But his temples still banged when he lay down on his bed. He thought he'd done all Mick had asked. What had he forgotten? What?

Now in the light of morning, he stared dully into his coffee cup. He thought back to his confusion over the call to the FBI, the fallen coins, his own humiliation. *No fool like an old fool,* he told himself bitterly.

Then, suddenly, Mick's words came flashing into his brain. Mick had said, "Don't try anything cute." Trying something cute, of course, had been exactly what Marco had done.

He thanked God that he'd used the pay phone because that number couldn't be traced. And he prayed God that his cuteness wouldn't backfire. He would rather give up his immortal soul than put Mick in danger.

Laura gave Montana his first stint as a teacher that morning. She let Trace skip his lessons and curl up on the sofa.

He was still sick, but stubbornly insisted that Jefferson read him the newspapers. Jefferson pretended to grumble, but settled in next to Trace and read aloud.

Laura sat with Rickie and Montana at the dining room table. She showed Montana how she tried to teach the concept of cause and effect.

"Tell me about this picture," she said, pointing at one in a series.

"Boy has big cookie," Rickie muttered, bored. He rocked back and forth in his chair and chewed his lower lip. He seemed jealous of his brother and kept wanting to turn around to look.

"That's right, the boy has a cookie," Laura encouraged. "Tell me about the boy's face. Say how his face looks."

"A smile." Rickie sighed.

She nodded to Montana, a signal for him to take over.

"Say if the smile means happy or sad," Montana said.

Rickie twisted in his chair, sighed again, and looked at the book. "Happy," he murmured, and he began to hum and tap his fingers against his face.

"Tell what makes the boy smile," Montana said. "Say what makes the boy happy."

Rickie frowned at the picture and chewed his lip harder. "Butterflies," he said for some unfathomable reason. "Butterflies fly."

Montana looked at Laura in grim astonishment.

Laura pointed to the picture. "The *cookie* makes the boy happy. The cookie makes the boy smile," she said patiently. "Now tell about this picture. Say who has the cookie."

"Doggy has the cookie," Rickie said and began to hum again and fiddle with the cuff of his sweatshirt.

Laura took him by the chin, made him look back at the book. "Tell about the boy's face. Say how the boy's face looks."

"Sad," Rickie said petulantly.

"Say why the boy is sad," Montana coached.

"Butterflies," Rickie muttered. "Butterflies, butterflies, butterflies."

"No," Montana said, shaking his head. "Say what made the boy sad."

At last, after four more tries, he got Rickie to say the boy was sad because the doggy had the cookie.

Then Rickie wanted to go to the bathroom. As soon as he was out of sight, Montana turned to Laura. "When's recess?" he asked in a stage whisper.

"You're in luck," she said, glancing at her watch. "It's in five minutes."

"Thank God," he said. "I had it easier busting crack dealers."

"You think you got it tough?" Jefferson called from the sofa. "I ran out of real newspapers. Now look what I'm reduced to."

He held up one of the old tabloids that had been stacked by the fireplace.

"He likes those?" Laura said dubiously.

"He loves 'em," Jefferson said with a put-upon look. "It's gonna rot my mind completely." He gazed at the paper in disbelief and shook his head. "My, my. What's that rascal Prince Charles gone and done now?"

Laura and Montana smiled at his mock gloom. Jefferson obviously felt at least a bit better, and Montana could see Laura's relief. Under the table he took her hand and squeezed it, as if to say, *See? We're going to be all right.*

She squeezed his hand in return, but her smile died. He knew what she was thinking.

Their time together was running out.

For recess, Montana and Laura took Rickie outside. Rickie took one look and immediately ran toward the barn.

"He's curious. That's always a good sign," Laura said. Montana nodded and together they set off after him.

The barn was small, but neatly kept, and its door was unlocked. Its air was scented with hay and the faint hint of horse. Straw littered the floor, a worn bridle hung from a peg, and a faded saddle blanket draped the door of a stall. An old-fashioned cast-iron bathtub stood in one corner under a faucet.

"Horses take baths?" Montana said, feigning surprise.

"They used it for a watering trough," Laura said. "My grandpa did the same thing. Only his was in the barnyard."

"Horses take baths," Rickie piped and climbed into the tub. He sat in it, grinning at them gleefully. He began to chant, "Horses take baths. Horses take baths."

Montana shook his head, but Laura only smiled. "Now see what you've started?"

He sighed and put his arm around her. She nestled more snugly into its crook and, while Rickie was crooning, gazed about the barn.

The place had served as a storage shed as well as barn. Sheets of rusted corrugated iron roofing leaned against one wall. An ancient tractor was parked near the bathtub.

An untidy collection of tires lay heaped in a stall beside a wheelbarrow and a tangle of hose. Overhead, the hayloft, thickly strewn with hay, sent fragrant motes dancing through the air.

Rickie, tiring of the tub, climbed out, his singsong words trailing off. He became intrigued by the ladder up to the loft and wanted to climb it.

Laura remembered her grandfather's farm and how much fun a hayloft could be. She let Rickie climb up and followed him to make sure his play was safe. Montana stayed below.

Rickie loved the hay. He fell into it, threw it into the air, crawled through it on hands and knees. Laura was touched by his delight, but could not forget that Montana paced beneath them like a sentry, his gun in place. A deep and terrible sadness nagged her. *Will we ever be free again?*

When she could finally lure Rickie away from the wonders of the loft, she let him climb down first. On some impulse, he sprang away from the ladder and Montana caught him. It was as if he trusted Montana to catch him without warning, and Montana had done it.

Montana whirled him around. He stopped and with his good hand, turned the boy's face to his. "Gecko," he said. "Iguana."

"Texas banded gecko," Rickie said with fervor. *"Big*

Bend gecko. *Banded* gecko. *Yellow* gecko." But he struggled to get out of Montana's grasp.

Montana released him, and Rickie ran outdoors. He threw himself down and began making a snow angel. "Leaf-toed gecko," he chanted. "Oscillated gecko. Ashy gecko. Reef gecko . . ."

Laura reached the bottom of the ladder. Montana took her by the waist, drew her to the floor, and turned her around. "I never had time to say good morning," he said, and gave her a brief kiss.

She was ashamed that such a quick kiss should make her short of breath. She kissed him back, just as quickly, and then they drew apart. Neither spoke.

Rickie lay thrashing in a snow bank, making a second snow angel. "Blunt-nosed leopard lizard," he caroled. "Leopard lizard. Spot-tailed earless lizard."

She strolled to the barn door and watched Rickie rise from the snow, then fling himself down again to a third angel. She felt Montana move behind her, so close that she could sense his warmth in the icy morning air.

She kept her back to him and her gaze on Rickie. "I keep wondering," she said. "What did they see that's worth all this killing? Or who?"

"I wonder, too."

Laura shook her head. "Who could they recognize? We went through almost all the mug shots."

"Almost," Montana said. "Not all."

Rickie leaped up from the snow, whirling around giddily. "Texas spiny lizard!" he shouted at the sky. "Granite spiny lizard! Crevice spiny lizard!"

He threw himself into a drift and flailed his arms and legs, making yet another angel in the snow.

Fear had been a constant presence in Laura's life for almost a week, a presence she'd tried not to admit. Now she found herself not only acknowledging, but bowing to it.

She spoke from between clenched teeth. "I want him to make angels, not to be one. He's so innocent. No one else could be as innocent as he and Trace are."

Montana gripped her shoulder. "Laura . . ."

She lifted her chin to a stubborn angle and tried to

ignore his touch. "I don't care what we pretend about you and me," she said. "But I always want to know the truth about them and what's happening to them."

"All right," he said, his mouth close to her ear. She felt the warmth of his breath, saw it ascend, ghostlike, toward the gray sky.

"All right, what?" she said.

"I've been thinking about the *World Weekly Record,*" he said. "It comes out today. Coast to coast, your pictures are out there. But I think that was an accident, a coincidence."

She looked at him in surprise, waiting for him to explain.

He said, "If the Colombians, or anybody else, wanted a paper to break the story, to force our hand, why the *Record*? It's a rag, it only comes out once a week, and it's national. They knew we had to be in Manhattan or damn close. That's task force jurisdiction. No—if they wanted to flush us out into the open, why not use a daily paper, a local one? The *Record* should be their last choice."

"But it still made us move. And Conlee said hardly anybody knew about the move. Unless he's lying."

"Right," Montana said.

The thought was a dark one and kept haunting her. Conlee, their one official liaison to the outer world, could be lying.

She stared at Rickie lying in a snow drift, laughing loudly and throwing snow into the air. The pines stood like a dark wall behind him. "It always comes down to the same question," she said. "Who do we trust?"

"We trust each other," he said. His hand moved to the back of her neck, rested there.

Neither of us is used to trusting anyone, she thought. *That's the one thing the fates didn't shape us for.* But she said nothing.

Rickie picked himself up and ran in wild circles. Snow had started to fall, and he held his hands out to catch it, raised his face to feel it, stuck out his tongue to taste it.

Laura watched him, moved by his apparent joy. He was a city child; he had never before experienced winter in the country. He spun about until he got dizzy and fell backwards into the snow again. He crowed with laughter and immediately began to make another angel.

But her heart felt as frozen as the landscape. "What happens if we do make it to Canada?" she asked. "We might never be able to go home again."

"Home is where you make it," Montana said.

Rickie was on his feet again, whirling and running. "Mole skink," he shouted in excitement. "Five-lined skink. Gilbert's skink."

She watched the boy thinking, *He can love life. He can. He has every right to live. He has to live.*

That afternoon Montana took the phone into the main bedroom to call Conlee.

"All right," Conlee said. "I can't hold it up any longer. They're slapping a federal warrant on your ass at midnight. That's it. The longer you stay out there—"

"Don't waste your breath telling me to turn ourselves in," Montana said. "Tell me what's worth knowing."

"Everybody's on the run," Conlee said, bitterness in his voice. "Dennis Deeds has disappeared from the face of the earth. Now the Mafia's after him because of the Scarlotti and Zordani killings. But he's the invisible man."

"What about Deeds's hit men?" Montana asked. "These so-called free-lancers? Have you got a line on them?"

"We're doing everything we can."

"Which means you know nothing—right?"

"Montana, you know what these people are like. The guys that did the hit may be back in South America. They may never set foot in this country again."

"Yeah, and they may be fifteen minutes away, loading their Uzis."

"They might be, Superman. So if anything happens to those kids, it's on your head. If you come in now, the bureau'll guarantee their protection. The bureau'll get them someplace so secret that—"

"The bureau had its chance," Montana said. "Tell me how Fletcher is."

"He can't walk, can hardly talk. He's still time-traveling. Thinks some nurse is his wife. Montana, you're going to be in big troub—"

"Your five minutes are up," Montana said. He hung up.

From the front room, he heard Trace coughing and Jefferson's voice, patiently droning out stories from the tabloids.

He knew Laura was at the table, having Rickie draw pictures of glad faces, sad faces. *Tell Laura what a frown means. Tell Laura what a smile means. Tell Laura what tears mean.*

Montana, grim, looked at his watch. The time was just after two o'clock. They had less than ten hours until midnight.

Then, from border to border, they would be wanted, all state and local police looking for them. And he would be a felon.

"Fuck it," he muttered to himself.

He opened the door and went out to the dining room table to try to help Rickie learn what smiles meant, what tears meant.

FOURTEEN

JORGE HEPFINGER WAS PASSIONATE ABOUT DETAILS. HE COL-
lected them, compared them, scrutinized them as lovingly
as a miser hoarding and admiring coins.

At his work he was tireless, his eye quick and discern-
ing. He could glance at a column of figures and instantly
see which fit and which did not.

No lead was too small, no connection too tenuous for
him to note. He had almost all the information that the FBI
did, thanks to the industrious moles of Mesius Estrada.
Fueled on coffee and obsession, he pursued his quarry
eighteen hours a day.

This morning Estrada had sent over the scaly-faced
Santander with a folder of raw data spirited from the bureau. "Stay," Hepfinger had told Santander. "I may need
you." And Santander, like the good dog he was, stayed.

Hepfinger devoured the new data greedily. It was the
file of phoned-in tips about the Valley Hope killings. Some
callers identified themselves but many were anonymous.
Some were concerned and responsible people. Others were
pranksters, and some were, quite simply, barking mad.

The calls came from everywhere, and went everywhere, to dozens of different branches of law enforcement,
to this headquarters and that.

The FBI plodded. Drearily it would shuffle through

these leads, one by one. But Hepfinger's mind did not plod. It flew, skimming at almost supernatural speed, swooping down on unexpected morsels of information with hawk-like precision.

After two hours of such high-flying and swooping, Hepfinger thought he'd seized on a lead that should be checked out quickly, before the bureau made its ponderous way in the same direction.

He turned in his gilded chair to face Santander, who sat on an expensive sofa reading a cheap magazine about crime. In screaming red letters its cover announced, "Crazy Dentist's Sex Slave Murders!" Santander looked at him, a wary curiosity in his flat eyes.

"There are two calls to two different agencies," Hepfinger said, patting the stack of faxes. "One's clear, one's garbled. They convey different information. Yet"—and he smiled his cherubic smile—"they were made minutes apart. By a whispering man. From the same pay phone."

Santander blinked, slowly, like a lizard. But he said nothing.

"A phone not far from Valley Hope," Hepfinger said in his jovial way. "I'll check it out. We may be taking a ride."

Santander nodded and turned his attention back to his magazine. He was not a man who cared for whys and wherefores. When action was needed, he would provide it.

Hepfinger picked up the cellular phone and dialed the number from which the two calls had been made. According to Hepfinger's information, the FBI had not yet noticed the duplication, had not yet traced the phone's location. With luck, it might not do so for hours, even days.

The phone rang a dozen times. At last a gruff voice answered. "Yeah? Ernie's Mobil."

Hepfinger's heart quickened, dancing in his chest. But he used his stodgiest voice. "This is Allen Kinsolving of New York Telecommunications. We've had a service complaint about this number. This is five-five-five, six-one-eight-oh?"

"Yeah?" The word was as much a challenge as an answer.

Hepfinger's body tingled, but he kept his tone superior

and slightly bored. "You say this is Ernie's Mobil? My note says this number belongs to Triple-A Storage. You're in the Bronx?"

"Queens," growled the man. "This is Ernie's, and we ain't had no complaint that I've heard about."

"Ernie's," Hepfinger repeated. "In Queens. But the number's five-five-five, six-one-eight-oh—right?"

"Yeah."

"All right," Hepfinger said smoothly. "My information must be mistaken. Thanks for your time."

The only reply was the sharp report of the receiver at the other end being hung up.

Hepfinger's blood raced with the excitement of the hunt. Somebody had used Ernie's pay phone to call both the police and FBI. He had told the police about the blue Bronco, and the FBI that a man, woman, and two children had gone to Philadelphia.

Neither the information about the Bronco nor that about Philadelphia had been made public. How had the caller learned these things? Who was this whispering man who knew so much?

Hepfinger rose and faced Santander. "We're going to Queens," he announced. "To make some inquiries. You have your gun?"

Santander nodded, his face impassive.

"Excellent," said Hepfinger, his eyes crinkling and his pink cheeks dimpling.

Rickie was restless, almost wild, by afternoon recess time. Laura and Montana took him out to play. "This time," she told Montana, "you're in charge. Completely."

They hiked a path that led through the woods. Rickie would dart first ahead of them, then behind them, changing directions like a rabbit.

The path ended at a large, snow-covered pond, almost large enough to qualify as a lake. Montana and Laura reached it first because Rickie had stopped to knock icicles from a thorn bush.

He came after them, running as hard as he could, then

skidded to a stop at the pond's edge. He squinted at the frozen water, scowling.

"Frogs," Rickie demanded. "Where are the frogs?"

Laura gave Montana a significant look.

"They—the frogs are asleep, under the ice," Montana told him.

"Asleep under the ice," Rickie repeated. "Under ice. Under ice. Under ice."

Ranged along the pond's surface, about twenty feet out from the shore, was a line of narrow little buildings.

"What's that?" Montana asked out of the side of his mouth. "It looks like an outhouse convention."

Rickie was fascinated by the tiny houses and tried to run toward them. He slipped and slid on the thick ice. Montana had to follow to make sure he didn't get so excited he went out of control and hurt himself.

"Hold it, chum," he warned. "Not so fast." Laura stayed at his side. "What is it?" he asked her again. "The Smurfs' winter places? Phone booths?"

"They're ice-fishing houses," she told him. "My grandpa had one. It's for fishing in the winter."

Montana looked dubious. "You sit in that thing and *fish*?"

Laura smiled. "Well, he didn't sit alone. He usually took a buddy and a radio and a six-pack. You cut a hole in the ice, you're sheltered from the wind and snow, and you catch fresh fish. It's a guy thing."

"Not this guy," said Montana. "I'll have pastrami on rye, thanks."

Rickie slid so wildly that he crashed into the side of one of the little buildings and fell. Montana picked him up, dusted the snow from his jacket, and warned him not to be so reckless.

But Rickie swooped and skidded on, more wildly than before. He discovered that one of the fishing houses was unlocked, and Montana almost had to pry him out of it.

Rickie was delighted with the little building. It had folding chairs stacked in a corner and a worn blanket hung from a nail on one wall.

"This isn't our house," Montana said firmly. "You can't play in here."

"Pronouns," Laura whispered. "Pronouns confuse him."

Montana sighed in resignation. "This house isn't Rickie's. Rickie can't play in the house. Come back on the ice."

Rickie agreed mechanically, wrenched away from Montana, and lost himself in more sliding. He slipped, skidded, spun, whooped. He careened, he fell, he laughed his raucous laugh, got up, and started all over again.

Laura shook her head. "When he wants to, he'll ignore pain. Once he fell down stairs and broke his arm. He never even whimpered. He wanted to go to lunch. It was time."

Montana put his arm around her shoulder. "When I talk to him like that it seems so damned unnatural."

She watched Rickie, then turned to Montana. "You get used to it. And you have to teach him all the time. Not to do dangerous things. Not to step into traffic. Not to break glass. Not to touch fire. He can be fearless about things like that. But he's scared of Santa Claus. And swans. And owls. Why? Maybe we'll never know."

Montana was silent a moment. "I'll take good care of him. I promise you that."

She lifted her chin and got the strained, stubborn feeling she always did when she spoke of separation. "I don't see how you can do it. Where will you get the money to live? Find a job? What do you do with him then?"

"We cross bridges one at a time," Montana said. "We do what we have to. That's all."

"Do we stay in touch? How can we—and still stay safe?"

"I'll find a way."

Her exasperation grew. "But how? And what if we can't ever go back? Do we stay apart forever?"

"No. We won't. But until then, we take it as it comes. That's it."

"That's it?" she asked, frustrated and irritated. "That's the only answer you can give?"

"That's it."

Rickie slid until he was too tired to go on. Then he crouched at the pond's edge and broke the stalks off dead cattails. The stalks were encased by ice, and each made a satisfying snap when broken. Fragments of ice cracked off, and he gathered them into a heap as if they were precious gems.

He was such a strong, handsome boy, she thought, his cheeks rosy with cold, his dark hair stirring in the breeze. What if she were never to see this child again? Or Montana. . . .

Montana seemed to sense her sadness. He drew her closer. She laid her head against his shoulder.

How odd, she thought, to depend on another human being again. After her divorce, she'd thought she never would. Even if the feeling of trust was an illusion, how good it felt, how comforting.

"I'll try to teach him, Laura. I can't be as good as you, but I'll do my best. I swear it."

She tried to swallow the knot in her throat. "You have to teach him to act as socially acceptable as possible. I mean, maybe you think I program them like little robots or parrots, but it's for their own good. So people aren't frightened by them, don't reject them."

"You've done a good job," he said. "A hell of a job. They're good kids."

"They *are* good kids," she said, turning her face to his. "They've got limitations, but they shouldn't be treated like freaks or outcasts. They're part of the human family, the same as you and me."

Montana kissed her. His lips were cold at first, and he held them against hers until both their mouths grew warm again.

Rickie, still crouched at the pond's edge, suddenly shrieked out a rhyme:

"First comes love, then comes marriage,
"Then comes Laura with a baby carriage."

Embarrassed, Laura pulled away and stood apart from Montana. "I'm sorry," she said, staring at the ice. "That's something else he learned on the playground."

He adjusted her jacket collar so that it stood up to keep her warmer. Rickie's taunting voice rang out again.

"First comes love, then comes marriage,
"Then comes Laura with a baby carriage."

Montana gave him a severe look. "Rickie, don't say

that. It's not polite. It's teasing. People don't like to be teased."

"People don't like to be teased," Rickie said mildly, staring at his handful of ice shards. "People don't like to be teased." Then he seemed hypnotized by the sparkling of the ice.

"We should take him back," she said softly. "He's getting cold."

"He doesn't act cold," Montana said.

"He is," she said. "He just doesn't know it."

"You're cold yourself," he said. "You're starting to shiver."

She hadn't realized it. She *was* shivering. And Rickie was reluctant to leave the pond, so at last Montana picked him up and carried him back to the house.

Rickie protested at first, but then became absorbed in his newest pet phrase.

"There's frogs in the bear hair," he sang loudly. "Frogs in the bear hair. Frogs in the bear hair."

He started shrieking, wild laughs that rent the air. Laura winced. "That," she said, "is the sort of thing he shouldn't do in public."

"Hey," Montana said with that false joviality adults reserve for children. "I—Montana has a game for Rickie. Be quiet five minutes. Look at Rickie's watch. Rickie can be quiet five minutes."

Rickie pulled up the sleeve of his jacket, glanced at his watch, and clamped his lips together. Then he stared up into the sky, his head rolling, his eyes squinted as if furiously counting something only he could see.

"That trick doesn't keep on working," she said to Montana. "It wears out fast."

"Hey," he said with the ghost of a smile. "Maybe it will for me. It could be guy stuff—a manly contest."

She shrugged and thrust her hands into her pockets. Montana didn't look unnatural or uncomfortable carrying the boy. And Rickie no longer resisted him. He had one arm draped loosely around Montana's neck.

Laura thought, *If only it could stay like this. If only it could be this way forever.*

.   .   .

Hepfinger, like a chameleon, changed to suit the situation. At Ernie's Mobil Station, he became "Detective Sergeant Curtis Enfield," and introduced Santander as "Sergeant Perez."

Hepfinger had a collection of official-looking business cards, identity cards, and badges. He could flash them so convincingly and speak with such authority that few questioned him.

The brusque, gaunt-faced attendant on duty wore a grease-stained jacket that had the name "O'Malley" embroidered in red script on the left breast. He was the person Hepfinger had spoken to on the phone; the curt, gruff voice was the same.

O'Malley was in his late forties and carried himself with an air of tough cynicism. He had the hard eyes of one who's seen much and believes little. But he did not question Hepfinger's authority, only looked at him and Santander uneasily.

Hepfinger said, "We're investigating two anonymous calls made from your pay phone last night. At eight sixteen and eight twenty-one. Do you recall anyone using the phone at that time?"

"I wasn't on duty last night," O'Malley said, and shifted his weight from one foot to another.

"Who was?" Hepfinger demanded. "Did he mention anything about a caller?"

O'Malley hesitated. Hepfinger sensed the man had tangled with the law more than once, and he was nervous, unwilling to cooperate, yet afraid not to.

"Billy was on duty. The only person I know what used the phone was Doc DeMario. He dropped some change. Billy picked it up. He put it in a envelope for him. It's by the cash register."

Hepfinger prickled with a thrill that was almost sexual. "Who's this Billy?" he asked in his most daunting tone. "How do I reach him?"

"Billy Frazetti. I don't know how to reach 'im. He's gone to Yonkers or someplace. For a wedding. Or something."

"Frazetti," Hepfinger said, writing this name down

neatly in a small black notebook. "And your full name is . . . ?"

"Dennis. Dennis O'Malley. What's this about?"

Hepfinger ignored the question and instead asked one of his own. "This DeMario, he's a regular customer?"

"Yeah, yeah," said O'Malley.

"From around here?"

"Yeah."

"For how long?"

"Years."

Hepfinger kept his expression sternly aloof. "Did this Billy say if DeMario made more than one call?"

Again O'Malley hesitated, resisting.

Hepfinger made his voice sharp-edged and insinuating. "Will we have to take you down to headquarters, Mr. O'Malley? I asked you—how many calls did DeMario make?"

O'Malley's eyes flashed, his nostrils pinched. "I don't know. I wasn't here. DeMario's old. He's harmless. Maybe his phone's broke or something."

"Exactly how much change did he drop?"

"How do I know? I didn't open the envelope."

"We'd like to see that envelope."

O'Malley's expression grew even more rebellious. "What's that got to do with anything?"

"Do as you're asked," ordered Hepfinger. "And this visit is confidential. Don't speak of it. Not to anyone. Or you'll be guilty of obstructing justice."

"*What?*" O'Malley asked, clearly alarmed and offended. "What the hell is this?"

"Do as you're asked," Hepfinger repeated.

O'Malley grumbled beneath his breath, but he turned and led Hepfinger and Santander into the station's cluttered interior. It was a small, overheated space and smelled pungently of gasoline. Its yellowed walls needed repainting, and the linoleum floor was tracked with slush and dirt.

Hepfinger watched hungrily as O'Malley stalked to the cash register. O'Malley picked up a white envelope gingerly, as if it contained dead cockroaches.

He handed it to Hepfinger, leaving dark fingerprints

on the paper. The envelope had a Mobil logo on its upper left-hand corner, and it was not sealed.

Hepfinger opened it delicately, not wishing to soil his hands. He poured the change into his palm: seven quarters, four dimes, two nickels—two dollars and twenty-five cents.

Hepfinger stroked his thumb over the money almost lovingly. "We'll keep this," he said. He poured the money back into the envelope, folded the envelope, and put it into his pocket.

Warily O'Malley watched him. Hepfinger said, "I'll tell you again. This visit was confidential. Mention it to no one."

O'Malley's face looked even gaunter under the yellowish lights. He pressed his thin lips together and looked from Hepfinger to Santander, then back again. Clearly he didn't trust them; just as clearly he wanted no trouble.

Hepfinger gave O'Malley a nod that was both a warning and a farewell. He and Santander left the office and got into Hepfinger's car.

"We go see the old doctor?" Santander asked in his dour way as he scratched his face.

Hepfinger nodded.

Afternoon was lengthening. Marco DeMario still felt hollow and spent from last night's exertions. He was plagued by guilt as well. Mick had told him not to get cute, but he'd gotten cute anyway, an old man spiting the advice of a younger.

All day long he had feared the authorities would track him down, question him. He'd sat in his silent house, taking frequent nips from the Chianti bottle to steady his nerves. Now when he held out his hand, it barely shook.

Just as he raised the glass to his mouth again, the quiet was abruptly broken. Someone knocked loudly at his front door. The sound seemed to rattle the very air.

Marco gave a start. *They've come for me*; he thought in guilty panic.

He rose on unsteady legs, made his way to the front window, and drew aside the curtain ever so slightly. A dark car was parked at the curb. Its polished surface reflected the light of the waning day.

Jesus, Mary, and Joseph, he thought sickly. *What have I done? Could they trace my calls from the pay phone?*

"You're a paranoid old fool," he told himself harshly. He realized that he was slightly drunk, and he had no idea who his callers really were or what they wanted.

If it really was the police he would brazen it out. He had lied to them once, and he would lie to them again.

He swung the door open and saw two men. One was round and fair and slightly rumpled. The other was lean and dark and had a serious case of cystic acne. They wore conservative suits and topcoats and equally conservative expressions.

Both men flashed badges, and the plump blond one said they were from the DEA, that they were running a backup check on all the sources the FBI had questioned. Just routine.

"May we come in, Dr. DeMario?" asked the fair man.

Marco nodded, fearing it would seem suspicious to refuse. But once they were inside, he regretted his choice.

He didn't like their looks, these two. There was something about them that was different from the FBI men, something that filled him with misgivings.

The men entered silently. The blond one kept his eyes on Marco; the other looked about the dim and dusty room. Marco gestured for them to seat themselves on his threadbare couch, but they remained standing, so he did, too.

"We only want to ask a few questions," said the blond man, studying Marco carefully.

"Ask away," Marco said, making sure he sounded bored, crotchety, and above all else, feeble.

The blond man smiled at him, a strange, boyish smile that made deep dimples appear in his cheeks. He reached into his pocket and pulled out an envelope. It bore a Mobil logo in the upper right-hand corner.

Marco's vision dimmed for a moment as if the blood rushed from his head. His heart raced; he felt it shaking his ribs, slamming against his breastbone.

"You lost something last night," the blond man said in a voice that was disconcertingly cheerful. "Remember?"

Marco said nothing. He reached out and clutched the back of the sofa to steady himself.

The blond man opened the envelope and spilled a clinking stream of coins into his palm. "You were making phone calls," he said. "You dropped these. You didn't bother to pick them up. Why? Were you frightened? Of what?"

Marco was shaken, but anger sparked within him, driving back the fear. "I didn't notice I'd dropped anything," he lied. "It was cold. I was in a hurry."

The blond man stepped closer to him, too close. The dark man moved closer, too, so that he was caught between the two of them.

"Why did you call the police? The FBI?" the blond man asked.

Marco didn't allow his gaze to waver. "I didn't."

The blond man smiled again. "The calls were logged. We know from which phone they were made and when. We know you used that phone. You called about Montana. Why? What do you know about him? Did he bring the black man here?"

Marco's chin jerked up defiantly. "I made some calls from Ernie's because my phone wasn't working. That's all."

The blond man stepped to the telephone and picked up the receiver. He dialed "O" for operator, listened a moment, then hung up.

"The phone works fine," he said without emotion.

Marco clutched the back of the couch more tightly. "It didn't last night."

The blond man gave Marco a pitying look and shook his head. "You know more than you're saying, Dr. DeMario. I'm afraid we'll have to make you cooperate."

He sighed and gave the dark man a significant nod. Before Marco realized what was happening, the dark man seized him, pinioning his arms painfully behind his back.

His shoulders felt wrested out of joint; he thought his fragile bones would snap. His pulses beat so furiously they rattled his body, and he wondered if he would have a stroke.

"Careful, Santander," the blond man cautioned. "He's old. Don't hurt him—yet."

These men aren't police, Marco thought dizzily. *These men are outside the law.*

Torturing an old man was a subtle art, Hepfinger thought.

You didn't want to kill him before he talked. Nor did you want him passing out or going into a coma. Such things were counterproductive.

So, for a while, Hepfinger used only psychological methods. He simply let DeMario sweat it out, let him wonder what was going to happen.

Hepfinger could tell that the old man knew plenty; he could see from his reaction to the Mobil envelope.

Hepfinger told Santander to restrain Marco, to keep him quiet while Hepfinger made a brisk search of the house. In his search, he found four things of great interest.

In the old man's bedroom were twin beds. One was rumpled and looked recently slept in, the other was neatly made.

When Hepfinger drew back the sheets of the made bed, he saw a large bloodstain on the mattress, its color still darkly fresh. He smiled, knowing the blood was probably Jefferson's. He remade the bed, more tidily than before.

On the glassed-in back porch, he found more bloodstains, a trail on the floor between the outside door and the door into the kitchen. The blood had seeped into the unpainted wood too deeply to be scrubbed away.

Upstairs he found a room that must have belonged to the old man's grandson. Hepfinger knew from his sources that Montana had been boyhood friends with this youth, Michael Kominski.

The room was like a dark, musty shrine, as if the old man had tried to stop time here. It looked as if he'd kept the boy's every possession, no matter how trivial.

And finally, under a dust ruffle of a bed in what seemed to be the guest room, Hepfinger found a child's toy. It was a small plastic lizard of bright yellow. He knew the twins had such toys. He smiled and slipped it into his pocket.

He needed no more proof. They had been here, and the old man had helped them. He went back downstairs to confront him.

"Bring him into the kitchen," Hepfinger told Santander, and Santander half pushed, half dragged the old man to the kitchen.

Hepfinger said, "Bring him to the sink. Put his hand on the cutting board. Palm up."

Marco struggled, but he was no match for Santander, who was tall, strong, and fifty years younger. Santander forced the old man's hand onto the cutting board.

Hepfinger opened drawers until he found the one that held the cutlery. He drew out the thinnest, sharpest knife.

He put the point of the knife at the edge of Marco's eye, and the old man went still, or as still as he could, for he was trembling.

"The children were here," Hepfinger said. "The black man was here. Montana and the woman, too. Yes?"

"No," Marco gasped.

Hepfinger picked up a glass salt shaker from the counter, and he held it before Marco's eyes. "The average house is full of implements of pain. Would you like me to cut off your eyelids? Pour salt in your eyes?"

A tremor ran through the old man's body, but he swallowed and said, in a shaking voice, "Fuck you."

Hepfinger laughed and shook his head. "Fool, they were here. I know it."

"They weren't," Marco said, almost panting. Hepfinger gave Santander a resigned look. Santander had Marco's right arm twisted behind his back, his left hand held down by the wrist on the cutting board.

Marco had made a fist, but he had little bodily strength, and Hepfinger could pry his fingers open as easily as if they belonged to a child. He crushed the fingers against the board, leaving the palm naked, exposed.

"If the black man wasn't here," Hepfinger asked. "Why is the mattress of the bed downstairs stained with blood?"

Marco's fingers twitched beneath Hepfinger's. "I had a nosebleed. In the night. The air's dry in winter and I—"

Hepfinger raised the knife and brought it down, driving it through Marco's palm, pinning the hand to the board. He kept the knife there and he twisted carefully, first to the left, then to the right.

"The black man was here," Hepfinger said. "I know it. There's blood on the back porch, too."

Marco's face had gone white and his knees sagged. Santander kept him standing upright.

Marco looked dazedly over the tops of his glasses at Hepfinger, and the expression in his eyes should have been supplicating. It was not. "Another nosebleed. I get them."

"The truth," Hepfinger challenged. "I want the truth. The children were here, too, weren't they?"

"What children?" Marco asked.

Hepfinger drew out the knife and set it neatly aside. He put his hand in his pocket, drawing out the plastic lizard. He took the lizard and forced it, headfirst, into the wound the knife had made.

Marco started to cry out, but clamped his mouth shut, strangling the sound in his throat. He stared at his impaled hand, the red blood welling around the yellow lizard.

"If they weren't here, what's this?" Hepfinger asked, twisting the lizard. "Look, old man, you're crucified on a child's toy. Now the truth. Where did they go? Is the black man with them?"

"I don't know," Marco said, his voice breaking. "The toy—it's my great-nephew's."

Hepfinger seized him by the jaw, squeezing hard. "I'll peel your cock and balls, old man. I'll pour salt on them. Tell the truth."

Marco kept his gaze fastened on Hepfinger's. "The black man died," he said. "That's the truth."

Hepfinger slapped his face. "That's a lie. The black man didn't die. Where is he?"

"They were taking him to somebody's home. Upstate. To leave him there."

"Where?" Hepfinger squeezed his jaw again.

"I don't know," Marco gasped. "They didn't tell me."

"Where did he take the woman and children?"

"They didn't tell me that, either."

"Money. What were they doing for money?"

"I d-d-don't know," Marco stammered. "They took all I had."

"How much?"

"F-f-five hundred dollars. Five hundred and twelve. It was all I h-had."

Hepfinger said, "What were they driving?"

"I—I don't know. I don't know cars. It was black."

"Where'd he get it?"

"I don't know. He didn't tell me. I was a prisoner in my own house. I did what they said, that was all."

"Hepfinger," Santander said, "he's bleeding a lot. He's bleeding on your shoes."

Hepfinger swore softly and stepped aside. Marco's wound seemed to be bleeding exorbitantly. Hepfinger picked up a dishtowel and thrust it at Marco. "See to yourself," he said. "Stop the bleeding. Santander, get more towels. I don't want to leave tracks."

Santander let go of Marco and backed out of the kitchen. Marco sagged against the sink, holding his hand over the drain, the blood coursing through the dishtowel. His mouth was twisted, his nose was running, and his glasses were askew.

He managed to turn on the water, but the flow from the tap didn't slow the bleeding, only turned the water a dark orangish-pink. It swirled, gurgling, down the pipe.

Marco gave him a strangely cold sideways look. Hepfinger didn't trust that look. He would have stepped to the old man, slapped him again, but he didn't want to dirty his shoes.

"You better not be lying, old man," he said. "I can skin your fingertips, your cock, your balls, cut off your eyelids."

Marco gave him another cold look. "Horseshit," he said. "I'd die of shock." He turned back to watching his blood flow down the drain. He shook, yet seemed suddenly to be eerily calm.

"What?" Hepfinger demanded. "Stop the bleeding, you old fool. You'll bleed to death."

Marco drew back the towel and stared at the blood

coursing from his wound. "You're finally catching on, aren't you, Einstein? I'm taking Coumadin, an anticoagulant. This blood won't clot. Nossir."

A rage seized Hepfinger so intensely that it momentarily dizzied him. "You're taking an anticoagulant? Then why do you drink, you ass? Did you want to kill yourself?"

Marco shuddered and kept watching the pink-orange water sluice away. "It wasn't a big concern." With the fingers of his good hand, he parted the wound so it bled even more profusely. He barely winced as he did so.

Hepfinger couldn't help himself. He stepped into the blood, seized Marco by the shirt, spun him around, and backhanded him across the face.

Marco's glasses flew off, his lower denture was knocked from his mouth, and he fell back against the counter. He also began to bleed from the corner of his mouth, not a trickle, but a steady, bright flow.

"Imagine," Marco said thickly, giving Hepfinger a crazy, bloody smile. "You were going to teach *me* about pain. Do you think pain scares me? My God. My God. You don't know anything about it. Amateur."

Hepfinger backhanded him again.

Marco's knees buckled and he collapsed like a cast-off rag doll into his own blood. His eyes were still open and his mouth worked, but the only sound he made was unintelligible to Hepfinger.

Santander came through the kitchen door and stopped dead. "What happened?"

"He's bleeding to death," Hepfinger snarled. "Let him. Break a glass and push a piece through his hand. Make it look like an accident."

"But—" Santander said.

"An accident," stormed Hepfinger, nearly crying with anger. "And wipe my shoes. Clean them."

Hepfinger stepped out of his shoes and padded daintily around Marco's twitching body. The old man's lips still worked spasmodically, his eyelids fluttered.

Hepfinger made his way angrily into the living room. He began going furiously through Marco's checkbook, the clutter of papers on his desk, the scribbled notes by the phone.

By the time Santander came from the kitchen carrying the cleaned shoes, Hepfinger was almost himself again. The old man hadn't thwarted him after all. He held a piece of paper that told him what he wanted to know.

"Is he dead?" Hepfinger demanded.

"Almost, the shaky old fuck," Santander said. "How'd he make you so mad? Didn't you want him to die?"

"Of course I did," Hepfinger said in disdain. "It's just he was so full of lies. He thought his secrets would die with him. He was wrong."

Santander blinked and set Hepfinger's shoes on the table. He gave him a look of sulky curiosity.

Hepfinger tapped his fingertips against the wrinkled paper. "He was careless. He had this in his coat pocket. Along with the change he had left for the phone. Old men are forgetful."

"Left what?"

Hepfinger managed to smile one of his little smiles. "It's yesterday's calendar page. There's the name and number of a drugstore here. A note that says, 'M. Boy and Jefferson flu, Goffstown, NH.' And more. About prescriptions."

"What's it mean?" Santander asked, scowling harder.

"That he phoned a prescription in yesterday. Last night, no doubt. Montana's in New Hampshire. He's got the boys. And the black man. But they're slowed down. It's sickness. Or they wouldn't need prescriptions. We've got them."

"New Hampshire's a big place," Santander muttered. "How can you find them, just from that?"

"Child's play," Hepfinger said. He sat down and slipped on his shoes. "What was he saying at the end, the old ass? Could you tell?"

The corners of Santander's mouth curved down. "It was nonsense. Something about 'We won.'"

Hepfinger shook his head at the folly. Lovingly he tied his shoelaces into perfect bow knots. He smiled to himself. "He was a stupid old man," he said. "He won nothing. Nothing at all."

FIFTEEN

EVENING WAS STARTING TO FALL. LAURA STOOD BY THE
kitchen counter, her arms folded nervously, her lips
pressed together. She watched as Montana knelt before
Rickie, trying to unjam the zipper on the child's jacket.

She'd worked hard to teach the boys to dress themselves for outside, but Rickie's red jacket had a stubborn
zipper that often baffled him.

She was familiar with the zipper; she could have
worked it with her eyes closed, but Montana had waved
her away.

"Let me do it," he'd said quietly. He intended to take
Rickie for the day's last outing by himself, without Laura
or his brother. He wanted to get the boy used to going
alone with him.

But Montana's bad hand slowed his progress with the
zipper, and Rickie fidgeted, confused and impatient. He
stared at Laura so accusingly that her resolve weakened.

"Let me help," she told Montana, "there's a trick to
it."

Montana shook his head. "No. He's got to learn to
depend on somebody besides you."

She leaned back against the counter again, hugging
herself more tensely. It was odd, disquieting, seeing her
place usurped.

Montana continued his struggle with the zipper. "*Laur-a!*" Rickie wheedled, pointing at his half-open jacket. "Laur-a—*fix zipper!*"

"Sorry, kid," Montana muttered. "Montana's gotta fix it this time."

He waggled the zipper's tag, and this time it traveled up the track, closing the jacket snugly up to Rickie's chin.

"Now where are your gloves, chum?" Montana asked. "Should I help you with them?"

Rickie shut one eye and stared at the ceiling. "Fruit flies are in bloom. I'll twink your wink."

Montana was saying things wrongly, unsettling Rickie, and Laura couldn't resist coaching. "Don't ask," she said. "He knows perfectly well how to put on his gloves. Tell him to. And use his name."

Montana gave a determined nod. "Okay. Rickie, put on your gloves."

Rickie kept staring one-eyed at the ceiling and rocking back and forth on the balls of his feet. "I'll twink your wink. I'll twink your wink."

Montana shot Laura an exasperated glance. "Make him look at you," she said. "Make him give you his attention. Then repeat it."

Montana took the boy's chin in his good hand, making Rickie lower his face so that his eyes were level with Montana's. "Rickie," Montana said, "put on your gloves. Put on your gloves now."

Rickie gave an irritated sigh, but he dug into his pockets, fished out his woolly gloves, and drew them on.

"Good," Montana said. "A big boy can put on his gloves. Rickie's a big boy."

That's it. Praise him when he does something right, Laura thought. *He's like anybody else—he needs praise.*

Montana rose, towering over the child. "All right," he said, "Rickie and Montana'll take a walk."

Rickie looked dubious about such a proposition. He cast a measuring glance at the hallway, then at Laura. "Laura come," he said. "Trace come. Laura and Trace come."

"No," she said stiffly. "Laura can't. Trace can't. Trace is sick. Rickie and Montana will go."

Rickie stood, looking troubled and hesitant. A strange knot formed in Laura's throat. "Go with Mr. Montana," she told the boy.

Rickie frowned, his smooth brow wrinkling, but he stalked toward the door, his snow boots swishing. Montana followed and opened the door. "Come on, Rickie. Let's go out. Should we make a snowman? Go to the barn? Or the pond?"

Rickie stopped on the threshold and his expression grew more bewildered than before. He looked back at Laura and held out his gloved hand to her, a gesture that showed he wanted help.

"Rickie, take Montana's hand," she said.

"Laur-a!" Rickie said, half pleading, half whining. He kept his hand stretched toward her, not Montana.

She tried to keep her voice even. "Rickie is the leader this time. Rickie decides where to play. Choose one place. The yard. The barn. The pond. The—"

"The barn," he said without hesitation. "Laura get Trace. Rickie wants Trace—and Laura. At the barn."

"No," she told him. "Go play now."

Rickie scowled, but he waddled out the door with the special gait of a child bundled in winter clothing. Montana followed, shutting the door behind them. She heard their footsteps crossing the porch.

A strange sense of emptiness seized her. She moved softly to the couch. Trace lay there, sleeping restlessly. All afternoon his fever had fluctuated, and he'd been miserable with a running nose and watery eyes.

All he'd wanted was for Jefferson to read to him from the stack of old tabloids. The papers littered the carpet around the couch in a garish spill.

She adjusted the afghan that covered Trace and felt his forehead, which was clammy. She gathered up the discarded tabloids and stacked them on the coffee table.

Jefferson, full of painkillers and cough suppressants, was taking another nap in the main bedroom. From time to time, in spite of the medicine, he had fits of coughing, harsh and wheezing.

She heard him coughing now and tried not to flinch; the big man's weakness frightened her because it seemed both unnatural and ominous.

She drifted to the kitchen window and stared out. Rickie and Montana had stopped halfway to the barn. Rickie's snow boot must have come unbuckled, because Montana was on his knees, working at it. It seemed to take him a long time—he was not used to such tasks, and his bad hand must slow him.

But at last Montana rose and offered Rickie his good hand. Rickie threw a backward look toward the house, as if he hoped to see Laura emerging with his brother.

He gazed for a long moment, and even from this distance she could see that he looked puzzled. But Montana said something to him and again offered the boy his hand.

To Laura's surprise Rickie reached out and took it. He seldom let anyone but Laura hold his hand. With that simple, single motion, he seemed to cross a bridge that led him away from her.

For the first time it hit her, very hard, that she and Rickie and Montana really would part. It had to happen; Montana was making ready for it.

The realization was acute and physical; it hurt, and she found it hard to draw her breath.

This is the start of good-bye, she thought. But she didn't allow herself to cry. She watched them walk away from her, man and boy, hand in hand. Neither looked back in her direction.

In a motel room in Queens, Santander lounged on one of the beds, eating salted peanuts and reading another true crime magazine. He had found a tube of prescription skin cream at Marco's and had applied it in liberal white patches to his face.

Hepfinger sat hunched over the desk, tapping at the keys of his computer. His cellular phone was at his right elbow, and a road map and his leather-bound notebook at his left.

Hepfinger pulled up an Internet menu on his computer

screen. "We're closing in on them," he said with satisfaction.

Santander gave him an idle glance. "How?"

"By performing an act of what's called 'negative capability.' I try to become one with my quarry. I try to sense what he fears, think as he thinks, plan as he plans."

Santander turned back to the magazine. "Whatever."

"He had prescriptions phoned to Goffstown," Hepfinger went on, enjoying himself. "He wouldn't ask for them unless he was desperate. That means somebody's sick—seriously. Who's most likely? The one who's already hurt. The black man. DeMario wrote his name by the prescription note."

Santander ate a handful of peanuts. "You always come back to the black man. *La verdad es que siempre estas con la misma cantaleta.* He's the song you always sing."

Hepfinger gave him a condescending smile. "Montana had no reason to drag him along. Unless he planned to use him some way. If Montana is clever—and he is—he will split up the twins. I think this is exactly what he plans."

"That doesn't help us find them."

"Yes, it does. Montana can't just go off with a kid like that. He'll have to learn to handle him. And the boy has to learn to accept him. These children don't like change. It interferes with the learning process. Ergo, for as long as possible, Montana will move them as little as possible. And to go underground successfully takes planning."

"They don't have time to plan."

"They don't have time not to. They can't use their own identities. They need new ones. And that's what they're doing now. Establishing new ones."

"So," Santander said, crumpling up the peanut sack. "They're somewhere near Goffstown. You don't need a computer to figure *that* out."

"But where near Goffstown?" said Hepfinger. "Use the process of elimination. The law's looking for them. Can they go to a motel? No. A hotel? No. Friends? Possibly. But we have a pretty comprehensive idea of who their friends are, and they know that. They would not want to put friends at risk. And there are five of them, after all."

Santander threw the crushed sack overhand into the waste container, like a basketball player shooting a basket.

"They could break into an empty house," he said. "Or force someone to take them in."

"Too chancy. Too messy. They'd be making themselves conspicuous." Hepfinger gave a dismissive wave of his hand. "Montana's a professional. He knows the simplest, safest thing is to acquire a normal, everyday address. By normal, everyday means."

"They're fugitives," Santander countered. "They have crazy twins and a shot black man and a white man with a crippled hand. Nothing about them is normal or everyday."

"If I were he," Hepfinger said, stroking his chins, "I'd rent a place, a house, out of the way. You can manage these things over the phone without ever coming face to face with a realtor."

Santander smiled, a rare occurrence. "New Hampshire's full of houses. What do we do? Knock on all the doors?"

Hepfinger nodded at his beautiful little computer. "In this country, they have a saying: 'Let your fingers do the walking.' I will. I hope they don't have to walk far."

He tapped on the computer's keys and the screen changed. He began to make notes in his notebook.

"What are you doing?"

Hepfinger smiled. "We live in the computer age. You've heard of the information superhighway?"

Santander frowned and shook his head. He'd heard of no such road.

"Electrons reach everywhere," Hepfinger said. "Most particularly into the marketplace. Including real estate. Even in places as godforsaken as New Hampshire. There's a system called Nynex. It lists realtors by area. I check the Goffstown area."

Santander saw a list in white and red and black and the name New Hampshire in large letters. He watched Hepfinger make notation after notation.

At last Hepfinger switched off the computer and took up the cellular phone. He dialed a number, casually, almost languidly, and began to talk.

Santander watched furtively, from the corner of his eye. Mother of God—was the fat man going to call every realtor listed on the stupid computer?

Santander thought that calling all those numbers would be not only impossible, but boring. And he would find it a strain to talk as perfectly as Hepfinger did. Estrada was lucky to have a man willing to do this drudgery. Santander wouldn't have stooped to it.

Hepfinger was presenting himself as some high-ranking DEA agent, saying he was calling about a confidential matter. He asked if a man of Montana's description had recently rented a place. He might have a wife and child or children. He would probably be driving a vehicle—a van perhaps—with out-of-state plates. Were there other realtors, other properties that might not have been listed on the Internet?

Santander finished his magazine, looked at the pictures two more times, then turned on the television to a soccer game, but it was boring, and he fell asleep. He was having a nightmare about the whores of Bogotá when Hepfinger woke him, a smile on his bland face.

"I've found them," Hepfinger said. "Get ready. We're getting reinforcements. Then we go after them."

Santander stared at him for a moment, groggy and disbelieving.

"Two days ago a man arranged to pick up a key for a rental cottage from a realtor in Hooksett, New Hampshire. His description matches Montana's. The renter mentioned a wife and child, but the realtor saw only him—he remembers because the man paid in cash."

Santander just kept staring. *Maybe it's true,* he thought. *He has powers. He's a* brujo.

"They're at a cottage two miles north of Hooksett. On Londonderry Turnpike. The second right after the Lucky Seven Motel is a dirt road. It leads straight to them."

"What if it isn't them?" Santander asked.

"It's them," Hepfinger said with perfect conviction. "He's using the name Michael Kominski. Which just happens to be the name of DeMario's dead grandson."

.   .   .

Laura tried not think of the future, to stay centered, to live as much in the present as she could. To keep busy, she'd volunteered to do the supper dishes alone. Even so simple an experience as sinking her hands into the soapsuds seemed sensuous and remarkable.

The men and the boys in the living room area were gilded by the glow of lamplight; it was getting close to the boys' bedtime and the scene was homey, deceptively domestic.

Montana lazed on the rug beside Rickie, playing a complicated form of solitaire that they scored with pennies. *He's doing it,* Laura thought. Hour by hour, he was winning Rickie's trust and the closest thing to affection the boy could offer.

Jefferson, looking depressed, sat on the sofa, a box of Kleenex at his elbow. He was slowly making his way through the tabloids, reading them aloud to Trace.

Trace, slumped beside Jefferson, still wanted to do nothing except be read to; he frowned and whined whenever Jefferson tried to quit.

When Trace rose and stamped into the bathroom, Jefferson saw the opportunity to escape. "I gotta lay down," he said. "I ain't good for *nothing.*"

He dropped the newspaper to the rug and started to rise. He moved like an old man who ached in every joint.

Rickie raised his eyes from the solitaire game and glanced at the cast-off paper. It had fallen open to a double-paged spread of celebrity photos.

"That's Moleman," he said without emotion, then turned back to the cards.

Laura, wiping off the dining room table, went still. She looked up sharply and drew in her breath. "What did he say?"

She watched as Montana took Rickie's chin in his hand and made the boy look at him. "Rickie," he said, his voice tense and careful, "where's Moleman? Show Moleman."

Rickie glanced toward the paper. "Moleman," he said, and impatiently stabbed his finger at the picture of a glamorous-looking young couple.

Then he turned over a red seven and put it neatly on a

black eight. Montana picked up the tabloid. "Mother of God," he said.

Laura forgot the table, the dishes, everything but what Rickie had said. Wiping her hands on her slacks, she hurried to Montana and knelt by his side.

Jefferson had sunk back into his seat and leaned over to peer at the paper.

Montana's expression was somber, and a vein twitched in his temple. He pointed at the photo. It was part of a gossip feature headlined "Behind the Screens."

In the picture a young couple in formal dress smiled brightly into the camera. The girl was a petite blonde with long hair and a full-length, clinging dress of sky blue. The young man was dark and handsome, and he had three moles on his left cheek, exactly as Trace and Rickie had described.

"My God," breathed Jefferson.

Laura read the caption beneath the picture. "Tori Byrd looks like the Blue Bird of Happiness in this stylish frock. The sixteen-year-old star of *Days of Our Lives* attends an AIDS benefit with steady Reynaldo Comce. The dashing Colombian is the grandson of his country's president."

The boy looked no older than seventeen or eighteen, and he had an engaging smile, wide and boyish. He somewhat resembled the film star Tom Cruise.

Laura's heart seemed to both plummet and to soar. She felt frightened and giddy and half faint. She took the paper from Montana and thrust it right in front of Rickie's face. "Tell Laura who the man is," she said, pointing. "Tell Laura about this man."

"Moleman," Rickie said, sounding bored. "Moleman shot walking man nineteen times. Bang, bang, bang, bang, bang . . ."

Jefferson's face was taut. "The grandson of the *President* of Colombia?" he said. "Christ. No wonder they're after us."

Montana stared wordlessly at the photo, and Rickie turned back to his cards. "Bang." He sighed peacefully. "Bang, bang, bang, bang, bang . . ."

Laura's chest tightened; she couldn't get her breath. She heard Trace come out of the bathroom.

Montana shot a glance in Trace's direction. "See if he'll verify it. Get Rickie out of the room."

She put her hand on Rickie's shoulder to get his attention. "Rickie," she said as evenly as she could, "go into the bathroom. Run the water in the sink for five minutes. Don't splash."

He glanced at his watch, gave something like a sigh, and rose, clutching a red plastic lizard. He dearly loved to run water, and she seldom let him. For a moment he looked down yearningly at the cards and pennies, but the lure of the water was stronger. He headed toward the bathroom, passing his brother on the way, but neither acknowledged the other.

Trace sat down on the sofa with a thump, looked at Jefferson's empty hands, and gave a vague frown. "Read," he demanded. He picked up a yellow lizard and twiddled with it. "Read papers."

Laura knelt before him. She put her fingertip over the moles on the young man's cheek before showing Trace the picture. She held the paper before him.

"Tell Laura who this man is." She held her breath. Without the moles, the picture might mean nothing to Trace; perhaps Rickie would have called anyone with similar marks Moleman.

Trace slouched listlessly, propped against pillows and turning the yellow lizard around and around between his fingers. He barely glanced at the picture.

She felt the drumming of her heart and pulses.

"Moleman," he murmured, letting his gaze drift back to his lizard. He frowned. "Jefferson read. Not Laura."

"Jefferson," she said softly. "You take the paper. Keep that part of the face covered. Have him show you."

The paper rattled slightly as Jefferson took it. He held it so his thumb covered the edge of the boy's face. "Trace," he said, his voice cajoling, "who's this dude here?"

Trace frowned impatiently. He poked the lizard's tail at the photo of the young couple. "That's Moleman. With moles. Moleman has a gun. He shoot it thirty times. The old man fall down. The people fall down."

Montana rose and bent over the boy, taking him by the shoulders. Trace flinched.

"The man in the paper—he's the one you saw?" Montana asked. "Are you absolutely sure?"

Trace's face screwed up as if he was about to burst into angry tears. He tried to shrug off Montana's hands, and his lower lip thrust out dangerously.

"Let me," Laura said, and Montana edged out of her way.

"This man in the paper," she said, smiling brightly. "Trace saw that man really—not just his picture? Tell about the day Trace saw the man."

Trace sighed resentfully and stared down at his own lap. "Moleman has a car. January eighteenth. The car has license number MPZ one oh four eight one nine. Moleman shoot the gun. The old man fall down. The old man fall down on the one hundred twenty-ninth step."

Then he raised his eyes and looked at the picture, his expression irritable. "Moleman," he said emphatically, "has *moles*."

He pushed Jefferson's thumb out of the way to reveal the moles on Reynaldo Comce's face.

"*Moles*," Trace repeated, then turned his attention back to the yellow lizard.

"Hoo, baby," said Jefferson. "He knew they were there. He didn't see them, but he knew."

Laura felt Montana's hand on her shoulder. He said, "Is he sure? Do you think he's right?"

She was so shaken, so excited, she felt light-headed. She looked up at Montana. "He's never wrong about things like this. Never."

"I may have seen his picture before," Jefferson said, picking up a stack of the papers he'd discarded. "He's always with that blonde. She's some soap opera chick."

"If you saw the picture before, why didn't Trace recognize him?" Laura asked.

" 'Cause half the time he's not lookin' at the pictures. He just listens. Christ. That's our Moleman? He's only a kid."

"He's old enough to shoot a gun," Montana said.

"But the grandson of the president?" Laura asked in bewilderment. "Why's he going around shooting people?"

"No wonder we're in trouble," said Jefferson.

"No wonder we're in trouble," Trace said in a sing-song tone, spinning the lizard. "No wonder. No wonder."

Laura put her hand over her stomach. She felt queasy. "What do we do?" she asked Montana. "Call Conlee?"

"No," he said. "We don't know if we can trust him."

"Will we turn ourselves in? Or keep running?"

"If we turn ourselves in, they can't keep us safe. We know that."

Jefferson sat, his head thrown back, staring at the ceiling as if dazed. "Hell, man," he said. "This is bad news. You don't just have an old Mafia man gettin' shot here. This is an international incident. A diplomatic disaster."

A shudder, cold and snakelike, crept down Laura's back. She touched Montana's sleeve. "What's this mean?"

His face was grim. "He's right. It's a diplomatic disaster. Nobody'll want it made public. Not our government, not theirs. Our relation with the Colombians is dicey enough."

"I never liked this diplomatic stuff," Jefferson muttered. "The government thinks if we don't baby the Cartels and the politicians they got in their pockets, we lose clout in South America."

"I don't care who this boy is," Laura said. "The facts need to be known. This is the truth they're scared of. This is what they don't want out in the open."

"This is the truth," Trace said mechanically. He shook Jefferson's arm so the paper rattled again. "Read," he ordered.

Jefferson ignored him. "Would Conlee believe us even if we told him? We still don't know if these kids' testimony is admissible."

"You have to tell somebody," Laura insisted. "Maybe once the truth's out, they won't want us any more. They can't prevent us from talking if we've already talked."

Montana shook his head. "Talking's not the same as testifying. Not in a court of law. If you or I say it, it's only hearsay. The authorities have to hear it from the kids themselves."

Tears of angry frustration sprang to Laura's eyes. "Put *them* on the phone, then—the boys, I mean. They can talk on the phone. You said you know they're taping our calls. There'd be a record then. It'd be official."

"Laura, I know how you feel," Montana said. "But it could still seem like you've coached them, that we've coached them. It wouldn't stand up in court without a judge okaying it, without a defense lawyer able to question them—"

Laura turned away from him, biting her lip, sick unto death of bureaucracy and the labyrinth of the law. She put her hand to her forehead in concentration.

"All right," she said. "Forget the courts. How about this? You've got the video camera. Make a tape of them. Make it, but don't let Conlee see it. Forget him and the lawyers, too. But make sure everybody else sees it—everybody."

A moment of silence followed. Both men stared at her. *Now I've said something incredibly stupid,* she thought. *Everybody's thinking how emotional and stupid I am.*

"Wait a minute," Montana said, putting his hand on her arm.

"I don't get it," Jefferson muttered.

"What's the difference if this isn't a mug shot?" Laura said, gesturing at the paper. "Tape the boys identifying the picture. Send the tape to somebody we trust. Have that person copy it and—and send it to every television network—newspapers, too. Then everyone would know, the whole country would see it. And nobody'd dare touch the twins. If anybody did, everybody'd know who was responsible."

Again there was a moment of silence. Laura didn't know if her idea was insane or inspired.

Jefferson massaged the bridge of his nose wearily. "Put her on the payroll, Montana. She's got it."

"Yeah," Montana said. He almost smiled at her, but not quite.

"Except," Jefferson added, "who do we send the damn tape *to*?"

"Not Conlee," Montana said. "Even if he's clean, somebody higher up would make it disappear. You know it, I know it."

"But if we have somebody copy it and send it out, it can't disappear. There can't be any cover-up," Laura reasoned. "And maybe, at last, they'd have to leave the boys alone."

Jefferson glanced up at Montana. For the first time, there was a trace of optimism in his expression. "I like it. How do we send it? Just by mail?"

"It's the only way we've got," Montana said. "And we should send it out as soon as possible, tonight, just in case."

The *just in case* gave Laura another shudder. *Just in case what? Just in case we're caught? Or we die?*

But she refused to utter such a thought. Instead she said, "How can we mail it tonight? The post office is closed. We don't have stamps—do we?"

Montana took his wallet from the back pocket of his jeans. He flipped it open. "I've got two. You got any?"

"No," said Laura, feeling foolish and vulnerable. How could she have known so much would depend on carrying a few stamps? *If we get out of this,* she promised herself, *I'll never go anywhere without a whole roll of stamps in my purse.*

"What about you?" Montana asked Jefferson.

"No, man."

Montana gritted his teeth. "Okay," he said, "I'll check out the post office. Sometimes a small-town post office keeps its lobby open. So people can get to their post office boxes. There should be a stamp machine. I can mail a tape and have it on the way."

"And what you gonna do if that stamp machine's broken?" Jefferson asked sarcastically. "Like most government stuff is?"

Montana shrugged. "Improvise. We've still got two stamps. I'll drop it in the damn box with two stamps and no return address. Whoever gets it has to pay the insufficient postage charge, that's all."

"But who can we send it to?" Laura asked, her throat so tight with anxiety that it ached.

Jefferson shook his head. "There's my mama. But I hate to drag her into it."

"No," Montana said. "It shouldn't be family. It

shouldn't be anybody obvious. But it's got to be somebody who's not afraid and that we can trust. Absolutely. Not Marco. I've turned to him too often already."

Laura's mind churned. She could think of no one.

"There's a retired agent I know," Jefferson said. "A real straight arrow. Most honest guy I ever met. But . . ."

"But what?" Montana asked.

"But he's got a bum heart. He was in the hospital again over Christmas. But I'd trust him with my life. Still—"

"No," Montana said. "Too chancy. We need somebody in good health."

They took turns throwing out one name after another. Laura had to go fetch Rickie from the bathroom and dry him off. She led him back to the living room and sat him down again with his coins and cards.

She'd run out of names, but Montana hadn't, and neither had Jefferson. At last they seemed stymied, too, and fell into thoughtful silence.

"Read," Trace begged, tugging on Jefferson's sleeve.

"In a minute," Jefferson said. "Let me think."

Montana's eyes narrowed. "Wait. I thought of somebody. A nun, a teacher. Sister Agnes Mary. I had her in high school. They transferred her to Sioux City, Iowa, a couple years ago. She runs the what-you-call-it. The school media center. She knows videotapes and stuff."

"A *nun*?" Jefferson said. "You're gonna drag a Bride of Christ into a drug hit conspiracy?"

"Toughest woman I ever met," Montana said. "Not afraid of the devil himself. She'd chew Clint Eastwood up like a stick of gum."

"How old is she?" Jefferson asked.

"In her late fifties, maybe. A spring chicken for a nun."

"You could get the tape to her?"

"Sure. I could call her old diocese, get her address, not give my real name."

Jefferson raised his eyebrow appreciatively. "A nun. Sister Mary Drug-Bust. I like the sound of that."

"Fine," Montana said. "Done."

"But you'll have to tell Conlee sooner or later, won't you?" Laura asked.

"After the tapes come out," Montana said. "Then we tell him."

"And after that?" Laura said, afraid to hope. "Do you think that once everybody knows, we can live normal lives again? And the boys will be safe?"

Montana reached out and stroked her hair. "I can't promise anything," he said. "I'm sorry."

She stared at him, wondering how long they could stay on the run. Their odds were growing thinner all the time, she feared.

But then Trace had a coughing fit, and coughed until tears came to his eyes. "Hurts," he said, his voice choked. "*Hurts.*"

Laura went to him and put her arms around him, and he let her, without protest. He coughed again, more raggedly. "Hurts," he repeated weakly.

She patted his back. "I know it hurts, sugar."

She carried him into the kitchen to get him a drink of water. "Go home," he pleaded between coughs. "Go to school, go home—please."

"Laura's brave boy," she whispered. "Don't worry. Laura's trying to get Trace home. Laura's here. Don't worry."

Santander was glad he wasn't the one driving. It was snowing, and the snow swirling in the headlights made him dizzy, filled his head with dark thoughts.

Estrada had sent three real *coqueros* to help with the killing, and they had arrived at the motel in a van. Now they rode in the back, talking laconically in Spanish. They were all in their late twenties, seasoned and sleekly efficient. Their names were De Mosquera, Alvirez, and Luppler.

De Mosquera was stout and squarely built, and Alvirez was hollow-cheeked and wiry. Luppler was a dandy, so handsome that his face was almost girlish, like Reynaldo Comce's. Santander found such handsomeness repellent.

The van was a brand-new Chevrolet, and it carried enough assault weapons and ammunition to take over a small town. There were also several ten-gallon cans of gasoline.

This time, Hepfinger had said with his gentle smile, the target must be hit. It was forbidden to fail. Now Hepfinger kept his eyes on the road and did not flick so much as a glance at Santander or the men in the backseats.

"Your orders are to keep quiet about this hit," Hepfinger said to the men in the backseat. "The Cartel denies any knowledge of it. Officially, you're hired by Dennis Deeds, understand? It's his kill."

"Hey, man," laughed Luppler, the pretty-faced one. "I know that. I'm not working for Estrada. I'm working for Dennis Deeds, man."

"Remember that," said Hepfinger.

"How far away are we?" asked De Mosquera. "It seems like we been on this road forever. I hate this fucking snow."

Hepfinger ignored the question. "I had to drive that road up there once before," he said rather dreamily. "I had to stop. There was a moose in the road."

"A moose?" De Mosquera echoed. Santander cast Hepfinger a dubious glance. He had never seen a moose except on television.

"A moose as big as the very devil," Hepfinger said. "He wouldn't move."

"Did you shoot him?" De Mosquera asked. Hepfinger kept his eyes straight ahead and smiled mysteriously at the swirling snow. "No. He amused me."

Santander settled more deeply into his seat and stared out the side window. He would never understand Hepfinger. He didn't want to.

"How far are we?" De Mosquera asked again. "How long before we're there?"

"Two hours," said Hepfinger. "We'll be there in two hours."

Two hours, thought Santander. His boredom gave way to edgy anticipation. For the first time, he allowed himself to dwell on the killing to come, to weave his private fantasies of sex and rage. He scratched his cheek so deeply that it oozed. But Hepfinger spoke to him, forcing him back to the present.

"Recite the plan. Have you got it straight?"

Did Santander only imagine, or was there condescension in Hepfinger's voice? "I know it," he said defensively. "Once we get on the road to the house, we cut the lights. Alvirez, De Mosquera, Luppler, me—we go by foot to the house. We take a look, make sure it's them."

"I'll wait in the van," Hepfinger said. "In case anyone comes down the road."

The pussy's job, Santander thought uncharitably. *He's not going to dirty his hands.* He wondered if Hepfinger thought he was above the scut work of an ambush, or if he simply wanted to keep his fat ass warm in the van. Santander wished the man had stayed behind at the motel. But Hepfinger was so fussy and old-womanish, he had to oversee everything.

Santander spoke from between his teeth. "If we can take down the two men by surprise, through the windows, we will. Then the woman and kids are easy. Afterward, we burn the house."

"What if the woman, too, has a gun?" challenged Hepfinger.

"It doesn't matter. We just shoot her."

"Those in the house—they are as good as dead," Luppler said from the backseat. His voice was full of bravado.

Hepfinger didn't seem to notice. He kept staring into the swirling snow. "They'd better be," he said softly.

SIXTEEN

LAURA WAS FILLED WITH ANXIETY, BUT SHE FORCED HERSELF to smile weakly. Jefferson stood at the edge of the braided rug, the video camera poised on his good shoulder.

Briefly her eyes met Montana's. He nodded encouragement. She sat down cross-legged on the rug with both boys.

"Lights, camera, action," said Jefferson.

She turned to the twins. Trace still wore his rumpled blue pajamas. "Tell me about Moleman," she said to Rickie.

She led Rickie through the whole scenario again, then Trace. Both talked reluctantly, but both identified the picture of Reynaldo Comce. Jefferson had found two more photos of the boy. They identified each, just as quickly, just as surely.

Finally, when Trace grew irritable with questions and seemed on the verge of exasperated tears, she looked at Jefferson and said, "I'm sorry. He's not feeling good. I don't want to push him further."

Jefferson said, "Beautiful, baby, beautiful." He switched off the camera and, with a wince, took it from his shoulder. "I think we got it all," he said.

"Couldn't have been better," said Montana. "Perfect."

Jefferson handed him the tape cassette, and Montana slid it into the VCR. "Let's see if we got it."

For a few seconds, the television screen was blue. The blue transformed into a gray, shifting confusion of lines. Then the images appeared, Laura sitting on the braided rug beside Trace and Rickie.

She watched the whole scene replay again until she looked up into the camera and said, "I'm sorry. He's not feeling good. I don't want to push him further."

Jefferson's voice said, "Beautiful, baby, beautiful," the screen turned blue again, and it was over. Laura's heart beat high and hard in her chest, and she realized she'd been holding her breath.

Jefferson had put the camera aside. The taping seemed to have energized him, given him back his edge. "We're in business, man," he said to Montana.

"You did great," Montana told him. "You missed your calling."

"Yeah," Jefferson said. "I should have been a cinematographer. An *artiste*."

Montana shot him a small, crooked smile. But Laura saw the men's eyes lock, and Montana's smile faded.

Neither said a word, but Laura knew the unspoken message that passed between them. *We are into big stuff here. We are into dangerous stuff. Very, very dangerous.*

She looked at the boys, sitting on the rug. Rickie's face was rapt and innocent as he stacked coins. Trace frowned in discomfort, and he sneezed so hard that his eyes filled with tears.

She picked him up and made him lie on the couch again, covering him with the afghan. "Laura's good boy," she said.

He hid his face in his hands and said nothing.

Montana parked the van in front of the town's brick post office. It was a compact structure, so small it seemed toylike. Its bare flagpole shuddered in the winter wind.

A dim light shone in the lobby. He got out of the van, the wrapped tape concealed beneath his jacket. He tried the door. It was open.

He stepped inside, found the stamp machine. No "Out of Order" sign was taped to it, and he offered up a brief prayer of thanks.

He went to the counter by the front window and weighed the package on the postal scale. Then he fed bills into the stamp machine, took out the booklets, and fixed enough stamps on the package to mail it to Sister Agnes Mary in Iowa.

He pushed the package into the mail drop. The tape was in care of the U.S. Mail now, and he wished it Godspeed.

Outside the post office he glanced up and down the street. No one in sight. The place was a ghost town. He got into the van and headed back toward the house.

He figured the tapes, given the weekend, would reach Agnes Mary in three days, four days at the most. It would take her at least a day to copy them and to express them to their final destinations. Maybe longer.

He had dictated a long letter to Sister Mary Agnes, and Laura had taken it down in her perfect schoolteacher writing. Montana asked the nun to send copies to the major broadcasters: NBC, CBS, ABC, FOX, CNN, C-SPAN, even MTV. He also wanted copies sent to *The New York Times*, the *Los Angeles Times*, the *St. Louis Post-Dispatch*, and the *Chicago Tribune*.

Agnes Mary was to delay only if she heard from him personally. He would identify himself by the code word "spitball."

Montana frowned and narrowed his eyes against the silvery flash of snowflakes whirling in his headlight beams. He stepped on the accelerator.

He didn't like leaving Laura and the boys. For some reason, he'd become hinky, haunted by the feeling that danger lurked nearby and was creeping nearer.

He shook his head to clear it. When he reached the house, he'd call Conlee to see if there were any new developments. He didn't know if Conlee was friend or foe, or how much they could believe in him. But he was the only liaison they had.

The snow swirled down more lightly now. He pulled

into the lane that led to the house. He was on the last lap of his journey, coming home.

Home, he thought. It was an odd name for it.

When Laura and Jefferson heard the vehicle pull up outside, they both tensed. Jefferson went to the window, lifted the edge of the blind, and peered out.

He nodded to Laura, signaling that Montana had returned. She heard the slam of the van door. Jefferson relaxed, but he kept his hand near his gun, just in case.

"It's okay," Jefferson said. "Let him in."

Laura went to the door, undid the chain, and shot the dead bolt back. Montana stepped inside, bringing a gust of frigid air with him.

"How'd it go?"

"We're in luck," he said. "The post office was open. The stamp machine worked. The tape's on the way."

"Did anybody see you?" Jefferson asked.

Montana shook his head. "Nobody."

She sighed in relief. Montana met her gaze, and one corner of his mouth twitched in an unborn smile. "Kids asleep?"

She nodded. Rickie had been tired and sleepy from playing outside. But Trace had napped throughout the day and had been harder to handle. Finally, after she'd read him almost the entire lizard section of the *Field Guide to American Reptiles,* he'd nodded off into restless sleep.

"Trace is better, I think," she said. "I hope he's through the worst of it."

"Good," Montana said. He shot a glance at Jefferson. "How about you?"

"I'll make it," Jefferson said. "I'm gonna hit the sack for a couple hours. Then I'll get up, stand a watch."

Laura felt an unspoken message pass between the two men. *They're worried,* she thought. *More worried than usual—why?*

"You don't have to," Montana told him. "I'm a light sleeper."

Montana, always serious about their security, seemed positively grim. So did Jefferson. A shiver, slow and cold, went up her spinal cord. *Do they know something?* she wondered. *Or just sense it?*

Jefferson said, "I slept a week's worth today. I won't sleep through the night. It'll do me good to take a watch."

Montana nodded, but Laura sensed a reluctance in him. "It's your call."

"Right," Jefferson said. "I'll probably dream the damn tabloids. Space aliens after me all night long. And bat-faced babies and Elvis."

He lumbered into the bedroom. Laura could see from the way he carried himself that he was still in pain.

She waited until he closed the bedroom door behind himself. "What's wrong?" she asked Montana. "Something's wrong. What is it?"

He shook his head, unbuttoned his jacket. "I don't know. It's just a feeling."

"Then why does Jefferson have it, too?" she asked. "Something must have happened. Something you're not telling me."

"There's nothing I'm not telling you," he said. "I just keep wondering what I haven't thought of. It's always the thing you don't count on that does you in. I get restless. He must, too."

She searched his face, wondering if he was lying.

He raised his good hand, touched her cheek, then stroked her hair, once, twice.

"Call it a sixth sense," he said. "When you're on the run, you live like an animal. You rely on cunning and instinct. Sometimes you sense something in the air. Maybe it's really there. Maybe it's not. But you pay attention."

"You mean it's better to be paranoid than sorry?" She found her hand was rising, almost without her volition, to rest on his shoulder.

"I wish it was just paranoia. But people really are after us. And that puts your nerve ends on alert. You know it. You feel it, too."

Animal cunning, animal instinct, she thought. *You sense something in the air.*

He said, "I'm calling Conlee. To see if anything's happened."

"But you won't tell him about the Comce boy or the tape?"

"No. Of course not."

She stood by him, tense, while he dialed Conlee's home number. He put one arm around her shoulders, pulled her close. She leaned against him and closed her eyes.

"Conlee, Montana here. Anything new?"

Conlee gave him a long answer, and Laura felt Montana's muscles harden as his arm tightened around her. She heard the faint noise of Conlee's voice, droning on like the inarticulate buzz of an insect.

Sensing something was wrong, she drew back and studied Montana's face. His expression was at first stunned, then angry.

"Shit," he said with violent passion. "I told you—"

She'd never seen him look or react this way, and it unsettled her. His side of the conversation consisted of curt, ominous questions: *In broad daylight? When? Who?*

"No leads? None? No, I'm not coming in. No way. I don't give a damn."

He hung up and looked at Laura. He was pale, his face taut, the look in his eyes so bitter it seemed cruel.

"What is it?" she breathed.

"Marco's dead," he said out of the side of his mouth. "They think somebody killed him."

Like a trap shutting, the room closed in on Laura. The floor seemed to pitch drunkenly beneath her feet. She clutched Montana's arm and stared at him, unable to speak.

His nostrils flared. "Some service station attendant named O'Malley got worried about Marco. He said he heard Marco'd been at the station the night before, acting shaky and disoriented. This O'Malley said he 'got a feeling.'"

" 'A feeling'?" Laura echoed.

"That's what he said," Montana muttered. "A bad feeling. He said the longer he thought about it, the more worried he got. He tried to phone Marco. Nobody answered. So when O'Malley's shift was over, he stopped by the house. It was dark, and Marco didn't answer the door. But when he looked in the garage, he saw Marco's car."

She gripped his arm more tightly, tears rising in her eyes.

He shook his head as if to clear it. "Then Marco's niece showed up. She was supposed to pick him at six-thirty, take him to a Knights of Columbus pancake supper. He should have been expecting her. She and O'Malley went to a neighbor's, asked them to call the police. The police found him. He'd bled to death."

A wave of horror shivered through her. "But how? How?"

Montana looked away, rubbed his eyes wearily with his thumb and forefinger. "A broken glass or jar or some damn thing. A piece went clear through his hand. But the coroner's not convinced it was an accident."

"But who'd hurt Marco?" She tried to blink back tears, but couldn't.

Montana kept rubbing his eyes. "The cops thought this O'Malley acted like he knew something he wasn't saying. So they grilled him. Finally he said he'd been worried because two guys'd come to the station, asking who'd used the pay phone last night. They were interested in Marco, took some money he'd dropped, warned O'Malley not to talk. They said they were cops."

He let his hand drop from his face, and gazed into her eyes, his expression hard as stone. "They weren't police, Laura."

"Then who were they?" Furiously she wiped a tear away. Her throat was choked and dry.

He swore. "I wish I knew. Somehow, some way, somebody got onto him. They had to be after us. They *had* to be."

"But how could they find him? Why did they do such a thing? He didn't know where we are."

"He knew New Hampshire. He knew Goffstown. That's too close for comfort." His eyes glittered, and he blinked hard, his jaw taut. He swore again.

She touched his face, but he brushed her hand away. He went and stood before the window, staring at the drawn curtains, his lips clamped together. A muscle in his chin kept jerking.

Laura watched him, not knowing what to say. "Do you think he told where we are?" she asked at last.

He turned and gave her a sharp look. "Never voluntarily. He'd never do such a thing. But who knows what they might have done to him? He's an old man, he's weak, he might—"

He stopped abruptly. "I keep talking about him like he's still alive. Hell."

He clenched his jaw and looked around the room, not meeting her gaze. "How'd they trace him? How'd they know he'd used that phone? They have to have inside information, lots of it. This is no bush-league outfit. No way this is just Dennis Deeds. This is big-time. They're probably closing in on us right now."

"Montana? I'm sorry . . ."

"Yeah, me too," he said and took a deep breath. "That and a buck'll buy us a cup of coffee, right?"

She winced and struggled not to shed more tears. "What did Conlee say?"

"The same as always—give up."

"But we can't do that."

"No. We can't."

"Then—" she swallowed "—maybe we should move. Now. Tonight."

For a long moment he seemed lost in his own dark thoughts. Finally he nodded. "Yeah. Can you do it? With Trace sick?"

"Better sick than dead."

"The kids'll be hell to handle if we yank them out of bed."

"I know," she said. "But I'll handle them." *I'll use the tranquilizers Marco gave us if I have to,* she thought with fatalistic resolve. *Oh, Marco, Marco . . .*

"Let's start packing," Montana said. He came to her, and took her in his arms, almost roughly. He kissed her on the mouth, a brief kiss, but hard. She kissed him back just as desperately.

It's like we're kissing good-bye, she thought, her throat tightening.

His hand moved to her hair, smoothed it. "If they're coming to look in New Hampshire, we'll leave New Hampshire. We'll go northeast. Maine, Cobscook Bay. Try to hire a boat to take us into New Brunswick. It'll be a bitch, but I think we can do it."

"We can," she said. "We have to. I'll pack the boys' things."

"I'll help."

Dazed, she thought they should be able to pack quickly; they'd done it so often that they had it down to a science.

She didn't want to leave the little house. For a short time, she'd felt almost safe there, as if they'd somehow come home. She couldn't be sure that running was wise, only that the impulse was too strong to resist.

Safety was an illusion. Only the running was real.

Montana awoke Jefferson as Laura finished packing the boys' clothes.

He put his hand on Jefferson's shoulder. He could feel the feverish heat of his body even through the sweatshirt. "Wake up," he said. "They got Marco. He's dead. I've got bad vibes about this place. We're moving on. You up to it?"

Jefferson propped himself on one elbow and shook his head groggily. "Hell, man—Marco? They got him? Who did? When? How?"

"We don't know anything for sure," Montana said. "Can you handle it? Moving, I mean? Or should we leave you behind? Last chance, Jefferson. I won't tell you where we're going. We'll just go. You can stay behind."

Jefferson sat up, ran his hand over his hair. "No, man. I'm with you. I've been feeling funny about this place myself, you know?"

Jefferson still looked sick, still sounded sick, but at least he was better than he'd been yesterday. Montana clasped his upper arm. "Okay. You're in. You're a fool, but you're in."

Jefferson swore. "Jesus, I'd like to see my own kids for a change," he said.

"Yeah," said Montana tonelessly and took his hand away.

Jefferson got up from the bed and strapped on his holster. "I'll help load the van."

Montana shook his head. "No. I can do it. Take some aspirin, get your shit together. We'll wake the kids when we're loaded."

He thought of Laura moving swiftly and softly about the boys' room. The boxes had been packed and unpacked so often that they had a beaten look. Together, he and she had taken down the curtains, the Looney Tunes plaques, the bulletin board, put them away again. *How many times have we done this?* he'd wondered, watching her pack sweatshirts and underwear. She worked with an efficiency that belied the anxiety in her expression.

He left Jefferson and went back to her. She was packing books now, and when she glanced at him, the look in her eyes made his heart twist in his chest. He wanted to hold her and promise her everything would be fine.

But there was no time for such things, and they both knew things might never be fine ever again.

"How's Jefferson?" she asked.

"He'll make it. He's tough," said Montana.

She gazed at Trace. He slept restlessly, sometimes whimpering. Once he'd opened his eyes and mumbled that he wanted a glass of water. But by the time she brought it, he'd fallen back into an uneasy doze.

Montana looked down at the boy. "He'll be all right," he promised. "We'll wrap him up good and have the van warm."

"I should give him one of Marco's pills," she said. He could tell how reluctant she was to do it.

He nodded. "Yeah. You'd better. What about Rickie? Can he sleep in a car?"

"Yes. But I don't know for how long," she said.

"Then maybe him, too."

She looked stricken and more than a little guilty.

He said, "We can't afford scenes, Laura. Or trouble. It's for their sake."

"I understand," she said.

Trace rolled over in bed, throwing his covers off.

When she tried to tuck them back in place, he struck sleepily at her hands. She tried to feel his forehead, but he
twisted away from her touch. His eyes fluttered open.

"Blue rhubarb, blue rhubarb," he murmured pettishly.
"Love is strange. Laura, give Trace *water*."

"Maybe I should give him the pill now," she said,
darting Montana a glance filled with regret.

"Yeah," Montana said. "Maybe you should."

Trace fought against taking the pill, and Rickie would
fight even harder. Laura was gentle but insistent. She finally got the pill down him.

"I'll pack the groceries and stuff," Montana told her.
"And start loading the van."

She nodded silently, trying to get Trace to lie down and
sleep again. Wearily he flopped back against his pillow,
and began to drum his fingers against his cheek.

Montana went to the kitchen and found Jefferson
rebagging the groceries. "I'll do that," Montana said.

"I can," Jefferson said. "I need to pull my share."
Jefferson's forehead glistened with perspiration. He moved
slowly, as if he ached. But he moved surely.

"You sure?" Montana asked.

"Yeah," Jefferson said, "but this is dicey, running off
in the middle of the night, the kid sick and all. You still
want to try to make it across the border?"

"I've got plenty of cash," Montana said. "It ought to
buy our way over. We'll hire somebody with a boat. Hell,
maybe it's easier doing it that way anyhow."

"Suppose the Canadians are looking for us?"

"It's a chance we take," Montana said.

"I promised my oldest boy I'd take him to Canada
someday," Jefferson said. "If the Blue Jays are ever in the
World Series again. He's crazy about baseball."

"Yeah," Montana said.

Jefferson said. "That's all he ever talks about. Baseball. He's got to see that Toronto stadium, 'cause Canada's
the only other country that ever won the series."

Montana nodded, but said nothing.

Jefferson shrugged his good shoulder. "How soon till
we're ready to go?"

"Not long," Montana said. "Maybe twenty minutes."

H epfinger cut the lights of the van. The snowy ground turned a deep bluish-white, full of shadows. Santander stared at the landscape dispassionately. The winter-dead trees and black pines that lined the roadside swallowed up the cold blue stretches of snow and hid it, but, unseen, it stretched on, covering the earth like a shroud.

"I can't see no house, man," said Luppler.

"And nobody in the house can see us," said Santander. "We walk from here."

Luppler shifted uneasily in his seat, staring out at the deep snow. "We're going to freeze our *cajones*."

"Maybe we should have made a side trip to L.L. Bean, bought you some snowshoes," De Mosquera said sarcastically.

"What's L.L. Bean?" Luppler asked, zipping up his suede jacket.

"It's this fucking big store," De Mosquera said. "It's always open, and it sells canoes and birdhouses and snowshoes, shit like that."

"Hand me a gun," Santander said to De Mosquera. "And a can of gasoline."

De Mosquera grunted in assent and passed him an Uzi. It was Santander's favorite weapon, elegant in its compactness. He got out of the van and stepped ankle deep into the snow. He did not allow himself to shiver.

Luppler, too, got out, and flinched when the snow covered his stylish leather shoes. He carried a Calico submachine gun. De Mosquera handed Santander and Luppler each a can of gasoline, then got out, a gasoline can in his left hand and a Calico slung over his shoulder. When he found himself up to his shins in snow, he swore.

"Shut up," Santander told him, and De Mosquera shut up. The squarely-built, silent Alvirez got out, too, but he was warmly dressed and had thick, high boots. He carried a Calico like De Mosquera's.

"I wish Dennis Deeds would do his own fucking killing," said Luppler.

"To the house," Santander said to the three men. "Stay to the side of the road. Hurry up. Let's get this done."

"It's fucking freezing, man," Luppler complained.

De Mosquera nodded and shrugged more deeply into his jacket. He had no hat, and he looked cold and a bit nervous. "There's only two men?" he said. "But armed. Just handguns, though?"

Santander said nothing. He hated repeating things. He nodded for them to start, and he brought up the rear.

They trudged toward the house. The snow had nearly stopped, a half-moon shone through the clouds, and the landscape reflected its light, making the night air luminous.

"This snow sucks," Luppler grumbled. "Who in their right mind would live here? I'm going to Florida when this is over. They're crazy to live in the cold like this."

Santander stayed silent. He, too, hated the cold, and once had not imagined the United States could contain such frozen, empty wastes. He had always thought the whole country to be as full of people as Miami or New York.

The snow crunched underfoot. It melted against his socks, burning his ankles, numbing his feet. Luppler was stupid, but he was right: Who with any brains would live in country like this?

But then, through the pines and naked trees, Santander saw a pinprick of light. The house. He took such a deep breath of air that the cold hurt his lungs.

Luppler saw it, too. "We got them," he said with satisfaction.

"Hey, man, it isn't over 'till it's over, you know?" De Mosquera said, his teeth chattering.

"Shut up," said Santander, but at last he found himself being swept up in the spirit of the hunt. His heartbeat sped, and for a moment he forgot about the freezing pain in his feet.

When they rounded the corner, his heart positively soared, for from there the house was clearly visible, and when he saw it, he knew this was indeed the place, and they were closing in on it.

All was as Hepfinger had guessed. In the carport a van was parked, not as big as the van in which Hepfinger waited, but big enough. In the front yard stood a snowman. And a snowman meant children.

Santander held up his hand to halt the men. "We split. We slip up on them. Alvirez, cover the back door. I'll take the front. Luppler, come at it from the east side. De Mosquera, from the west. Check the windows first. Quietly. If you get a clear shot, especially at more than one of them, take it. But make it count. Understand?"

"Make it count," De Mosquero repeated, his teeth chattering harder.

Santander emphasized his order. "Get as many down as you can. Then we set the house on fire. Be careful and we should suffer no casualties."

"What if nobody can get a shot at any of them?" Luppler asked, a frown on his pretty face.

"The same thing. Set fire. If they try to escape, shoot them. Watch out for the men. They'll come out shooting."

"We can back off, t-take cover. Be in the shadows, b-behind trees," De Mosquera offered.

Luppler said, "I am a man. I won't back off. I'll stand in the open and kill my enemy like a man."

"Even if he's only eight years old," Santander said dryly.

Luppler gave Santander a conceited little smile. "Enemies are for killing," he said. "No matter how old."

"Enough talk," said Santander. "Go. Now." His breath ascended heavenward like a visible prayer.

They began to move toward the house, to converge upon it.

SEVENTEEN

LAURA SHUT THE CARTON OF BOOKS, AND MONTANA LIFTED it and stacked it against the wall. They had packed as quickly and as noiselessly as possible. They hadn't been noiseless enough.

From Rickie's bed came the rustle of sheets, the sound of a body restlessly shifting, and a child's sleepy complaint: "Too much light. Too much *light*."

"Uh-oh," Laura said and darted Montana a worried glance.

Rickie had awakened. He pushed himself to a sitting position, squinted and scowled. He rubbed his eyes and scowled again.

When he saw the packing boxes, he stiffened and glared, as if confronted by mortal enemies. He sensed the threat of confusion, disorder, and change. "No," he said belligerently, drumming his fingertips against his cheek. "No, no, no, no, no, no, no."

"I'd better get a pill down him, too," she said *sotto voce*.

Montana nodded grimly.

"Put on your slippers," she told Rickie. "Laura's going to take Rickie to the kitchen for a glass of orange juice."

She stretched out her hand to take his, but he shook his head and refused to meet her eyes. He shoved his feet into his bedroom slippers. "Pee-pee," he said in a truculent voice.

"Fine," she said, dropping her hand to her side. "Rickie goes to the bathroom like a big boy."

He rose, still tapping his fingers against his face, and shuffled off to the bathroom, muttering under his breath.

"I won't strip his bed yet," she told Montana. "It'll just upset him more. I hope Jefferson hasn't packed the orange juice."

"Want me to go see?" Montana asked.

"No. I'll do it." She sighed resolutely and said, "We're almost ready."

Only the Bugs Bunny lamp remained to be packed, along with the bedclothes.

Montana said, "I'll warm the van up, start loading."

But he paused for a moment and gazed down at Trace. The boy lay on his back, one arm thrown out across the bed. His eyelids flickered and he frowned in his sleep as if he was dreaming restless dreams.

He won't be able to understand another move, Laura thought. *Neither of them will.*

"How long will it take for the pill to affect Rickie?" Montana asked. He had on his jacket.

She shook her head. "I don't know. It took about fifteen minutes to work on Trace."

She heard the toilet flush. "I'll give him the pill, sit him down in front of the TV, then help you load." She took her jacket from the closet and slipped it on.

"Maybe I should carry him out to the couch," Montana said, nodding at Trace. "So you can strip this bed, too."

"Good idea," she said. "Let me get him into his sleeping bag, first."

"I'll help."

Together they pulled away the bedclothes, lifted Trace, and laid him on the open sleeping bag.

She heard the bathroom door open and shut and the sound of Rickie's slippered feet running down the hall toward the kitchen. She started to zip the sleeping bag shut.

"Orange juice, orange juice," she heard Rickie tell Jefferson.

She finished fastening the bag, then straightened. "I'll go give him the pill," she said.

Montana bent to pick up Trace to carry him to the living room.

Jefferson's voice, oddly tense, came from the kitchen. "Montana! I heard something outside. By the kitchen window."

The alarm in his tone prickled Laura's skin.

Montana stepped back from the bed, leaving Trace lying in the sleeping bag. He moved toward the door, his hand going to his holster.

Instinctively Laura followed, but he put out his arm, barring her way. She froze in the doorway, gazing down the hall toward the living room. She could see nothing.

Montana drew his gun and inched quietly down the hall. He had the tautly alert air of an animal preying.

Laura's blood drummed in her ears. *No,* she thought, sick with dread. *Not now. We've come so far.*

"Get back," Montana said over his shoulder.

Like a thunderclap striking in their midst, a barrage of gunfire ripped apart the air. Laura screamed and flinched convulsively against the door frame.

For an eternal second she saw Jefferson framed in the doorway at the hall's end. With one hand he gripped his gun, aiming it in the direction of the kitchen window. He fired, once, twice.

With the other hand, he seized Rickie by the shoulder, and half flung, half pushed the boy into the hallway. Rickie stumbled and fell, sprawling to the floor, crying out in protest.

Another fusillade of gunfire shook the air. Jefferson was flung back against the wall at the hallway's far end, blood spurting from his chest and shoulder. He propped himself drunkenly against the wall, and raised his badly trembling arm. Once again he shot in the direction of the window.

Laura screamed, "No! No!"

Jefferson still held his gun in his right hand, but he quit shooting. He stared down dazedly as the blood from his chest poured onto the green carpet. It spilled down his body and turned the carpet a wet, dark scarlet.

He's bleeding to death, Laura thought in horror. She tried to run to him to staunch the streaming blood. But Montana's arm shot out, blocking her.

"We've got to help," she cried, struggling to force her way past him. But her words came out like meaningless noise.

"Stay back. Get Trace. Get ready to go out the window."

"But—"

Jefferson still leaned heavily against the wall, a surprised expression in his eyes. He turned to face Montana and tried to speak. Instead of words, a bloody froth bubbled from his mouth.

"Help him!" Laura cried frantically. She tried to wrench past Montana, but he gripped her tightly and held her back.

With a slow gesture, like that of a weary ballet dancer, Jefferson turned his face to Montana and held his gun toward him like an offering. Slowly it slipped from his fingers and fell to the floor with a soft thud.

With a sigh, a terrible sound that gurgled with blood, he crumpled to the carpet, leaving a running smear of crimson, as wide as his body, on the wall.

"Get Trace," Montana ordered harshly, pushing her toward the boys' room.

He went to retrieve Jefferson's gun, leaping back as gunfire erupted again. He grabbed Rickie, who was screaming, and scrabbled back to the boys' room.

He pressed Jefferson's gun into Laura's hand. It was slippery with blood. "Take this," he yelled above the gunfire. "Use it."

Laura lifted Trace awkwardly, sleeping bag and all. Montana had Rickie in his arms and was at the window, heaving it as high as it would go. Rickie tried to twist away from him, still crying. Montana had wrapped him up in the red bedspread and it was trailing on the floor.

Montana lunged, his shoulder knocking the storm window out into the snow. The gunfire was so loud and insistent that Laura could not hear the crash of the window tearing loose.

We're all going to die, she thought, clutching Trace more tightly.

The window was a large one, set low, and Montana fired out of it twice, then nodded for her to go. The next thing she knew, she was halfway to her knees in snow, struggling not to fall or drop Trace.

Trace stirred fitfully in her arms, but didn't wake. Then Montana was beside her. The gunfire had stopped. She heard the crash of the front door being kicked in.

Someone was yelling, "Luppler! Luppler!"

"Don't say anything for twenty minutes," Montana said fiercely to Rickie. "It's a game. For twenty minutes. Don't say anything."

Rickie's lip trembled with anger and frustration, but he stared at his watch, which glowed in the dark. He kept staring, as if losing himself in its numbers.

Please, God, Laura prayed. *Make him stay quiet. In the name of the Father, Son, and Holy Ghost. Please. Please.*

"The barn," Montana said in her ear. "Keep low. Head for the trees. Stay in the pines until we can make a run for the barn."

Bent low, looking from side to side, he ran toward the pines, which loomed like a black and jagged wall in the moonlight. She followed blindly, Trace heavy in her arms.

She saw a man raise himself from the snow. She hadn't seen him before, but there he was, lifting himself, pulling himself upright, then taking a lurching step in their direction.

"They got out the side," he screamed. "They're getting away, you assholes!"

He had a gun, and he raised it as he took another drunken step. Laura ran more wildly, and tried to keep her body between the gunman and Trace.

But Montana stopped abruptly, turned, squeezed his trigger. The spurt of his gunfire flashed once, twice, as the report roared.

Laura didn't look back. She plunged in among the pine trees and kept running until she was deep inside the stand.

Then Montana was beside her again. "Don't stop," he said. "Go right."

"Did you kill him?" she asked, panting for breath.

"I think so," he said. "But there's more."

More, she thought darkly, too breathless, too frantic to talk. It had sounded like an army battering down the door of their house.

Vaguely she was aware of men's voices carrying across the night air, coming from the direction of the house. Her lungs burned, and hampered by Trace's weight she kept stumbling in the snow, which in places was drifted to her knees.

Montana took the lead. She tried to follow in his footsteps, but it only made her stumble more. The snow had soaked through her jeans, had gotten into her mukluks.

She wondered how long she could keep running. The voices in the background were louder now, clearer, although she couldn't understand what they were saying. Her blood banged crazily in her ears.

They're following us, she thought drunkenly. *They're following us, and I can't go much farther.*

But then, mercifully, Montana stopped. They had reached the edge of the woods where the pines most closely bordered the barn. Her heart hammered, her breath coming in ragged gasps.

The barn seemed millions of miles away, as if it lay on the other side of a vast arctic waste. Crossing that endless space, there would be no place to hide.

"Where are they?" she asked. Speaking tore at her chest and parched throat.

"They're in the pines, too," he said, wrapping the bedspread more snugly about Rickie.

A bedspread, she thought in despair, *a bedspread isn't warm enough*.

In the shadows, she could just make out Rickie's confused face. His chin quivered, and tears glinted in his eyes.

"Shhh," she said softly and pointed to her watch. He sniffled, but he nodded. He understood and gazed unhappily at his own watch. He choked back a sob.

"Good boy," Montana encouraged, and hugged the boy more tightly to him. "Good kid."

He turned to Laura, bending close to her. "We have to run for the barn. Are you up to it?"

She nodded, although in truth she was exhausted and shuddering from both cold and fear.

"Okay," he said. "I'll go first. I don't want them to get us both in their sights at once. If I make it, then you come. Stay low and run for all you're worth. Got it?"

She nodded again. Her teeth had started to chatter. She took a deep breath. "What if you don't make it?"

"Try to circle back to the house. Get to the van. And get away. Here." He put his gun under his arm, fumbled in the back pocket of his jeans for the keys, and tucked them into her jacket pocket.

"Okay," he said. "I'm going for it. I love you."

"I love you," she managed to say, her voice choked. Her vision blurred with tears that she blinked back, but he was already gone from her.

He ran with sure strides. He and Rickie looked so alone, so vulnerable in the snowy emptiness that her heart seemed to freeze.

She found she was holding her breath and forced herself to let it out. Then she heard an explosion; to the east the night sky filled with an orange-red glow.

"Oh, my God," she whispered.

They'd set the house afire. She thought of Jefferson, shot down without a warning or a chance. The house would become his funeral pyre. *Jefferson, I'm sorry. So sorry.* Again she blinked back tears. She forced her numb hand to clutch Jefferson's gun more tightly.

She realized, with a start, that Montana had disappeared from view. He'd made it. It was her turn. The empty white space yawned before her, and the child in her arms seemed impossibly heavy.

Then she heard a man's angry voice yelling something. In her confusion, she could not tell how far away it was.

"The bastard's in the barn," the man cried. "I saw him."

"Why didn't you shoot, *stupido*?"

"I saw him go in is all. He was there—he was gone. He's inside. He was carrying a kid with him, I think."

"Is the woman with him?"

"I don't know, man."

One of the men stepped out of the pines and into the moonlight. He was perhaps forty yards from her. If she ran for the barn now, he would get a clear shot at her.

Then a second man appeared, perhaps another ten yards farther away. Like the first, he carried an assault weapon.

Trapped, Laura watched them. She stayed where she was, holding Trace and trembling.

I won't give up, she thought. *I won't let us die without a fight.*

Santander was high on the excitement of killing. His blood throbbed. But his thrill was spiked with anger.

Luppler had had a chance for both the black man and one of the boys. But like the fool he was, he'd been shooting either scared or wild, and despite emptying fifty rounds into the house he'd killed only the man.

Now they'd lost De Mosquera—the white man had hit him first in the leg and then in the head, leaving De Mosquera with his skull shattered, his brains spattered across the snow.

Luppler had stayed behind to torch the house. Its light blazed the night sky in the east. Snow fell lightly, and the orange light gave it a pleasing eeriness.

Now he and Alvirez had at least the white man pinned in the barn, and maybe one of the children. Santander's guess was that the other two were with him, as well. The four were cornered like rats, and the rats, both big and little, would soon be dead.

Santander was too smart to rush the barn, for the man, after all, had a gun. But little good it would do him.

"Luppler!" he shouted over his shoulder. "Over here! The *yanquis* are in the barn! Bring the gasoline."

In a moment, Luppler appeared, sprinting awkwardly through the snow. He carried two cans of gasoline and the Calico slung over his shoulder.

Good, Santander thought with satisfaction. *He didn't use up the gas.* Perhaps Luppler was not such a fool as he seemed.

Santander's plan was to strafe the barn. They would shoot it so full of holes that anything inside, even anything so small as a field mouse, would be blasted to bits. They had ammunition enough to do it; they had enough ammunition to kill a platoon of men.

When they finished shooting, Santander would send Luppler to douse the barn with gasoline so that their enemies were finally consigned to hell in flames. Santander would have Luppler do it just in case, against all odds, the man survived and could still shoot.

Luppler reached them, panting. He handed a gasoline can to Santander. It felt half full, maybe five gallons left.

"The other can," Santander said. "It's full?"

"Yes. The house—" Luppler said, gasping for air. "The fire didn't want to take. But it did—Mother of God!"

Luppler seemed vivified and excited by the fire, which burned fiercely in the background. His eyes flashed in the moonlight, and his girlish face had turned hard and wolfish.

"They're in there?" Luppler asked, nodding toward the barn.

"Yes," Santander said. "Shoot the shit out of it. Start from this side. We need to get closer. Just a little. Stay out of pistol range."

Cautiously, they moved nearer. If the *yanqui* was fool enough to fire on them, they would see where he was, and would riddle that place with bullets. They would fill the wall with so many holes that it looked like lace.

"Enough. Here," Santander said. The three of them stopped, spread out slightly, like men at practice on a rifle range. Luppler set down the full gasoline can, and Santander put down the half-empty one.

They put their weapons to their shoulders. Santander's Uzi held thirty rounds; Luppler's and Alvirez's Calicos each held fifty. In their first burst, they would fire over a hundred bullets into the barn. They would fire a thousand before it was over.

"Start at the bottom," Santander ordered. "Rip it apart."

At that moment, a popping noise came from the pine

woods. Three sharp reports barked on the night air. Simultaneously, something hot buzzed Santander's cheek, like a bee of fire.

He'd seen the flash of gunfire out of the corner of his eye. *The woman—it had to be. And less than forty yards away.* Rage filled Santander. He spun angrily, aimed into the woods, and squeezed the trigger.

Alvirez caught on immediately, and joined him, opening full fire. Luppler simply stared at the woods, his mouth open. Together Santander and Alvirez fired eighty rounds into the pines.

"The whore," Santander said with contempt. "She hit me." He rubbed his stinging cheek.

"I thought she was in the barn," Alvirez said, sounding offended.

"You were wrong," Santander snarled. "I want to make sure she's dead. And see if she has a kid with her."

"What about the barn?" Luppler asked.

Santander looked at the blood that darkened his fingertips. His cheek had only been grazed, but it *hurt*. He would find the whore, and if she wasn't dead, he would set her on fire and burn her alive. If she had those imps from hell with her, he'd burn them, too.

"Keep firing at the barn," he said from between his teeth. "Do it until you're sure he's dead. Then set it on fire."

He slipped another magazine into the Uzi and made his way toward the woods, carrying the half-full can of gasoline. He moved carefully, ready to hit the ground in case she fired again.

He hoped he'd already hit her and she was lying in her own blood in the snow with the kids beside her, shot to pieces. Even if she was dead, he would burn her, and with pleasure. But first he would do all the obscene things that he could think of to her body. That would be her punishment and his pleasure.

He began to move more boldly. No more gunfire spurted from the pines. She—or what was left of her—was his for the burning.

.   .   .

Laura had taken cover to shoot, crouching behind a boulder of granite. When the men opened fire on her, she instinctively dropped flat to the ground, throwing her body over Trace's.

She and Trace were virtually buried in snow, and it burned her face and hands with cold. The bullets ricocheted off the granite with wild pinging sounds; they ripped bark and branches and needles from the pines.

The noise from Jefferson's gun had almost deafened her, and then the barrage of the men's bullets made her ears ring even more hellishly.

She thought of Trace, sick and still feverish, lying beneath her, crushed into the snow. He could die because of this; he could catch pneumonia and die. And she would have let it happen.

Then the men's guns went silent, and the silence seemed as loud as the gunfire. She waited a moment, counted to thirty, then peeped cautiously around the boulder. Her heart churned sickly. One of the men, the one who'd been nearest, walked purposefully toward her hiding place. He carried his large gun and a can like a gasoline can.

She licked the snow from her cracking lips, wiped it from her cheek. She pulled Trace to her, laying his cold face against her breast. She wrapped the sleeping bag more securely around him.

She picked up Jefferson's gun, not knowing how many more bullets it held. Jefferson had fired at least three times, and she'd fired three times, but she wasn't sure she'd kept count right. Did she have one shot left? Or more? Or none at all?

She'd hit none of the men as far as she could see. The knowledge made her sick with failure. Now one was stalking her, and the other two were raising their weapons again and aiming at the barn. They fired, and their volley roared, incessant, terrifying. She winced, breathing hard and chewing her lip.

She could wait for the man approaching her and try to shoot him when he was near enough. But she wasn't sure she could hit him; she was shivering too hard. And the gun barrel was clogged with snow. Would it even work?

Lead him away from the others, she thought, watching the man. *Get him away from the others. That's one less for Montana to face. If Montana's alive, maybe he can handle only two of them.*

If Montana was alive.

The other two men had reloaded and were sending another hail of bullets into the barn.

"My God," she said to herself hopelessly. "My God."

How could Montana and Rickie survive such a firestorm?

The lone man was still walking toward her, straight for her without wavering, drawing closer with a horrible inevitability.

She stood, her legs unsteady, and hoisted Trace so that his head rested against her shoulder. She was no longer cold, no longer exhausted, no longer weak. Sheer adrenaline drove her, and she ran harder than she'd ever run in her life.

Sometimes she stumbled in the drifts, but she always caught herself and kept running. The pines were thick, and the wind and snow stung her face. Then, through the dark trees, she saw the flat, white sweep of the pond.

The snow that fell on the pond's flat face drifted like surf before the wind.

If I cross the pond, I won't leave tracks, she thought, trying not to panic. *But I'll be in the open.*

Then she saw the ice-fishing houses, standing like frail sentinels on the pond.

She remembered that the door of one was unlocked.

Montana, waiting for Laura, had watched for her from the darkened barn through a crack in the door.

Come on, he'd thought. *Run for it. Now. Now. Now.*

Then he saw the two men emerge from the woods; he saw their assault weapons; he heard the explosion of the house. Stunned, he watched as the eastern sky flared orange.

And Laura—she was out in the pines, half to her knees in snow, alone with Trace.

She could not make it to the barn. She could not make

it to the van. The house burned so brightly that surely the van, next to it in the carport, was burning, too.

He held Rickie and felt a sickening dread. He knew what would happen next. The men would strafe the barn until they were sure he was either dead or wounded. Then they would burn it to the ground.

Rickie struggled. Montana knew the kid was cold, disoriented, and frightened by the absence of Laura and his brother.

Rickie made low, inarticulate sounds in his throat, but he hadn't spoken a word. He stared resentfully at his watch, and Montana could feel the frustration building to explosion level in the kid.

"Twenty more minutes," Montana told him. "You stay quiet twenty more minutes."

Rickie's eyes flashed with disbelief and his chin quivered. "Twenty more minutes," Montana said with ferocious intensity, trying to convince the kid. "Some bad men want to hurt us. We're hiding. Rickie has to be quiet."

Rickie, tears in his eyes, doubled up his fist and hit Montana in the shoulder as hard as he could. "Twenty minutes," Montana told him. "Be good. Twenty minutes."

Then, his eyes adjusting to the darkness, Montana saw the old cast-iron tub used as a watering trough. By God, no bullet would go through that.

He saw the sheets of corrugated iron roofing leaning against the wall.

Hell, he thought, he'd barricade the two of them. He'd take the kid and burrow behind all that iron as if they were a pair of cockroaches.

He holstered his gun and flung together a primitive, ramshackle fortress of roofing sheets around the tub. It was a pathetic shelter and a desperate one. It was all they had.

Montana was about to drag Rickie into the makeshift foxhole when he heard an unexpected sound.

Gunshots—handgun shots. Three of them.

My God, he thought, *Laura—is Laura shooting? They'll kill her in a minute.*

He allowed himself a swift glance out the door. There were three men now, and they were carrying gas cans.

Two of the men turned to fire into the woods. The barrage was followed by a moment of silence more silent than any he'd ever heard.

The man nearest the woods reloaded, picked up one of the gas cans, and with deliberation stalked toward the dark and silent pines.

He's going after her, the bastard. And any second the other two will start firing on the barn. One's already leveled his gun at it.

Montana dived for the cast-iron tub, dragging Rickie with him, and pulled a sheet of roofing over the two of them. He curled up as tightly as he could in the cramped space, his body wrapped around Rickie's.

Gunfire roared again, relentless and thunderous. Bullets ripped into everything around him. He heard them tearing through wood, ricocheting off metal, hammering the sides of his makeshift shelter, raining on its roof.

The bullets were an endless fiery hail. Sometimes the sound paused, only to burst out again, inexorable and ear-splitting.

He held Rickie more tightly. Bullets struck the rafters, raining chunks of wood and splinters down on the iron sheeting. Then the target must have been the loft, because the air was stifling with the dust and haze of hay drifting down.

Rickie coughed, but Montana barely heard him. How many rounds had been fired? A thousand? More? His ears rang so hard he could hardly think, and hay dust filled his nostrils, his throat, his lungs.

Then, as if by miracle, the world went silent again. His heart beating hard, Montana knew why. They were changing positions, probably drawing nearer as well.

Rickie coughed and sobbed. Montana didn't know if the kid was scared or angry, but his small body flailed, fighting hard to get away. He couldn't. Montana held onto him so tightly he feared he might hurt him. But he had no choice.

Laura, he thought in despair. If they'd hurt her, he'd kill them, even if he had to come back from the dead to do it. He swore he'd do it, even if they killed him.

But then there was no time to think because the bullets

tore through the walls again, deafening him. All he could do was hang onto the kid and pray. He heard wood ripping, metal ripping, and cast-iron ringing like a gong in his ears.

Then the rafters rained chunks and splinters down on them again, and he shielded Rickie as best he could. The barn shook with the onslaught, as if it were a massive creature systematically being riddled to death.

Montana's teeth rattled; he felt the barrage vibrate his innards and the very marrow of his bones. Then the loft was under attack again, and the air thickened with dust and shattered hay. If he and Rickie weren't shot to death, they'd choke.

He couldn't hear Rickie's coughing in the uproar, but he could feel it, convulsing and contorting the kid's body. "It'll be over soon," he yelled in Rickie's ear. "It'll be over soon, and then we'll go." He knew he yelled in vain. He couldn't even hear himself.

There was another pause. The silence rang like a great bell in Montana's head. Rickie's coughs had weakened until they sounded like the coughs of a cat. Montana wondered if the kid was going to pass out.

Then they were strafing the barn again, from yet another direction. Bullets crashed through wood, shrieked against metal. The fusillade came in hellish staccato beats.

He told himself to hang on, just hang on. Soon they'd be sure he was dead. They'd have to approach the barn to douse it with gasoline. That would be his chance to take them.

More pieces of rafters hurtled down on the sheeting. Montana was vaguely aware that his cheek was bleeding. He gagged and choked as another assault on the loft, a long one, filled the air with another suffocating cloud of dust and hay. Rickie went limp. *He's passed out*, Montana thought. Maybe he's better off.

Then the eerie, ringing silence descended again. This time the silence lasted. Montana wanted to get into the loft because he'd have the advantage of height and surprise.

The gunmen were probably approaching the barn. If they were smart, they'd be cautious. They'd take their time. But he could not take his time. He needed to move fast.

Carefully, he raised his head. He thrust his gun into the holster, picked up Rickie's sagging body, and made for the ladder. He climbed into the loft as quickly as he could, Rickie over his shoulder. The ladder was metal; its rungs were bent by bullets and one was chopped raggedly in half.

He dropped the kid faceup in the hay. The dust was still chokingly thick, but there was nothing he could do about it. He rose, drawing his gun.

He heard men's voices. They were approaching the front of the barn. Were they coming in to check the bodies? To count them?

He moved to the east door of the hayloft, which hung slightly open. The wooden bar that had held it fast had been shot off. It swung back and forth in the breeze, creaking slightly.

He stepped over to it and gazed down. Two men were just below him. Only two, he thought. He remembered the third man had gone into the pines after Laura and Trace. His jaw clenched.

They entered the barn. He moved softly to the edge of the loft. He could just make them out in the haze and the shadows. They could see little, he knew.

He started to take aim, knowing he had to get this right, he could make no mistakes. They had him outnumbered and outgunned; if he missed, he wouldn't get a second chance.

Then he heard Rickie stir in the hay, sigh, and give one of his little cat coughs. The sound seemed louder than all the gunfire of the night.

But the men, treading carefully through the hay and splinters, did not seem to hear.

Stay quiet, kid, Montana prayed, setting his teeth. *Stay quiet and let them move just a little nearer so I can get two good shots. That's all I need. Another sixty seconds. Two good shots.*

He steadied his gun hand with his scarred one, braced his legs slightly apart, the good old Weaver stance he'd learned in the police academy.

Come on, baby, come on, he thought, waiting for the

man in back to step just a little more into the open. *Two more steps and you're mine.*

But the man in the rear hesitated, looking around the shattered barn. He held his weapon ready.

"I don't like this," Montana heard him say. "Where are the bodies?"

"Maybe they're up there," said the man in front. He nodded toward the loft. If he'd looked hard enough, he would have spotted Montana through the haze and the shadows, waiting to get both men in his sights.

The man raised his weapon. "Maybe we should shoot straight up for a while," he said.

No, Montana prayed. *Thirty seconds more. Give me thirty seconds more and step this way. Just a few feet closer.*

At that moment, behind Montana, Rickie began to scream. He screamed on and on, like a lost and tortured soul.

EIGHTEEN

SHOTS RANG, ECHOING ACROSS THE NIGHT, COMING FROM the direction of the barn.

Santander heard the roaring crash of magazine after magazine being fired. Luppler and Alvirez were strafing the building into fragments. Santander felt a surge of satisfaction, but only a small one. What he wanted most was the woman.

His cheek stung where she had shot him, *la puta*, the slut, the whore. And now she was eluding him. He'd followed her tracks to the edge of the pond, and there they'd disappeared.

A shifting veil of snow scudded over the pond's flat surface, making footprints impossible, making tracking her impossible if she'd fled that way.

Shacks stood on the ice, and he knew what they were: fishing houses. Had she disappeared into one of them? Was she that scared, that foolish?

If she was there, he would find her, and when he did, he could kill her as slowly as he liked and any way he liked.

But what if she was trying to outsmart him? What if she had cut across the ice to head into another section of woods, throwing him off her trail? He rubbed his cheek and tried to outguess her.

If he stopped to search the houses, she could be running farther, every second putting more distance between herself and him. How would he pick up her trail again?

But he had to investigate. Perhaps she was trying to get the drop on him. She could shoot him through a door cracked open. Or perhaps she was simply exhausted.

He set down the gasoline can, raised the Uzi, and emptied its thirty rounds into the little houses, ripping a line of bullet holes right across their middles. He shot up the nearest house the most, so much that it actually danced on the ice, shifting its position almost a foot.

Devils and hell, he thought, lowering the gun. He would never know if she was in one unless he looked. He reloaded the Uzi, moved to the first house, and tried to ease open the door. It was locked.

Methodically he poured shots at the lock. He stepped to the side of the building and sprayed it with bullets, top to bottom, until the gun was empty again. He reloaded and kicked in the door, his gun ready, just in case she was inside, wounded yet still able to shoot.

But the house seemed empty. He lit his cigarette lighter and took a closer look by its flame. The bullets had knocked over two chairs and riddled an old coat that hung on a peg. A pair of fishing rods had been jarred from a crude rack and lay on the ice.

He backed out, leaving the open door creaking in the wind. He went to the next house. It, too, was locked. Once more he took aim and squeezed his trigger until the locks were blown apart; the door groaned and swung inward.

He systematically poured the rest of the thirty rounds into the interior. Then he put in an another magazine of ammo, kicked open what was left of the ruined door, and looked inside.

This house was even emptier than the other. It held nothing but a rusted tackle box dented and pierced by bullets. The wind whistled through the holes in the wooden walls. He lit his lighter again to make sure.

Nothing. He moved on to the next house.

.   .   .

Montana didn't have time to think why the kid was screaming. He looked down at the two figures obscured by drifting dust and shadows. He fired.

He fired eight times in rapid succession. No one fired back. He saw one man crumple, toppling forward into a heap. The other staggered backward, out of sight. Montana thought he'd hit him more than once, but wasn't sure.

Rickie shrieked more wildly and desperately, but Montana didn't let it register. He eased along the edge of the loft until he could see the second man, who lay fallen across a bale of hay. His head and one arm hung motionlessly over the bale, and Montana saw the hay darkening with blood.

The other man lay just as still, facedown on the floor. Montana took no chances. He emptied his gun into the two bodies.

Then he took a fresh clip of ammunition and slid it into the automatic. Keeping it aimed toward the bodies, he climbed awkwardly down the ladder.

Above him in the loft, Rickie still wailed and shrilled, but Montana ignored him. He knelt by the first man, rolled him over, felt for a pulse in his neck. There was none.

He went to the second man, and pulled him off the hay bale, onto the floor. He turned him over and felt his throat. There was no pulse there, either.

Montana felt no emotion except a weary cynicism. There was at least one gunman left, and he'd gone after Laura. And Rickie was up in the loft, screaming bloody murder without stop.

Montana shoved his gun back into its holster and climbed back to the loft. Rickie had scuttled to its farthest corner and sat, hugging his knees and banging his head against the ruined wall. His dirty face was streaked with tears, and his voice was raw.

Montana went to him, knelt by him, tried to draw him into his arms. Rickie cried harder, striking and kicking wildly. His cries grew so fierce they strangled in his throat, too shrill for his vocal cords.

Montana seized the boy by the shoulders and shook him, at first gently, then hard. "Rickie," he said, "stop—

stop. Tell me what's wrong. Are you hurt? Tell me where you're hurt."

Rickie shook his head and kept on crying, a terrible sort of crying because it made only high, choked shrieks and moans.

"Tell me where you're hurt," Montana pleaded. "I'll help."

Rickie shook his head and wept even more wildly. He pointed toward the center of the loft. At first Montana could see nothing. But Rickie kept sobbing and pointing, and seemed close to going into convulsions.

Montana rose and stumbled through the hay. The air was still thick with dust, and his head vibrated from the thunder of so much shooting. Rickie's screams only made it ache worse.

Then he saw it. Lying in the hay, its great, shattered wings spread, was a large gray-and-white owl. Bullets had torn its body half apart. But its head was almost untouched. Its sharp beak hung open as if it had screamed out in anger when it was hit, and its great eyes glared emptily at the rafters.

A bird, Montana thought. *A big, damned bird.*

He picked up the mutilated thing, and Rickie shrieked even more hysterically. The poor kid must have come to and found himself staring at the owl, his worst nightmare come true.

Montana moved to the loft door, kicked it open, and flung the bird as far as he could. Then he turned and went back to Rickie. This time he didn't let the kid fight him off. He gathered Rickie into his arms and held him so tight that the boy couldn't struggle away.

"It's gone," Montana kept repeating until Rickie finally quieted to tired, hiccoughing sounds and cried against his shoulder. "It's gone."

"Where?" Rickie snuffled. It was the first coherent thing he'd said. "Where?"

Montana remembered Laura comforting the boy about the picture of the swan on Stallings's tie. "Japan," he said from between his teeth. "The owl flew to Japan. It's gone now."

Then Montana heard the staccato of gunfire from the direction of the pond.

Laura huddled in the dark, four houses away from him. She couldn't see what he was doing, but she knew.

When the man had fired the first time, she'd been crouching on the icy floor, holding Trace tight. The bullets had missed her head by only inches.

When she'd first darted inside carrying Trace, she'd knocked against something leaning against the back wall. The rattle and unexpected contact had terrified her until she'd remembered what it was—chairs, folding chairs, stacked against the wall.

She'd cowered with Trace and hidden in the corner behind the chairs. She'd prayed that if the gunman opened the door, she and Trace would be concealed. He might not see them, he might go on.

But she'd underestimated him. He was methodically blasting the fishing houses into pieces, and she knew he would find her, perhaps kill both her and Trace before he even opened the door. She'd been foolish to hide in the house, for now they were trapped.

Her heart racing, she knew she had no choice. She must try to shoot him first. Her hands were numb, she was shaking, and she didn't even know if Jefferson's gun held any bullets.

Before tonight she had never shot an automatic. She'd been taught to shoot a revolver that held six bullets in its chambers. Automatics had clips, not chambers, but different automatics had different sizes of clips. Did she have two bullets left? Ten? None?

It didn't matter, she told herself; it was the only chance they had, and if she had any bullets, she'd have to hit him with the first shot. If she missed, he would know where she was, and he'd rip their fragile little shelter to shreds.

Freezing air flowed through the holes that gunfire had already torn through the walls. The holes were big and ragged, and she tried not to think what such bullets would do to a child's body or to hers.

She moved as soundlessly as she could, leaving Trace's

motionless body hidden behind the chairs. Crouching, she reached the door and eased it open an inch. She saw the gunman, and her heart felt as if a hook had caught it, hauling it out of her chest.

He stood with his back to her, aiming at the fourth fishing house. He was only two houses away from her and Trace.

Do it now, she thought. *Fire. Hit him in the back. If that doesn't kill him, shoot him again.*

He stood, his back still to her, reloading the Uzi.

Now—now! she thought. But again she hesitated, paralyzed by the enormity of what she was doing.

Then, very deliberately, she aimed for the center of his back. She bit her lower lip so hard she tasted blood. She squeezed the trigger.

"Shh," Montana told Rickie. "We have to get Laura and your brother. Shh."

"No more shooting," Rickie said, scrubbing the tears from his eyes with his fists. He sounded both angry and exhausted, and his voice was a raspy whisper. He'd screamed himself hoarse.

Montana took the boy's chin in his hand. "Don't cry," he ordered. "Don't talk. Don't make a sound. If you cry, the owl might come back. You have to make the owl stay away. Be quiet. Is your watch running?"

Rickie looked too terrified to speak, but he raised his wrist and looked at his watch with fearful eyes. The watch, Montana saw, still worked. Its luminous second hand swept slowly round the face.

"Be quiet for thirty minutes," Montana ordered. "Understand? Thirty minutes. Be quiet so we can get Trace and Laura."

Rickie's lower lip twitched, and fear and dismay shone in his eyes. But perhaps he was too spent to cry again. Or perhaps Montana's intensity had gotten through to him. He sniffled and looked sick with fright, but he made no other sound.

"Okay," Montana said. "Quiet. For thirty minutes. Even if there's more shooting, Rickie stays quiet. Now come on. I'll give you a ride. Put your arms around my neck. Hang on tight."

He held the boy to his shoulder. Rickie hung on tensely, hiding his face against Montana's neck. Awkwardly Montana climbed the ladder out of the loft.

Gaining the floor, he kept his right arm around Rickie. He bent and picked up a Calico that lay by one of the men. The guy had an ammo belt across his chest like a Pancho Villa bandit. Montana helped himself to a few extra magazines, just in case.

He heard gunshots again, a spattering of them. They came from the direction of the pond. Hurriedly, he pulled the dead man's jacket off and wrapped it around Rickie.

Rickie stared down at the corpses dispassionately, as if he didn't understand who or what they were and didn't care. He looked away from them and nervously up at the loft, as if he feared another owl might appear and swoop down.

Montana moved to the barn door, which stood open, its wood perforated with bullet holes. He looked about.

His mind spun crazily. He couldn't leave the child. But how in the hell could he take a kid to stalk a killer?

"You've got to do everything I say," Montana whispered. "Do what I say, and don't make a sound—remember?"

Rickie's eyes filled with tears, his face crumpled, and he put his hands over his ears. But he said nothing. He said not one word.

"Rickie has to save Laura from the bad man," Montana said. "Rickie has to save Trace, too. Stay quiet."

Rickie looked forlorn and kept his ears covered. He suppressed a sob.

"That's a good kid," Montana said. "That's a champ. Help me now. Help me, Rickie. Help Montana."

Montana hoisted the kid to his arm and hoped they wouldn't be mowed down crossing the snow. He ran for the pines, hugging the boy fast against him. From the direction of the pond came another spattering of automatic fire.

And then one gunshot, different from the others.

Laura, he thought, running harder, his breath tearing his lungs. *Laura.*

. . .

The gun kicked in her hand, almost knocking her backward. The shot's crash deafened her and resonated through her nerves like electric shock.

Horrified, she saw the man was still on his feet, but his body had hunched strangely. Then he vanished—lurching for cover behind another fishing house.

Frantically she kept firing in his direction, again and again. She didn't realize she was crying; she just kept shooting because it was the only chance they had.

She didn't know how many times she fired or if she hit him. She shot blindly, out of raw, frightened instinct.

Then the gun was empty. It only clicked when she squeezed the trigger.

She went dead still, listening. Her ears rang, but she could hear no sound but the sweep of the wind across the pond. The ghostly veils of snow flowed silently across the pond's surface. shifting, weaving. Of the gunman, she saw nothing, heard nothing.

God, let him be dead, she prayed. *God, please let him be dead.*

She knew her prayer was evil, but she didn't care. She realized her eyes burned, her cheeks were wet, her nose was running. She wiped her nose on her jacket sleeve, rubbed her free hand across her cheeks.

She looked at the gun in her hand, held it out, and tried to fire it again. There was only a click. She tried again. Another click. It was truly empty.

If the man was dead, she could take his gun. What her next step after that should be, she didn't know. She couldn't think clearly.

Behind her Trace stirred. "Mama?" he said sleepily. "Mama?"

"Shh," she said softly, automatically, "Laura's here." He stirred again and was silent.

She heard no more shooting from the direction of the barn. When had it stopped? The noise had paused before, but never stopped; it had sounded like a war. The silence didn't seem like peace to her. It seemed like death.

She suppressed a sob. Still holding the empty gun, she cautiously pushed the door open more widely. She would have to see if the man was dead. He'd never fired back. He must be dead. She must have hit him. Thank God she'd hit him.

Fearfully she stepped from inside the door and started to inch toward the house he'd disappeared behind.

Suddenly he was there, looming before her, his gun raised and pointed at her head. Her heart leaped insanely. She tried to scream but couldn't.

"Bitch," he said. "Whore. That's twice you've hit me." He took a limping step toward her. "You'll pay, devil's whore."

She could think of nothing to do but throw the gun at his head. She hurled it as straight and hard as she could. He turned to dodge it, and it struck him in the shoulder.

When it fell to the ice, he kicked it aside savagely. He strode toward her. She tried to shrink back from him, but he drew back his hand and hit her in the face so hard she felt a tooth break.

But the pain was phantomlike; she barely felt it. Fear was stronger. He hit her again, this time so violently that she was knocked off balance and fell heavily against the inside back wall of the fishing house.

"Stay there," he ordered. "If you want to make a run for it, try. I'll shoot your legs off."

She was too dazed to move. She lay on the ice as he backed off, keeping his gun trained on her. When he turned away and headed toward the snowy shore, she had the irrational desire to seize Trace and run.

But she was too weak and shaky to rise, let alone carry a child. She knew he meant what he'd said. He'd shoot her legs from beneath her. But whatever he did to her next, she knew, would be worse.

He hadn't seen Trace yet. Perhaps he wouldn't. Maybe even if the man killed her, he wouldn't find Trace. And maybe somehow against all odds, Montana would be all right, and *he* could save Trace.

It occurred to her hazily that Trace might be safer if she did run, only without him. If she ran, the gunman would shoot her out there on the ice or in the snow. He might not even come back to this place.

She crawled on her hands and knees to Trace, took off

her jacket, and laid it over the sleeping boy. Then she dragged herself to the door. If she could pull herself up by the door frame, then she would *make* herself run. She could do it. She knew she could.

But suddenly the man was there again, and once again he hit her so hard that she knocked against the back wall and fell to the ice.

She looked up at him. In one hand he still carried the gun. But in the other he had what looked like a gasoline can.

He took a limping step toward her. "Now, whore," he said from between his teeth, "we're going to have some fun."

She stared at him. Clouds dimmed the moonlight, and she couldn't make out his features. "What are you going to do?" Her voice shook.

"Maybe I'll shoot you in the legs, so you can't move," he said. "Shoot you in the hands, too. Then throw gasoline on this house. Set fire. You won't even be able to crawl away. You'll lay there and burn up alive."

"Why don't you give me a fair chance?" she said, her voice shaking harder. "Let me run for it."

"No. I like where I got you," he said. "Where are the others? The man was in the barn. He's burning up now, too."

"I'm a fast runner," she said. "You're afraid you couldn't bring me down. You don't have the *cajones*."

"The man," he said, stepping nearer. "Was he alone? Did he have one boy with him, or two? Where are the boys?"

"The boys are with him," she lied. "Let me run. You really don't have the *cajones,* do you? You can't shoot well enough. You're a coward and a bad shot, afraid to take a chance."

"Anybody else here?" he asked. "What's behind the chairs?"

Painfully she moved so that her body was between him and the chairs. "Nothing, she said. She could taste the blood in her mouth, and it tasted like despair.

"You don't *act* like nothing," he said contemptuously. He grabbed her by the arm, hauled her up, and threw her against the opposite wall so hard that for a moment she saw only darkness and spinning lights.

But when her vision cleared, he'd pulled the chairs away and Trace lay, unconscious and helpless, wrapped in the sleeping bag and jacket. The man reached into a pocket, pulled out a cigarette lighter, and flicked it on.

He stared down at the child's face with a satisfied twist to his mouth. He was, Laura saw, a cadaverous-looking man with hollow cheeks and a scarred complexion. The lighter's flame made pinpoints of reflected fire glitter in his eyes.

"Is he dead?" the gunman said. "Did I kill him?"

"No," she said fiercely. "He's medicated."

"Wake up," he said, bringing the light nearer Trace's cheek. "Wake up and die, *muchacho*."

He's going to burn him, Laura thought with a surge of anger. She lunged for him and struck his hand away with all her might.

She pushed herself between him and Trace, and she tried to wrest the gun away.

He called her a name in Spanish, snatched the gun from her grasp, and backed off. He spewed a long string of foreign curses at her.

Then he straightened and said, "Whore. For that, I throw the gasoline on you and the child."

He flicked the lighter on again. "And then I will set you on fire. Both of you."

He took a step backward, putting the lighter back in his pocket. He picked up the gasoline can and deftly, with his gun hand, he unscrewed the top. Laura snatched up her jacket from Trace, and when the man threw the first splash of gasoline at them, she held up the jacket as a shield.

"It's toreador you want to play?" he sneered. He tried to jerk the jacket from her hand. She struggled to hold it.

"*Toro, toro,*" he mocked her. "You're a fighter. You don't want to die. That makes it more fun to kill you."

Laura kicked at him, but she didn't let go of the jacket. He pulled so hard, she felt as if her fingernails were tearing out.

"Whore!" he cried and let go of the jacket. Then he lifted the Uzi to strike her with the barrel.

"Stop right there," a quiet voice said. "Drop the gun, fucker. Or I take your head off."

Laura dropped down, shielding Trace again. Her eyes widened, and her heart beat so hard she thought it would explode.

"I'm counting to three," said Montana's voice. "One. Two—"

But the man didn't drop the gun. He whirled and shot. Montana shot, too. She couldn't see him clearly, but she saw the orange-white flash of gunfire.

She pressed into the corner, keeping as low as she could. The gunman stopped firing. He staggered forward a few steps. Then he fell face forward on the ice.

The silence seemed louder than the gunfire. "Montana?" she called, her voice small. "Montana?"

"I'm here," he said. He stepped from behind the nearest of the fishing houses. All she could see was his silhouette. He moved toward her, something peculiar in his gait.

He stopped by the gunman's prone form, knelt, and turned him over. She rose, shaky, and made her way toward him. He held up his hand, signaling her to stop.

She paused, shivering, three or four paces from the gunman. He lay on his back in a twisted heap, breathing in gasps. A dark puddle formed on the ice beneath him. He lifted his hand a few inches as if his fingers were trying to claw a hold in the empty air.

The moon swam out of the clouds, and by its bluish light, she saw the man's eyes were open. He glared at her as if in his mind he was burning her, killing her.

Montana grasped the front of the man's bloody jacket, pulled him up so that his body arched in pain. "Who sent you?" he demanded. "Can you hear me? Tell me, you son of a bitch. Who sent you here to die?"

The gunman's glare, not quite focused, turned to Montana, and his mouth worked spastically.

"Who sent you?" Montana said through clenched teeth. "Whoever did it got you killed. They murdered you. Who did it? Who?"

The gunman's hand groped for Montana's. He said, his voice rasping, "We will kill you yet. You and your whore and your maggots. We never quit. Never."

Montana slammed him back against the ice. "Don't make me beg, bastard."

Numbed, Laura watched as Montana stuck his right thumb into a deep, open wound in the man's shoulder. She flinched at the strangled sound the gunman made.

"Montana," she said, "don't—please."

He ignored her, gouged the wound more deeply. "Tell me, damnit. Who sent you?"

The man's back arched again. His mouth worked frantically. He said something that sounded like "H-h-heffinger."

"Hepfinger?" Montana said with venom. "Jorge Hepfinger? Who else? You want to die easy? Or you want to die hard as you can?"

He drew the gunman's body up and slammed it against the ice again. "This is the fucking angel of death talking, kid," he said, bending closer. "Hepfinger and who else? Who, goddamnit?"

"M-mesius Estrada. That's all. Let me die in peace. *Madre de Dios. Madre de Dios.*"

Montana's lip curled. "What about Reynaldo Comce? Is that why they sent you here? To protect Comce? They let you come here to die for Comce? For a pretty little rich boy?"

"*Sí, sí,*" the man said, wrenching the words out. Again his hand clutched at the air. "*Reynaldo es un asesino . . . Reynaldo, no mí . . . deseo madre . . . deseo mama . . .*"

"What about Isaac Conlee of the task force? Is he in on this? Is he one of yours?"

"*No. No. Por favor . . . el dolor, el dolor . . .*"

"Who else is out there?" Montana demanded, lifting him by his jacket front again. "How many of you came? Are there more?"

The dark eyes rolled upward. The gunman's mouth went slack, he gave a long, rattling sigh, and his hand fell lifeless to the ice. His mouth still open, he lay with his eyes reflecting the cloud-dimmed moon.

Montana released his hold, letting him fall again to the bloody ice. He stared down at the bony, pitted face.

"Is he dead?" Laura asked. She could feel no horror, no shock; she could feel nothing.

"Yeah," said Montana. "He's dead. Remember what he said. About Comce. About Hepfinger and Estrada. It's important."

He shook his head and rose. He came toward her, limping slightly.

"Wh—who are Hepfinger and Estrada?" she asked numbly.

"Bad guys," he said and reached for her. "Laura, I'm sorry. I had to get it out of him. Remember the names. Remember those names, all right?"

Then she was in his arms. He gasped with pain. Her hand moved under his jacket, and his shirt front was sticky when she touched it.

He kissed her, but she wouldn't let him hold her close. "You're hurt," she said in alarm, drawing away and looking into his shadowy face. "Where?"

He kept one arm around her shoulder. "He got me in the ribs." She could hear him trying to bite back the sound of pain in his voice.

"How bad?" she asked.

"Hey," he said with a forced laugh. "I'm still standing. That's what counts. All that counts in the end is who's standing."

She looked at the dead man. She started to move toward him, but Montana held her back. "What do you want?" he asked.

"His shirt," she said. "I'll take his shirt, wrap your ribs. You're bleeding—"

"Later," he said. "I left Rickie in the woods. He's alone. Is Trace all right?"

She nodded mechanically, feeling like a dreamer who cannot escape from a nightmare. "Yes—yes. I'll get him. Then we'll get Rickie. And then we'll—we'll—"

She stopped. What would they do? The van was probably burned up. The house was gone.

"These guys got here somehow," Montana said. "Take his gun. There may be more of them."

"More?" She couldn't take any more. She forced herself to reach for the gun, and her stomach pitched when she touched it. But she took it.

She set it aside long enough to put her jacket back on

and button it all the way and turn up the collar. Its fur was damp from gasoline. She didn't want to think of that or talk of it. She knelt and took Trace into her arms.

Awkwardly she took up the gun again and stood. What a combination for a portrait, she thought darkly. *Woman and child and Uzi.*

"I'll carry him," Montana offered.

She shook her head. "Save your strength for Rickie."

Together they moved to the edge of the pines, began to follow the trail of his footsteps. The only sound was the wind and the crunching of the snow.

She'd been afraid to ask the question, but she forced herself. "Is Rickie hurt, too?"

"No," Montana said. "He's cold, he's confused, but I don't think he's hurt. But he saw an owl. It scared him."

What these children have seen, she thought, a wave of bleakness sweeping through her. *What they've been through.*

"He was more frightened of a dead owl than the dead men," Montana said.

"Dead men," she said with peculiar detachment. "You killed them?"

"Yes," he said.

"Good," she said. She didn't have the energy left to marvel at her new callousness.

"I'm sorry I couldn't stop him sooner," Montana said. "I couldn't get a bead on him. He wouldn't come out of the damn shack. Did he hurt you?"

"Some," she admitted. "I was too scared to feel it, mostly."

Her jacket reeked of gasoline, but she tried to ignore it.

She said, "I was scared for you. It sounded as if they shot the barn apart. How did you keep from getting killed?"

Haltingly he told her. "I never want to be in another bathtub as long as I live," he said with feeling. "I don't even want to see one."

Suddenly there was Rickie, standing by a tree trunk, shivering and looking at his watch. "Rickie!" she cried and ran toward him. "Rickie, it's Laura. And Trace. We're together."

Rickie looked up at her and gave her a weak smile. Laura almost stumbled in the deep snow, but in a moment she was at the boy's side.

She let the gun fall from her shoulder and pulled him to her in an awkward hug. She held both him and Trace as tightly as she could. She kissed Rickie's icy cheek.

"Tell me how you feel," she said. "Tell me if you hurt."

He wriggled in her embrace, but didn't answer. "Rickie," she said, drawing back and studying his confused face. "Laura's so happy to see you. Tell Laura if you hurt anywhere."

"He won't talk yet," Montana said. "The time isn't up yet."

Tears of pride stung her eyes. "Rickie, you're a good, good boy. One of the best little boys in the world."

Montana bent and picked Rickie up. The boy didn't like it, but he allowed it.

"Yeah," Montana said, and he couldn't keep the emotion from his voice. "You're a good boy, pal. You're a good kid. The best."

Laura knew it cost Montana pain to carry the child. He limped badly, but he said nothing.

Together they kept to the edge of the woods and made their way back toward the house.

It flamed upon the night, filling the sky with its eerie, dancing light.

NINETEEN

IT'S TOO MUCH TO TAKE IN ALL AT ONCE, LAURA THOUGHT. Numbed, she stood in the shadows at the edge of the clearing, hugging Trace to her, staring at the fire.

Parts of the house's skeleton still stood black and broken among the high flames, but the roof had caved in and the walls tumbled down in ruin.

The carport roof had collapsed on the van, and the van itself was a torn and blackened shell, its interior full of leaping flame.

We've lost Jefferson. He's gone forever, she thought dully. Smoke poured up from the blaze in dark billows, and its acrid stench filled the night.

Jefferson, a good man, full of kindness and courage, was dead in that inferno, his earthly body burning. She would never again hear his deep voice grumble or chuckle or joke, never again see his expressive eyes, his rueful smile. Her throat ached. For a moment she squeezed her eyes shut.

The house was gone, the van was gone. Everything that had sustained them during this endless chase was gone, literally up in flames.

She was stunned by shock and a sense of helplessness. The loss, especially of Jefferson, was too much to comprehend. Her mind simply could not accept it.

For reasons beyond logic, the only thing she could truly grasp was that the boys' possessions were lost. All those fragile, childish things that had given their world the illusion of order—destroyed. The patterned sheets and curtains, the cartoon plaques, the books, the toys, the battered Bugs Bunny lamp, the videos and maps and marbles and jars of pennies. All gone.

She opened her eyes again. Montana leaned against the trunk of a tall pine, clutching his side and watching wordlessly.

He had set Rickie down, and the boy was so rapt by the spectacle of the flame that he clearly did not understand what was burning. *At least God gave you that,* she thought. She bent and brushed a kiss against Rickie's cheek. He didn't seem to feel it.

"Rickie's going to be fine," she told him mechanically. "We're all going to be fine."

Montana spoke. "We're too near the light. We should get back."

The firelight flickered over his features and lit the grim expression of pain he tried to mask.

Without speaking, she backed further into the woods until she and Trace were deep within the shadows again. Even there, she could feel the heat from the monstrous fire.

Montana, the assault weapon slung over his shoulder, straightened. "Come on, kid," he told Rickie. "We're too close. It's dangerous."

Rickie stood as if rooted until Montana gripped the boy's shoulder and forced him to turn away. Rickie kept turning back to stare, but Montana urged him on.

With growing concern, Laura saw that Montana walked slowly, his limp more pronounced. The right leg of his jeans was shiny with blood from his side.

"We've got to do something about your wound," she said.

He shook his head. "Later. We've got to get out of here."

She nodded. In a dreamlike way she recalled the dead men whose bodies lay scattered in the night. Somewhere, not far down the lane, they must have left a car, a vehicle of some sort.

In the same surreal, hazy way, she remembered Montana saying there might be more gunmen. *More.* It really was too much to bear; she really could not think of that.

She looked at Montana and listened to his labored breathing. She set her jaw, shifting Trace's weight. The gun she hated so much hung over her shoulder. The child was heavy, the gun awkward, but she had to keep carrying both.

"We go by way of the woods again?" she asked Montana. "Right?"

He shook his head. "I'll go alone. Stay with the kids. I'll get the car and come back for you."

He had leaned against a tree trunk again.

"Let us go with you," she said. "You're hurt, and—"

He cut her off. "No. You've seen enough for one night. So has he." He shot a look in Rickie's direction. The boy stood staring back over his shoulder at the fire, still mesmerized.

"I'm afraid for you," Laura said.

"I can go faster without you," he said.

He seemed to wrench himself away from the support of the tree. He walked past her, one hand clamped to his side, the other steadying the gun. He walked too straight and too carefully, like a drunk fighting not to stagger.

"Montana . . ." Her voice trailed off because she was overwhelmed by new fear. She suddenly realized that he could not carry Rickie if he wanted to. He could hardly carry himself; he was hurt worse than he'd admitted.

He made a good fifteen paces through the pines. Then he stumbled, and her heart stumbled with him.

He paused, swayed, then straightened and kept on. But his careful gait was deteriorating, and he lurched as he walked. He stumbled again, and this time he fell to his knees in the snow.

"Oh, God, no," she breathed.

She ran to him, her steps awkward in the drifted snow. But by the time she reached him, he'd risen again. He stood, swaying a moment, then plunged on crookedly.

"Don't!" she begged.

He drove forward, but he gained only another dozen yards. Then he sank again, pitching forward into the snow.

She ran after him and fell to her knees as he struggled to rise again. She could see his blood, a thin stream of it, trickling into the snow.

"You can't go on," she pleaded. "You'll bleed to death."

His breath was ragged. "Don't leave Rickie alone. He could go too close to the fire."

"I'll bring him to you. You keep the boys. I'll go for the car."

"No," he said, struggling to rise. "Somebody might be there."

She shifted Trace to her left arm. With her right hand she gripped Montana's shoulder and hung on hard, too hard for him to spend the energy to fight her.

"If you go, you'll bleed to death," she said from between her teeth. "And then what good are you to us?"

It was the one argument that would give him pause, and she knew it. She pushed her advantage. "What happens if you fall over and die, Montana? We'll freeze to death waiting for you. You'll kill us all."

"There might be somebody waiting," he said through clenched teeth. "He'll be armed."

"And if there is, how much protection are you?" she demanded. "Lie down. I mean it, lie down. I read about a woman who got shot and would have died, except she fell in the snow. It slowed her bleeding."

He tried to protest, but she made him sink down into the snow. He lay on his back, his teeth gritted, his hand bloody against his ribs. "Lie there," she said. "Don't move. I'm going to lay Trace against you and get Rickie. And then I'm going for the car."

"Christ, Laura," he said, his voice a groan.

She lowered Trace so that his body was nestled against Montana's. Carefully she adjusted the sleeping bag so that it kept the snow from touching his face. She felt his forehead. It was burning hot.

She drew the sleeping bag more securely around him, covering his face from the cold air. She did not know what else to do for him.

Then she rose, waded back through the snow to

Rickie, and half carried, half dragged him to where Trace and Montana lay.

She knelt before the boy. "Rickie," she said earnestly. "Listen to Laura. Laura has to go away. Stay right by Montana. Don't move away until I come back."

"Cold," Rickie said, clearly miserable. "Cold. Go *home*."

He did not look at her, but back toward the glow of the fire. For the first time she realized he had no covering for his feet except his slippers. She felt sick with dread, and took his face between her hands.

"Don't move away until Laura comes back. Now come here. Take snow like this—" She pushed snow against Montana's bleeding side "—Keep the snow on Montana's side. Where Montana's bleeding. Rickie, keep snow there."

Obediently he crouched by Montana, pushing snow against the wound with his bare hands.

"That's Laura's good boy." She brushed a kiss on his cheek, but he flinched away from the contact.

"*Cold*," he said again, even more unhappily than before. But he stayed kneeling by Montana, his hands in the snow. He intended to mind her.

She turned to Montana. She ran her hand over his cheekbone, touched the corner of his mouth. "I'll be back. Don't die on me. Promise."

"Laura—" he said "—be careful. Don't be afraid to shoot. If somebody's there, ambush him. Don't let him see you—"

"I won't," she said. She touched his face one last time. "I mean it. Don't die. Please."

She stood and took the gun, the hated gun, from her shoulder and into her hands. She set off, moving as swiftly as she could through the shadows. Behind her she left Montana and Trace lying in the snow and Rickie, stolidly kneeling, pressing the packed snow against Montana's side.

The car phone rang. Hepfinger answered and heard Estrada's impatient voice.

"What's going on?" Estrada demanded. "Why haven't you called? Haven't you found them?"

"We found them, all right," Hepfinger said cheerfully. "The house is burning. There's been a good deal of shooting. They must have put up a fight."

"The shooting's over?"

"Yes. They must be cleaning up, getting all the bodies in the fire, something like that."

"Go check," Estrada ordered. "And when you're sure it's done, call me."

"Of course," Hepfinger promised in his chipper way. "Rest easy. I'm taking care of everything."

He switched off the phone with a sigh. He was more than ready for the twins and the others to be dead. It would be, as the Yankees put it, a feather in his cap. To have followed them this relentlessly, to have tracked them with such swiftness?—His praises would be sung, loudly, long, and oh, so sweetly.

Hepfinger folded the hinged receiver back into itself and put it back on the charger. He rolled down the window slightly and listened. There was only the wind's long, lonely sigh and creak of icy tree limbs. No more shooting.

He supposed, idly, that Estrada would have the three gunmen killed—Luppler, De Mosquera, and Alvirez. That way there would never be any danger of their talking of this night.

Perhaps Estrada would even have Santander killed; it would not be a bad idea. Santander was a bit perverse, Hepfinger suspected; he was not pleasant, and he was so damnably ugly. Hepfinger would have him shot for his complexion alone.

The chill night air flowed through the open window, and Hepfinger shivered a bit. He rolled the window back up and sighed. The van was warm and toasty, and he had lovely classical music on the CD player, Liszt's "Mazeppa," the Symphonic Poem Number Six.

But manfully he switched off the music, struggled into his coat, and pulled on his fur-lined gloves. He took a black watch cap from his pocket, pulling it down securely to cover his tender ears.

He reached to the back and took up a gun, an Uzi such

as Santander favored. He took an ammunition belt and slid it jauntily over his shoulder. Then he looked down the road one more time. Nothing out of place. No movement of any sort except the trees in the wind and the play of shadows on the snow.

Hepfinger was a meticulous man, so he would trudge the cursed quarter mile to the house through the woods, not the road. He certainly would never drive into a potentially dangerous situation; it would be far too conspicuous. This sort of caution at the expense of his own comfort had kept him the assassin instead of the assassinated.

He was glad he had let the others do the killing tonight. For one thing, it was too cold out to enjoy such diversions, and for another, he truly had no stomach for strenuous killing tonight; his supper of extra-crispy fried chicken had roiled his digestion. He loved rich fast food, but hated the heartburn it always gave him.

And, deep down, he was still secretly vexed over Marco DeMario. Hepfinger prided himself on his genial disposition, but DeMario had put him out of sorts.

He had meant to kill the old man eventually, of course. He knew a dozen ways to make it look accidental, even with the wounded hand.

But DeMario's excessive bleeding had taken Hepfinger badly by surprise. Hepfinger had misjudged the situation, his stride had been ruined, and he was still cross when he thought of it.

Yes, he would be relieved to get to Boston and on the plane that would take him safely back to Atlanta. Santander and the others would fly to New York; the Cartel men in Boston would dispose of the van; and then, once Reynaldo Comce was taken care of, this episode would be over. Closed.

Hepfinger tapped his fist against his chest, belched softly, and opened the door of the van. He would take the long, annoying walk to see that the killing was properly done. But he had been sitting in the van a long time. First, he would urinate. He faced away from the wind and unzipped his trousers.

·   ·   ·

Laura had run through the pines as lightly as she could, trying to make little noise. She kept her body low and stayed as near the road as she could without being seen.

But she was tired and ran awkwardly, wasting effort, and her footsteps crunched loudly in her ears. Her side hurt as if a knife were thrust into it, and her legs seemed more leaden at every forced stride. She was frightened and desperate, but she could not shake off the feeling that she was a ridiculous child playing soldier in the pine woods.

She'd run off, perhaps leaving Montana to die. *Please, God, don't let him die.*

Trace lay abandoned and feverish in the snow. If she didn't get help, he would catch pneumonia; his lungs would fill, and he wouldn't be able to breathe. *Please, God, don't let him die.*

She had left Rickie behind, exhausted but obedient, with nothing on his feet except his slippers and with his bare hands in the snow. He wouldn't move until she returned. What if she didn't come back? He would stay until he passed out from cold and exhaustion, and he would freeze to death where he fell. *Please, God, don't let him die.*

What if she did find a car standing there empty but without keys? What if the keys were with one of the fallen men? She would have to retrace her steps, search the dead, perhaps all of them, and she'd lost track of how many dead there were.

She shuddered spasmodically. There was no time to turn back. Time was running out.

Please God, don't let them die.

The farther she ran, the more hallucinatory the world seemed. What if the car was waiting—but miles away? Sheer adrenaline and willpower kept her moving, but how long could she last? She was dizzy with breathlessness. Her lungs burned, her ears roared, and strange, tiny lights snapped at the edges of her vision. She already felt faint enough to fall, and tired enough never to get up.

But then, glimmering in the moon's unsteady light, she saw *it*. A van was parked at the snowy roadside.

She'd been so intent on running, she'd almost passed by, not even seeing it.

Slow down! she commanded herself. *Think straight. You have to get this right. You won't get a second chance. Montana can't save you this time.*

She backtracked a few yards, until she could clearly see the van through the trees. She forced herself to move as quietly, as economically as possible. She breathed in gasps even though she struggled not to gasp, to be silent. Her head swam; her knees threatened to buckle.

But then the door of the van opened, and a man stepped out, locked it, then put the keys in his pocket. He was a fat man with an ammunition belt slung over one shoulder and a gun much like hers over the other.

He turned, standing in profile to her, and unzipped his pants. She watched, strangely embarrassed to see him urinating in the snow.

She crouched and raised the gun, trying to get him in her sights. The gun wasn't enormously heavy or bulky, but it was strange to her, and she was shaking so hard she couldn't hold it steady.

Tears of frustration welled in her eyes. She couldn't help it; the gun jittered and jumped in her hands. This wasn't like shooting at the man at the fishing houses. He had threatened her and Trace's lives, and shooting had been an instinctive act, one of survival.

The van's driver zipped up his pants, took his gun from his shoulder, and stepped in her direction.

He's coming into the woods, she thought in panic. *He's coming straight for me.*

Had he heard her? No, he moved too casually, lazily, almost reluctantly.

She wouldn't have to kill him if she wounded him so that he couldn't shoot—she could aim at his arm. But that wasn't possible because she couldn't hold the gun that steadily.

She would have to aim at his body and fire repeatedly. *I have to kill him in cold blood. I have to kill him now.*

He moved through the trees in her direction, slowly, almost daintily, watching where he set his feet. He held his gun ready.

Images cascaded through her mind like cards falling from a pack. She saw old Mr. Zordani, his chest turning into gory wreckage before her eyes.

She saw Becker standing at the gate at Valley Hope, his fingers suddenly turning to red stumps. She saw Jefferson staring in stunned disbelief as his lifeblood poured out, soaking the green carpet.

She saw Montana bleeding in the snow, Trace nestled unconscious beside him, and Rickie crouched beside them, his hands in the snow.

She smelled the sharp scent of gasoline on her jacket. These men would have burned her and Trace to death. These men would have murdered them all.

The man was only four or five yards from her. She held the gun as steady as she could. The words Montana had so often said spun through her mind: "We do what we have to do." For the first time, she understood him, completely and perfectly. *We do what we have to do.*

She squeezed the trigger, firing again and again.

The man rose up on his toes, almost as if he were a mime ascending invisible stairs. Then he danced a few stumbling steps forward, his arms flailing. His gun flew off into the shadows. He started to fall forward, his arms thrown out as if in amazement. He seemed to fall in slow motion, taking forever to hit the snow.

She fired until she had no more bullets. Then the gun was silent, and the man lay facedown in the snow.

She crouched as if paralyzed, still squeezing the trigger, even though the gun had gone silent. It had kicked hard, bruising her shoulder, but she was only vaguely conscious of the pain.

The man did not lie completely still. He rolled to his side; his legs twitched.

Laura rose, her own legs weak. She went to his gun, which lay beneath a pine. She picked it up. Then she walked to the man's side and looked down at him, feeling hollow and unreal; *I did not do this thing. This is a dream.*

He was breathing, but irregularly, and each time he inhaled or exhaled, he made a broken, sucking noise.

His leaking blood stained the snow. Blood dribbled

from his chest and upper arms. His fingers fluttered weakly, like those of an old man picking feebly at nothing.

She knelt beside him. Gingerly, she turned him on his back. Her stomach pitched with nausea. His chest was a ruin of blood. She had done that to him.

He stared up at her, his gaze glassy and unfocused. *"Quién es usted?"* he said in a choked voice. "Who are you?"

Her hand trembled as she reached to his jacket pocket for the keys. "I'm Laura," she said mechanically. "Laura's here."

"Puta," he gurgled. "Devil's bitch. Help me. Help me—*socorro!*"

He cursed her at the same time he begged her for help. Tears burned her eyes again, blurring her vision. She forced her hand more deeply into his pocket.

Her fingers closed around the keys, and she drew them out, her hand shaking.

He seized her by the hand, his grip surprisingly powerful. "You—" he said, in an accusing, angry voice. "You—*you*. You're nothing but a teacher of idiots. That you should do this to me—to me—"

His body convulsed, and his legs kicked impotently.

"Nothing but a little teacher," he said between his teeth and kicked again. "A woman. Nothing but a woman—"

Then, his gaze looking past her, he went still. The rasp and sucking noise of his breath ceased. His hand fell away from her wrist.

"I killed you," she whispered in disbelief. And then, even though it was irrational, she said, "I'm sorry. I'm sorry."

She stood, her knees shaking, and made her way, stumbling, toward the van. She fumbled with the lock, finally got it, opened the door, and climbed in, slamming it behind her.

She put the key into the ignition, and stepped on the gas. The thing started. Her heart wrenched from its too-swift pace and missed a beat. She searched for the head-lights, found them, and switched them on. Grinding the gears slightly, she put the van into drive. It lurched forward. She was not used to a vehicle this large and power-ful; her blood jarred fearfully in her veins as she stepped on the accelerator.

As swiftly as she dared, she drove back toward the fire. She stopped parallel to the place in the woods where she had left Montana, Trace, and Rickie.

She kept the motor running and opened the door. When the overhead light came on she noticed, for the first time, the phone. *The phone,* she thought. *Get help.*

She picked it up, her hand trembling harder than before.

She knew they were on the run, that they shouldn't ask for help, but she had no choice. Montana might die if she didn't. And the boys needed more help than she could give.

She willed her hand to be steady so that she wouldn't misdial. She punched out the emergency number, 911.

A man answered almost immediately. "Merrimac County Sheriff's Office."

"I need help," Laura said, her voice tight. She couldn't get her breath, and her chest hurt. "There's a man shot here. Bleeding badly. The house is on fire. There are two children in the snow—and some—some people are dead."

"Ma'am, try to be calm. Where are you?" he asked.

"Outside Hooksett. Off the Londonderry Turnpike. Listen, this man is bleeding a lot. I'm going to drive him into town. Is there a doctor there? We need an ambulance—"

"Ma'am, don't try to move him. Let us. Now tell me exactly where you are. Stay calm. Talk to me."

"He's lying in the snow," she protested. "He'll freeze. I can get him to the van. I can get to Hooksett, but we need an ambulance. And police. All kinds of police. Every kind. Please—help us. He's been shot."

"Ma'am, I'm dispatching that order. But don't move him. We can get an Emergency Medical Treatment and an ambulance to you in a few minutes. Give me your location and stay where you are. Do you hear me? Stay where you are."

"Send the closest doctor, the closest police," she insisted, fighting tears again. "Hurry. This man's a federal attorney. We have children with us. Th—there are three men dead, maybe four. Maybe more. The house is burning."

There was a moment of silence. "Jesus Christ, lady, what *is* this? Where are you? Pinpoint it for me."

"Londonderry Turnpike," she repeated. "Two miles out of Hooksett on Daniel Road . . . Hurry—please."

"We'll be there, lady. We'll be there. Hang on."

Numbly she hung up. She wiped her eyes and took a deep breath. Leaving the van door open, she ran on unsteady legs into the shelter of the pines.

She found Rickie still kneeling, pushing handfuls of snow against Montana's side. He was shaking and crying.

"Rickie," she ordered. "Laura's here. Get in the van and sit down. Hurry. Do it now."

He nodded and rose shakily. He staggered toward the glow of the headlights. She knelt beside Trace. Montana lay next to him, his eyes closed.

"Montana," she begged, "can you hear me? I've got the van. I've called for help. They're coming for us."

His eyelids fluttered, opened, but he didn't turn his head. "Laura?" he said dully.

"Yes. Lie still until I get back."

She snatched up Trace and carried him to the van. She carried him awkwardly because she had hardly any strength left. She unlocked the back door and lowered him to the seat. She tried to tuck the sleeping bag around him more snugly, but made a bad job of it. He shuddered and coughed in his sleep.

Rickie sat crouched in the front seat on the passenger's side, hugging himself, still crying.

She climbed in beside him, searched for the heater, and turned it on. "It's all right now," she told him. "Cry if you want. But you can be warm now and rest. Laura's here. Laura loves you. Laura will take care of you."

She got out, shutting his door and Trace's. She labored back through the snow to Montana. She found him kneeling, trying to raise himself. The snow was dark with blood beneath him.

"Lie down," she said, crouching beside him. "Help's coming. It'll be here soon. Lie down. I'll try to stop the bleeding."

He ground his teeth as he sank back to the snow. "Laura," he said, "what happened?"

He lay clutching his side and shivering. She stripped off her jacket and covered him with it. "There was a man," she said, trying to tuck the jacket around him more snugly. "I—I shot him."

"Oh, God," he said and shuddered. "God. D-did he hurt you?"

"No. He never saw me until it was too late."

His body gave a convulsive jerk. He squeezed his eyes shut. She seized his hand and squeezed it.

"Laura?"

"Yes?"

"Is he dead?"

"Yes," she said, feeling hollow and lost.

He convulsed again, and his hand tightened around hers.

"But—" he gasped "—you called for help?"

She lowered herself next to him and laid her cheek against his. "I'm sorry," she said. "I had to. I'm sorry."

He turned his face so that his lips were close to hers. "Listen," he said. His voice sounded drunken, but she sensed the urgency in him. "Don't say anything about killing him. Promise me that. Don't implicate yourself. Tell them only the basics. And get the word to Conlee. Tell him about Hepfinger and Estrada. Say it's a conspiracy to murder."

His face contorted and his body stiffened in pain.

"Montana?" she begged, clutching his lapel.

He drew his breath in sharply. "Tell Conlee about Hepfinger and Estrada. Conspiracy to murder, tell him that. But not about Reynaldo Comce. Not yet. Promise me that."

"Not about Reynaldo Comce," she repeated.

She didn't even know who Hepfinger and Estrada were, and she no longer cared about the tape or Reynaldo Comce or anything except the people she loved.

"Promise," he said. "You've got to."

"I will," she said, laying her forehead against his. "I promise. Now be still, Montana, please."

"No," he said. "Listen. If I can't talk—if something

happens, wait till the tape comes out. Don't say anything about Comce until then. Maybe I can—maybe I—you've got to trust me. Can you—"

"I promise," she said "Lie down—please."

He sank back to the snow again. His hand went to her shoulder, tightened spasmodically, then went inert and fell away.

"Montana," she breathed, frightened, "don't die. You promised!"

He did not respond.

Behind her the house still burned, casting its queer light on the softly falling snow.

In the distance a siren keened, drawing closer.

Desperately she gripped Montana's hand. It was a futile gesture.

From another direction another siren wailed, coming for them. Soon they would be in custody.

The whole run had been for nothing.

TWENTY

FOR LAURA, THE NIGHT PASSED IN A HAZE OF UNREALITY. She realized, dimly, that she was in some sort of shock. She could walk, she could talk, but she felt numb, divorced from herself.

It had seemed to take an eternity before the ambulance came. It took another eternity for them first to load Montana and Trace into the ambulance, then to help her and Rickie.

Rickie refused to go to anyone except Laura, so she held him during the ride into Manchester. He buried his face in the curve of her neck, sucked his fingers, and would look at nobody else.

In Manchester, they let her stay with the boys, but wheeled Montana, still unconscious, away. She stared after him, dazed and distracted.

"Honey," a nurse said kindly, "that boy's heavy. Let me take him. You sit down, let a doctor look at you."

"No," she said, hugging Rickie closer. "I take care of him. It's my job. Call Isaac Conlee. Tell him the names Estrada and Hepfinger. Conspiracy to murder. Tell him that."

The state police shot question after question at her, but she remembered Montana's injunction and told them only the barest details.

They kept asking, "What happened?"

"Some men tried to kill us. Call Isaac Conlee of the Organized Crime Task Force in Manhattan. Please."

Why?

"We saw a murder. They didn't want us to testify. Call Isaac Conlee of the task force. Please."

Who were the men who had attacked them?

"I don't know. Two men named Estrada and Hepfinger sent them. They should be arrested for conspiracy to murder. Tell Isaac Conlee. Please."

The interrogation dizzied her, made her head ache. The questions kept coming, wave after wave of them. Who was she? Who were the boys? Who was the wounded man? Why were they in New Hampshire?

"I can't talk about it any more. Except there was another man with us. His name's Jefferson. They killed him. He was a good man. He saved one boy's life. I—it's wrong he's dead."

Whenever she got to the part about Jefferson, she cried.

At last they stopped trying to question her.

The rest of the night, time passed in a slithery, unearthly way. She thought she'd been tranquilized, and Rickie, too. It seemed to her she slept, but she couldn't be sure. Waking and dreaming were equally disjointed and unreal.

The next day was little better. She was told that Trace had a touch of pneumonia and Rickie's fingers and toes were frostbitten. She couldn't stop watching the boys for signs of more serious illness or injury. She watched over them as fiercely as a tigress guarding her cubs.

Rickie was hyperactive; Trace was unsettled and irritable. She had her hands full with them. She concentrated all her energy on the boys so she would not have to think of Jefferson or Montana.

When she let herself think of Jefferson, she went on a crying jag that she couldn't stop. When she thought of how badly Montana was hurt, she was frightened nearly sick. A nurse assured her that Montana was fine, but she didn't believe her. She no longer believed anything or anybody except Montana.

That afternoon, she was told that she and Rickie and Trace would be flown by helicopter back to Manhattan, to a bigger hospital. Against her wishes, a nurse sedated the boys with shots. She herself refused to be tranquilized.

A doctor said Montana was in fair condition and would be taken to the same hospital that afternoon. She didn't really believe him.

At the Manhattan hospital, she and the boys were put in a room guarded by U.S. marshals. Two men who identified themselves as members of the task force came to question her.

She thought of Jefferson, and once again tears overpowered her. "I can't talk about it," she said. "There are some men named Hepfinger and Estrada. They committed conspiracy to murder."

"Now, Laura," one of the men from the task force said, putting his hand on her arm. "What exactly did the twins see? Do you know? Why would Estrada want them out of the way?"

She looked at his hand on her arm as if it were a large and poisonous spider. She set her chin at a stubborn angle even though her voice was choked. "Where's Montana? *How* is he? Is he here?"

The man patted her arm. Perhaps he thought his touch comforted her. It didn't.

"Montana's here," he said reassuringly. "And he's fine. Just fine."

She didn't believe him.

"Laura, I understand," he said. "But right now let's think of you. You've been through a lot. Is there anything we can get you? Anything you want?"

She took a deep, shivery breath. She straightened her back and looked him in the eye.

"Yes," she said as evenly as she could. "I'd like a Bugs Bunny lamp and two sets of sheets with Daffy Duck and Sylvester and Tweety on them. And matching curtains. I want a bag of fifty plastic lizards, a Chinese checker game, and two quart jars of pennies."

He looked at her as if she were certifiably mad.

She set her jaw stubbornly. "And I want them now," she said with feeling. "I want them *right* now."

They wouldn't let him see Laura. They kept telling him she was fine, but they wouldn't let him see her or talk with her.

It was the same with the kids. The boys were in good condition, they assured him. But he hadn't seen this for himself; he wasn't allowed to.

His hospital room closed in on him like a prison cell. The only touch of cheer was ironic, a cheap bouquet of red carnations from the task force office. Technically, he was under arrest.

The door was guarded by two federal marshals, and Montana's only visitors were lawmen. Detectives from the New Hampshire State Police came, as well as those from New York. FBI investigators took their turn, and DEA agents, and two men from the task force.

During their earliest visits, Montana was groggy and doped by pain, and he told them little. First, he said, get Estrada, get Hepfinger. The charge was conspiracy to murder, he said. When the two Colombians were in custody, he said, then he might talk.

The lawmen nodded wisely and informed him that they would pursue all leads. Then they tried to pry more information from him. They might as well have gone outside and talked to the rocks.

Everything Montana heard about Laura and the twins was hazy and imprecise. Laura and Rickie, he was told, were in "excellent" condition. Trace, fighting off pneumonia, was "good."

One of the task force men showed Montana a copy of the *World Weekly Record*. He'd never had a chance to see it.

On page six was an overblown story about how the twins and Laura had been forced into hiding. Their pictures were there, enlarged, fuzzy, but clearly them, for all the world to see.

Montana had turned away wearily and stared at the wall. This was the story they had tried to outrun. They had failed. Now everyone knew about her, about the boys. But no one would tell him anything.

At last, the second day after the shootings, Montana had a visitor who might be privy to some answers. Conlee appeared, but he looked about as concerned, genial, and charitable as a carrion crow.

Montana had four pints of nice, fresh blood in him, and he could sit up without the world spinning around, but the effort hardly seemed worth it. His head ached, his ribs ached, his whole body ached. He cast an unfriendly look at Conlee.

Conlee sat down without being asked. "Tell me what happened at Hooksett," he said brusquely.

"I already made a statement," Montana said, surly. "I've got nothing to add. Did you get Estrada? Hepfinger?"

"We'll come to that," Conlee answered. "First, what in hell happened? I want to hear it from you."

Montana didn't intend to talk about Hooksett. He hauled himself into a sitting position, even though it made his head bang. "I've got my own questions," he said. "What have you done about Hepfinger and Estrada?"

"I said later. Give me your version of events. The woman won't talk. She won't say anything except the same goddamn thing: Hepfinger and Estrada."

Good for her, Montana thought. "How is she? And the kids?"

"They're fine," Conlee said sourly. "Except she's stonewalled us for two straight days. What the hell do you know? Or pretend to know? What did those kids see?"

Montana eyed Conlee coldly. "It's not just what they saw. It's what we heard. That bastard on the ice, whoever he was—"

"Santander," Conlee said. "His name was Santander. He was one of Estrada's men. Yeah, he's connected to the Cartel, all right."

"I told you all along the Cartel was in this," Montana retorted. "He named names. He said enough to make the Cartel nervous, very nervous."

"Fine. But *why's* the Cartel in it?" Conlee demanded. "All the Colombians we haul in say the same thing—this wasn't their problem. The problem belonged to Dennis Deeds."

"Dennis Deeds couldn't find his ass in the dark with both hands," Montana said contemptuously. "He couldn't know about Valley Hope without the Cartel's help. And he couldn't have tracked us to Hooksett."

"Then answer me this. Why the hell do the Colombians *care* if the kids saw some nickel-and-dime hit man hired by Deeds?"

"Because it wasn't any nickel-and-dime hit man," said Montana.

"Then who the hell was it?" Conlee demanded.

"Somebody you'll never touch," Montana said. "The CIA won't let you. So the name doesn't matter—to you. But it does to the Colombians."

"What're you talking about?" Conlee demanded. "You're talking like you want to cut a deal with the Colombians, for God's sake."

"Exactly," Montana answered. "And I want you to contact them and say just that. We made a tape. The twins are on it. They identify the guy. Positively. Tell the Colombians we can make this tape public at any time. Unless they meet our demands."

"*Your* demands?" Conlee said in disbelief. "Who do you think you are?"

"A man with a bargaining chip," Montana said. "I'm making them an offer they can't refuse. If they want the tape suppressed, I want four things."

"Four things," Conlee mocked. "The Taj Mahal, an emerald mine, eternal life, and what else—Ecuador?"

"First," Montana said, "have you got Estrada, and second, what about Hepfinger?"

"Estrada, no," Conlee said, his expression going bitter. "He went to Colombia by private plane."

"Since when?"

"Since the other night."

"The night we were ambushed?"

"Approximately," Conlee admitted.

"Approximately," Montana jeered. "Listen to you, Conlee. All right, I want four things. Estrada's one of them."

Conlee gave a mirthless snort. "We've got federal warrants out. But we'll never extradite him. Not from Colombia. You want him, you're going to have to wait for him to get cocky and come back to the States."

Montana went silent for a moment. Then, very deliberately, he picked up the vase of carnations from the bedside table. He drew back his arm and hurled the vase at the opposite wall. Glass shattered, water drenched the wall, and glass, water, carnations, and fern spilled to the floor.

Montana was grandstanding, and he knew it. But he'd gotten Conlee's attention.

"Fuck your warrant and fuck extradition," he told Conlee. "I said I want Estrada. I want him, or the tape's made public. If it embarrasses the CIA, you take the fall."

"Montana," Conlee snarled, "why should the Colombians listen to you?"

"Because they *have* to listen," Montana said. "And they know it. I said I want four things. The second?—I want Hepfinger."

"We're going to have a little talk about that—later," Conlee said without emotion. "I think we can meet that demand. What else?"

Montana wondered what Conlee meant, but he didn't stop to ask. "I want to know who leaked our relocation to Valley Hope. I want to by God know that. And fourth—I want the safety of the twins and Laura Stoner guaranteed. I mean *guaranteed*. Anything happens to them, the tape is made public."

"Montana, you got delusions of grandeur—"

"Four things, Conlee. Four things or that tape airs in less than a week. And nobody but me can stop it."

Conlee held up his hand to silence Montana. "This is ludicrous. I'm supposed to call Diego Carmago? Tell him he has to meet the demands of some half-assed assistant attorney—"

"Precisely."

"—and I don't even know what's at stake? Come clean, Montana. What exactly do you know?"

"No," Montana said. "When your people know a secret it doesn't stay secret. What you protect doesn't stay protected. I'm going around you. It's the only way left."

Conlee was silent for a long moment. He stared with distaste at the water stain on the wall. "I'll see what I can do," he said.

"Yeah," Montana said. "You do that."

On this same day, in a hospital in Tahiti, Burton Fletcher had been told about his sons. He was distraught when he heard what they'd been through and exasperated that he hadn't been informed sooner.

Burton could both walk and talk now. He walked with feeble, uncertain steps that sometimes veered sideways when he meant to go straight. He talked with hesitation and a slur, and he had odd gaps in his memory.

He could not, no matter how hard he tried, remember how he had come to be in a hospital in French Polynesia. He had trouble remembering why he'd been in French Polynesia in the first place. His emotions were raw and unstable, and he had fits of weeping.

When he fretted during daylight hours, he was comforted by a pretty little part-Tahitian nurse named Marie Therese, who took special interest in him and gave him sympathy.

It was Marie Therese who broke the news to him about Rickie and Trace. She knew only the sketchiest outline of what had happened and ended with, "Your sons were in trouble, but now they're safe and well. You'll soon be well, too."

Other people told him the same thing. His sons had been in serious danger, but now they were fine and under protection.

The twins, he was told, were in a hospital, just as he was, but they weren't hurt. They were presently being held for observation, and their teacher was with them. People said he owed a debt of gratitude to this woman, that she had helped to save their lives. She and a man had done it, and another three men had died trying to protect them.

The thought of his children in peril, of people risking their lives for them, caused Burton to cry. He wanted to go home. He wanted to see his two sons again. He realized that he loved them, even though he knew they could not return his love, not in expected ways.

He had been wrong and foolish to reject them. When he was hurt, he'd had complex dreams of how happy he had once been with them and with his wife. They were all that was left of Mary Catherine. She would hate that he had turned from them. He had hated himself for it.

Burton insisted on talking to his sons by phone. Marie Therese helped him put through the long-distance call and held his hand while he talked to their teacher and to them.

The teacher, Laura Stoner, sounded guardedly upbeat. She assured him that the boys were fine. "Right now they're restless, that's the worst. They're full of energy. If we had chandeliers, they'd swing from them."

"How are they—emotionally?" Burton asked in his halting way. Marie Therese squeezed his hand. "I—I was told there was a fire? And shooting?"

Laura Stoner paused. "They're confused. And disoriented. But they're coping. Trace doesn't know what happened that night. He just knows that now things are different. Rickie gets upset when we try to talk to him about it. He puts his hands over his ears and says, 'No bang-bang night.'"

Burton's eyes filled. His voice shook with emotion when he asked, "Can I talk to them?" Marie Therese nodded encouragingly.

"Of course," the Stoner woman said. He heard her instructing the boys what to say.

Then his son's voice came over the line, making him shudder with yearning for happier times. "Hello, Daddy. This is Rickie. I love you."

Rickie's words were flat and mechanical as a parrot's. He was saying only what he'd been taught to say. But tears spilled over and ran down Burton's cheek. "Hello, son. I love you, too."

"I love you, too," Rickie repeated.

"I'm fine," Burton managed to say. "How are you?"

"I'm fine," said Rickie. "How are you?"

"Fine, son, fine. I—I'm sorry you had a bang-bang night."

"No bang-bang night," Rickie said with surprising emphasis. "No, no, *no*."

"That's right. No more bang-bang night. Not ever. Only nice nights from now on. Daddy loves you."

"Bang-bang-bang-bang-bang-bang-bang-bang-bang-bang," Rickie said in a high, disturbed voice. "Bang-bang-bang-bang—"

He kept repeating the word until Burton felt like nails were being hammered through his heart. He bit his lip to keep from sobbing.

Then Laura Stoner was back on the line. "I'm sorry. I'll let you talk to Trace now."

Then Trace was on the line. "Daddy, dinosaurs sing and dance. Miss Piggy sings and dances. Miss Piggy is a puppet."

"Sure, she is," Burton answered with false heartiness. "That's absolutely right. That's one-hundred-per-cent correct. Miss Piggy *is* a puppet."

"Kermit the Frog is a puppet."

"Yes, yes. That's true, too," Burton said. "Listen, son. I'll be coming home soon. I've had a little accident, b-but I'll be fine. I'll come to see you soon. Real soon."

"The Cookie Monster is a puppet," Trace said. "Kermit the frog rides a bicycle. Frogs ride bicycles."

"I love you very much," Burton said. "And I'm coming home soon. I love you, son."

Trace said, "I love you, son. I love you, son."

Laura Stoner was on the line again. "Hello?" she said. "Hello?"

Burton choked up. Marie Therese clung to his hand and wiped his cheeks with a tissue.

Burton was tight-throated when he spoke again. "Miss Stoner, I lay here in this hospital, and I couldn't talk right. I hurt, but I couldn't talk right. And I understood what my sons go through. I know what happens now when your brain won't work, your words won't work. It was a terrible experience. But I learned from it."

She said, "They try. They work hard. They're good boys, Mr. Fletcher."

"What you've done for them," Burton said. "I can't thank you enough. Never. Whatever you want—it's yours.

A car. A diamond. Diamonds. Pearls and diamonds. You tell me what. It's yours."

She was silent a moment, and he sniffled unashamedly.

When she spoke, her voice was hesitant. "There is one thing I'd like. I've thought about it a long time. I've thought about it hard. Could you promise me something?"

"Anything," vowed Burton.

She paused again. "I don't want you to separate them —ever. They're so alone, except for each other. I think they came into the world together for a purpose. Let them stay together. Nobody should have to be all alone."

Burton, surprised at her request, almost lost all control. "Yes, yes. You're right. Nobody should have to be all alone."

"You promise?"

"I promise. I swear. Yes. I promise." Burton dissolved into tears.

Marie Therese took the phone from him. "I'm sorry," she said in her accented English. "He's overcome. It's very hard for him just now. Thank you and good-bye. We will talk to you again soon."

She hung up and put her arms around Burton. He put his face against her breast and wept like a child. She held him and said, "Your sons are all right. You'll be all right, too. Shh, now. Shh."

Four more days passed. Laura was exasperated at being held in the hospital. The marshals wouldn't tell her when she and the boys could leave or where they would go next.

"We're working on it, ma'am," was all they would say.

They guarded the doors; they accompanied her and the twins outside when the boys took walks. They flirted with the nurses, and the nurses flirted back. They were kind to the boys and deferential to Laura, but they told her nothing.

All she knew was that Montana was no longer in the hospital. He'd been released. But where he had gone, she didn't know; he'd sent no word, nor had anyone else. She was allowed to make no calls and could receive them only from Burton Fletcher. She felt isolated, abandoned, bereft.

"Where is he?" she kept asking the marshals.

Their reply was always the same. "We weren't told, ma'am."

Yet she had a tense feeling that things were happening, things she didn't understand. Over a week had passed, but the twins' tape had not been released. Hadn't Sister Agnes Mary received it? Or had Montana contacted the woman and told her to suppress it, at least for the time being?

Laura didn't know. She could only trust that Montana knew what he was doing.

By the time Laura and the boys had been in the hospital for nine days, it seemed like nine eons to her. She sat by the room's metal desk, rereading yesterday's newspaper and wondering what life was like in the real world.

The twins sprawled on Rickie's bed, clutching their plastic lizards and watching cartoons on television. Their days had settled into routine. Mornings, they did lessons, took a walk, talked to the doctor. Afternoons, they did lessons, talked to the psychologist, took a walk, watched cartoons. After cartoons would be supper, and after supper another walk, then videos and bedtime books.

She often thought of a poem she'd read in high school. In the poem, a woman had been locked inside a tower and forbidden to look upon the world. She was only allowed to see its reflection in a mirror. Laura felt like that imprisoned woman, cut off from life.

But then, that ninth afternoon, there was a knock on the door frame, and she looked up, grateful for any break in the day's tedium.

Montana stood there.

Her heart seemed to tumble down a long hill.

He wore a dark suit and tie and topcoat, just as he had the first time she'd seen him. His dark hair was slightly wind-tossed, his gaze steady. He was gaunt and solemn, but to her eyes he looked wonderful.

"Hello, Laura," he said, not smiling. "Long time no see."

She couldn't speak. Another man stood beside him, a shorter, more compactly built man who looked Hispanic.

He had graying hair and an expression as sober as Montana's, but Laura hardly noticed him.

She rose from her chair as if in a dream, her eyes locking with Montana's. "Look, boys," she managed to say, "Montana's here. Say hello."

The boys, lost in watching a cartoon cat chase a canary, didn't seem to hear her.

"Are you—all right?" she asked Montana. Her knees felt unsteady beneath her, and her heart banged crazily in her chest.

"Yes. Are you?"

"Yes. But I'm tired of being here. Are they sending us somewhere? Will you come, too?"

She wanted to throw herself into his arms, but she seemed incapable of moving and feared if she touched him he would vanish.

But he came to her, put his hands on her upper arms, and at his touch, her blood bolted through her veins. He was real and he was here and she was with him again at last.

But still he didn't smile. He said, "Are you ready to go home? For good?"

Home, she thought dizzily. She didn't really understand what the word meant any more. *Home?* She could go *home?* She stared at him in incomprehension.

"It's over," he said. "Finally. We can take the kids back to school. Now. As soon as you're ready."

"Do you mean it?" She was swept by a mixture of disbelief and rising joy. "Really?"

"Really," he said.

"But how?" she asked. "How can it be over? Just like that?"

He shook his head. "It wasn't just like that. It's taken time. It's taken red tape. But it's done. Nobody's after you. Or them. You're safe."

"But how?"

He handed her a copy of *The New York Times,* folded to an inside page. A neat circle in red ink had been drawn around one brief story.

Laura took the paper, not understanding what he meant.

"Read it," he said with a nod. She dropped her gaze to the paper.

STARLET'S BEAU KILLED IN AIR CRASH

BOGOTÁ, Columbia—Reynaldo Comce, 18, the constant escort of U.S. television starlet Tori Byrd, was killed Saturday in a plane crash near Bogotá, Colombia. Comce was the only grandson of Cesar Perez de la Garza, president of Colombia.

Comce, formerly a student at NYU, made gossip columns when he romanced Byrd, 16, an actress on the soap opera *Days of Our Lives*.

Authorities speculate that an electrical malfunction caused the crash. Also killed was the pilot, Mesius Estrada, 32, a family friend. Estrada was owner and manager of *El Tesoro del Oro*, a New York gallery specializing in South American art and antiquities.

Laura looked at Montana warily, unsure if she could believe the story. "Reynaldo Comce is dead? And Estrada, too?" she asked. "Isn't that too much of a coincidence?"

"Not such a coincidence," he said. "We wanted them both. This is how the Colombians gave them to us. We sent our own forensics man down to check. It's Comce and Estrada, all right."

She stared at him, bewildered. "They killed Reynaldo Comce? But his grandfather . . ."

"Laura, these guys'd kill their own mothers. Comce and Estrada both screwed up. Badly. The Cartel made them pay."

The newspaper slipped from her grasp, and she let it. Her hands rose, shakily, and settled on his shoulders. The dark wool of his overcoat was rough beneath her fingers.

"What does it mean?" she asked him. "I don't understand."

"It means it's over, Laura. Really."

The other man spoke. He showed her his badge. "Miss Stoner, I'm Al Pastrana, FBI. We've been moving through unusual channels this last week."

She turned back to Montana in confusion. "What about the leaks? We couldn't trust anyone—what about that?"

"We're plugging the leaks. And the worst one—that one we got rid of a long time ago, without even knowing it."

He paused, the corner of his mouth turning down. "We were bugged. From the time we left the station house."

"Bugged?" She was stunned. "Who did it? How?"

"The cop named Valentine," he said. "He's dirty. He's been on the Colombians' payroll for months. He called them from your phone when he went to pick up your things at the school."

She remembered Valentine, a big, sarcastic man, with bulldog eyes and oily, thinning hair. It was as if he'd existed in another lifetime, one that seemed far more innocent than this. He'd helped destroy that innocence.

Montana's hands tightened on her, and he drew her closer. "They told him exactly what to do. He picked one of the kids' videos, and when he went out for an early supper, he took it. He left it in a restroom in a luncheonette. While he ate a man named Esdra Ibarra came in, ordered a cup of coffee, and pretended to use the restroom."

Pastrana said, "The bug they used was minute. It could fit under the inside seam of the cardboard video box. Valentine went back to the restroom after Ibarra, picked up the video, took it back, and put it with the others. So, you see, you were electronically monitored from the first. But the tapes were lost in the shuffle after Valley Hope."

Laura remembered Valentine sitting at her desk, smirking in superiority at her and the boys. A bitter, sick feeling flooded her. "Do you have him? Did he confess?"

"We've got him," Pastrana said with a nod. "The man who was killed near the van—" his piercing dark eyes flicked her up and down "—was a high-ranking member of the Cartel. His name was Hepfinger. He specialized in information. In his suite at the Plaza we found transcripts of the tapes from the bugs. He labeled his sources. He was meticulous about keeping sources straight. We got the people who leaked that information and how they leaked it. Including Valentine."

Montana's mouth took on a cynical line. "And Valentine's telling everything he knows so he can cop a plea. Singing like a bird."

She shook her head. "That was the leak? A video box? The box for a child's cartoon?"

"Right," Pastrana said. "They were eavesdropping the whole time. They just didn't want another hit in the heart of the city. So they waited till you were on the move to Valley Hope."

"Jorge Hepfinger left a lot of sensitive material lying around that suite," Montana said. "It led us to two major leaks in the task force. And two in the FBI. We've got the people in custody."

"Everything tied into Estrada," Pastrana said. "And we've got a material witness who'll testify that Estrada conspired to murder. That he engineered Valley Hope and sent Hepfinger after you."

"A witness?" Laura asked.

Montana gave a small, bitter laugh. "Dennis Deeds. He knew the Cartel was going to make him the goat in all this—a dead goat. With both the Cartel and the Mafia after him, he rolled over to our side. The irony is that he'll testify in the cases against the informers. He'll end up in the Federal Witness Protection Program himself. Probably wind up running a diner in Dubuque."

Pastrana said, "We've pieced together the story. Estrada made one mistake. He told Deeds to hire three would-be assassins, nothing but kids. In turn, they made a mistake. They let Reynaldo Comce come along for the fun and pull the trigger. From there it snowballed into an avalanche. They all got caught in it."

Montana raised his hand and stroked her hair lightly. "You and the kids are safe now," he said. "I mean it. Really safe."

Pastrana cleared his throat. "We've got a guarantee from Diego Lopez-Portilla Carmago that neither you nor the boys are threatened in any way. We have this in writing."

He reached into the inside pocket of his suit jacket and drew out a legal-sized envelope. He handed it to her.

"Go ahead," Montana said. "Read it."

With nervous fingers, she opened the envelope, and took out the copied page from a fax machine. The message, written by hand, was in elegant and high-flown Spanish, and she felt too confounded to translate it.

"I can't—I can't—" she stammered.

Pastrana took it from her. "May I?" he asked. Then he muttered, "Damn. I forgot my glasses."

He held the paper at arm's length and said, "This begins with the equivalent of 'To Whom It May Concern.' It's from Carmago. He says. 'Three individuals have been singled out for my particular attention, and they are Richard Mark and Trace Francis Fletcher and Laura Ann Ferris Stoner.

"Whoever will harm so much as a hair of the heads of any of these three, his name is marked, his hours are numbered, and his soul is damned to everlasting hell. All three are held in my most especial esteem and enjoy my personal protection, and the lasting esteem and protection of me and mine as long as the rivers run to the seas. I am yours in God, Don Diego Lopez-Portillo Carmago."

Laura looked at Pastrana, thunderstruck. Her throat constricted. "Is it real?" she asked. "Where did you ever get such a thing?"

"It wasn't easy," Pastrana said. "Trust me on that."

She turned her gaze to Montana. "You mean, we're now under the protection of a *drug lord*?"

"You might put it more tactfully," Montana said. "But yes. And nobody is going to want to mess with this man. Nobody."

"But how on earth did you do this?"

"Very diplomatically," Pastrana said.

Montana said, "As far as we officially know, Reynaldo Comce was never with the men who hit Zordani. He wasn't there, he wasn't anywhere near there, he was completely disassociated from it, and later he died tragically by accident, an innocent boy struck down in the flower of his youth."

"But you know and I know—"

He put his finger to her lips. "You and I know it. But we say nothing."

Confusion filled her. "But aren't we guilty of—of collusion or something?"

"No," he said. "Like Pastrana said, Estrada set it all in motion. Now he's dead. And so are the men who murdered for him. They're dead, all of them. The ones who killed Zordani, Becker, and Stallings. The ones who killed Marco and Jefferson. Justice has been served as far as we can ever reach. There's nothing more we can gain."

"Two of the Colombians' heaviest hitters are downed," Pastrana said. "Estrada and Hepfinger. Besides that, we rooted out Cartel moles in two agencies, and we got Deeds into the bargain. We can't get to the Cartel heads, but we've made them promise the safety of you and the boys. It's as good as we'll do."

She stared up at Montana, trying to read what he'd left unsaid. "The tape . . . ?" she asked.

He looked into her eyes but said nothing. Sister Agnes Mary must still be holding it ready, like a terrible swift sword.

As if Montana could read her thoughts, he nodded. "Yeah," he said. "Yeah."

She held his gaze, her heart beating hard.

He said. "Are you ready to take the boys home? To take them back to school again?"

"Yes," she said, fighting to keep her voice steady. "Oh, yes. I want to take them back."

"Can I help you pack?" he asked.

"Yes," she said. "Please. Only—we don't have any boxes."

"Yeah, you do," Pastrana said gruffly. "I got a car full. I'll bring 'em up."

"I'll help," Montana said, but he didn't move, and he didn't take his eyes from Laura.

"Stay where you are," Pastrana said, resignation in his voice. "I'll get one of the marshals. And this," he said, handing the envelope to Laura, "is yours."

She took it and stared at it in wonder. "Just like that," she murmured. "Just as easy as that."

324 / BETHANY CAMPBELL

"Not just like that," Montana said. "And like he said, *not* easy."

"It wasn't any harder than teaching a snake to tap dance," Pastrana said. He turned and left the room. Laura was too stunned even to think of thanking him.

"How's the lizard-and-penny business?" Montana asked, pulling her closer.

"Brisk," she said, then blinked back tears. "Oh, Montana, where have you *been*?"

"Part of it was called 'being debriefed,' " he said. He nodded at the envelope in her hand. "And they didn't want me to have any contact with you as long as it was possible for this thing to become a case. But it's not a case. It's over. That's final."

"All this time, you've been doing that for us?"

His expression grew sober. "That. And I went to see Jefferson's ex-wife. And his kids. To talk to them."

"What did you say?"

"That he saved us. He warned us that something was up. He saved Rickie's life. He fired the first shot for us. And that one of the last things he talked about was his kids and how he missed them. He was a hero, and he loved them. I told them that."

"Good," she said, and swallowed.

"I went to Marco's grave, too," he said. "He's with Mike now. And his wife and daughter. They're together."

She turned her face away.

"Hey," he said. "Don't cry. Don't—please. Okay?"

But there was no time to cry, because the cartoon program was over. Its spell over the boys broke, and they clambered off the bed and raided the closet for their jackets and gloves, ready for their afternoon walk.

They didn't seem surprised to see Montana, but Rickie frowned as he zipped his jacket, as if hazily remembering something. "Montana," he said in an accusing tone. "Montana fall down in the snow, and Rickie got *cold*."

"Sorry, Rickie," he said. "I got cold, too."

Trace's face brightened. "Blue rhubarb," he said. "Blue rhubarb. A clown can bend."

Rickie gazed at the ceiling thoughtfully. "A clown can bend. Love is strange," he said. "Strange. Strange."

"Indeed, it is," said Montana.

He put his scarred hand under Laura's chin, and tilted her face up to his. He lowered his mouth so that it nearly touched hers.

"Let's take the kids home," he said.

The playground was roisterous with children, the air split by their laughs and shouts.

The late March sky glowed flawlessly blue and the breeze was alive with the hint of spring. The old forsythia bushes that flanked the school's main entrance were full of yellow buds, and a robin pecked in the gravel.

Montana strode across the schoolyard, nodding to the teachers and children. In truth he barely noticed them; his attention was fixed on Laura, who hadn't seen him yet.

She stood in profile to him, by the swing set. She had on a tweed coat that she wore unbuttoned, and her long hair fluttered, glinting with red in the sunlight. Her hands were thrust casually into her pockets, and she laughed at something the little boy on the swing said.

Beyond her, Rickie and Trace hung on the bars of the schoolyard fence, staring intently down the street. They looked identical, except that Rickie's jacket was red, Trace's blue. Almost simultaneously they glanced down at their military-style watches, then off down the street again.

Laura watched the little boy named Lionel pump his swing higher and higher. The iron chains creaked as he moved back and forth.

"Laura," Lionel cried excitedly, "are you watching? Look how high I go! Look! Look at me!"

"I'm watching," Laura assured him. "That's good, Lionel. That's wonderful, and I'm proud of you."

She turned, and when she caught sight of Montana, she smiled, and he found himself smiling in return.

He came to her side, took the lapels of her coat, drew her nearer, and stared down into her eyes. He didn't kiss her because the kids would get rowdy and silly if he did, and the other teachers were watching.

"Hi," he said. "I was in the neighborhood, so I thought I'd come see my best girl," he said.

"Hi." She ducked her head, shy because she knew people were looking at them, some slyly, some boldly. She busied herself with picking a piece of lint from the sleeve of his overcoat.

He said, "My mother always says if a woman does that, picks threads off you, stuff like that, it means she cares. Do you?"

"You know I do," she said and found another minuscule piece to pick away. Then she lifted her eyes and looked at the twins, clinging like sentinel monkeys to the fence. She nodded in their direction. "Did Rickie and Trace see you? Do they know you're here?"

"They saw me. They just didn't get too excited, that's all."

His gaze followed hers. The boys' cheeks were bright from the cool air, their dark hair was tousled, and their bright jackets fluttered in the breeze. Trace's expression was empty, but placid. Rickie's lips kept moving, as if he was mumbling to himself.

"Their father's coming to see them again this weekend," Laura said.

Montana caught her hand in his, lacing his fingers through hers. A frown line appeared between his brows. "About last night," he said, "I didn't mean to push you. You know that, don't you?"

She looked at their joined hands, her face pensive. "I know. And I don't mean to be stubborn. It's just that it seems too soon. After all we've been through, I'm not sure either of us is thinking straight. I wouldn't want for us to jump into something, and then have you regret it."

He lowered his face so that she had to meet his eyes. "I would never regret it. Never."

"But you might," she said with feeling. "You have to remember that I can't ever—"

"Laura! Laura!" cried Lionel. "Look at me! I'm even higher! Laura, look at me! Look! Look!"

"I see you, Lionel," she said, nodding. "That *is* high. Good job!"

"Laura, no!" shouted a little girl, running toward the jungle gym. "Watch me instead—see what I'm going to do."

"I see you, Heidi," Laura called. "Be careful now." Heidi chortled wildly and kept running.

Laura turned back to Montana. "I'm sorry," she said. "What I was trying to say was that you should think hard about this, because I can never have children, and—"

He put his hands on her shoulders and gripped her tightly. "Laura," he said, "look around you. Just look. You do have children. Do you understand me?"

Startled, she raised her eyes to his. He held her gaze and raised his hand to touch her face.

He nodded. "You have children; you always will. They need you. And you'll be there for them."

Her lower lip trembled. She bit it and said nothing. He kept his hand resting against her face. He smiled, and at last she smiled back.

Around them the chatter and laughter and excited shrieks of children's voices echoed. The swings rose into the air and fell back again, rhythmically, the seesaws went up and down, and Heidi had climbed up the monkey bars and hung by her knees, singing loudly.

The children's noise mingled with the scuffling sound of traffic from the streets, the rumble of trucks, the fainter sound of cars. In the distance, a siren wailed.

Rickie and Trace did not seem to hear or notice. They clung to the bars of the fence and waited, looking expectantly down the street. It was nearly 2:07, and time for the nice old gentleman to appear.

Mr. Zordani did not appear, of course, but the boys kept patiently waiting for him until the recess bell rang, and Laura came to take them inside the building. "Laura's here," she said, holding out her hands to them. And they went with her, back to the safe and predictable world of her classroom.

ABOUT THE AUTHOR

BETHANY CAMPBELL is the nationally bestselling, award-winning author of over thirty romances. A two-time winner of the Romance Writers of America's prestigious Rita Award, she has won every major award in her field, usually more than once. She has taught Literature and Creative Writing at Eastern Illinois University. Her humorous pieces and articles have been published in magazines such as *Good Housekeeping,* and she has also published more than fifty poems in literary magazines. Ms. Campbell collects cartoon art, belongs to the ISHTAR fan club, and like all Arkansawers, is an avid basketball fan.

You won't be able to put it down.

The new romantic thriller
from the nationally bestselling

BETHANY CAMPBELL

Coming from Bantam Books in Fall 1996

Carolynn Blue was a tough, quick-thinking risk taker, and she was willing to do what it took to survive. But when she agreed to work for a private investigator who was looking for a missing girl, she didn't know she would be entering a world where danger could wear any face, and where nothing was what it seemed. . . .

A private detective's office should be behind a mysterious door, its window blinded by frosted glass. This doorway should be in a poorly lit hallway in an upper story of an old building, preferably in the most sinister section of downtown Los Angeles.

That's what Carrie thought.

She wanted a 1940s-ish atmosphere: venetian blinds slicing the dusty sunlight, a smart-ass secretary with a whiskey voice, and a detective who looked like Humphrey Bogart or Robert Mitchum or, at the very least, Jack Nicholson.

But this detective agency was on the sleepy main street of Fayetteville, Arkansas, in the bright white stucco building that had once housed the Jolly Baker's Shoppe.

The interior had been remodeled in the style that Carrie thought of as Godless Office Modern. The linoleum was blandly colored, the furniture all angles and steel, the walls white, the lighting stark. But if she tried, she imagined she could smell the ghostly scent of freshly baked bread haunting the air.

The secretary at the reception desk was plain and matronly enough to preside over the office of a fundamentalist church. She wore a ruffled blouse, bifocals, and her blue-tinted hair was trained in waves so stern they might have been cast metal.

"Mr. Ivanovich has a client right now," the secretary said. "He'll be with you shortly."

It was lunch hour, and Carrie was the only other person in the waiting room, so she sat on the hard tan sofa with its plastic upholstery and steel arms and legs.

The secretary unwrapped a sandwich that smelled of tuna fish and pickles and began to nibble daintily at one triangular half. Idly Carrie picked up a *Time* magazine that was six weeks old and had a dark, moody cover. It showed a photo of two wounded young soldiers, half lost in shadows, their eyes bandaged.

"Vietnam," stark letters announced. "Twenty years later, it haunts us still."

Indeed it does, thought Carrie, with a pang. *But only some of us.*

She didn't want to touch the pages, didn't want to read about Vietnam, see the pictures. Almost superstitiously, she set the magazine aside. She took up one of the glossy pamphlets that said BURNSIDE INVESTIGATIVE AGENCY, HAYDON D. BURNSIDE AND ASSOCIATES, HAYDON D. BURNSIDE, FOUNDER AND PRESIDENT.

She did not allow herself to smile at the formal portrait of the sleekly fat Haydon D. Burnside, who looked righteous, self-satisfied, and smug.

His poor associates, thought Carrie, reading the names of these lesser personages. There were four associates, and the name of the man she was to see, Joseph Ivanovich, was printed at the bottom of the list, last and presumably least.

Ivanovich, however low on the pecking order he was, might have part-time work for her. She didn't know what it was, but she was curious enough and broke enough to check it out. "Wotthehell" was Carrie's motto. It had brought her through much.

Carolynn Cornell Blue was forty-five, with blond bangs, freckles, and blue eyes that saw much, missed little. She was a lean, windswept tomboy of a woman, dressed for her job interview in the only skirt she owned, which was, of course, made of denim.

Her short-sleeved blouse was light blue and freshly, if haphazardly, ironed. She'd had to search half an hour to find her steam iron and had at last discovered it in the bottom drawer of her file cabinet next to a folder marked "Irony."

Carrie no longer wore a wedding ring. Her husband had died ten years ago, leaving her with two sons, fourteen and thirteen, to raise and educate. She'd taught high school, and during summer holidays she'd worked at whatever job paid best, usually as a cocktail waitress. Once when both boys had taken summer jobs in a nearby city, she had driven a truck. Wotthehell.

When Joel, her younger son, had finished college last year, Carrie thought, *All right, boys, it's my turn now.* She'd always wanted a master of fine arts degree. She'd been accepted by several schools, but she chose the University of Arkansas because she'd spent the happiest two years of her girlhood in Arkansas and could not resist returning.

Carrie knew it was dangerous to go looking for the lost glow of halcyon days, but she was not afraid to take chances. She'd taken them all her life and learned she fared best when she followed her heart.

Once, long ago it seemed, she had been flirtatious and had delighted in playing the games that men and women play. She knew she still had an offbeat sex appeal, but she no longer bothered to wield it. Twice since her husband's death she had taken lovers, one for two years, the other for three.

She had parted amiably from both but wasn't looking for a replacement. Relationships demanded so much attention; they claimed so much time; they needed such endless nurturing. For the present, she didn't think of herself as between men but temporarily *beyond* them. Now that her sons were launched, this time was her time, and she wasn't interested in romance. Romance she'd had. She wanted completely new frontiers.

Hearing a door open, she looked up from the Burnside pamphlet with its catalogue of services: Surveillance. Criminal, Civil, and Workman's Compensation Cases. Witness Locates. Divorce. Child Custody. Background Investigations.

A young woman had exited from the farthest office and fumbled to pull the door shut behind her.

The woman was tall, brunette, and extremely beautiful. Carrie was sure she had seen her on campus before—a cheerleader? A beauty queen?

The girl—she was no more than twenty—was dressed to expensive perfection in a dark green silk pantsuit. Gold glittered from her earlobes and wrists and at her throat. But her eyes were swollen, her expression stricken, and it was obvious that she had been crying uncontrollably.

Why? Carrie thought, with a frisson of alarm and curiosity. What could the girl have learned inside that office that had made her weep so bitterly?

The secretary looked up, saw the girl's distress, and glanced discreetly away. Delicately she lifted the second half of her sandwich and took a precise bite.

The girl pushed open the thick glass door of the waiting room as if desperate to flee and escaped into the hot June sunshine outside. She disappeared down the street, and Carrie stared after her in pity and wonder.

The secretary chewed her sandwich. The clock ticked. Then the office door opened a few inches, but Carrie couldn't see who was inside. A masculine voice with a southern accent said, "Give me a minute before you send in the next one, Alice."

"Yes, sir."

The door shut again. The secretary did not make eye contact with Carrie. She dawdled over her sandwich, giving it all of her concentration. At last she carefully bundled the crusts up in the wrapping, making little crackling noises.

She opened her purse, took out her compact, grimaced at herself in the mirror, inspected her teeth, then refreshed the powder on her nose. She clicked the compact shut, returned it to her purse, clasped her hands together before her on the desk in a businesslike pose. She cleared her throat.

She nodded, reacknowledging Carrie's existence. "He'll see you now."

Carrie rose and went to the farthest office door, wondering if she was expected to knock. She raised her fist to rap smartly on the door frame.

But the receptionist said, almost pettishly, "No, no. Just walk in."

So Carrie walked in. A tall man with straight brown hair, graying at the temples, stood behind the desk. He looked up with an expression that was half frown, half displeased surprise.

He had a glass of water and a wet handkerchief with which he dabbed at his shirtfront. He'd made a large damp spot on his chest, but he hadn't succeeded in wiping away the streak of cherry red lipstick smeared there. When he saw where her gaze had settled, he looked more resentful than guilty.

Carrie narrowed her eyes, wondering if he'd made advances to the girl. Sexual harassment was all too common at a college and in a college town. It was something that infuriated her; she'd never stood for it, and she never would.

The man looked Carrie up and down, his expression stony. It seemed as if he could read her mind and didn't give a damn what she thought, that the lipstick was none of her business.

Carrie considered the truth of this. It *was* none of her business. Yet the weeping girl had registered not only on her sympathy but on her lively imagination. Just what had happened in this office?

Ivanovich made one more ineffectual wipe at the lipstick smudge, then tossed the handkerchief aside. He kept his eyes fixed on Carrie. They were brown eyes touched with hazel green, and they didn't waver. He had straight thick eyebrows, a well-shaped jaw, an adequate nose, but his mouth was too wide for handsomeness and it had a sarcastic slant that looked permanent.

He wore no jacket, and his white shirt was better pressed than her blouse. The shirt was open at the throat, and his tie had been cast onto his desk. She saw why. The tie was of pale blue silk, and it, too, was smudged with lipstick.

Hmm, thought Carrie and wondered again precisely what had happened between him and the girl.

Ivanovich saw her looking at the tie, picked it up, and stowed it in his top desk drawer, away from her curious gaze. "You must be Carolynn Blue," he said with false pleasantness. "Professor Goldwell told me you were observant."

She thrust her hand out to him in greeting. "And you're Joseph Ivanovich. All Goldwell said is you're a detective. And you might have part-time work for me."

He shook hands, firmly but briefly. He gestured at the chair opposite his. "Have a seat."

She sat, crossing her legs with almost military precision and making sure the unfamiliar skirt didn't hike up her legs.

They were still good legs but nothing like the girl's, she was sure.

Joe Ivanovich sat, too, settling into a swivel chair that was oak, not metal. He showed no interest in her legs, but he studied her face as if determined to read more of her character than she wished to reveal.

He said, "I have work to offer, yes. You're one of the people Goldwell recommended."

"People? He recommended more than one of us?"

He nodded, showing no emotion. "Yes. But it's not a competitive thing. I need a couple of people who can write, who can be . . . creative. Preferably women."

Why does a detective need writers? she wondered. *And why, specifically, women writers?*

Her expression must have indicated she was puzzled. He rubbed his jaw reflectively, opened a manila folder, stared at the top page.

"Goldwell faxed me a copy of your application to the writing program. He says you have a more varied background than most students."

"I'm older," she said. Ivanovich was a prospective employer and, by law, she didn't have to tell him how old, but she didn't care. "Forty-five."

"Hmm," he said, looking faintly surprised. He darted a quick glance at her bare left hand, so quick that she almost missed it.

"I'm a widow," she said, although she didn't have to tell him that, either. "I've got two sons. Both out of college now. I decided it was time for me to go back—"

He raised his hand, gesturing that he didn't want to hear. "I'm interested only in your work background. You really were a policewoman at one time?"

She raised her chin slightly. "I was an officer. For two years."

There was a beat of silence between them. *Two years that were several millennia ago,* she thought. When she'd started, she had been little older than the pretty girl who had just left in tears.

"You were in law enforcement, too?" she asked. "Before . . . this?"

He ignored her question. "Tell me about being an 'officer.'" He put an ironic spin on the word that she didn't like.

She decided he was overbearing and impressed by his own superiority, but she had her own way of handling such men. Let him underestimate her; the more he did, the bigger the surprise he'd have coming. She gave him a wry little smile to disarm him with her dimples.

"It was in Parkview, Nebraska. I was mostly a meter maid," she said. "I'd go around the town square giving out parking tickets. Help with traffic during the homecoming parade, the Fourth of July fireworks. That's about it."

"You went to the police academy?"

She gave a deprecating shrug. "Yes. I did."

And in the written exam I was first in my class, you condescending bastard.

"Did you ever use a gun?"

She smiled again, as if marveling over the oddity of her own past. A meter maid had little use for a gun, but she'd worn one; all the officers had.

And once in a while, when the men needed inconspicuous backup in an undercover drug bust, she would be drafted. As soon as the drug money changed hands, that was the signal for her to whip out the gun. She'd pulled it more than once. She'd never had to shoot it."

"I never shot anyone," she said. "Or anything. Well, a rabid skunk once. I felt bad about it afterward."

She paused, showed him her dimples again. "I won't need a gun for this job, will I?"

"I was just curious, that's all. Why'd you quit the force?"

Because it was the early 1970s, I was the only woman, and the police force of Parkville, Nebraska, was full of male chauvinist pigs, just like you.

"I lost my taste for it," she said. "I decided to go back to college."

"And then you taught? High School?"

Carrie nodded and looked brightly innocent. Teaching high school demanded nerves as steely as any police officer's and perhaps greater overall toughness.

"All these other jobs? Cocktail waitress? Store clerk?" The sarcasm vibrated in his tone. "House painter?"

"Schoolteachers don't get paid much. I had two boys to raise. I worked summers."

"Truck driver?" he said dubiously.

"It was just a florist's delivery truck," Carrie said. "It wasn't an eighteen-wheeler, a big rig or anything."

"Anything else?" he asked, his green-brown eyes narrowed as if the better to measure her.

"Tutoring," she said. "Baby-sitting. Whatever came along."

She didn't add that she'd also written stories for the "true confession" magazines. The magazines paid her five cents a word, never gave her a byline, and nobody knew that she stayed up late at night writing the stories. Not even her sons. Certainly not Howland Goldwell, head of the creative writing program. He would have a fatal attack of aesthetic revulsion if he knew.

Ivanovich looked at his file on her and again rubbed his jaw. "You live out by the lake?"

She did. She rented a two-bedroom fishing cabin from an elderly lawyer who no longer used it. The cabin was isolated, a bit ramshackle, and had a possum living under the front porch. But it also had a million-dollar view of the lake, and she loved the place more than any house she'd ever lived in.

Ivanovich raised his eyes to meet hers again. "You live all alone out there?"

Her heart gave an inexplicable skip. He wasn't handsome, she didn't like him, but he made her hormones wake up, stretch, and say, *How long have we been asleep?* She resented it.

"I live alone and like it," she said. "So what's this about? What kind of job is this? How much does it pay?"

"You have a phone? A computer? A modem?"

"A phone, yes. A computer, yes, if you're charitable about it. A modem is that gizmo that you hook up between a computer and a phone? So you can get access to the Internet and things? No."

He cast a discreet glance at her legs, then met her gaze again. "We can take care of all that if you're interested. Can you navigate the Internet?"

Carrie's heart sank like a stone. If the job depended on computer literacy, her chances were gone. She could use a word processing program for writing, that was all, and her computer was twelve years old. Her sons considered it prehistoric and called it "T. Rex," the dinosaur.

"I know nothing about the Internet except that it's there," she said carefully. "But I can learn if I have to. I'm a quick learner."

Ivanovich's mouth kept its sarcastic slant. "Goldwell said that, too. What you'd have to learn isn't hard. You could get it down in a day or less."

Relief danced giddily through her veins.

Ivanovich said, "Do you know what virtual reality communities are? Specifically the one called Omega MOON?"

Carrie lifted an eyebrow. Joel, her younger son, had played around with the virtual communities, which went by strange acronyms like MUDS, MUSHes, MOONs, MOOs, and TinyMOOs. And she'd heard students talk.

"I know a little," she said. "Omega MOON's supposed to be the biggest and most sophisticated. People take on characters. It's like a giant masquerade."

He nodded, picked up a back issue of *Newsweek* magazine, and handed it to her. "There's an article on Omega on page thirty-seven. Read it. That is, if you're interested. I need a couple of women to go on Omega as characters."

Carrie accepted the magazine but gave Ivanovich a curious stare. "Go on Omega MOON? As a character? Why?"

His expression became unreadable. He put his elbows on his desk, tented his fingers. His hands looked strong and surprisingly sensitive. "I've got a client," he said. "He was interested in a girl on Omega MOON. She's disappeared."

"From Omega?" Carrie asked.

"Disappeared completely," he said, watching her face as if gauging any change of expression. "Her name's Gretchen Small. She's a sophomore at Memphis State. She vanished just after spring semester was over. We know that three weeks ago she booked a round-trip flight to Chicago. She went but never used the return ticket. And after that we know nothing."

The rest is silence, Carrie thought, with an ominous little prickle deep in her bones.

She said, "Her disappearance has something to do with Omega MOON?"

"She met another guy on Omega. Maybe the wrong guy. My client's worried. Her character's been erased from the MOON. He claims she never would have done that."

"Who was this man, the other man she was interested in?"

"We don't know. That's why we need you."

The copy of *Newsweek* slipped from Carrie's lap and fell to the floor. She hardly noticed. "Wait a minute. You want me to be *bait*?"

For the first time his mouth took on the trace of a smile. "It pays six dollars an hour. You work as many hours as you can. Mostly at night. That's when the action is. You go on Omega. You chat up guys. Are you interested?"

She swallowed and reached to retrieve the magazine, her thoughts racing. She had only one class this summer, grammar, which she ought to be able to pass without much study. She'd spent eighteen years pounding grammar into students' stubborn heads.

If she could work thirty-five hours a week at six dollars an hour, she could make over eight hundred dollars a month—eight hundred dollars! The sum staggered her.

Her car's transmission sputtered and groaned and clanked, threatening to go out; her CD player had been broken for months, and she fiercely missed playing her favorite music. She could buy the books she'd been yearning for, even some new record albums, put money in the bank, get Joel a decent birthday present—

She put the magazine back in her lap. "It's not dangerous, of course?"

Ivanovich's aura of mild scorn vanished. "If I thought it was dangerous, I wouldn't ask you to do it."

He spoke with such rough conviction it startled her. She thought she saw something new come into his eyes, but she couldn't quite understand what it was, flickering there in the depths.

"Use your head and you'll be safe," he said. "Nobody can find out who you are—unless you tell them. Omega gives you total anonymity, if you want it. Use it."

She thought about this and nodded slowly. "And the man? The one this Gretchen Small supposedly went off with? He had total anonymity, too?"

"Yes. The Internet's full of people damn near impossible to trace. Besides that, characters on Omega can change. The one she'd taken up with was called Joachim the Beggar. He may be back, posing as another character. He might be anybody there, male or female."

Carrie frowned slightly. "He'd pose as a woman?"

"There's a lot of gender-bending. Nobody has to be what he says he is. If you go on, you'll be approached by both men and women. Some of these 'women' are men pretending to be lesbians."

"You mean people are going to . . . to try to . . ." she groped for a polite way to phrase it.

"Seduce you," Ivanovich said. "They'll offer sex then and there. You'll have to get used to it."

" 'Then and there'? What's that mean?"

"It's called MOON sex. It's like phone sex, except they use words on the computer screen, not voices."

Carrie, not usually easily shocked, blinked hard. "MOON sex? You mean people *type* dirty to each other?"

"The joke is that they type one-handed," Ivanovich said but didn't elaborate.

He didn't have to. Carrie had a vision of a pimply,

aroused college student furiously typing erotic messages to a stranger while touching only the keys—and himself.

"Computer sex? You don't expect me to do that, for God's sake?"

"Gretchen Small didn't go in for MOON sex—as far as we know. So play hard to get. Unless you think there's good reason to do otherwise."

"You're serious? If I go on Omega, I'll be propositioned? Maybe repeatedly?"

His gaze met hers coolly. "Count on it."

She couldn't quite believe it and laughed. "But Omega's full of college kids. I'll be old enough to be their mother."

"They won't know that. Everything's illusion on the MOON. You're one more illusion."

Carrie nipped the corner of her lower lip thoughtfully.

Ivanovich watched her. "Goldwell says you think fast, write fast, that you're more mature than the others. He thinks you can handle this."

Carrie shook her head. The thought of sitting at the computer night after night, lying to college boys, flirting with them and leading them on, filled her with profound distaste.

Ivanovich, his face harder than before, opened his desk drawer, took out a snapshot, and handed it to her.

As she stared at the photo, a frown line etched itself between her brows. The picture showed a plump, busty girl with frizzy hair and a long chin but beautiful eyes.

"This girl's missing. She may be dead," Ivanovich said. "We've got good reason to think so, and that the guy who did it is prowling Omega. And maybe other virtual communities as well."

Carrie gave him a sharp glance. "Dead? Why do you think so?"

"We'll get into that later. Now—do you want to help us try to find this guy? or not?"

She studied the snapshot again. Except for the extraordinary eyes, Gretchen Small was not attractive, not in the least. But that wasn't what interested Carrie. What struck her was the insecurity in the girl's face, the vulnerability of the mouth, the hope and fear in the eyes.

Carrie had seen that expression on other young faces, and it always filled her with pity and sorrow. The expression said, *I am lost, please love me. I would do anything to be loved.*

Carrie studied the naked need in the girl's eyes. Young, inexperienced people that lonely could make terrible decisions; they could be misled, tricked, exploited, even destroyed. She remembered one of her high school students from nine years ago.

The same desperate, needy look had shown in Shannon Flannery's gray eyes. One night at a teen dance she accepted a ride home with a stranger. Four days later her nude body was found caught in a raft of snags in the Missouri River. Petite, thin little Shannon who still had braces on her teeth and wrote poems about springtime and kittens and puppies. Sixteen years old. The killer had never been found.

A bitter sadness filled Carrie.

"I'll help you look for him," she said.